The
Tattered
Black Book

The
Tattered
Black Book

Lexy Duck

atmosphere press

Chapter 1
Early Morning, October 21, 1951

It was raining hard when we arrived. Mother got out of the car then sheltered me under her umbrella and we hurried into the house.

"Auntie, we're here!" Mother called from the vestibule as she shook off her wet raincoat. "Where are you, Auntie?" she shouted. She looked toward the kitchen before she turned to face me. She told me to take off my coat while muttering under her breath, "We are running so late, and this weather isn't helping."

My parents were taking my two older sisters to see a new exhibit at the Philadelphia Museum of Art. My oldest sister saw an advertisement for the exhibit in the newspaper. And she begged Mother to take her because she knew Mother would enjoy the exhibit too.

Mother thought about it then talked to my father and sisters about it. And they decided to make a day of it. They'd have lunch at Schrafft's after the exhibit then go to the Franklin Institute and catch the afternoon show at the Fels Planetarium. So, for the next week that is all anyone talked about. No one invited me. My middle sister was going because "she knew how to behave," they said. But I couldn't go. I wasn't old enough. I'd get bored and spoil everything, so I had to stay with Auntie.

"I'm right here, Diana. I'm right here," Auntie said, entering the vestibule.

She stood in the doorway to the vestibule, watching my mother with her shoulders back and her chin up. Her posture was impeccable. She was tall and slender without a discernible curve to her frame. She wore a pale green dress dotted with small flowers and accented by a white collar and cuffs that she had starched and ironed until they were perfect. Its skirt flared from her waist and was hemmed below her knees covering her calves. Lyle stockings covered her legs and her feet were laced into highly polished leather Oxfords with two-inch heels.

Her hair had grayed over the years and her dark hazel eyes change color with every movement of her head. They were sometimes green, sometimes brown, and sometimes a combination of both. And the rimless glasses she always wore perched on her majestic straight nose seemed to intensify their color. Her skin was white to the point of being translucent, yet there was a pale, pinkish tint to her cheeks. She cut her hair short, in a bob, and it fell in soft gray and white ringlet curls around her face. And when she smiled her eyes twinkled and she revealed a mouth full of straight white teeth. She was so proud of her teeth because at her age she still had every one of them. She wasn't a beautiful woman, but she had an inner beauty that exuded from her every pore.

"Why such a commotion?" Auntie asked. She removed her apron and leaned down to kiss me. She lifted her head and looked at my mother. "Diana, you are in a huff this morning."

"We are running late. I want the girls to enjoy every minute of this whole day, and I dallied a bit too much this morning," my mother said.

"Now, child, stand up straight and take a deep breath," Auntie said to Mother. "And settle down this instant. It's early yet. You have plenty of time to get everything in."

"Why can't I go? I want to go too," I said, stomping my feet.

"Danielle, I've had enough. We've been through this a hundred times. Now, I expect you to be good for Auntie. Do you understand me?" I shook my head and said, "Yes, ma'am." Mother nodded. She smiled and touched my cheek. She turned to Auntie. "We will be back, I'm thinking, sometime around five. Is that okay? I hate to leave you with her. She's in such a snit this morning."

"You have a good time, and don't give us a thought. Danny and I will do fine. We will have supper ready when you get back. Won't we, Danny?"

I didn't answer. I scowled, trying to stop my tears as my mother bent down and kissed me. I looked into my mother's eyes as one small drop escaped from mine. She smiled and pinched my cheek. "Be good for Auntie," she said. She reached over me, kissed Auntie, then she went out the front door, waving goodbye as she left.

Auntie turned and looked down at me with her arms folded in front of her. "So, you're in a snit this morning," she said, smiling.

"That's what Mother says," I replied with a tinge of belligerence. "I'm not, though. I wanted to go, that's all." I tried to hide my tears so Auntie wouldn't see them.

"Well, why don't you read or play with your toys while I finish what I'm doing in the kitchen. Then may . . . be," Auntie said, stretching out her final word. I looked at her, knowing good things usually would follow. "Then, if you are good, I'll ask Fireman Harriman to show you the new hook and ladder truck that arrived last week."

"The Sugar Bowl too? Can we go? Will you take me for ice cream too, please?"

5

Auntie chuckled as she always did. She never laughed aloud. Ladies don't laugh like that, she said, so she chuckled her chuckle that always made me laugh. "You can if you may, Danny. I'll be twenty minutes or so. I'll be in the kitchen." She hung my coat on the hook and left the vestibule, walking through the middle room on her way to the kitchen.

I followed her from the vestibule into the large, square middle room. Dark, hand-hewn, peg and groove planked flooring lay under my feet. And a long staircase with dark treads and white risers was against the wall to the right. A bronze man, three feet tall, stood atop the newel post at the end of its banister. The man was holding a big round glass ball over his head. The ball looked like a globe of the world. Auntie called the man Tiffany. Mother called him Atlas.

Straight ahead a large archway led to the formal dining room and the kitchen. To the left of the archway was a massive, carved wood chest. It looked like it was two different chests stacked one on top of the other. The bottom half had three big drawers running the whole length and width of the chest. The top half was much smaller. It had three drawers across the front with two tall glass doors above. Behind the glass doors were some of Auntie's favorite books.

To the left of the chest, in the middle of the wall, was a large window dressed in sheer white panels that reached the floor. An over-stuffed leather rocker was in front of the window and a Tiffany floor-lamp stood next to it.

Behind me was a small, narrow, burgundy tufted bench with a short back and narrow seat. Beside the bench were two doorways. The one on the far left led back to the vestibule and the other one opened into a large formal parlor at the front of the house. That room was used on special occasions for entertaining special guests only. Auntie always referred to it as the front room and I wasn't allowed to play in there.

On the floor in the middle of the room was a fringed round Oriental rug. The light background of the rug against the dark flooring accentuated its intricate pattern and made its colors pop. In the center of the rug was a round oak table surrounded by four straight-backed chairs. Hanging from the ceiling centered above the table was a large fruit bowl Tiffany chandelier. When it was lighted its apples, oranges, and grapes sent out rays of colored light like a kaleidoscope.

I put my bag of things on the table and sat down. I was disappointed and a bit disgruntled that I had to stay behind but I knew it was always fun at Auntie's house. I loved going to the firehouse with her. She knew all the firemen. She lived across Federal Street from Engine Company Number 9. Her husband had been a fireman with that company, and he died when my mother was in high school. He was always referred to as Uncle. Auntie and Uncle raised my mother from the time she was three years old. Before Mother came to live with them Auntie said she was a ragamuffin running wild, roaming the streets. She told us lots of stories about Mother, but I didn't want to hear them today. I wanted to do something special too.

I lay my hands on the tabletop one on top of the other and put my chin on them. In my head, I heard Auntie say, "Patience is a virtue." I knew I had to be patient and wait until she finished whatever she was doing.

I opened my bag and rifled through the stuff I brought.

I looked at one thing after the other before I tossed each one aside. Nothing interested me at all. It was all the same old stuff. And I was bored with it. There had to be something that was new and different to do. I got up and walked around the room.

I ran my hand over the top of the table; then I touched the man on the newel post. I walked to the tufted bench and felt its velvet upholstery. I knelt on the rocker and looked out the window to see if the rain had stopped. Then I stood staring at the old carved chest.

I looked up at glass doors where Auntie kept her books then down to the three drawers under them. The first one was where Auntie kept the paper dolls my sisters loved to play with. And the one in the middle had her collection of matchboxes that I always played with. The last one had the coloring books and crayons all of us used. *Same old stuff*, I thought and lowered my eyes to the bottom half of the chest.

Curiosity gnawed away at me as I stood looking at them. And, the longer I looked the more intriguing the contents of the drawers became. I had to see what was inside. *But could I?* I thought, *Auntie never told me I couldn't.* So, I spread my arms wide and took hold of the knobs of the first big drawer. I held my breath and pulled hard.

The drawer gave way, sliding out of the chest with a force I didn't expect. Its weight knocked me down to the rug, and the drawer landed on top of me. Two linen tablecloths and an old album tumbled onto the floor beside me. I pushed the drawer to the side and sat up. The album had opened to a page with a photograph of a tall, muscular man in uniform, leaning on a fire truck. The man's head was sideways so all I saw of his face was his profile. *That's Uncle*, I thought, and I turned the page, looking for more pictures of him and the firehouse.

I leafed through the album and saw pictures of women I didn't know who wore high button shoes. And men who wore high starched collared shirts and waistcoats under their jackets. I'd never seen pictures like these before. Some of the images were reproduced on tin and some on a thick, board-like photographic paper. I leafed through a couple more pages looking for more photographs of fire trucks. But when I didn't find more, the album didn't interest me. I set it aside and turned my attention to the drawer, trying to figure how I was going to slide it back in place. I turned the drawer to the side and a tattered, old black book, along with a faded photograph, fell to the rug. I had no idea where they came from until I flipped the drawer over and saw a ripped envelope pasted on the bottom.

I put the drawer down and picked up the photograph. In it I saw an older Indian man standing beside a young Indian man. The two men were with a woman who didn't look Indian at all. I had no idea who they were. The older man wore a fringed shirt and trousers and an elaborate headdress. I assumed he was the Chief because the young man's headdress was smaller, and his clothing was different. The young man was dressed almost the same as the woman. They both wore white robes with wide beaded belts. The belts were tied around their waists so that the ends dangled down the front of their robes. The only difference between them was the garments I saw beneath their robes. He wore white fringed pants and she a full length white fringed dress.

I wondered who they were and why they were dressed like that. I figured it had to be something special. But what, and if it was so special why was the photo hidden? Why was the photo with the black book? And why were they stuffed into an envelope that was pasted under the drawer in Auntie's chest? I had no clue, so I began searching the pages of the black book for answers.

I was in third grade and I read printed books well above my grade level. But the writing in this book was something I'd never seen before. It was handwritten by someone with a fine cursive script. And I didn't understand it.

So, I scanned the pages for anything I could decipher. Some entries had printed letters interspersed so I was able to figure out the words. As I read, I saw what I thought was an Indian name, Mil-tey-wok-en. Sounding the syllables out, I said the name aloud as Auntie came into the room.

"Miltëwakàn? Child, where did you . . ." she stopped, immobilized by the sight of the book in my hands, and stood with her mouth wide open. Several seconds passed.

"What did you do?" she asked.

"It fell out. I wanted to see what was in it and it fell out. That's all."

"That book. You have no right." She wrenched the book from my hands and pressed it to her breast. She bent her head down and held the book to her heart as if she were holding on to the most precious thing in life. Tears fell from her eyes.

"I'm sorry, Auntie, I'm sorry." I felt so bad. I didn't know what I had done to make Auntie cry. I scurried around the room, trying to put everything back where I found it. "It's . . . it's when the drawer came out these fell to the floor too. I saw the Indians. I wanted to know . . ." I hesitated before I tried handing Auntie the picture.

I had never seen Auntie cry before. I felt so helpless. I had no idea what I should do. I watched as she walked to the rocker and fell into it. She laid the book and photograph in her lap and traced the image of the young man with her finger over and over again. After a long while, she raised her head and beckoned for me to come to her side. She stroked my cheek and said, "Well, child, you've opened quite a can of worms." She leaned back in her rocker and closed her eyes. All I could hear was the squeak the rocker made as it moved back and forth until she whispered, "I've kept this secret for over sixty years. Maybe that's long enough." She opened her eyes and smiled at me. "Don't look so worried, child. I'm not going to scold you." She sighed and closed her eyes.

A few more moments passed until she added, "It never occurred to me that after all these years today would be the day."

I waited until she looked up at me again before I asked, "The day for what, Auntie?"

"Achimwi, Danny. In Lenape, it means to tell a story, one that happened a long time ago. This book is the story of an Indian boy who dared to do what one Caucasian girl's father deemed unforgivable."

"Did you know them, Auntie? Did you know the Indians in the picture?"

"Yes. Yes, I did. When I was a girl a Lenape tribe lived not far from here. They still have a large cooperative farm that they own and operate today."

"Lenape? Is Mil-tey-wok-en Lenape? In the book, it

said Mil-tey-wok-en.″

After a long pause, she uttered the name Miltëwakàn and paused again. As she opened her eyes, she turned her head and looked at me. "The Lenape never say his name. He was the Chief's son."

"Is that him in the picture?"

"Yes." She paused and, holding the photograph so I could see, she pointed to the young man. "Yes. That's Tey. Everyone we knew called him Tey."

"Is that the Chief, and the lady, Auntie? Who is the lady?"

"Yes. That's Tey's father Aihàm or Chief Golden Eagle. And the lady, Danny, well, the lady is—she's—she's called Charlotte."

"Did you know her, Auntie?"

"Yes, I did, Danny. I knew her very well; seems like a lifetime ago." She paused and as she traced the face of the young man her eyes glazed, and her voice softened. "Chulëntët. That's what Tey called her. It means little bird. She loved watching the mourning doves bill and coo. She thought it was a beautiful thing to see. He said she billed and cooed when she was with him, so he called her his little bird. Chulëntët. And she called him Tey. When they were alone, she called him Tey eholàk. He taught her how to say that. In Lenape, it means Tey, the one I love."

"Their story, Auntie, will you tell me their story?"

"Their story," she said and looked at me for several moments until a warm smile parted her lips. "Oh child, their story, well . . ." She paused, settled into her rocker, and closed her eyes. I sat down cross-legged on the rug in front of her and waited for her to speak.

"Their story begins—" Auntie hesitated as she opened

the black book. She leafed through until she found some loose pages tucked in it. I watched her eyes as they skimmed over the pages; then, she smiled.

"Their story, Danny—their story begins in 1883 when a Caucasian girl named Charlotte and a full-blood Lenape Indian boy named Miltëwakàn meet in . . ." She hesitated and closed her eyes for a brief moment. "You see," she said, "their relationship was forbidden because he was Indian." She stopped, lowering the pages, and looked at me. "Do you know anything about the Lenape Indians, Danny?"

I shook my head no. "I never heard of them."

"Well, you must. Your mother is part Lenape. So are you. Did you know that?"

"Me? Well, no. I knew she was part Indian but not me."

"Your mother's a quarter and that makes you one-eighth Lenape."

"Were there lots of Indians living around here when you were a girl, Auntie?"

"Yes, there were. They were known as the Delaware Tribe, Danny, because they lived along the river. That's how they got their name. They were once a part of the great Algonquin Nation. There were tribes in Delaware, New Jersey, and Pennsylvania, too. They were peaceful, friendly tribes and they trusted the settlers to trade equitably. Then they discovered the settlers were duping them. They realized they signed away their valuable lands in exchange for worthless trinkets. And they got angry."

I sprang to my feet and imitated someone pulling back on a bow to shoot an arrow. "Then they went to war. They scalped them," I said, "like Cochise and Geronimo did. Didn't they, Auntie? I read about the Indian wars in my encyclopedias."

"No. Not like that, Danny," Auntie said as she took hold of my arms. "Now sit back down and don't do that again."

"Why, Auntie?"

"Because the Lenape would never do that. Not without provocation. Not without cause or a good reason."

"But you said the English settlers took their land. Isn't that a good reason?"

"Well, yes. Actually, it was the reason why the Lenape, and the rest of the Algonquin Nation, sided with the French in 1755. They went to war to get their lands back. Unfortunately, that war didn't end well for the Lenape. They were defeated badly."

"Then they went to Little Big Horn. Didn't they, Auntie? They fought Custer, didn't they, Auntie?"

"No, child. That happened many, many years later. After the French War came our revolution. We expelled the British from America. Then some brilliant men drew up the Constitution and a new government was born. And that is the government that makes the laws we live by today. Unfortunately, Danny, some of those laws are good and some are quite bad. One of the worst ones ever enacted was the Indian Removal Act of 1830. That law gave the white man the right to force Indians off their property. Then they relocated them out west on unsettled, barren lands called reservations. I've heard a few of the elder tribal members say these 'reservations' resembled hell here on earth."

Auntie paused. She tilted her head, first to one side then the other. She sighed then pursed her lips. "What inhumane things man does to man." She said and she shuddered. "That law angered the Indians." She continued, "And every time it was enforced, they became angrier. And many waged war against the white man."

"At Little Big Horn?"

"Yes. There too. But some of the Lenape tribes didn't fight. Some of them never fought in any war. They hadn't spilled one drop of blood. So those clans had the choice to stay or go to a reservation. If they chose to stay, they had to swear allegiance and abide by our laws. If they did, they could keep their hunting and fishing rights. And they could stay on the lands they once owned. Some refused and were sent to reservations. But some remained. Their settlements were near here and in Pennsylvania, too. Tey's clan was one of them. They built their own town and still have a lovely community a few miles down the pike from here. In 1883, they were unique because they were citizens of the United States."

I jerked my head back and stared into Auntie's eyes. "Wait a minute. Citizens?" I asked.

"Yes. Citizens. Why?" Auntie said, questioning me.

"They were already, weren't they?" I said, cocking my head to the side and scrunching up my brow.

Auntie nodded and smiled. "Well, Danny," she said, "according to some they were, but not according to others."

"I don't understand. Why, Auntie?"

"Well, child, it's complicated. It all boiled down to each person's interpretation of the 14th Amendment to the Constitution. Countless bitter fights happened because of it. One side believed the amendment meant the Indians were citizens. But the other side vehemently opposed this interpretation. They believed that the amendment didn't have anything to do with the Indians. They believed that it only gave citizenship to the freed slaves born here. Well, for years the wars continued, both the physical battles and verbal ones raged. Attorneys filed lawsuits on behalf of the Indians. And advocates went to Congress to fight for their rights. Then, in 1924 the Indians were granted citizenship. That's when Congress finally passed the Snyder Act.

"All the while, hatred for them grew. Those opposed mocked and taunted the Indians. They called them horrible names and used atrocious slurs when referring to them. They couldn't stand the sight of Indians. And, Danny, unfortunately, Charlotte's father was one of those people."

"Her father didn't like them, Auntie, not any of them?"

"Not any of them, Danny, no matter what tribe they came from."

"Why not, Auntie?"

"Because of a horrible incident that took place when Charlotte's father was fourteen. His name was Tobias. And on this particular morning, Tobias was helping friends in a neighboring town. Back then people lived in constant fear of hostile renegade Indians. These Indians sought retribution from the white settlers who they thought stole their lands. So, they pillaged towns and murdered the innocent inhabitants indiscriminately. And on this day, a band of renegades raided the town where Charlotte's father lived. They scalped every white man, woman, and child in the town. And Tobias' whole family was among them. When he returned home, he had to bury his father, mother, two sisters and baby brother. So, from that day until the day he died, he sought revenge. He harbored a hatred for Indians so deep nothing could appease it. That's why he forbade Charlotte from associating with Indians.

And he was adamant about it. She could not associate with anyone who had even a single drop of Indian blood in their lineage. That included the peaceful Lenape."

"Then how did she meet Tey, Auntie?"

"Charlotte met Tey on their first day in school. They were both seven years old at the time. Tey was allowed to go to the English School because his father was chief. So, his father brought him every day. Then, after Aihàm finished delivering his produce and goods to homes and businesses in town, he came for Tey. And every Tuesday, without fail, he delivered produce to Charlotte's mother. After school let out for the summer Tey came along with his father to help. So, while Tey's father conducted business with Charlotte's mother, Tey and Charlotte were together."

"Wait a minute. Didn't you say that was forbidden?"

"Well yes," she paused. She tilted her head and smiled. "And, well, no, Danny, because Tobias never knew the children played together. Charlotte's mother never told him. She didn't think there was any harm in innocent children playing together. But buying produce from Tey's father was permissible. You see, Tobias believed Indians were the lowest life form on the evolutionary scale. 'It is,' as he often said, 'the natural order of things for God has ordained they grovel in the dirt for their daily bread.' He had no problem with Charlotte's mother doing business with the Indians as long as she kept them in their place. So, every Tuesday she bought produce from Tey's father. And every Tuesday Tey and Charlotte were together. And as the years passed, the bond between them grew stronger and stronger. They became inseparable, and their relationship blossomed.

"When Tey was old enough, he made the deliveries alone, and Charlotte knew on Tuesday she would see him, rain or shine. She looked forward to it. They were seventeen now and neither one went to school any longer, so it was hard for them to see each other. They would meet now and again on the sly but in those days, nice girls didn't do things like that. Sometimes they would plan to be at a certain place in town at a certain time. Still, as much as Charlotte wanted to meet him, she was always worried that her father would find out.

"But Tuesdays—they had their Tuesdays—and they looked forward to them. That was the one time they were sure that they had at least a few minutes together. Then baseball started again, and things changed.

"A new baseball league formed, and the Phillies came back to Philadelphia. Neither Charlotte nor Tey cared much for baseball. They only wanted to go to the Phillies game so that they could see each other. It was the perfect excuse. When there was a home game on Sunday, they could spend all afternoon together. So, when Tuesday came, they made plans to meet at the first Phillies game of the season.

"If I remember correctly, that Tuesday was. . ." Auntie opened the black book and turned pages till she found the one she was looking for. "Yes," she said and smiled, "It was Tuesday, April 10."

Tuesday, April 10 – Sunday, April 15, 1894

Charlotte Wickham watched through the front window of her house as his wagon pulled to a stop. He jumped out of the wagon to the ground and walked around to the back. All

Charlotte could see was his hat until he rounded the corner at the rear of the wagon. When he came into full view she chuckled with delight.

Tey was a tall, muscular young man with beautiful sun-tanned skin. He jerked his head sideways, moving his long, silky black hair from covering his black sultry eyes. He waved and smiled at her when he noticed Charlotte in the window. She smiled back and waved as her heart fluttered in her chest. He opened the rear gate and set to work unloading baskets of fruits and vegetables.

"He is the most gorgeous thing I think I have ever seen," she whispered, forgetting where she was for the moment. The instant the words left her mouth she held her breath and glanced back, looking around the room. She exhaled loudly when she realized her mother wasn't anywhere in sight and turned her attention to Tey once more.

"Charlotte! Charlotte! Do you hear me, Charlotte?" her mother called from the kitchen.

"Coming, Mother," she answered, and she turned and walked through the house to the kitchen.

"Hurry, girl. Tey is here and we'll have lots of canning to do."

Charlotte stood in the doorway to the kitchen and watched for Tey through the window. When she saw the top of his head, she hurried around the table to hold the door open. He squeezed through the doorway with his arms filled with baskets of vegetables. When their bodies touched, he paused and caressed her with his eyes, then walked into the room and placed the baskets on the table. He turned to face Charlotte again and smiled. A slight blush colored her cheeks, and she nodded her head in his direction.

"Good morning, Chu – ah, Charlotte," Tey said as he nodded his head almost in a slight bow. "I brought beautiful asparagus and spinach this morning. It looks like we are going to have good crops this summer."

"They look delicious, Tey," Charlotte said. She walked to the table, picked out a stalk of asparagus and lifted it to her nose to smell its earthy freshness. She chuckled and looked at Tey.

"Best we've ever grown," he said, smiling at her.

"They'd better be," Miriam said. "Or your father will hear from me."

"Yes, ma'am, Mrs. Wickham. I'll tell him."

Miriam Wickham was a robust woman in her early forties. She was inches shorter than her daughter with graying brown hair she tied back in a bun. Her gold wire-rimmed glasses were always askew on her nose and lent a benevolent glint to her sky-blue eyes. She seldom smiled in public because of her chipped front tooth. And she always spoke in a stern, authoritarian manner that put those who didn't know her on guard.

She reached into her apron pocket and retrieved an envelope. "Make sure you do and give this to him. Tell him I expect nothing but the best. You may go now, Tey." And she handed him the payment envelope.

"Yes, ma'am," he said and bowed. He turned and looked at Charlotte. He smiled, touching his tongue to his lips as if he could taste the air around her. "Charlotte, you are going to the game Sunday, aren't you?"

"Wouldn't miss it. It's their first Sunday game this season," Charlotte's voice was full of excitement. She knew she'd be spending Sunday with Tey. She turned to watch her mother. "Everyone will be there, Mother. Everyone."

Miriam looked at her daughter. She studied Charlotte for a moment. Then she turned her attention to the vegetables on the table. "Tey," Miriam said. "Remind him he owes me one bushel of sweet corn. And a peck of tomatoes from last season. And next week I'll need strawberries, peas, and whatever is ripe as soon as you pick them."

"Yes ma'am, Mrs. Wickham. I'll have them on the wagon. You can choose whatever you like. Will that suit you?"

"That will be fine, Tey. Don't forget to remind him about the tomatoes and corn."

"Yes, ma'am, I will." Tey nodded to Mrs. Wickham and looked at Charlotte as he hid his gloves beside the boxes of vegetables. "See you there, Charlotte." He nodded his head, turned, and left the kitchen. He walked to the street where his horse and wagon stood waiting. He leaned against his wagon, watching the empty walkway on the side of Charlotte's house, and waited.

Charlotte sighed and moved toward the vegetable baskets. She touched Tey's gloves lying on the table. "He forgot his gloves, Mother." She picked them up and ran through the kitchen door and around her house before her mother could stop her. She hollered to Tey and he smiled at the sound of her voice. As she approached, he stood straight with his shoulders back. He grinned and walked to meet her.

"Your gloves, Tey. I'm sure Mother is wise to this," she said as she reached him.

"Thanks, my Chulëntët. I guess we'd better think of another way . . ." He hesitated. "Sunday, Charlotte, I can't wait till Sunday." He gasped to catch his breath as he looked into her eyes. Charlotte's almond-shaped, green-brown hazel eyes always dazzled him. When she smiled, he fought the insatiable urge to kiss her full red lips. He longed to touch her silky golden-brown hair that fell in soft curls to her shoulders. She was tall and slender and reached his nose when she stood next to him. And her complexion was creamy white, unblemished, and perfect. She was the prettiest thing he had ever seen. He'd been in love with her since grade school.

Charlotte extended her hand, holding the gloves. Tey reached for them. For one moment they clasped their hands, lingering as their eyes locked together.

"Charlotte! Charlotte! Do you hear me, Charlotte!"

"Yes, Mother. I'm coming." She shrugged and smiled at Tey. "Must go. See you Sunday, Tey. That's all I'm thinking of too. I can't wait, so don't be late." She turned and walked along the sidewalk that led to the kitchen.

Miriam Wickham studied her daughter as she walked through the kitchen door.

"That ploy stops now. Do you hear me? Charlotte, I don't like the way you look at that boy. And I don't like the way that boy looks at you. He needs to know his place. Your father will not allow such a relationship. Do you understand me? Your father forbids it. You know that. No fraternizing with Indians. Your father has warned you again and again."

"I know, Mother, I know. But . . . Mother, I intend to be nice to them whether you and Papa like it or not. I don't see any reason to hate them. Tey is free—as much a citizen as me—or you. His people, Mother, God created them—like you and me. They can't all be bad no matter what you say. They can't be. Tey can't help being Lenape any more than

I can help being English."

"Charlotte, how many times do I have to tell you to stay away from him? Getting involved with Tey will only bring you grief. Why would you consider relinquishing your station in life to be with him? What's the attraction? What's your infatuation with that boy? Why can't you get interested in one of your own kind? Why don't you like Henry Tomlinson or Theodore Benedict? Nice boys with futures. And Teddy; Charlotte, there's a boy who adores you. He follows you around like a lovesick puppy. Why won't you give them a chance?"

"Because I can't stand them, that's why. They . . . they . . . why do you and Papa think just because you like their families, I should like them too? I can't stand the sight of Henry. He spits at me when he talks and . . . and Teddy, Teddy is so dull. He's nice enough but, Mother, he is as dense as that wall. He . . . Oh, Mama, why won't you understand? I'm nutty about him." Tears ran down Charlotte's cheeks as she put her face in her hands.

Miriam walked around the kitchen table and took her daughter in her arms. "But I do, Charlotte. I do understand. I was once seventeen, you know, and in love like you."

Charlotte lifted her head and looked into her mother's eyes. Miriam sighed and whispered, "There was this boy—I thought I would die if I didn't have him." Miriam hesitated, closing her eyes. For a brief moment, her face changed. She trembled as if she had remembered something long forgotten. "But, Charlotte," she said, turning to look into her daughter's eyes. "I knew I had to do what was right; what was expected; what was respectable. Getting involved with an Indian boy is asking for trouble. I don't care how handsome or smart he is or how much in love you are. I like Tey. He's a fine boy, but a relationship with him is forbidden, as forbidden as the fruit in Eden. So, stop this nonsense. Right this minute. We have work to do."

Miriam stepped away from her daughter and dropped her arms to her skirt, smoothing her apron. "There's canning to do. I need help putting up these vegetables before your father comes home. Charlotte? Are you listening to me? Charlotte. We've got work to do." Charlotte nodded, and Miriam turned and walked to the sink.

Thoughts flooded Charlotte's mind as she walked to the sideboard to get an apron. *Why, Mother, why must I? Why must I do what's right, what's expected, what's respectable? Why can't I do what's right for me?* She felt her anger percolating. *It's the same old argument every time. Obey your father's commands. Do what your father says. But Father says no Indians because they are savages barely tamed from wild beasts. He distrusts Catholics because they are Papists and answer to no one else, not even God. And he refuses to even consider my befriending a Negro or Jew.* Charlotte closed her eyes and heard her father's words echo in her head. *"A good, white skinned, God-fearing Protestant boy who knows the Bible and keeps its laws. That's what you need Charlotte."* I hate it! she thought and slammed the sideboard drawer shut. *How many times have I heard that? But nothing they say satisfies my heart.*

* * * * *

On Sunday, the Philadelphia Phillies were playing their first home game in Camden. The stringent Pennsylvania Blue Laws forbade many things and playing sporting games of any kind happened to be one of them. So, the city of Camden was happy to accommodate the Phillies and the revenues that the games brought in. The city fathers had the old Camden Merritts' ballpark redesigned for the "New York" style game. They added new seats and renovated the enclosures. They built new concession stands and landscaped the lawns. And as the improvements took shape the excitement grew. When Sunday came, Phillies fans squirmed in their pews in anticipation of the first pitch of the season.

After church services, fans from miles around flocked to the ferry dock. They cheered as each vehicle containing a Phillies player rolled off the ferry. And they walked alongside the carriages all the way to the ballpark. Once at the ballpark, the fans took their seats or spread blankets on the lawns. At 12:45pm the high school band marched onto the field. The band accompanied a local vocalist or glee club as they sang a medley of patriotic songs. Then at 1:00pm the Mayor walked onto the field and took his place midway between the mound and home plate. He gave a short speech before throwing out the first pitch. Finally, the Phillies took the field and the crowd roared their delight. The umpire behind home plate hollered, "Play ball!" and the game began.

After church Charlotte hurried home to pack her picnic basket to take to the ballpark. When she finished, she joined her mother in the front room to watch for the first carriage to arrive. Charlotte's house was the favorite meeting place. It was closest to the ballpark and had facilities for the horses and buggies.

When the first rig arrived, Charlotte and Miriam went out to greet them. As each rig arrived, the boy escorted his date to the front porch. After he secured his rig in the portico on the side of the house, he joined the girls. Miriam and Charlotte served lemonade and cookies to those waiting. When the last buggy pulled up, Charlotte excused herself. She went to the kitchen to get her basket. A few moments later her mother followed her inside.

"Charlotte, where's your escort?" her mother asked. "By my count, you are the sixth girl and there are five boys outside. You packed such a large basket I was sure someone I'd approve of would be escorting you, but I see no one. Who are you meeting at the park?"

"Meeting at the park? Mother, Millie never packs en..."

Miriam turned her daughter toward her. She lifted Charlotte's chin so she could stare into her eyes. Charlotte felt her cheeks burn and she turned her head in embarrassment.

"Don't even try to lie to me, Charlotte. If your father finds out..."

"Finds out what, Mother?" Charlotte asked defiantly. "That he was at the game too? What's wrong with that? Tell me, Mother, what's wrong with that?"

Miriam shook her head from side to side. "You are hardheaded and strong-willed. So much like your father." Miriam took hold of her daughter's arms and shook her. "I should forbid you to go right now."

"Are you, Mother? Are you going to forbid me? Go ahead, I'll find another way. I will see him, Mother. I will. You know I will."

"Don't do this, Charlotte. Please listen to me for once

in your life. If your father even thinks your escort is Tey, that lad is in deep trouble. He will make Tey's life miserable. You know that's true. Don't do this, Charlotte."

"Mama, he won't find out."

"I won't lie to him; not even for you."

"I know that, Mama. I know that." Charlotte kissed her mother on the cheek and started for the front door. "Please don't worry," Charlotte said, turning to face her mother. "It's my friends and me enjoying the ball game and he happens by. That's all, Mama. That's all Papa has to know. Mama, that's all he needs to know."

"I hope you are right. Charlotte, remember that you leave this house a good girl. My daughter, I beg you, come home that way."

Charlotte smiled and opened the front door.

"Charlotte!" her mother shouted.

"Yes, Mother. I understand." She turned and looked at her mother. "I promise. I will." She blew her mother a kiss and joined the group, and they walked from the house toward the ballpark.

* * * * *

Charlotte and her friends found a nice spot on a rise behind third base and spread their blankets. They were a close-knit group who had known each other since first grade. They often kept secrets between themselves that their parents never knew. They never tattled on each other. For them that was unthinkable.

After the group settled in, the girls passed around the delicacies they'd made. While the girls talked about the new dresses and shoes they saw in Philadelphia, the boys discussed the rules for the New York Style of play and who was in the game's starting line-up.

The Providence Grays were playing the Phillies. The Grays were a formidable team, but the Phillies fielded a Hall of Fame outfield. The trio, Ed Delahanty, Billy Hamilton, and Sam Thompson were considered the best in the league. Jack Taylor was the starting pitcher and he was a strikeout artist. And Tuck Turner was on the bench for backup if needed. The boys agreed the Phillies couldn't lose.

Charlotte looked around as the top half of the first inning was ending. She worried that Tey wasn't coming to the game. Seeing him was the reason she was there.

When the top half of the inning ended Taylor had held the Grays to one hit. Everyone in the crowd got to their feet and applauded the Phillies as they left the field. Charlotte was adjusting her skirt to stand up with the crowd when she heard a familiar voice. "Afternoon everyone." he said as he offered her his hand. She looked at the hand before she raised her eyes to meet his. Tey smiled. "Afternoon, Charlotte." His smile made his eyes twinkle and he nodded his head. "May I help you up?" He wore corduroy trousers and a woolen over-jacket the same as the other boys.

"Thanks, Tey. Where have you been? Are you hungry?"

"Charlotte," Millie Hertzog, Charlotte's best friend and confidante, said. "Your father just walked in. He's with the Mayor in the VIP seats. Be careful."

Charlotte looked toward home plate at the VIP seats and saw her father. At supper the night before, he'd mentioned that he hadn't accepted the Mayor's invitation.

He said he didn't think that he would be going to the game. So, seeing him in the VIP seats made her angry.

"Damn," she said under her breath.

"Easy, Chulëntët," Tey whispered and a smile curled his lips.

Charlotte looked at him. A blush that started at the base of her neck colored her cheeks. "Yes. But he said he wasn't coming. He's spoiled everything." After a moment she smiled. "Well, at least have a bite to eat, Tey. I made most of this for you anyway, so let's sit down."

By the top of the third, the Phillies were leading the Grays by five runs. Tey and Charlotte talked, laughed and held hands as they shared the picnic she had prepared. They rarely glanced at the game. Yet the whole time Tey watched Charlotte's father. Late in the inning, he leaned his head toward Charlotte's. He moved his index finger in the general direction of the VIP seats and whispered in her ear. "Looks like your Papa's leaving. Once he does, will you take a walk with me?"

Charlotte looked toward the VIP seats and smiled. She turned to Tey. "Where? Any place special?" She laughed. He nodded and turned his attention to the VIP seats. "You think he'll be back?"

"No. Last night he said he had a meeting about the old Cooper Mansion. They want to renovate it and turn it into a library and make the grounds a park. The city council wants my father to make the deal. Papa has a meeting with the heirs tomorrow so he will be busy for quite a while this afternoon." Tey got to his feet and offered his hand to Charlotte.

"Let's go see what they're talking about. The mansion's down there." He pointed in the direction of the house.

"It's boarded up, isn't it?"

"Yes, it is but there's a way to get in." He turned and looked into her eyes. "It's safe. No one will see us there. Will you come with me?"

Charlotte nodded in agreement and turned to her friend. "Mil?"

"Don't worry; I'll take care of your things. But Charlotte, be careful. And make sure you're back before the game ends." she said, motioning toward the group, "None of us want to face your mother if you're not there. Please."

"We will be. Thanks, Mil. Thanks, everyone."

"You're dotty; you know that, don't you?"

"Maybe so. But Mil, I can't be because this feels so right..." Charlotte shrugged. She smiled then turned away. She took a few steps and stopped. She turned back to face her friend and said, "If Papa comes by . . ."

Millie waved at her. "We'll cover for you. We always do, so don't worry. And don't forget to be back before the game ends."

* * * * *

Tey led Charlotte around the old mansion to a set of French doors in the rear of the house. He took out the knife he always carried tucked in his boot and pried open the door. The house was dreary and dark and smelled musty and old. Tey took hold of Charlotte's hand and led her through a dank, dark, empty room. They walked through a doorway into a huge, sunlit, elegant front entrance foyer.

The sunshine streamed into the room through clear leaded glass windowpanes. The rectangular panes surrounded the massive mahogany front door on her right. And on her left was a sweeping central staircase with dark stair treads and white risers. It ascended to meet an intricately carved fretwork balcony on the second level. In the center of the foyer stood a large, round mahogany table on an Oriental rug. A huge crystal chandelier dangled from the second-floor ceiling above it.

"We're going up here," Tey said and started up the stairs. "Watch the third step. The boards are loose." He looked at Charlotte and stopped. "Charlotte, are you all right?"

"I don't think we should do this, Tey. We shouldn't be here."

"It will be fine, Charlotte. No one comes by; at least, no one has ever come in that I've seen. I come here a lot and, well, I've made a place here, a spot that's ours. I was hoping I could show you. Please come upstairs with me. Please, Charlotte. Nothing's going to happen. Please."

Charlotte climbed the stairs and followed him to the second-floor landing. Tey took her by the hand. They walked toward a huge, circular leaded glass window at the end of a long hallway. They turned into a room as they neared the end of the hall. The room was bright and cheerful. There was a flowered down-feather bed and coverlet on the floor with feather pillows placed on it. He turned to Charlotte and shrugged. "What do you think?"

"You did this?"

"Whitewashed the walls and the floor and bought the pillows from Mrs. Havernathy for a penny. Got the feather bed at Woolworth's and brought the blanket from the farm. I stay here a lot. Do you like it, Charlotte?"

"It looks so nice, Tey," she said, turning around,

looking at what Tey had done. "Why do you stay here?"

"Nights I work at Esterbrook. They won't let me in the boarding house, and it's too far to walk home so I stay here. There's even running water."

Charlotte chuckled and turned to look at him. There was a hunger, a desire burning in her eyes, and Tey walked as close to her as he could until their bodies touched. Charlotte reached for his face and held it in her hands. She pressed her lips against his. Tey wrapped his arms around her, kissing her on the mouth and the neck as he laid her down on the coverlet. She stroked his hair and touched his cheek as deep thoughts clouded her eyes.

"What, Charlotte? What are you thinking?"

She sat up. "Oh, Tey. What are we going to do? We can't stay here. We can't stay anywhere. Last week when the Macasse's saw us I was sure they'd tell Papa. I want you so much, but we can't keep doing this; we can't. My mama knows, and Papa, Tey, I'm so torn. I don't want to deceive him but he is wrong and I am afraid of what he'll do if he finds out."

"Oh my, Charlotte. I thought . . . I'm sorry. I don't want to pressure you, Charlotte, I love . . ."

"Don't be sorry, Tey. This place; what you did; it's . . . well . . . it's, it's just, I don't think I'm . . . Tey, I don't want to lead you on, to make you think that I would . . ."

He put his finger across her lips. "I don't. Charlotte, I don't. You didn't make me think anything. I want to love you with all my heart. Is that so wrong?" Tey watched her expression for a second before getting to his feet. He walked to the window. He stood there for a few moments. As he turned toward her, he said, "I guess this is a bad idea, isn't it?"

Charlotte got to her feet and walked to him. "No, it isn't." She took hold of his hands and wrapped his arms around her waist. "Hold me, Tey. Please hold me."

He looked into her eyes and kissed her nose and lips. "We should go back," he whispered. Charlotte nodded, and they left the room.

They walked side by side, glancing at each other, not saying a word until they reached the ballpark. "Charlotte, do . . . do you think we could, ah . . ."

"Yes," she interrupted and turned to look at him. "Yes, we could."

"Would you, Charlotte? You'd meet me there . . . to be together . . . would you?"

"Yes, Tey, I would." A smile started at the corners of both their mouths and spread till they were beaming at each other. The crowd inside the ballpark roared their approval. "I guess we'd better go in," Charlotte said, and they walked to where their friends were watching the game.

It was the bottom of the eighth with one out and two men on, and the Phillies were leading eleven to two. Charlotte and Tey sat side by side, holding hands. They didn't care who won or lost. They only wanted the baseball game to never end.

Chapter 2
Mid-morning, October 21, 1951

Auntie sat up in her chair. "I'd like to stop for a few minutes, Danny. It's time for a cup of tea and maybe some milk and cookies too. I made a batch of sugar molasses ones this morning. Are you interested?"

"Yes, please. I'm hungry. Mother was in such a rush I couldn't finish my cereal," I answered, springing to my feet.

Auntie laid the book and photograph on the table and went into the kitchen. I walked to the window and looked out. It was raining even heavier than it was when I arrived. I thought if it doesn't stop, we wouldn't be able to go to the firehouse.

I followed Auntie into the kitchen and sat at the kitchen table, watching her without saying a word. She moved with grace and barely made a sound as she brewed the tea and set a plate of cookies in front of me.

"This morning I baked a rhubarb pie for your mother. She loves rhubarb pie. It's so seldom your whole family is here for supper I want to make a special meal. So, I'll need your help getting supper together. How's that sound?"

She smiled and sat down at the table across from me. She reached across and patted my hand. As she removed her hand from mine, she took hold of the sugar bowl that was in the middle of the table beside the creamer. She removed its lid and scooped one spoonful of sugar from the bowl. She stirred it into her tea and poured a tiny bit of milk from the creamer into the mixture. She lifted the cup to her mouth with her pinky finger extended and took a sip.

"Perfect," she said, replacing the cup in her saucer. She leaned forward and put the lid on the sugar bowl before she again lifted her cup.

"Does that mean you won't finish the story? About the Indians?"

"No, but what about the firehouse? I thought you wanted to see the new truck." she said before she took another sip.

"It's raining too hard to go."

"And the Sugar Bowl? No ice cream either?" she asked as she placed her cup on its saucer.

"The story, Auntie. I want hear the story."

"It's quite long."

"Please?"

She smiled and nodded her head. "Yes, all right then. Where were we? Do you remember?"

I shook my head yes. "He had shown her the place in the mansion and they went to the ballpark. Auntie? Did the Phillies play in Camden often?"

"Yes. That summer and fall anyway. I don't remember when the Blue Laws changed."

"Blue Laws? Who cares?" I interrupted, "I want to know about them. Did they go to the ballpark again?"

"Yes." She chuckled. "Yes, they did. They went every Sunday that there was a game. Charlotte and her friends met at her house, and together they walked to the park. The group often went places together so Charlotte's father didn't suspect a thing. They always picnicked at the same spot, right behind third base. And Tey always wandered over and joined them. Charlotte's friends knew she and

Tey were in love, and they also knew how much Tobias Wickham hated Indians. But friends trust friends to keep secrets, and this secret they kept well.

"So, while they were at the game Charlotte and Tey made no overtures towards each other. They patiently waited until they were sure they were safe from Tobias Wickham's scrutiny. Then they'd leave the group at the park and walk to the old mansion. On the way, they were careful that no one would suspect they were together. Once inside they knew they were safe from prying eyes and they'd climb the stairs up to their secret place. But Tey was getting impatient. He wanted an answer to his question so on Sunday, April . . ."

Sunday, April 22 – Sunday, April 29, 1894

As soon as they had entered the room Tey took Charlotte in his arms. His lips pressed against hers as he guided her to the feather bed and laid her down.

"I want to love you, Charlotte. I want to love every inch of you. Let me love you."

"Tey eholàk. I love you so much. But we can't. Not yet."

He covered her lips with his and kissed her nose before rolling to the side. He lay beside her, breathing heavily for a few moments. "I love you, Charlotte. With all my heart I love you. When will you let me love you? Please, make up your mind and tell me when. I need to know. This limbo is impossible."

"I know, Tey," she said. "I love you too. But we can't. Not yet. Not until we wed."

"I know. I know. You promised your mother."

Charlotte rolled on her side to face him and she

touched his cheek. "It has nothing to do with Mother. It has to do with us, Tey. What if we never can wed? What if it is impossible for us? Did I tell you that Teddy asked Papa if he could court me? I raised a ruckus when Teddy told me. I told Papa to stop imagining any relationship between Teddy Benedict and me, ever. Papa got so angry and said I'd better choose soon, or he would do it for me. He is threatening to send me to Saint Mary's Convent School. I heard him tell Mother. He said they can't take me until next fall. He told Mother that it's unnatural for a female my age not to even consider seeing a boy like Teddy or any of the others. He thinks the Papists—the Papists! As much as he hates them, he thinks the Papists can 'straighten out my thinking.' That's what he told Mother. Tey, he thinks I don't like boys. He asked Mother if I did. Can you believe that?" She laid her head on his chest close to his shoulder and traced his mouth with her finger.

Tey laughed. "A convent! Don't like boys? You? If he knew." Tey rolled on his side and faced her. He furrowed his brow as he studied her face and seemed to be in deep thought for a few minutes. Charlotte looked into his eyes and asked him what was wrong.

"He should know, Charlotte. He should hear it from me. I want to talk to him. Please, don't stop me. Charlotte, he might listen. I may be able to make him understand. I've been thinking about this a lot. I want to walk into his office tomorrow morning. If there are people around, he'll have . . ."

"Have you arrested!" she interrupted. "That's what he'll do! Or he'll have you thrown in jail! Or kill you on the spot! He hates you! He hates the thought of you. You know that. He hates all Indians, just hates them. Listen to me,

Tey. Please don't do anything rash. There is no talking to him about it. He won't listen. He told me he would kill any savage that dared touch even one hair on my head. And if I ever allowed it, he'd kill me along with him. I thought it bluster but it's not. He's heard something because two nights ago at dinner he asked me about you. He said someone saw us together and he said there were rumors. The look on his face, Tey, sent a chill up my spine. He grabbed my arm so tightly I thought he'd break it. Then Mother stepped between us and was almost cut by the knife he was holding. He shoved her aside and stepped towards me again. He clenched his jaw and said if he found out even one word of the rumor was true, he'd burn your village to the ground. Then he stared directly into my eyes and in a barely audible voice that was so menacing he said, "I'll see you in your grave first, girl!" Oh, Tey, he'll kill us both. I'm sure of it. He frightens me so. He's scared me before but not like this."

"Now don't you see? We have no other choice, do we? We must do it my way."

"I don't know. I'm so torn. How can I betray my father like that? And my mother, Tey, I don't want to hurt her. She's dreamed of giving me a beautiful wedding. I'm her only child; she's poured everything she has into me. Tey, there has to be another way."

"How, Charlotte? Do you have a better plan? How else are we ever going to be together? It works. Next week you will be eighteen, and you won't need his consent. If you want, we can wait until you are sure your father will be out of town for a few days to do it. If he's out of town, maybe we could convince your mother to come. We could ask. There's no harm in asking if that's what you want.

Chulëntët, it's the only way. No one else will go against your father. Everyone in this town is afraid of him. My plan will work. Charlotte, it will work."

"How can it, Tey? I won't live a lie and I refuse to live in sin."

Tey got on his knees. He sat upon his feet and lifted Charlotte onto her knees, setting her in front of him. He took her face in his hands, and he looked into her eyes. "Charlotte, listen to me. Please listen to me. It works. Even in God's eyes it works. So, hear me out. Because my father is Chief, the state has named him magistrate of our community. He has the authority to do lots of things. He can perform weddings, Charlotte. He is the law by your rules and by ours: the leader, the elder who everyone looks to. I talked to him. He said he would marry us as long as we agree to marry in the ways of my people. He wants his son to have the full rite. I know you consider it heresy, but it's not. It's the only way. And once done, your father cannot change it. Once done we cannot change it. The eyes of God will see us. You and I will be one forever. What does it matter if the rite is Lenape? God is God, Charlotte. He is the same whether yours or mine. He will bless us. I love you. I want to marry you. Isn't that what you want too?"

"Yes, Tey, that's what I want too. I want to marry you more than anything else. But I'm so afraid to do it. I'm so afraid because my father . . . he will find us. No matter where we go, he will find us and . . . and he will destroy you. I won't let that happen. I'd rather give you up than have Father—" Charlotte flung herself into his arms and sobbed.

"Hush, Chulëntët, hush." Tey stroked her hair and rubbed her back until her tears subsided. He kissed her forehead and said, "There's a game next Sunday. Think about it this week. And give me your answer on Sunday."

Charlotte looked into his eyes and nodded her head yes.

"We'd better go, my little bird. Are you ready?"

Charlotte sighed. "I love you very much."

"I know," he said and smiled at her. "You and I are one. I don't think anything known to man could ever change that." He leaned down, kissed her on the lips and burst out laughing.

"Why are you laughing?"

"It's the strangest thing. A picture of two little children flashed in my mind." He smiled at her and shrugged. As he got to his feet to offer Charlotte his hand, she pulled him down to the bed.

"Tell me. Tell me what you saw, Tey. Was it us?"

"Yes. Yes, it was. Do you remember the first day we met? We were seven years old. We stood across the room from each other. Do you remember?"

"Of course I do. You came and sat next to me on the long wooden bench in old Madam Tiller's room. You kept looking at me out of the corner of your eye. You didn't think I noticed, but I couldn't take my eyes off you either."

"You were so pretty. I finally got the nerve to hold your hand."

"What made you think of that, Tey?"

"From that moment till this and for the rest of my life there will be no one but you, Charlotte. There can never be. Let your father do what he must. He can never take you from me. Only God can do that. Don't fear what we cannot control. As far as I am concerned, whatever time we have together is worth whatever pain it costs. So, marry me, Charlotte. Let's choose a day, and I'll have my father make the preparations. Think long and hard this week, and please say yes, Chulëntët."

* * * * *

All week long Tey worried that Charlotte would say no. Alone at night in the big mansion he practiced what he'd say to convince her otherwise. He wrestled with his feelings and the uncertainty that bedeviled him. But by Friday he settled his thoughts. He made up his mind she'd definitely say yes. Feeling confident, he focused on the questions and problems Charlotte would pose. He wanted to be ready with the answers and solutions that he knew Charlotte needed.

Still, when Sunday's game time came his confidence faded. He hesitated as he approached the group searching for the something witty to say. A hint of nervousness was in his voice as he tripped over his first few words before sitting next to her. *How beautiful she is*, he thought as he searched her eyes for some sign. He saw nothing. He reached for her hand. She pulled away and pointed to something in the distance as she spoke. She laughed and talked with everyone, rarely looking in his direction. She didn't say a word after they left the ballpark. Only a few stolen glances passed between them as they walked to the mansion. In silence they climbed the stairs and walked to their secret place. Anxious and agitated, Tey could no longer restrain himself.

"Did you think about it, Charlotte?"

"Of course! Nothing else."

"And?"

She put her arms around his neck. "God is smiling on us, Tey. Your plan will work." She leaned in and covered his lips with hers, lingering. They kissed several times until she moved, kissing her way to his ear. "Of course I will. You knew I would..." she whispered, then hesitated. She moved back so she could look into his eyes. "Didn't you?" she asked.

Hot red streaks spread from his neck to color his cheeks. He shrugged, turned his head to the side and smiled. Charlotte smiled, giggled then laughed. "Did you think otherwise?"

"You ah . . . you had me wondering."

"Me? Why?"

"You were so cold. I thought that. . ."

"Tey. I was afraid . . . with everyone there . . . I was afraid I'd say . . . Oh Tey, I'm sorry if you thought . . . you silly goose," she said as she released her arms from around his neck. She took hold of his hands. She gently pulled him toward the feather bed. "I was afraid I'd tell you there because I'm bursting with good news, Tey. Everything seems to be falling into place. Father took on a new client. He told us all about it at dinner Friday night. He said his new client wants to build a plant in Chicago of all places. But he is having problems with water rights along the shores of Lake Michigan. He needs the water to cool his machinery, but the city of Chicago opposes it. So, Father has to go to Chicago once a week until he resolves all the issues. He said he must meet with the city officials each step of the planning and building of the plant. Tey, it's an omen! It all works in our favor. He gave Mother a calendar with his travel dates marked on it and I copied it down. Now we can pick the date for our wedding."

They studied each travel date on Tobias' schedule. They counted and recounted the hours between his departures and his returns. Then they eliminated all trips less than two nights long. And they narrowed the remaining ones down to three. Out of those three dates they chose Tuesday, July 17, 1894. It was the perfect date, they thought. Tobias would board the train for Chicago in the morning at 9:37. And he would be out of town until the evening of the 20th, arriving home at 6:32pm. They'd have three days together before Tobias came back to town. They decided that Charlotte would see her father off at the station. Then, after his train left, she would take a cab to the clearing outside of town where Tey would be waiting. Aware that if Tobias Wickham got wind of this they would be in grave danger, they set a new plan in motion.

* * * * *

Charlotte walked ahead of Tey all the way back to the ballpark. It was the bottom of the eighth when they arrived. Charlotte stomped to her blanket and flopped down. A few seconds later Tey said his goodbyes and left the park.

Millie looked from Charlotte to Tey then back again as if her head were on a swivel. All the while she waved off the other girls' gestures urging her to find out what happened. Bewildered she went to Charlotte's side.

"Charlotte?" she whispered.

"What!" Charlotte snarled.

"Calm down. I just thought you might want to talk. That's all."

Charlotte took hold of Millie's hand. "Sorry Mil."

"What happened?" Millie asked, "It might help if you

talk about it."

"A beast, that's what he is. I should have listened. Everyone told me." Charlotte cried out as she put her face in her hands, pretending to weep. "How could I be so wrong?"

Millie put her arms around her friend. "It's for the best Char. You know that."

Charlotte nodded her head and looked up at her friend. "Yes. You're probably right."

* * * * *

Tey and Charlotte were not seen together after Sunday. They met in the old mansion when they could. Every moment of their lives was now cloaked in total secrecy. No one could know what they were up to, not even Charlotte's mother. But Charlotte was having great difficulty with that. Escaping Miriam's prying questions created a huge dilemma for her. Confiding in Miriam was inconceivable, yet lying to her she found impossible.

Miriam knew Charlotte was sneaking out of the house and suspected she was meeting Tey. She confronted her daughter every chance she got, and she threatened to tell Tobias if she didn't stop. Still, Charlotte was sure Miriam's words were simply idle threats. *She knows I've been with him, yet she hasn't said one word. Why would she tell him now?* she thought. So, when next confronted, she wrapped her arms around her Mother's neck. She whispered in her ear, "Mother, you don't want to know. Not yet. I will tell you everything when it's time. Please, it's best you know nothing now, so let me be." And she ran from the house and did not return for hours.

Alarmed and frightened for her daughter, Miriam

worried night and day. She felt she must stop Charlotte before she made the biggest mistake of her life. She worried that Tobias would hear rumors about Charlotte and suspect something. And she worried that she'd be the one that would let that something slip.

Miriam knew in her heart her child was on a path leading to much sorrow and pain. Still, she had raised her daughter to think for herself. From the time Charlotte was able to utter her first word, Miriam taught her to say what she meant. She told her to never fear speaking her mind. That's the way, she instructed her, she'd get what she wanted, and she should accept nothing less. She pounded into Charlotte's head that women were equal to men. She should never feel as though she wasn't as bright, intelligent, or important as the male of the species. "Someday women will have equal rights," she said. "But it will never happen if women of your generation don't stand together and demand it."

Miriam taught her well. She marveled at the ease at which Charlotte stood her ground and often went toe to toe with her father. But Miriam knew what Charlotte contemplated now was beyond the pale. Charlotte could never change her father's mind about interracial unions. That argument she would never win because his prejudice ran deep; so deep it scarred his very soul.

He harbored a vile hatred and she'd seen its handiwork many times before. She knew it was impossible for him to ever understand Charlotte's feelings. And she knew he would never accept it. Ever! So, Miriam prayed and prayed. She hoped against all hope that what Charlotte was doing wasn't what she was thinking. Still, deep down in her heart, she knew.

Chapter 3
Lunchtime, October 21, 1951

Auntie stopped. She removed her glasses and clasped the bridge of her nose between her thumb and middle finger. She closed her eyes for several seconds before she put her glasses on again. She looked at her watch and noted the time. "Oh my, Danny, it's near lunch time already. I'd better get cracking, or I won't have supper ready when everyone gets here. I have that Lebanon baloney you like and fresh sliced white cheese. How does that sound?"

"Super, Auntie. And mustard too, please."

"I was thinking the same thing, on some nice rye bread with caraway seeds," Auntie said and chuckled.

We didn't say much during lunch. I kept thinking about Charlotte and what Charlotte's mother may have been thinking.

Auntie's voice broke into my thoughts when she said, "Let's shell the peas while we talk."

"Sure. I like to shell peas."

Auntie cleared the table and covered it with a linen cloth. She went through the back door to the pantry. She brought in a big brown bag full of bright green pea pods bursting with peas. She dumped the contents of the bag in the middle of the table. Then she handed me a bowl and put a bowl at her place at the table.

"Nice and fresh. I knew you were coming so when the huckster came by yesterday, I bought the rhubarb for the pie and these peas. Nice supper we will have tonight. I'll put the roast in the oven in an hour and we'll peel the potatoes at three. Yesterday I went to the bakery after I dropped a pound cake off at the firehouse. I bought that nice crusted bread that your father likes. So, we will have that too. How does that sound to you, Danny?"

"They're Mother's favorites—fresh peas with mashed potatoes and gravy and rhubarb pie. You think about Mother a lot, don't you, Auntie?"

"Yes, and you and your sisters, too. And your father. Every one of you."

"I guess that's what love is, isn't it Auntie? Thinking about each other. That's what it is, isn't it?"

"Yes, it is, Danny. That's a big part of it."

"Is that what Charlotte's mother did? Think about her, Auntie?"

"Well, yes. I suppose she did."

"You said she hoped it wasn't what she was thinking. What was Charlotte's mother thinking, Auntie?"

"What was she thinking? A mother's intuition, I guess. She thought, because of all the secrecy, that her daughter and Tey were planning to run off together. Of course, she was right. That was exactly what they were planning to do and Tey had the perfect place in mind.

"You see, two years earlier Tey accepted an apprenticeship at Esterbrook Pen Company. By January 1894, Tey had proved that he was quite capable. His foreman was a young man named Saul. Saul talked to Tey about applying for admission to an engineering program. Saul was a graduate and knew all about it. Both Rutgers College and the College of New Jersey offered the program."

"You mean Rutgers University, don't you, Auntie?

Mother wanted to go there."

"No, Danny. Rutgers wasn't a university in 1894. It was a private college. And the College of New Jersey didn't become Princeton University until 1896. Still, it was always referred to as Princeton. But university or not, they both were good schools in 1894. And Saul knew both schools offered a variety of scholarships. He went to school at Rutgers on scholarship. He also knew that both schools offered ones specifically for the Native American people. And he knew Tey needed a scholarship to defray the cost of his education."

"Did he get it, Auntie? For Rutgers, I mean?"

"Yes. Saul forced Tey to apply. He threatened to fire him if he didn't. You see, Saul thought Tey had exceptional abilities. He felt that Tey was a perfect candidate for the programs. He told Tey so many opportunities had opened for him after he graduated. He was sure the same would happen for Tey. So, with Saul's help and encouragement, Tey applied to both schools. He heard from Rutgers in April. He had been accepted into the Work/Study program on scholarship and his classes started the first week in September."

"The same as Pop did when he went to Drexel, Auntie? He worked after school. Mother took care of us, and you helped."

"It was very much the same thing, Danny. But, Tey and Charlotte wouldn't have anyone to help because they had to move to New Brunswick. That only added to the doubts Tey had about going to Rutgers. Tey was a very responsible young man. He knew he had to find a way to provide for his new wife. He had to figure out how he would pay for their food and lodging along with the books and supplies he'd need.

"The scholarship only covered the cost of tuition along with an offer of employment in his field of study. But it didn't guarantee that the participating employer hired Indians. And finding a place to live was another problem. The college subsidized housing suitable for a couple; however, Indian students were not allowed to live on campus. They had to take a flat in town instead. Still, as they drafted their wedding plans, they decided it was the best way to get away from Tobias. So, Tey accepted the scholarship at Rutgers.

"They planned to spend a day or two in the wedding cottage that Tey's parents were preparing, and then they would be on their way. They'd leave Tobias Wickham and Camden behind to get settled into their new life together in New Brunswick. But this all changed in July. Tey kept one very important secret from Charlotte until their wedding night."

Auntie stood up with the bowl of peas she had shucked in her hand. She reached over to my side of the table and picked up the bowl of peas I had shucked. She took both bowls to the kitchen sideboard. When she returned to the table, she stood a moment, smiling, and watched me. Then she gathered the linen cloth that covered the table. She made sure all the pea pods stayed inside.

"I'll use those to make a nice soup," Auntie said as she swept the gathered cloth to her side of the table with her arm.

Curiosity was gnawing away at me. I had to know, so I reached over the table and took hold of her hand. "What, Auntie, what didn't he tell her?"

She chuckled as she took the tablecloth to the sink.

"Well, Danny," she said as she sat down at the table. "What Tey didn't tell Charlotte was he received a letter from Princeton. He jumped at their offer and declined the one at Rutgers. Tey made it a point to tell no one. Tey was sure if no one knew where they were Tobias Wickham could not find them, and Charlotte would be safe.

"Now everything was set, and Tey approached his father, Aihàm, about performing the ceremony. His father agreed. And Tey's mother gathered materials to make the garments that he and Charlotte would wear. His community members began preparing the ceremonial grounds for the wedding and feast. And, at Charlotte's request, Tey asked his father to include the white man's exchange of rings. Aihàm, reluctant at first, looked for a suitable place to insert it in the Lenape rite. But as the date for the nuptials neared, Aihàm grew more and more apprehensive. He was having second thoughts. He knew the power that Tobias Wickham wielded, and he feared for both his son and his son's prospective bride. He wanted to see the two together. He had to know in his heart that the power of this union would withstand whatever was to come. He told Tey he must meet Charlotte before he would agree to the final details and perform the ceremony.

"Tey arranged for his parents to meet Charlotte on a Wednesday as I recall." She opened the black book and leafed through. "Yes," she said, "It was Wednesday. Wednesday, June ..."

Wednesday, June 27 – Tuesday, July 10, 1894

The clearing was small with plenty of grass and a deep well for watering horses. There was a small, covered pavilion with a table and two benches nestled in the pine trees. Travelers relaxed under the pavilion while their horses grazed and rested. The clearing wasn't visible from the road and many who went by missed it because they didn't know it was there.

Tey and Charlotte arrived at the meeting place early. It was hot for the last week in June, and not a breeze blew in any direction. Charlotte took off her bonnet and laid it on the table. Tey brought her a cup of cool water from the well, and they sat down to wait for his parents.

"Hè nkwis (hello, my son)," Tey's father said as he walked from the pinewoods.

"Hè nuxat (hello, dear Father)," Tey said as he stood up. He reached for Charlotte's hand. Charlotte rose to her feet and walked with Tey.

"Charlotte," he said, smiling. "You remember my father. Father, my beautiful Chulëntët." He said while turning to face his father. "Please, Father, speak English so my Chulëntët understands. Where is. . ." He stopped when he saw movement in the pines as a woman emerged. Tey let go of Charlotte's hand and walked to the woman and hugged her.

"Anati (dear Mother), please speak English so Charlotte understands. Come," he said, leading her to Charlotte. "My Mother, this is my Chulëntët."

Charlotte nodded her head and said hello. They said nothing in return. They stood motionless staring back at her. Unnerved by his parents' expressionless faces she looked to Tey's for help. Her mind shouted *say something—anything please!* Still, nothing changed and no one said a word. She didn't have the slightest idea what the protocol was or what was the acceptable thing to do or say. As she looked from one to the other a disquieting anxiety grew in the pit of her stomach. She tensed and her body trembled. She felt the sweat trickle down her back. She stuttered as she searched for the right words to say. I must prove myself worthy of Tey, she thought. But another voice in her brain yelled *STOP . . . Stop it this minute . . . just say what you feel . . . say it from your heart.*

"It . . . It's . . . It is a great pleasure to see you again, Aihàm," she said as confidence trickled into her speech, "and to meet you, Tey's Mother. I hope someday you will think I am worthy of your son. I know you're worried about my father; well, so am I. So is Tey. My father is a wealthy and powerful man. He can cause many problems. But please understand I do not want to marry Tey to spite him or in any way hurt him. I love my father, but he is wrong about Tey." She turned toward Tey and took hold of his hands. "On all things concerning Tey, my heart wields the power, not my father . . . because I love your son. He and I have been in love since we were seven years old." She squeezed Tey's hand and smiled at him. She turned back and looked at Tey's parents. "This is not a passing fancy. This is not a game I choose to play for fun. No. This is real. This is for the rest of our lives. Together. We do not go into this blindly. We know life will not be easy for us. We know people will object to this union, but we still wish to take this step. Tey and I want to become one in the eyes of God. Please, please do us this honor. Please give us your blessing."

Charlotte pursed her lips, bowed her head, and turned to face Tey. Tey smiled at her and nodded in approval. He gazed into Charlotte's eyes and spoke with a quiet resolve. "We are one, my Father, my Mother. I hope you will honor our wishes. We will be husband and wife under white man's law. Someone somewhere will say the words and file the papers that join us for eternity. We know in our hearts that there is someone who will do us the honor." Tey turned and looked into his mother's eyes. Then he turned his head, moving his eyes from his mother's to his father's. His body followed until he stood facing his father. In a quiet, prayerful voice he said, "We wish that person to be you, Father."

Tey's parents studied their son and Charlotte for a few moments. They spoke in Lenape and instructed their son to wait. They turned and walked into the pinewoods.

"What's happening, Tey? Where are they going?" Charlotte asked.

"Shush, Chulëntët," he whispered. "They go to talk. Now let me listen. They will now decide."

She listened, hoping to understand something, but they spoke only in Lenape. Tey leaned toward her and whispered, "My mother is upset you call me half a name. But Father told her that is the white man's way. Shush. They talk more . . . they talk of your courage." Tey chuckled.

"What, Tey?"

"They think you have spunk. Hush, wait; they speak more . . . pretty, they both agree that you are pretty . . . and Mother worries you can't cook, and Father thinks you are too skinny, wait . . ."

"What else, Tey, what are they saying?"

His parents turn their backs towards Tey and Charlotte and spoke softer than before. Tey strained to hear what they were saying. He took a small step and leaned his body in the direction of his elders. He listened. He reached for Charlotte's hand as a smile began at the outside corners of his mouth. He straightened to his full height walking back to her. And he put his finger across Charlotte's lips to silence her. He cocked his head sideways, listening for another moment. His eyes sparkled as the smile spread across his face. He looked into Charlotte's eyes as he held her face in his hands. He kissed her forehead and then her lips. "Looks like we're getting married. They like you." He took her in his arms, and they kissed, releasing the fervent passion they had locked inside. And, for the moment, in their reverie, the world and everything in it disappeared. Nothing existed but the two of them.

Without warning, Tey reeled his whole body around assuming an aggressive, threatening posture. In one fluid movement, he pushed Charlotte, holding her behind his back, protecting her. He reached in his boot and drew his knife. His expression was fierce. He glared out, ready to fight his assailant until he recognized his father. Embarrassed, he realized it was his father's hand he'd felt touch his shoulder. He shook his head and relaxed his stance. He smiled and addressed his father in Lenape. Then he listened while his father replied, nodding several times.

The two smiled and stepped towards each other. They clasped arms, each holding the other's forearm. They spoke then laughed. Tey nodded then walked to his mother and they hugged. He kissed her cheek and spoke to her. Then he returned to Charlotte's side. "Now it's our turn. Do as I do." He took hold of Charlotte's hand and said, "Thank you, my Father. Thank you, my Mother. You have honored us." He whispered to Charlotte, "Now you say it." Charlotte nodded and said, "Thank you both for this honor." Tey bit his bottom lip and grinned. "Now, Chulëntët, go embrace your new parents; first, my father, then my mother." Charlotte did exactly as Tey asked, then returned to his side. "It is done," he said. The men clasped arms once again. And Tey's parents disappeared into the pinewoods as silently as they had arrived.

Tey helped Charlotte into the buggy and steered his horse toward the road. They rode for a while in silence. Charlotte kept looking at Tey, hoping he would fill in the details, but he didn't look at her. He smiled every so often, but he didn't volunteer any information. He kept his eyes on the road ahead. Curiosity was getting the better of her, and she finally couldn't stand his silence one moment more. "Tey, don't just sit there. Tell me everything they said. Is the date still July 17th? Are they going to call me Chulëntët and not my Christian name? What's happening? Talk to me."

Tey's laugh came from way down in his belly as he wrapped one arm around her, pulling her close. "Everything is as we planned. July 17th will be our day. And yes, Charlotte, when we wed you become part of the Lenape. You will be introduced to everyone as Chulëntët and that is how you will be addressed from that moment on. That is the name I have chosen for you. You are my little bird. It is our custom."

* * * * *

The days flew by for Tey and Charlotte. Each time they met, Charlotte brought a piece of clothing or two hidden under her outer garments. Tey took them to the farm and put them in a steamer trunk. Still, as the time came closer, Charlotte's anxiety surfaced anew. Guilt tormented her so much that she feared she would surrender to her father's will. Tey did everything he could but still Charlotte's apprehension grew. She worried, prayed and hoped that what Tey said was true and everything would work in their favor in the end. Still the guilt she felt over betraying her father weighed heavily on her heart and her fear of his reprisal was ever-present in her mind.

July 4th arrived, and Charlotte started counting the minutes that remained. Her emotions fluctuated from moments of overwhelming joy to devastating frailty. One moment she'd picture herself in her happy-ever-after fantasy. Then the next she'd see herself as the most despicable person on earth. Her nerves frazzled. Abject fear of her father fenced with her love, want and desire for Tey. It was impossible for her to think, reason or speak clearly.

At dinner on the 5th, Tobias Wickham turned to his wife and said, "Oh, my dear, I've changed my schedule for the next few weeks." Charlotte's face went ashen. Miriam looked at her daughter and felt Charlotte panic. And she knew Tobias' sudden change of plans was the cause. Without taking her eyes off her daughter, she asked her husband, "How so, Tobias? Won't you be going to Chicago as you planned?"

"Why yes, of course. And you are to accompany me, Miriam. My client has a summer retreat along the shores of Lake Michigan. He has invited us for a working holiday. He believes I need to enjoy the splendor of the lake and see how massive it is. Then, as he said, I will be more inclined to understand his position. He thinks I will fight harder for him with the officials in Chicago. You've never been to Chicago, have you, Miriam?"

Charlotte stared at her dinner plate. She didn't breathe or move a single cell in her body as she listened to every word her father said.

"Why, no, I haven't." Miriam reached out and put her

hand on Charlotte's. "I would enjoy seeing it." Charlotte looked up. Her eyes met her mother's and, in that moment, that brief moment, Charlotte sensed her mother knew her secret. "Charlotte can stay with the Hertzog's. I will arrange it. You and Millie will have a great time, don't you agree, Charlotte?"

Charlotte shook her head, trying to regain her composure. "Yes, for sure, Mother. Don't worry, Papa. It will be all right with them. And I will be fine, just fine." She looked into her mother's face, and Miriam tilted her head and smiled.

"When will this be, Tobias?" Miriam asked. "I must make preparations."

"Saturday a week. That's the fourteenth. We will return Saturday two weeks hence, that is the . . ."

"Twenty-eighth," Charlotte whispered. She closed her eyes and dropped her head to her chest. She sighed in such relief it alarmed her father.

"Yes, the twenty-eighth—on the afternoon train that arrives at 3:43. Will that be a problem, Charlotte? You seem distressed."

"No, Papa, no problem at all," she said, looking at him. "That gives . . . ah . . . Millie and me two full weeks. . . ." She smiled and under her breath whispered, "Two full weeks."

Tobias looked at his daughter curiously. He always had been frustrated by her emotional postures and even more so as of late. Still, he wasn't alarmed. He shrugged it off and turned to his wife. "Miriam, that gives you adequate time to prepare, doesn't it?"

"Yes. Of course. I will have everything in place, Tobias." Miriam turned to her daughter and asked, "Will you, Charlotte?"

Charlotte looked into her mother's eyes. It was unmistakable. She knew. "Yes, Mama, yes I will."

* * * * *

The following Tuesday Tey pulled his wagon filled with produce to a stop in front of Charlotte's house. He filled his arms with baskets of fruit and vegetables and walked around to the kitchen door. Once inside he placed them on the table. He and Charlotte chatted, as they did every Tuesday. They talked about the coming Sunday game, Millie's new beau Charles, and Henry's job offer.

Unable to wait a second longer Miriam hollered, "Stop! Both of you. Stop this nonsense and say not one word. You will hear me out. I will say this once, and never speak of it again." She smoothed her apron as she raised her head, squaring her shoulders. She looked at her daughter. "I will tell no lies, but I will withhold my suspicions until I know, in fact, they are true."

She turned to Tey and looked him in the eyes. Without malice, she said, "Tey, he will hunt you down like a mad dog and feed your remains to the wolves. You do know that."

Tey, his brow furrowed as he listened to every word Miriam said, answered, "Yes, ma'am." He bowed his head respectfully.

Miriam turned to her daughter. "Charlotte, he will lock you away for the rest of your life or until he is sure you will succumb to his will. He will find a way to break you. He will find a way to destroy your spirit. He will never let you be. You do know that."

Charlotte nodded her head. She scowled and bit the side of her mouth. "Yes, Mama," she answered in a whisper.

Miriam looked from one to the other and took a deep breath. She held it for a few moments then blew out her cheeks, expelling the air through her puckered lips. Once more she looked from one to the other. She clasped her hands in front of her and said, "Then I have nothing more to say. Except for this. If you insist on doing what I suspect, I give you my blessing. I wish not to know a single detail. If I do not know, I cannot lie. I will pray that God watches over you every moment I live. But from this day forth, we will never mention this again." She turned and walked to the doorway of the room. She stopped in the doorway and with her back to them she shouted, "Tey!"

Tey's head jerked in her direction. "Yes, ma'am," he answered.

"Take care of my daughter, or I will hunt you down personally."

"With my life, Mrs. Wickham, with my life."

Miriam nodded and continued to walk from the room.

Chapter 4
Early Afternoon, October 21, 1951

"How did she know, Auntie?" I asked. "How did Charlotte's mother know?"

Auntie smiled. "I guess she figured it out because Charlotte was being so secretive about what she was doing. And Miriam knew every time she left the house a few of her clothes disappeared. So, like all mothers, she pieced it together and arrived at that answer. Which, of course, was correct."

Auntie got up from the table and opened a drawer. She rummaged through it until she found the cooking implements she was looking for. She placed them on the table. She held one in her hand and said, "Now Danny, it's time we peel potatoes. Do you know how to use this peeler? Have you ever tried?"

"No. Mother said it would peel the skin off my fingers right to the knuckles. She never showed me how."

Auntie smiled and walked onto her back porch and down into her root cellar. When she returned, she was carrying a sack of potatoes. She set the sack on the table and spread a layer of newspaper in front of me. She smiled down at me and said, "So, let me show you how to use this peeler." Auntie placed the peeler in my hand and held her hand on top of mine as we cut the first strip of peel from the potato. "Like that. Make sure the blades pivot downward and stroke across the potato like, yes, that's it. Keep your fingers away from the blades. That's perfect. Do you think you can do that while I peel onions and carrots?"

"Sure I can. I can do anything, can't I, Auntie? I've got spunk—like Charlotte. Don't I, Auntie? Don't you think I have spunk too?"

"Sometimes when you assert yourself, I see bits of Charlotte in you. Yes. You do have spunk, but you still have to learn when to use it. And you have to learn when to reconsider, like Charlotte."

"Reconsider? Reconsider? Charlotte? Did she reconsider? Didn't she get married?"

"Yes. Yes, she married Tey and it was a beautiful, beautiful wedding. That photograph you found someone took on the day of their wedding."

"Did you go, Auntie? Were you invited?"

"Yes. Yes, I was there, Danny. It was a day filled with emotion that began when Charlotte kissed her mother goodbye on the platform and watched the train leave the station on that very special morning of Saturday, July . . ."

Saturday Morning, July 14, 1894

Miriam and Tobias Wickham boarded the 9:38 express to enjoy two weeks along the shores of Lake Michigan. Their daughter stood on the platform, waving goodbye as the train left the station. Miriam, on impulse, opened the window and leaned out, shouting to her daughter, "I love you! Be happy, my child."

Tears streamed from Charlotte's eyes as she blew her mother a kiss and shouted back, "I love you too, Mother, I love you!" She put her hands on her mouth to stifle her sobs. *Those may be the last words I ever hear my mother say, and today could be the last time I ever see her.* Those thoughts resonated in Charlotte's brain, and her whole body shook.

She whispered aloud, "I may have said the last thing I ever say to her." A cry escaped from her lips. She bowed her head trying to stifle the sobs that were writhing inside her. And, as she turned to leave the platform, she reeled, bumping into a man standing in her way.

"Pardon me, sir," she said, her voice quaking with sorrow. "I was unaware of your presence and . . ." She raised her head and looked at the gentleman. At first glance, there was a familiarity about the man, but she wasn't sure who he was. She narrowed her gaze and looked into his eyes. His business suit looked brand new. He wore a starched collar and a tie that was properly knotted and tucked under his vest. A bowler hat sat at an angle on his head of short barbered hair. And brand-new polished shoes were on his feet.

"It's quite all right, Miss Wickham," he said, worried yet trying to smile at her. "You seem distressed. Please let me help you. Allow me to escort you to your carriage or to a place where you can rest."

Charlotte had to look away. She had to stifle the urge to burst out laughing at the unexpected sight of Tey standing in front of her. It took several seconds until she got herself under control and was able to look at him.

"Thank you, sir, I would appreciate that," she said. Trying not to smile, she took his arm. They walked from the train platform to the street where a covered Hansom cab was waiting for her. Tey opened the door, helped her in, and climbed in beside her. Charlotte told the driver to move on and as the cab trotted from the station, she reached for Tey. Her lips pressed against his with an impatient longing. He fondled her bodice until Charlotte pulled away. "Not yet, Tey. Tonight. Tonight, you may do whatever you choose. But now, please don't fluster me. We still have more to do until we are free of this charade."

He sighed, nodding his head. He sat upright and fixed his tie as she straightened her skirt. They turned and looked into each other's eyes. Several minutes passed before Charlotte said, "I didn't recognize you." Her voice was soft and still quivering with the passion he aroused. "It took me a minute to realize it was you. Where did you get these clothes?"

He smiled, cocking his head. A devilish timber crept into his voice when he answered, "I'm going to university, Charlotte. I must look like I belong. What do you think? Do you like it?"

Charlotte laughed and nodded her head. "You look spectacular. What will your parents say? Have they seen you dressed like this before?"

"No. But I've told them I must dress this way. They understand. But tonight—tonight, I will dress like every nervous Lenape groom waiting for his bride." He looked into her eyes and after a long moment, he furrowed his brow.

She pulled away, searching his face. "What, Tey?" she asked.

"Your neighbors. When I am with you when we arrive, do you think they will recognize me? Will they tell your father?"

"Tey, I didn't recognize you, but tell Father? Yes. I'm sure of it. And on a beautiful morning such as this, I expect they will be outside on the porch."

"Then, who will you say I am? How will you explain my presence?"

"Oh Tey, I hadn't given that a thought. I don't know. I thought we'd arrive about noon at dinnertime and everyone would be inside. I hadn't thought we'd be arriving earlier."

"In that case, we must prepare. Charlotte, if you must make introductions, you will introduce me as . . . as Taylor Aihàmson." She jerked her head around and stared at him. She tried to speak when he placed his finger across her lips. "Listen first, then ask anything you want. We must agree on this before we arrive at your door. So, Charlotte, if I am not recognized and they press you, say I am an old friend from school. That we met by accident this morning at the station; you were distraught, and I offered to see you home. None of that is a lie. It is all true. And if you must introduce me, I will be polite, but I won't face them, and I will take my leave. I will go to our meeting point and wait for you. So, my love, finish packing and meet me at the first watering hole, the very first one. Charlotte? Are you listening to me?"

"Taylor Aihàmson? Taylor Aihàmson, Tey?" she asked, wondering if he was joking.

"Yes. That's the name I used to complete my application for school. Saul said I must not use my Lenape name. He said they wouldn't even consider me if I did. So, he and I put our heads together and thought of Taylor Aihàmson. Charlotte, I chose Taylor because it was the closest name I could think of to Tey. I wanted to have a name like it so when you addressed me you wouldn't have to think what to call me. Tey, Taylor, it works. And well, Aihàmson . . . I took my father's name, Aihàm, and I am his son. Saul said in his culture they take the father's name and add 'son' to the end of it. So that's what I did. I am now Taylor Aihàmson. What do you think? Do you like it? I'm getting used to it. Saul calls me that now. He was trying to help me get used to it. And I am and, Charlotte, I like it."

Charlotte laughed as she slipped her hand under his.

"Mrs. Taylor Aihàmson. It has a nice ring to it, Tey. I like it too."

"A few more hours, my love."

"Tey, I'm so happy we moved the date up. I don't know what I would have done until Tuesday. We traded the full moon for three more days. What could be more perfect?"

"Nothing, Charlotte. Everything is ready. Tonight, in the moonlight, nothing could be more perfect. Even my mother agreed tonight was a perfect time for a wedding: our wedding, Charlotte."

* * * * *

Neighbors watched from their porches as the carriage approached the Wickham house. Tey jumped out after the carriage came to a stop and helped Charlotte step down. Charlotte started toward her front door when the neighbor next door greeted her.

"Good morning, Charlotte. My, you are out and about early this morning."

"Good morning, Mr. and Mrs. Rayford. Yes, I am. I saw Mother and Father off at the train station. They went to Chicago for two weeks."

"Will you be alone in the house dear?"

"No, ma'am. Mother arranged for me to stay with a friend. I'm going to finish packing now."

"Well, that is wonderful dear and who, may I ask, is your attractive escort?"

"Oh, please excuse me, Mrs. Rayford. I didn't mean to be impolite. May I present Taylor Aihàmson. Taylor, this is Mr. and Mrs. Rayford. Taylor and I are old school friends. I was a bit overcome, and he helped me at the station. He thought he'd better see me home."

"Pleased to make your acquaintance." Tey said, bowing and tipping his hat to the side so that the Rayfords couldn't see his face. Tey turned to Charlotte and asked, "May I be of any more service to you, Charlotte?"

"No. I'm feeling fine now. Thank you for your help, Tey, ah, Taylor."

"It was my pleasure. Now, since you are home and there are plenty of people around to call upon, I will take my leave. It was so nice seeing you again, Charlotte. May I call the next time I am in town?"

Charlotte chuckled and smiled. "Please do, Taylor. I would like my parents to meet you. Goodbye." Charlotte had to bite her bottom lip to keep from laughing.

Tey leaned forward in a slight bow and tipped his hat. "Good day," he said to Charlotte and the Rayfords and walked down the street. Charlotte watched him walk away as Mrs. Rayford said, "He seems like a well-bred young man, Charlotte. He lives out of town?"

"Yes, he does, Mrs. Rayford."

"Pity, dear. A nice young man."

"Yes, he is," Charlotte said, watching him fade into the distance. She sighed and said, "I don't mean to be rude, Mrs. Rayford, but I must finish packing. Father will be angry if this cab bill is more than he expected." She turned around and addressed the cabbie. "I won't be long. I'll call when I'm through. Thank you for your patience." She ran up the front steps, unlocked the door, and went into the house.

Charlotte finished packing and stepped onto her front porch. The cabbie carried her trunk from the house and tied it on the back of his rig. As she waited, she noticed there wasn't a neighbor in sight. *Everyone must be having dinner,* she thought. *Too late now,* she sighed and locked the door. The cabbie helped her into the cab, and they drove off.

They drove along the old Blackwoodtown Road until they reached the first watering hole. The cabbie pulled his horse onto the access road and helped Charlotte down from the cab.

"He never said we'd be going this far, Miss," the cabbie said.

"This is as far as you go," Charlotte said as she reached into her little bag. She took three coins from her purse and handed them to the cabbie. "The first is to compensate for the extra distance. The second is in payment for your services in two weeks' time. And the last is a thank you for your diligence. Now, if you'll get my trunk you can be on your way back to town."

"Here, Miss? You want me to leave you here?"

"Yes. My friend will be along any minute."

"If you say so, Miss, but it ain't safe out here. Injuns, you know. You're sure, Miss?"

"Yes. Thank you."

The cabbie shrugged. "It's your neck, Miss." He went to the rear of the cab and untied Charlotte's trunk. He climbed into the driver's seat and said to Charlotte, "You're sure, Miss? You sure it's all right for me to go?"

As Charlotte answered, she heard the sound of horses' hooves in the distance.

"I'm sure. My friend comes as we speak. Don't forget our arrangement."

The cabbie nodded his head. "I won't, Miss. I gives you my word and I means to keep it. I'll be at the station two weeks hence at 3:43 in the afternoon like we agreed." And he coaxed his horse onto the path and pulled away. The cab turned from the access road onto the main highway. The cabbie headed toward town as a wagon with a young man dressed in working clothes pulled in.

Tey jumped from the wagon and swept Charlotte into his arms. He kissed her and held her close to him. "In a few hours, Chulëntët, in a few more hours you will be mine. I love you with all my heart."

Tears streamed down her cheeks.

"You're crying," he said, holding her at arm's length. "Chulëntët, why are you crying?"

"I'm so happy, Tey. I've been so scared Father would find out. But now, when I saw you, I knew. I knew, Tey. I am so in love with you, my Taylor, no. I can't call you that yet. You are my Tey. You will always be my Tey. I love you so."

Chapter 5
Late Afternoon, October 21, 1951

"We're back! Auntie, we're here!" My mother shouted from the vestibule. After my father and sisters hung up their coats, they followed Mother into the kitchen. As soon as Mother entered the kitchen, I ran to greet her. I threw my arms around her neck and hugged her with all my might. Mother took my face in her hands and kissed me. "Were you a good girl for Auntie?" she asked.

"Yes, I was, wasn't I, Auntie?" I said, looking at her.

Mother smiled at Auntie. "You do have a magic way with her. She was in such a snit this morning I was sure she'd give you nothing but grief today."

"She and I have an understanding, don't we, Danny?" Auntie said, smiling at me. She turned back to tend the food cooking on the stove.

"We are early so don't rush on our account. We cut the day short because the weather was abysmal. So, what can we do to help?" Mother asked as she walked to Auntie's side.

"There's a table to set, and if they are ready the potatoes need mashing. And the brown gravy you make will go nicely tonight."

"Girls," Mother said, addressing my sisters. "You heard Auntie. The table needs setting."

Mother put her hand on Auntie's shoulder, insisting she bend down. She kissed her on the cheek, tied on an apron and helped her finish preparing supper.

All through dinner, my sisters babbled about the

things they did in Philadelphia. They described the paintings they liked at the art exhibit and the show they saw at the Planetarium. But I wasn't listening. I picked at my food, deep in thought. The story was all I was thinking about. So, when dinner ended, I had no idea what had been said. Nothing had registered in my brain, not even my mother putting a bowl of ice cream in front of me. I just sat at the table, deep in thought with my forearms crossed on it and my chin resting on them. My brain was in overdrive. I knew I had to find a way to get Mother's permission to stay overnight with Auntie. I knew that was the only way I'd get to hear the rest of the story.

My father was the one who sensed my preoccupation. He nudged my mother, pointing out that I hadn't touched my ice cream. And that was a rarity because ice cream was my most favorite thing in the world. Mother watched me for a brief time before asking, "You've been so quiet, Dan. You barely touched your dinner and now no ice cream? What's wrong?"

"Nothing. I want to stay, that's all. Can I, Mother, can I stay here tonight?"

"But we're going to Uncle David's tomorrow. You don't want to go?"

"No. I want to stay here. Please."

"Well . . . I suppose . . . if it's alright with Auntie. . . ." Mother said as she turned to her aunt. Feeling uneasy, Auntie rose from the table to escape Diana's probing eyes. She walked to the sideboard and played with the folded dish towels. Several long silent moments passed as Mother watched her aunt. Mother's brow was knit, and she was biting her lip.

"What did you promise her, Auntie?" Mother asked.

"Nothing. I had no idea she'd ask," Auntie said without turning around.

Perplexed, Mother asked me, "Then why? Why all of a sudden, Dan? What happened? Something must have happened today that changed your mind." Her eyes were locked on Auntie's back. "What did you do?"

"Nothing. Auntie told me a story. That's all. Didn't you, Auntie."

Auntie turned around and walked back to the table without answering.

"That's all we did. She told me a story, and I want her to finish it, that's all. She didn't finish it. You didn't, did you, Auntie?"

My Mother's eyes sought her aunt's. Confused but wary she asked, "A story? She's told you lots of stories. You've never reacted like this before. What's so special about this one that you want to stay?"

"Indians. She never told me one about Indians before. That's what's special. It's about a Lenape Indian boy."

Mother gasped. For a moment I thought she couldn't breathe. A long second passed until she exhaled. She breathed in again and this time, she exhaled between puckered lips like she does when she is very upset with me. She sat straight in her chair, not moving her eyes from Auntie's. "And a girl?" she asked. Her voice was quivering, and her words were tinged with hurt as if I had wounded her. "Was there a girl in the story? A girl named . . ." She paused, then she hurled the name, "Charlotte?"

Shocked by the inflection in my mother's voice and not sure what I should say, I just answered yes and waited. My curiosity was aroused. How did she know? I wanted to know. So, I asked, "Do you know the story?"

"I do, Danny," Mother said, staring at Auntie. "I read the story in a book." Anger crept into her voice. "An old, tattered black book when I was thirteen. I found it. It was hidden under a drawer . . . in a torn envelope."

The emotions in my mother's voice intensified as she spoke. It was as if she were reliving the moment she had found the book. Her words were measured and quiet and were filled with pain and an outrage she must have harbored for years.

"Someone pasted the envelope to the underside of a drawer. The drawer is the first one in the bottom half of tall chest. The chest in the middle room and there was a photograph with it. A photograph of two Indian men, and a woman, a white woman was standing between them."

My mother glared at her aunt. With each second that ticked by Mother's torso stiffened as anger flared in her eyes. Auntie didn't move a single muscle in her body as she watched my mother. Her face was expressionless.

There wasn't a sound in the room. No one moved. No one even breathed. The silence was so cacophonous I put my hands over my ears to stop the ache. The silence didn't break until Pop rose from the table and ushered my older sisters from the room. When he came to get me, Mother said, "No, Daniel. Danny stays. She is part of this now. It appears she is the *chosen one*. Auntie has decided Danny is . . . is . . ." Tears welled in her eyes as she flicked her hand at him. And, not moving her eyes from Auntie's, she gestured for him to go and leave us alone.

Auntie sat down. The two women continued staring at each other. They said nothing. And no discernible expressions were on either one of their faces. As I looked from one to the other, I thought, *How amazing. They look so much alike. I'd never noticed it before.* It was so apparent as I watched them. Their facial features, their posture, everything about them seemed oddly the same.

I had no idea how that could be. They were not blood relations. Mother's father was Auntie's brother, but he was adopted. When Auntie was nineteen years old someone left a six-month-old baby on her mother's doorstep. Auntie's mother adopted the boy and raised him as her own. That baby was Mother's father.

It mystified me. I couldn't understand why this story angered Mother and why her actions upset Auntie so much. I felt deep down in my heart that there had to be more to this story. And every second I watched them I became more convinced. The answers were in the pages of the old, tattered black book. I was positive it would explain why, at this moment, the two women glaring at each were so affected by its discovery. I moved my eyes from my mother to Auntie. I watched a tear trickle down her cheek. Then another tear followed. She wiped them away and lowered her head.

"You never told me you found it." Auntie said, her voice barely audible.

"No . . . you never told me," Mother said in a tone filled with sadness yet peppered with bitter sarcasm. I never heard my mother speak like that before. I jerked my head around to look at her as Mother spat the word "why," with such venom it rocked me back.

"I vowed, Diana. I promised on Welles' life that . . ."

"He died in 1918—the year after I was born. They were gone. They had died. So, what vow? Who did you promise? Why such importance that . . . that . . ."

Auntie interrupted, "We thought . . . everyone thought

we were . . . we . . ."

"Were wrong! That's what you were. You and Uncle were wrong!"

The two women sat glowering at each other for an interminable amount of time until Mother stood up. Her body was rigid. Her shoulders were back. She turned to me. "Yes, of course, you may stay if Auntie still wants you." There was anger, outrage, resentment, and a definite painful hurt in her tone. "But the girls and I will finish the dishes and go home." She turned to go to the middle room and took one step forward. "It's up to her, Dan," she said with her back to me. She called my sisters and they came into the room. Without another word said, they washed, dried, and put away the dinner dishes.

Mother folded the three dish towels and placed them on the sideboard. "Tell your father I'm ready to go home, girls. I'll be right there," she said to my sisters. The words were said in such a crestfallen, dispirited way all I wanted to do was reach out to her. She stood at the sideboard for a few more moments before she turned to face her aunt. "I don't know what I am feeling right now. I'd always hoped you'd tell me. I need time to think." Her voice quivered with a wretched sadness, yet I could feel anger eating at her. She walked past Auntie and stopped. She turned and walked back to me. She kissed the top of my head. "I'm not angry with you. Honestly, I'm not." She walked to her aunt's side. She stood there for a moment as tears came to her eyes, and she spat out the words, "I'm so damn jealous right now! I can't think straight."

Mother turned to walk away as Auntie reached out and took hold of her hand. "Then stay, Diana. Send the girls home with Daniel and stay."

Mother stood still for a long time. Then she raised her head, squared her shoulders and straightened her back. She cocked her head from side to side and pursed her lips. She bit down hard on her bottom lip. She turned to look at her aunt and asked, "Why? To clear your conscious?" She accentuated her words with an uncharacteristic caustic sarcasm.

I watched Auntie. She didn't cringe or flinch at my mother's words. She simply looked into my mother's eyes and said, "Or to right a wrong. Please stay and let me try."

My mother didn't move. I heard her take several breaths one after the other for a few moments before she asked me, "Where are you in the story, Dan? The wedding . . . have they married yet?"

"No," I answered. "They are at the first watering hole. I guess that comes next." I looked from my mother to Auntie and asked, "Doesn't it, Auntie?"

My mother was looking at her too. "Yes. That comes next," Auntie said, looking at Mother. "Diana, please stay."

"That's why I want to stay. I want to hear her tell what happens." I said.

My mother nodded her head in agreement and, as if she were speaking to herself, said, "Yes. I want to hear her tell it too—there are so many blanks—I want to hear every last bit." A tear trickled down Mother's cheek.

Mother walked into the middle room and asked my father to take my sisters home. She told him she would let him know tomorrow when to come for us. I heard her say, "It's a long story. Auntie still has a lot to tell, and there are a lot of questions that need answers."

"I don't understand, Diana. You know this story. Why are you so upset?"

"That's just it, Daniel. I don't know it all. Tomorrow. Let's talk about it tomorrow."

* * * * *

The middle bedroom in Auntie's house was at the top of the stairs and the bathroom was to the left of it. Auntie called the bathroom the "necessary." Further down the hall to the left was Auntie's room. It was the largest bedroom and the only one in the front of the house. To the right was a small bedroom Auntie used as her sewing room, and at the end of the hall was Mother's bedroom.

I loved going into Mother's room. It was fun to look at all her thing and try to imagine what she was like in her high school days. I knew she excelled in many sports and I knew she starred in many school plays. But archery was her thing. She worked hard to become a world-class athlete and she even earned a place on the USA Olympic Team. Her dreams of gold died when she found out she was pregnant with my oldest sister. Still, Auntie kept all her medals and trophies displayed around her old room and the walls were still covered with her certificates and photographs.

Mother took me upstairs to get ready for bed. She ran my bath and chose pajamas for me from extra clothes she always kept for us at Auntie's. After I had bathed and changed into pajamas we returned to the kitchen and sat around the table. Both the book and the photograph were lying in the center of the kitchen table. Mother lifted the photograph from the table and seemed to study it.

"How does a cup of tea sound, Diana?"

"I'd rather a stiff drink, but that will do fine," Mother said, still studying the photograph.

Auntie walked through her back door and down into her root cellar. A few minutes later she emerged carrying three brown bottles caked with dust. She put them in the sink and washed the dust from them.

"Did you start drinking, Auntie?" Mother asked and laughed.

"They're from when you were pregnant. It's Porter Ale. Will it do?"

"Is it still good?" Mother asked, leaving the table. She walked to Auntie's side and opened a bottle. She poured a bit of the liquid into a glass and looked at its color. She took a sip and smiled. "Still quite good. Thank you. This should relax me enough so I don't act too obnoxious." Mother took the other two bottles and placed them in the Frigidaire. She brought the opened bottle and the glass to the table and took her seat.

She stared at Auntie for a few moments before asking, "Do you understand my anger at all?"

"Diana, my oath wasn't until the day they died; it was until the day I died. I swore on Welles' life and the life of his progeny. So, I was bound."

"If I had told you I found the book, would you have told me?"

"Yes, yes of course. I . . . ." Auntie paused. She studied her hands. She smoothed her fingernails with her thumbs then rubbed her palms together. Finally, she put her hands on the table and clasped them together. Then she looked up at my mother. "I knew. I found you, asleep in the front room, curled in a ball on the divan. You had the book in your arms. I thought I'd wake you but . . . but you were so rebellious at that age. If I had, we would have argued. So, I waited and watched for a sign from you, but you said nothing. So, I said nothing . . . as we tended to do in those days. But today, Diana, today just happened. When Danny found the book and asked . . . I thought . . . I thought it was time."

My mother studied her, then she reached for the book and picked it up. A few pages dangled from the book's binding and Mother nudged them back into place. "I have questions. I used to imagine all sorts of things."

"Ask them. I'll answer to the best of my recollection."

Mother leafed through the book, coaxing more pages back where they belonged. She stopped on a page that was half full. "Here," she said. "The narrative stops. The next page is the wedding. The writing is different. It looks like the details were written later."

She turned the book around and handed it to Auntie. Auntie looked at the paragraphs on the page and smiled.

"Yes, they were. There wasn't time for writing on their wedding day. There was so much to do, so much happening. Still, it's all here, about that beautiful day. And it was a beautiful day for a wedding. It was Saturday, July . . ."

Saturday Afternoon & Evening, July 14, 1894

Charlotte and Tey rode along the old Blackwoodtown Road for an hour. As they went deeper into the pinewoods, Charlotte turned and looked at the road behind them. She wondered if she would ever see civilization again. The road ahead narrowed and the overhanging branches played with the sunlight as they neared Tey's town. The Lenape called their town Kuwehoki, which meant pine tree country. *Perfect name*, she thought as she strained to see anything ahead. There was nothing that looked familiar to her. Then, with each turn of the wagon's wheels an object began to emerge from the road surface ahead. *Are my eyes playing tricks?* She watched that object begin to take on a familiar shape. As the shape became clearer, Charlotte was able to make out the top of a chimney. The chimney grew taller and soon the rooftop it was on became visible. The rooftop grew into a cottage, and she saw another cottage across the road. A house appeared and more houses came into view, and the road widened into a street that opened onto a town square.

Charlotte looked back and forth, trying to take everything in as the town spread before her eyes. She was dumbfounded. She looked at Tey in amazement. It had never occurred to her that the Lenape lived like she did in Camden. She saw single story cottages and two-story homes lining the streets. The houses had manicured lawns and white picket fences. In the village center were stores, a doctor's office, a city hall, and a post office. She noticed a firehouse, a police station, and even an ice-cream parlor. People walked the streets dressed the same as everyone Charlotte knew in Camden. Charlotte was pleasantly surprised, and she looked at Tey.

Tey saw the surprise in Charlotte's eyes. He tossed his head back laughing. "See, we're not such savages after all." They continued on through the town to the town square. Town's folk were busy decorating the square. They were weaving fresh cut flowers in, around, and through sculpted bushes and trimmed trees. Men were setting up tables around the periphery of the town square. And women followed behind covering them with colorful cloths. And a third group was arranging fresh cut flowers in the center of each one. On the other side of the tables, toward the center of the square, blankets were laid out on the ground. Each blanket was woven in a different intricate pattern in bright colors. And benches placed in a circular formation surrounded a fire pit that was in the center of the square.

Charlotte reached out and touched Tey's arm. "Is that where . . .?" she asked. Tey smiled and shook his head yes. "Please, can we stop for a minute? I'd love to walk through, if that's all right." Tey stopped the horse and helped Charlotte down from the wagon. She walked ahead of him, pausing to touch the first table. Charlotte smiled and nodded at a woman who was spreading the cloth. She took the other end and helped the woman smooth it on the table.

Charlotte looked toward the center ring. She turned to Tey and asked, "Is that where, Tey? Is that where we will make our vows?" Tey nodded and watched her.

"How beautiful this is," she said. "I wish Mama could see it."

Tey put his arms around her. "Don't, Charlotte. This is a happy day. Don't clutter your mind with sad thoughts; only think of tonight. Tonight," he said, straightening his back. He took hold of Charlotte and turned her around so that her back was against his chest. He held her with one arm as he pointed with the other.

"We meet in the center and become one." He turned her and pointed to a particular house facing the square. "To-night, I come from my uncle's house." He turned her around and pointed in the other direction. "And you come from my mother's house. Soon," he said, turning her so he could look into her eyes. "The women will take you from me. You must bathe so you smell sweet and pretty for me tonight. And the men take me to do the same.

"You will be dressed by my mother, and I by my father. My mother has made garments for us to wear—even under-garments. She agreed to make them in white and designed yours to cover you as you asked. They are not traditional because, as she said, this is not a traditional wedding. Still, the garments are beautiful. You will approve. When it is time we meet in the center where I barter for you. Traditionally, the bride price is set when betrothed. But since we skipped that part my mother insisted I barter for you tonight. For some reason she wants me to, so I agreed. After that Father will say, well, he has changed that too. They like you. Father wanted to accommodate your wishes. It will be many parts Lenape to suit the elders of our community, but my father has inserted your words.

"Then they pass the pipe and we feast and dance until once again they take you from me. They will prepare you for our first night together. When they finish, we again meet here, in the middle. From here they take us to the pinewoods where my father and mother have prepared a wedding cottage for us. We stay there three days. No one will bother us. Each day food will be left at the door for us, but we will see no one. After three days we return to the house of my mother and have breakfast with my parents. After that, we go on our way. That's it. That's the whole plan." Tey shrugged and grinned.

"How lovely, Tey." Tears came to Charlotte's eyes.

"Don't cry, my love," he said as he held her face in his hands and kissed each eye.

Men and women gathered around them. "They have found us," Tey said and laughed. He kissed her forehead. "And so, it begins. I will see you in the circle tonight." Charlotte smiled at him as the women of the village ushered her from the square. They led her to the house that he had pointed out—the house of his mother.

Before she entered the house, she glanced across the

square. She got a last glimpse of Tey as he disappeared into his uncle's house. Charlotte took a deep breath, exhaled, and squared her shoulders. She braced herself for the unknown that was waiting beyond the front door.

Tey's mother opened the door and greeted her. "Welcome," Tey's mother said. She bowed and made a sweeping gesture with her arm. "Please, come in. This house is now your home." Charlotte nodded her head and said thank you, fumbling for a name so she could address the woman. She hadn't thought to ask Tey and she was a little embarrassed that she could not think of a single thing to say. The only name she knew was Aihàm, but she didn't know if Aihàm or Tey had a surname. She wondered if she should call her Misses. She felt a panic begin to bubble in her gut as she looked at the face of this woman who soon would be her mother-in-law.

Tey's mother read the panic in Charlotte's eyes. She smiled as if she could see into Charlotte's thoughts, and she touched Charlotte's hand. "I am called Kishkikwentis," she said. "In your world, I am called Violet." Charlotte, confused yet afraid to ask for clarification, nodded. Violet read Charlotte and explained, "I was purple the day I was born hence, the name. You may call me Violet if you choose." Charlotte's shoulders relaxed and she smiled. "Thank you," Charlotte said as she thought; *now it's your turn. You need to talk—to make conversation. You must talk to her, so speak.*

"Ah and . . ." Charlotte hesitated and continued, "Is there a story how Tey . . ." She stopped. She couldn't breathe. The blood drained from her face and she closed her eyes. *How could I make that gaffe? Half a name—she hates it.* She opened her eyes and looked at Tey's mother. "Sorry, I am so sorry," she said.

Violet's expression was warm. She didn't appear angry. Violet tilted her head to one side and said, "Continue. Finish your thought." Charlotte wet her lips with her tongue and swallowed hard. She cleared her throat and said, "His name, I mean, is there a story how Miltëwakàn got his name?" Violet studied Charlotte as if she were looking into her soul. A moment later she smiled and chuckled out loud. She took hold of Charlotte's hand.

"Yes," she said. "His naming day was a beautiful one. I did not wed until late. I was unworthy. I was told I would bear no children. Aihàm knew. Aihàm knew of my life. Still, he chose me. I was empty for many years before the Creator looked upon us. On the night we heard his cry, we wept. It was a joyful sound. Aihàm took him from my arms, held him high and gave thanks to the Creator for blessing us with such a wonderful gift. And so, our son is named Miltëwakàn. It means gift." Violet smiled and turned to walk toward the kitchen. "Come," she said as she walked away. "It is time to bathe."

Charlotte immediately followed. As she walked from the front door toward the other end of the house, she passed a parlor on her left. It was furnished with carved end tables and upholstered chairs that were on either side of a large sofa. The furniture was arranged facing a stone hearth and fireplace that was on the wall on the far side of the room. The staircase on her right led to the upper floors and the long hallway in front of her led to a large kitchen. A long oval dining table was in the center of the kitchen. Beyond the kitchen was a huge necessary with two washstands and an over-sized claw foot tub. A small wood burning furnace was attached to one end of the tub. And water from a cistern on the roof circulated through the furnace heating the bath water. A braided rug was on the floor and several towels and a cotton robe were on a small table that stood next to the tub. Facing the tub was a padded bench with a straight-backed chair beside it. And outside the back door was a private commode chamber. It had a William Howell water closet that, at the pull of the chain, drained into sewage pipes under the house.

After Charlotte entered the room, Violet instructed her to remove her garments. Violet leaned over the tub to test the water and poured in bath salts and lilac-perfumed oils. Charlotte felt so uncomfortable. It had been years since anyone bathed her. Even her mother hadn't seen her naked since she was eight years old. *But this is his custom. I cannot offend his mother. I must do this. I promised him,* she thought as she began to disrobe as modestly as she could.

Violet breathed in the sweet fragrance of lilacs that billowed from the steamy tub. As she turned her head, she detected the acrid scent of Charlotte's disquieting unease. It tainted the air and Violet knew Charlotte's discomfort. She sat back on her heels and said, "Perhaps it would be best if I left you." She stood and turned to leave the room. Charlotte held the robe around her as she reached out and touched Violet's arm. "No, don't. Please. I promised Tey." Charlotte gasped. "I, I mean—"

"Chulëntët, ah, Charlotte," Violet said, feeling every bit of Charlotte's discomfort. "If we talk a few minutes, would that help ease you?"

Charlotte nodded her head and words tumbled from her mouth. "Yes. Please. I'm sorry. I don't mean to be a problem. It's just . . . he asked me to. He said it was a ritual. I don't want to disappoint him. I . . . I . . . " Charlotte's eyes filled with tears.

A tear rolled down Charlotte's cheek and Violet caught it with her thumb. She laid her palm against Charlotte's cheek. "Today is not a day for sadness. Today is a happy day. It is not a day for tears. If the bath makes you unhappy it will not be done. Today, I will only do what makes you happy."

"But he told me it is a ritual. That I must or you will be upset."

Violet smiled and laughed. "What my son told you is not correct. Yes. Between a Lenape bride and her mother, it is a ritual. But today our rituals change. I see no reason this one cannot change too. When you are ready you will bathe . . . or not, as you like. Does that agree with you?"

Charlotte shook her head. "Yes. Thank you. I don't want to cause any problems." She looked into Violet's eyes and felt compassion, an affinity that soothed her. "Thank you," she said in a low, soft voice.

Violet took hold of Charlotte's hand and led her to the bench. "So please, sit here and we will talk." They sat, not speaking for a while until Violet interrupted the awkward silence. "Now, what shall we discuss?" She looked at Charlotte for a response. When none came, she said, "I have a question. I would like to know . . . I am not scolding you, is that understood?"

Charlotte furrowed her brow and asked, "What? Have I done something?"

Violet smiled and shook her head. "No, Chulëntët, you have done nothing. I want to know how he came to be called Tey. Will you tell me this?"

Charlotte smiled and tilted her head to one side as the memory played in her consciousness. "Yes. It happened a long time ago. We were so little: seven years old. It was the first day in old Madam Tiller's classroom. She was a nasty sort. She always had a long switch in her left hand and slapped the table in front of you with it. The sound was frightening. Tey was sitting next to me. He was holding my hand. Madam Tiller started with the first child on the bench. That was Theodore Benedict. She demanded he, followed by each one of us, stand with correct posture and recite our full name.

"When she got to Tey, he stood up. She said, 'I see we have a Lenape in the room. No funny Indian names in my classroom. Do you understand, boy? You will speak English. Now, what is your name?' She was baiting him. But Tey stood straight and tall. He wasn't defiant or anything like that. It's like he was proud to be who he was. So, with respect yet unafraid, he said, 'My name in English is Miltëwakàn,' and he emphasized Tey so hard it felt like he spat at her. She glared at him for a few moments. Then she said, 'Well, Master Mil Tey Walkin, you so much as step one inch out of line . . .' She slapped her switch on the table while saying, 'This will speak for me.' But Tey didn't flinch. Instead he nodded his head as if bowing and answered, 'I understand, Madam. I understand perfectly.'

"Violet, Tey was magnificent. He didn't cower at all. He didn't even blink. He stood up to her; at seven years old he stood his ground, and it was she who backed away. At that moment he became my hero. I fell madly in love with him. And I love him more and more each day."

"And so, he is known as Tey in the white man's world." Violet said, whispering, "Nkwis, chìpëtun pilaechështët." She looked at Charlotte and saw bewilderment in her eyes. She touched Charlotte's hand. "This means my son, a courageous little boy." Violet turned away as a tear formed in her eye. She nodded her head and said, "Wëlët në èluweà." She turned to face Charlotte. "Chulëntët, those words mean it is good what you said."

She walked to the tub to tend to the water. In a moment or two, she turned to Charlotte. "Wanìshi. Wanìshi means thank you." She studied Charlotte's face for another long moment. "Maybe you would like to remember our word 'wan ìsh she.' You may find reason to say wanìshi many times tonight." She smiled and, as she watched Charlotte, her smile changed. She asked, "Please. I do not mean to pry. Still, I would like to hear what you answer. My son—what do you call my son when you are alone, when you embrace?" Charlotte could feel herself blushing. She closed her eyes for a moment before looking into Violet's and said, "I call him the words he taught me. He is my Tey eholàk."

Violet smiled. "It is good you call him what he taught you. I will call him what you taught me. He shall be my Tey nkwis. It means Tey, my son." Violet smiled at Charlotte and Charlotte smiled at her. "Now," Violet said, "Tey ehòlënt, your beloved, is waiting for his Chulëntët. Charlotte, how much longer do you wish him to wait?"

Charlotte laughed and walked to the tub, "Not one minute longer, Missus, ah, Violet," she said. "Thank you . . . no . . . wanìshi."

Violet's smile spread across her face and she laughed. She said, "I think you feel better now. Yes?"

"Yes. You make me feel like I belong."

"Only you can make you feel like you do not. So, come; it is time to bathe. I shall leave you now." As Violet turned to go to the kitchen Charlotte said, "Please stay . . . I belong because I know you will show me the way. Please stay. It is tradition, isn't it?"

Violet smiled, "Because today I act as your mother, yes.

It is tradition. Now bathe. Time grows short. There is much to do."

As Violet bathed Charlotte she told her the details of the ceremony to come. "First, the ceremonial fire is lit. The ceremonial pipe is put on the altar stone in the fire pit. My son comes from his uncle's house, and you come from here. I am with you. We meet in the center ring. My son offers gifts. When the gifts are enough, I accept the gifts as payment for his bride and put your hand in his. Once done, Aihàm and the priest sachem enter the ring. Aihàm asks the question that the law has him ask. The state leaders say both man and woman must answer 'I do.' It is not a part of our tradition. Aihàm said this is the time for the rings. He has never done this. Can you suggest how?"

"Yes. Of course. When we purchased the rings, the jeweler explained the double ring ceremony. He said it is being done all the time now. He told Tey that it is a new twist on the old Algonquin traditions. Did he lie to us?"

"It is our custom to give jewelry but not of this type. He could be mistaken, but I am not sure, so tell me of this new tradition."

"Well, Tey puts a ring on the third finger of my left hand. He pledges to wed me for richer or poorer, in sickness and in health, forsaking all others till death do us part. Then he vows to wear the ring as a symbol of our love and commitment. After he finishes, I do the same, placing the ring on Tey's hand."

Violet pondered for a few moments. "I like this new tradition. Instead of beads, there is a ring that has meaning. We have never seen this. Chulëntët, you must lead my son through the giving of rings tonight. Aihàm does not know the words and I may not remember what you said. Will that suit?"

"Oh, yes." Tears welled in Charlotte's eyes. "Thank you so much for allowing this. It means a great deal to me. Tey and I have practiced the words. And this, this is perfect."

Violet had to look away so Charlotte would not see the tears that were in her eyes too. She cleared her throat. "Now, that is settled."

"Yes," Charlotte answered. "And Tey and I will be man and wife."

"Not yet. You must sign the paper required by law. Aihàm has it ready. Once done the men pass the pipe and you are one and we feast. Now Chulëntët, you must dress."

Violet helped Charlotte from the tub and dried her soft, smooth, milky white skin. She applied soothing, sweet smelling oils all over her body. She went to the closet on the far side of the room. One by one she took Charlotte's garments from the closet. She helped Charlotte step into a white silk panty that went from her waist to her knees. Violet slid a matching white silk scoop-neck sleeveless under-blouse over Charlotte's head. When it was in place it reached her waist. Next, Violet helped Charlotte into a form-fitting, scoop-neck sleeveless sheath. Its fringed bottom touched the floor and the white leather used to make it was soft and supple. Around the neckline was a broad strip of ornate beading. The beading continued all the way down the front and encircled the hemline above the fringe. A wide beaded sash in the same pattern went around Charlotte's waist with the ends left to dangle down the front. Then Violet put a narrow-beaded band around Charlotte's head to hold her hair away from her face. Next, she helped Charlotte into a white silk robe with dark blue piping. The piping started behind the neck. It ran down the front, around the hemline and up the other side and met at the back of the neck. Finally, Violet knelt and helped Charlotte into white beaded moccasins. When Violet got to her feet, she took several steps backward. She scrutinized the garments for loose ends then smiled, admiring her new daughter-in-law.

"Come. See yourself." Violet took Charlotte by the hand. She led her through the kitchen where many women were preparing the evening's feast. She led Charlotte into the great room in the front of the house. A full-length mirror hung on the wall next to the doorway leading to the front door. Violet turned Charlotte toward it and stepped aside. Charlotte gasped. How beautiful I look, she thought as her eyes filled with tears.

"No tears, Chulëntët. My son doesn't want to see puffy eyes." Charlotte put her hands to her mouth as if in prayer and turned to Violet. Without thinking she threw her arms around Violet. "How can I ever thank you? How beautiful you have made me." All Charlotte heard in her brain was a resounding no and she released her hold on Violet and stepped back. "Forgive me. I should not have been so demonstrative."

Violet cocked her head, frowning. She seemed to be in deep thought. After a few seconds, she asked, "This word, demonstrative, what is the meaning?"

Charlotte wondered why she asked and said, "Well, it means an emotional display, or in a very expressive manor, gushy even."

Violet tilted her head to one side again as she pondered Charlotte's reply. A few moments later she asked, "Feelings of love, and to touch with affection?"

A slight smile was on Charlotte's face when she said, "Yes. Hugging spontaneously with love and affection is exactly right."

A smile spread across Violet's face. "Then it is good to be demonstrative." She turned toward the kitchen. "Now come. There is much to learn tonight." She led Charlotte into the kitchen and helped her take off her robe. Charlotte sat down at the kitchen table and Violet sat across from her. The women were busy working on the food for the feast and seemed to pay no attention to them.

Violet placed her palms on the table in front of her and cleared her throat. She looked at Charlotte and stared into her face for a long time. An older woman who had been watching walked to Violet and whispered into her ear. Violet spoke to the woman, and the woman responded. Violet, with her eyes diverted, said, "My son is pure. I would know if he were not. He has been asked many times, but he has refused." She looked at Charlotte.

Charlotte put her head down to hide her embarrassment. *My mother should be talking to me now, but I need to know. I need to know what will happen. I must talk to her.* She took a deep breath and looked into Violet's eyes and whispered, "Me too."

A wide smile spread across Violet's face and she sighed in relief that what she believed in her heart was in fact true. She spoke in Lenape to the older woman. After the older woman answered Violet asked, "Chulëntët, do you know what happens tonight?"

Charlotte dropped her head as she felt the hot red blush climb up her neck and paint her cheeks. Mumbling, she answered, "I have read things. And, well, girls talk."

Violet smiled. "Today we will explain." As Violet and the older woman told Charlotte what to expect, her embarrassment waned. She listened and asked a question. Without hesitation, Violet answered. Encouraged, Charlotte asked another and whatever Charlotte asked, Violet answered. In response to a question Charlotte asked, another woman came to the table. She told her a risqué personal story, and everyone in the kitchen laughed. Soon the women in the kitchen were telling Charlotte stories one after the other. After each one they erupted in wails of laughter. Charlotte relaxed. She didn't understand everything they joked about, but she laughed with them and felt a part of it all.

Then Violet stood and everyone in the kitchen stopped talking and laughing. She saw Aihàm walking along the hallway, approaching the kitchen. "Do not stop," Aihàm said, smiling at everyone as he entered the kitchen. "It is a good sign to hear laughter on this day." He motioned to Violet, and she went to his side. They spoke and Aihàm left the house a few minutes later. Violet turned to everyone in the kitchen and said, "It is time."

The women finished what they were doing. One by one they left to take their places outside, leaving Charlotte and Violet alone in the kitchen.

"It is time, Chulëntët," Violet said, placing her hand on Charlotte's shoulder. "Are you ready?" Charlotte smiled at her and shook her head. Violet helped Charlotte put on her robe and made sure that Charlotte looked perfect. She led Charlotte to the front door, took her by the hand and watched for Aihàm to give the signal for them to proceed. When Violet saw the signal, she squeezed Charlotte's hand. And together they left the house and walked toward the center ring. Charlotte's heart pounded with every step. Her groom approached from the other side of the square with his uncle by his side. *How handsome he is,* she thought. His clothing was exactly the same as hers except he was wearing trousers and a beaded headdress. The garments they wore were the same in design and in every detail, down to the last bead and blue stripe on their robes.

Charlotte and Tey locked eyes as they neared the center ring. At the edge of the ring, Violet stopped and told Charlotte, "You stay here." Violet took one more step forward into the ring and said to her son, first in Lenape, then in English, "Why have you come?"

Tey answered in Lenape followed by English, "To offer gifts for the hand of Chulëntët so that you will favor me above all others."

Tey turned to his uncle and took a large stack of woven blankets and coats from his arms. He placed them beside his mother. She shook her head no. Tey turned again to face his uncle. This time he handed Tey bracelets and necklaces made of gold and silver. Stones of zircon, amber, bloodstone, spinel, amethyst, opals and pearls adorned them. Tey walked to his mother and placed them on the pile of woven things. Again, Violet shook her head from side to side and said no. Charlotte looked at Violet, questioning why. She leaned toward Violet and whispered, "Accept him." Violet eyes fixed on her son as she said, "Quiet. You have no say in this."

Charlotte looked at Tey pleading, wondering what was happening. Tey's eyes fixed on his mother.

"Be patient, Chulëntët. This is our way. Kishkikwentis is your mother today. It is between Kishkikwentis and me," Tey said. "She determines the bride price." Tey studied his mother for a moment longer before turning and walking to his uncle. They spoke for a minute, and his uncle left the ring. Tey and his mother said nothing. They each stood their ground, watching one another for many minutes, waiting for Tey's uncle to return.

Tey's uncle was riding a beautiful dapple-gray horse when he returned. He tied it at the edge of the square, unsaddled it, and carried the saddle with a rifle in the scabbard back to the circle. He handed them to Tey. Tey took the saddle and rifle, laid them on the growing pile of offerings and looked into his mother's eyes. Violet hesitated a moment before saying, "No. Her price is more." Charlotte gasped. "Quiet, Chulëntët," Violet said.

Tey looked into his mother's eyes, studying her for several moments. "She is worth more than this after so short a time?" Tey asked in Lenape and English.

"Her worth is not yet known but what I know and what my heart feels demands a greater price than this."

Tey bowed from the waist. "You do me honor, my mother. I thank you." He turned and walked from the ring to the horse that his uncle had tied outside the square. He led the horse into the ring and placed the reins in his mother's hands. "I give you my horse and all my worldly goods. What I have left to give is my life, and that I pledge with all my heart to Chulëntët."

Violet swallowed hard to stop her tears. She looked at her son as a single drop trickled down her cheek. She reached behind her and took hold of Charlotte's hand. As Charlotte stepped forward, Violet placed Charlotte's hand in his. "It is done," she said, and she stepped out of the ring.

Charlotte looked into Tey's eyes. Emotion bubbled up inside her and she could not even breathe. She gasped and reached her other hand for his as he took hold of both of hers. Tey smiled and whispered, "Just your words remain to say. Smile. It is done." Charlotte breathed and smiled as tears came to her eyes.

Aihàm and the priest sachem entered the ring. Aihàm stepped forward. He said, "Miltëwakàn, Chulëntët, the law demands that each of you declare that you wed of your own free will. Do you now so declare?" Both Tey and Charlotte answered, "I do."

Aihàm took the two gold rings from his pocket and placed them in the palm of his hand. He held his hand out to the couple. Charlotte and Tey each took the other's ring. They vowed to love and honor, for richer or poorer, in sickness and in health, forsaking all others, till death do them part. They placed a ring on the other's hand and concluded their vows with, "I wear this ring as a symbol of my love and commitment."

They turned to Aihàm and he led them to a small table. There they put their marks on the license required by the State of New Jersey. He led them back to the center ring. He guided Charlotte to stand on the right side of the ring and Tey to stand on the left side. The priest sachem then entered the center of the ring. He retrieved the ceremonial pipe and moved to the open fire. With great pomp he lit the pipe and took one puff then another. Then he held the pipe skyward and moved it down to the earth, all the while chanting as he moved. He moved the pipe to the north, to the east, to the south, finally acknowledging the setting sun in the west. After a few moments of silent prayer, the priest sachem handed the pipe to his Chief.

Aihàm took a puff and handed the pipe to Tey. He took a puff and handed the pipe to the first man in the outer circle of elder men. Then he passed it on until every man had taken a puff. When the pipe returned to the priest sachem, he raised the pipe skyward once more. He stood in silent meditation for several moments. He then placed the pipe on the altar stone by the fire and left the circle. Aihàm walked forward. He spread his arms, pointing to Charlotte on his right and Tey on his left and presented them to the gathering. He walked to Charlotte and kissed her cheek. He smiled and nodded, then turned and walked to his son. They grasped arms and stood looking into each other's eyes for a moment. Then Aihàm turned to those gathered once more and invited them to feast.

One by one, each guest greeted Tey and Charlotte. After the last guest left, Tey and Charlotte walked to each other until their bodies touched. They stood in the center ring, gazing into each other's eyes, holding hands, not moving, not saying anything. Then Tey bent down and kissed Charlotte on the lips. They kissed for a few moments before they both began laughing, relieved that it was all over.

"We're married, Charlotte. We are actually married. I love you, Charlotte."

"I love you, Tey. I've dreamed of this day, of marrying you, since I was seven years old."

"Was this day everything you dreamed?"

"Yes, and more. But for a little while, I was afraid your mother would not accept your offer."

"Yes. She would not agree until she got what she wanted. You must have impressed her today. She likes you."

"What was it she wanted?"

"She wanted me to pledge my life to you. She wanted to hear me say it our way."

"I could have saved her the trouble. I've known that since we were seven."

Violet walked to Charlotte and Tey. She put her arms around both of them and kissed each one. "Come eat," she said. "You have a long night ahead of you."

Chapter 6
Evening, October 21, 1951

"Diana, is Danny asleep?"

"No, I'm not," I said, lifting my head from the kitchen table. "I was listening to every word. I want to hear the story. I want to hear every bit of it. Please don't make me go to bed."

"Okay, sweetheart," my mother said. "We were checking. That's all. You haven't moved for a while, and we thought you'd dropped off and would be more comfortable in bed."

"No. I had my eyes closed trying to see it—the village, the wedding, Charlotte's dress, but most of all, Violet. I was picturing what she looked like. I wanted to see her like Charlotte did, to see everything."

"Well, it's time for a cup of tea for me and a few cookies for you, Danny. A little pick-me-up will be perfect right now. Diana, what will you have?"

"The Porter. I'll finish it. Nothing else, thanks."

"Yes please, Auntie. Are there any cookies left from this morning?"

"Yes, there are. Diana, you sure I can't get you anything?"

"Knowing more, that's all I want. I want to know everything about them. And her father. He had to find out. What happened?"

"Yes, of course, he found out. But that happened much later. Should I skip ahead, Diana?"

"No. No. I want you to tell it the way it happened. Every

detail. Leave nothing out."

"Then next comes the three days—the three beautiful days they spent in the wedding cottage. Violet told them it was she and Aihàm that brought the food. And on one of the trips they got a glimpse of them standing together, unclad. They had their hands clasped by their sides, fingers intertwined, with lips touching. The sight of them, Violet said, brought tears to her eyes. *How much in love they are*, she thought. Three beautiful days they spent together without another human being anywhere. They loved, they made love, and they planned. And on Wednesday, July . . ."

Wednesday, July 18 – Saturday, July 21, 1894

On the morning of the fourth day, Tey and Charlotte had breakfast with Aihàm and Violet. They talked about the wedding and the comments people had about their ceremony. Tey and his father talked about his horse and rig and about how long to work the animal before stopping. But when pressed to talk about the route they chose to take, Tey hedged. "It is best you know nothing," he said. "We will make contact and let you know what we are doing when it is safe. But for now, my Father, my Mother, it is best you do not know."

After breakfast Tey and Charlotte gathered their things and walked to the door. Before they left Charlotte turned to both of them. "My parents are in Chicago until the afternoon of the twenty-eighth. They arrive on the 3:43 train. They have no reason to shorten their trip. I left two notes with a friend. I've asked her to post them at specific intervals. They, especially Father, should suspect nothing. But once my father arrives home, the wrath of kings will be upon us."

Charlotte paused and clasped her hands in front of her. She looked at Violet and Aihàm. "In our book, the Bible, there is a section called Proverbs. One verse, 16:14, reads: *The wrath of a king is as messengers of death: but a wise man will pacify it.* Please Aihàm, Violet, do as it says in Proverbs. Do whatever you must to pacify him, or I fear he may burn this village to the ground."

* * * * *

Tey and Charlotte boarded their wagon and headed north on the Burlington-Salem Road. They planned to travel ten hours each day, hoping to cover a distance of thirty miles. Tey knew they were pulling a light load. Still, he thought it would be best to keep their horse at an easy pace. He knew the road was long and sometimes not in good condition. They had eighty miles to travel. Tey planned the route so that they would spend each night along the way in a town that had a nice tavern or inn. He even made contingency plans in case they needed to add more days to their journey.

Tey figured they would travel fifteen miles at most their first day. Then they would stop for the night. He'd heard that there were suitable accommodations in that town. He also heard no one would refuse them lodging because he was Indian. As luck would have it, a little after six that evening Tey stopped in front of an appealing house. There was a sign in the front yard advertising that there were rooms available. A little further down the road, Tey saw a livery stable. He would be able to board their horse and wagon for the night. They agreed that the house looked nice, and Tey knocked on the front door. A woman who Tey guessed was in her sixties answered the door. He asked if she had accommodations and a meal available for the two of them. The woman was obliging and showed them the room. They agreed on a price, and Tey left Charlotte to get settled while he tended to their horse and wagon. When he returned, he found Charlotte standing outside. Their overnight bag was on the ground beside her.

"Why are you here? With our case? Charlotte, what's wrong?"

"The proprietrix's son is a very nasty man. He hates Indians as much as Father. He said I could stay but that you were not entering his house. So, I called him a nasty name, stomped from his house and waited for you here. Are you angry with me?"

Tey laughed. "Well, Mrs. Taylor Aihàmson, you may have to get used to that."

Charlotte frowned. "I'm not sure I can ever get used to that!" As she looked at him her anger turned to concern. "But what will we do now?"

"No need to fret. While I was at the stable, I talked to Mr. Trask, who owns the Livery. He said if we had any trouble here, and he must have suspected we would, to come to the Livery. He said he has a room that we could have for the night. And he said we could get a fine supper for a reasonable price across the street at Miss Lily Mae's. So, my love, let's stroll to the Livery."

They ate a hearty meal at Miss Lily Mae's. They purchased muffins for breakfast and a loaf of bread and her jam to have for lunch as they traveled the next day. At sun-up the next morning, Tey paid Mr. Trask and thanked him for his hospitality.

They started north, staying on the Burlington-Salem

Road. Before noon they reached the Burlington-Shrewsbury Road. That road led to Trenton, not New Brunswick.

They found a good resting place where they could water and feed their horse. They opened Miss Lily Mae's jam and slathered it on their bread and ate and laughed and talked.

"We are covering good distances," Tey said to Charlotte. "The roads are much better than I heard, and our mare is having an easy time of it. We may get to the Bordentown Road before nightfall."

"The Bordentown Road? That's not the road to New Brunswick, is it? You told me a different one. Is this shorter?"

"Charlotte," Tey paused and took hold of Charlotte's hand. "We are not going to New Brunswick." He bit his lip and watched her.

Stunned, Charlotte glared at him. "You lied to me. Did you? Did you lie to me? Where are you taking me? You said you were going to school. Is that a lie too?"

"Charlotte. Charlotte. Listen, please. I didn't lie to you. I simply withheld the truth until now. Yes, I am going to school but not in New Brunswick. We were going there until I got another offer. The other offer was a scholarship plus a small stipend to attend Princeton. So, I accepted Princeton and turned down Rutgers. I thought if you slipped and mentioned New Brunswick, your father would be looking in the wrong place. Please don't be angry with me."

Charlotte was not placated. "Don't ever do that again. Don't ever again keep things from me. Promise me. This is going to be hard enough. The prejudice yesterday overwhelmed me. I've never known that before. It was frightening. No. It was terrifying. So, I want to know, Tey, we must know the true facts every moment about everything, or we won't make it. Honesty must be the one thing that never falters between us. Keep nothing from me. Promise me, please promise me."

Tey took her in his arms. "My darling Charlotte, I am so sorry. I promise. You will know my every thought from this moment on. I promise you."

"Good." She leaned backward, studying his face. "Good. That makes me breathe much easier." She paused as a slight smile curved her mouth. "Now," she said looking into his eyes as her lips moved into a wide smile. "Tell me about Princeton. Am I actually married to a Princeton man? My father attended Princeton. That's where he read law. I'm so proud of you. Tell me, how did it happen?"

"Saul. He made me apply there too. He told me he'd fire me if I didn't, so I did. I didn't tell you because I thought that if I wasn't accepted it might disappoint you. Well, I still had the offer from Rutgers. Then the letter came. So, I answered it as soon as I read it. I sent it by express and accepted before they could change their minds. They sent a letter back the same day with the particulars outlined. Charlotte, they are giving us a flat of our own. We pay nothing as long as I keep my grades up and they pay me four dollars a week for food, clothing, whatever we choose. They accepted me into a program called the Re-education of the Native Peoples. A government grant pays for the program. With my stipend and the wages I will earn, we will do fine and there is no need for you to find work. I now can provide for my beautiful wife. So, don't be angry with me, Charlotte. We are fine, aren't we?"

"I still want to work, Tey. I want to contribute. I have no intention of sitting home all day while you work yourself to a frazzle. I will find work."

"But, Charlotte. What will people think if I allow my wife to work? It is a man's job to support his family. I should forbid you . . ."

Tey was cut off by Charlotte's uproarious laughter. She finally said to him between giggles, "Forbid me. Go right ahead and see where that gets you."

Tey shook his head and grinned as he looked into her eyes. "Father warned me you would be a handful. He knew the moment you spoke in the clearing that you have a mind of your own and . . ." He drew her head toward his. He kissed her and whispered, "I love it."

* * * * *

They next day they arrived in Trenton, where they stayed overnight. Early the following morning they went on to Princeton. They arrived shortly before dinnertime and found their assigned housing. He stopped their wagon in front of the house. It was a large, four-story brick house, one of many in a long row. He walked up the front steps and knocked on the front door. As Tey stood there waiting, a young man came bursting through the door almost knocking him down.

The young man was tall, attractive, and well dressed. "Sorry, old man." he said. His accent had similar intonations as the British but Tey was sure it wasn't. "Are you looking for someone?"

"Yes. The proprietor. Can you show me where..?"

The young man broke in. "There's no proprietor here. Are you making a delivery?" The young man looked Tey over up and down. He turned, looked to the street and saw Charlotte, then turned back to Tey. "Or is your assigned housing in this building?" he asked.

"Yes. We have a flat here," Tey answered.

The young man relaxed and laughed. "I suppose you're another misfit they don't want on campus. No matter, you're welcome here, so go in and find your flat. If they didn't send you a key, it is in the room. My name is Butcher, by the way, William Butcher," he said, smiling. He offered his hand for Tey to shake.

Tey smiled back. "Tey, ah, Taylor Aihàmson," Tey said, shaking hands. "This is my wife Charlotte," he said as they walked to the wagon. Mr. William Butcher tipped his hat in Charlotte's direction, "Nice to meet you, ma'am." he said. "Sorry for the mix-up but one can't be too careful these days. No matter now anyway." He glanced at his pocket watch. "Sorry I can't stay and chat, but I've got to run. I'm meeting Martin at the pub. Martin's in 304. Nice fellow. Very congenial. I'm in 302, by the way; if you need anything, just knock on my door." He waved and walked down the street.

"Seems to be a friendly sort, this Mr. William Butcher, doesn't he? Odd accent, though," Tey said as he helped Charlotte down from the wagon. He hesitated a moment as he pulled the paper from his pocket and read the address. "We're in 301. Looks like we will be neighbors. Let's go in, Charlotte, and take a look at our first place together."

They climbed the front steps and walked into the entry foyer. The foyer was large and painted a stark white. Large brass mailboxes lined the right wall and a long, dark wood library table was on the left. A dim hallway ran down the left side and two flats opened on to it. On the right side, beyond the mailboxes, was a wide staircase that lead to the upper floors. Tey and Charlotte sprinted up the two flights to their flat. Tey opened the door and stopped Charlotte from entering.

"Wait," he said. "I must carry you across. I'm told that brings good luck." He laughed and swept Charlotte up into his arms and walked into the room. He placed her feet on the floor, and they stood there looking around. To their left was a large bay window with a round table in front of it and a tall brass lamp in the center of the table. On each side of the table was a crook neck reading lamp behind an overstuffed chair. Across the room from them, against the far wall, was a tester bed without a canopy drape that was large enough for two. On its frame were soiled pillows and a tired looking mattress that looked like it had seen better days.

Charlotte walked to the bed and pounded the mattress with her fist. "Not too bad. No clouds of dust. After I flip the mattress and put our feather bed on top, it will be nice and comfortable. But, Tey, these pillows must go. They look like dozens of people have drooled all over them." She picked one up and said, "Ugh. That's disgusting. We will make do tonight but they get replaced in the morning."

Tey laughed and agreed as Charlotte tossed the pillow back on the bed. She turned to her right and walked to her kitchen. On the left began a bank of upper and lower cabinets that had white wood doors with brass pulls. Charlotte opened each cabinet and looked inside. She found all the dishes, eating and cooking utensils and pots and pans they would need. "Everything's here! Everything, Tey." She moved to her right and bent down to peek into the oven of the three-burner gas stove that stood next to the cabinets. She turned to Tey. "They even thought to include a striking block and a set of long wooden matches for lighting the oven." She took another step to the right and stood in front of the deep sink that was next to the stove. Again, she smiled. "Look, Tey, spigots for both hot and cold water." She bent down and moved back the drape across the front of the sink. "There's even plenty of space beside the pipes for washing soaps." Then she opened the doors of the full-sized four-door icebox that stood next to the sink. "Look at that! Tey, it drains into the pipes under the sink. You won't have to empty the pans for me."

She walked to the far right and opened a closed door. Behind the door she found a small necessary room. A hand sink hung on one wall and a free-standing commode with a chamber pot was beside it. The sign on the wall said the necessary equipped with sink, bathtub, and flushing commode was at the end of the hall. The sign went on to say it had hot and cold water and the four flats on their floor shared it. She closed the door and walked to the small oblong table that stood between the kitchen and the bed. It was in front of the entry door and there were four straight back chairs around it. Above the table, a lamp with a single light dangled from the ceiling.

She turned and smiled at Tey, who was still standing in the doorway. She looked to his right and saw a built-in armoire that was six feet long and stretched from floor to ceiling. It had drawers on the bottom and two full-length mirrors on the doors above. To his left stood a large chest on chest that was five feet wide and six feet tall. It had five large bottom drawers and seven smaller drawers on top. A large, colorful, oval braided rug was under Charlotte's feet. It extended from under the kitchen table to the bed, covering most of the hardwood floor. There was another oval braided rug on the other side of the bed. That one was halfway under the round table in front of the bay window.

"Oh, Tey," she said as she spun around. "I love it. We have everything we need. I'm so excited. Once we make this place our own it will be wonderful. You'll see. Come." She ran to him, grabbed hold of his hands and tried to pull him out the door. She looked into his eyes. "Come on. Let's get our things. Come on, Tey." He threw his head back and laughed. "Yes, my love. Let's do it," he said.

After they emptied the wagon, Tey went to find a livery stable. While he was there, he was able to sell the horse and wagon. When he returned, Charlotte was putting the finishing touches on their flat.

"What have you done?" he asked, smiling and laughing at the same time.

"Do you like it, Tey?"

"Charlotte, yes, yes I do, very much. It looks like home," he said, beaming at her.

"Did you find a place and get a fair price for the horse and wagon?"

"Yes. The stable master was quite generous, I thought. He paid forty dollars for our horse and twenty-five for our wagon. He asked that I throw in the leather. He knew good Indian hide when he saw it. So, I did, and he gave us an extra five dollars. So, with that, we have seventy dollars. That doesn't count my savings from working at Esterbrook. I'm hoping we can do well enough and not touch that. But if we must, we must."

"Seventy dollars is a lot of money, Tey. If we are sensible with our purchasing, we will be fine until we start working and wages start coming in. But we do need to buy staples and pillows. I've made a list. Did you see a grocery or a mercantile on your way?"

"No. But since you've got everything put away already,

let's stroll around the town and stop for a bite to eat. Charlotte, my stomach has been talking to me for the last hour or so."

"Mine too. After we eat, we can explore and get what we need on the way back."

"First, let me hide the extra money."

Tey rocked back and forth with each step he took as he walked across the floor. "What are you doing?" Charlotte asked.

"Looking for a loose floorboard, but I'm not having any success. I'll hide it here for now." Tey pulled out the bottom drawer of the chest on chest and looked at the underneath of the drawer. He rolled their extra cash into a wad and shoved it in an old stocking he found in the drawer. He got on his knees and placed the stocking so it lay against the back of the chest, and he replaced the drawer.

"Unless someone tears this room apart, the money will be safe there."

"Do you think we have to worry about that, Tey?"

"I don't know. Father said to be cautious. So, I'm being cautious."

Charlotte nodded her head and chuckled. "Now, my Tey eholàk, please let's find a place and have supper."

Chapter 7
Later That Evening, October 21, 1951

Auntie stretched, arching her back as she stood. She walked around a bit, turning her body from side to side, and asked my mother if she wanted a cup of tea. My mother said no, that she preferred to finish her Porter, and I asked if I could have ice cream. Mother said no because it was so late. "You'll never sleep," she said. It was ten thirty. Mother looked at me and asked if I was ready to go to bed.

Ready for bed! I thought. *No! I was not ready for bed.* It irked me that she would even ask.

"Now? Charlotte and Tey are in Princeton and Tobias Wickham is coming home. He's going to find out that Charlotte's gone, and he's got to be mad at her. Isn't he, Auntie? He goes to the village doesn't he, Auntie? Does he burn down the village, Auntie? What does he do? Mother! I got to know what happens. I can't go to bed now. Please don't make me. I want to hear the rest of the story. Please."

Auntie placed the pot of tea she had brewed in the center of the table and sat down. She looked at my mother and they both smiled. "Yes," Mother said. "I want to know too, so on with it Auntie."

Auntie chuckled and, in a move that surprised both Mother and me, she put her elbows on the table.

"Well," she said and paused. There was an impish grin on her face when she added, "Well, Danny, he was very, very, very angry." She played with her tea until it was perfect before taking a sip. "That's perfect. Diana, the next time you go to that store please bring me another tin of this.

I am enjoying it."

I looked from Auntie to my mother and to Auntie again in disbelief. I wanted to hear what happened. I couldn't believe she was talking about tea. "Auntie," I said, raising my voice quite indignantly. The look in her eyes told me I may have crossed that fine line. So, I quieted down and, pleading, I asked, "The story, please tell me. Please, please . . . you said he was very, very, very angry. Well, what happened? What did he do?"

Auntie looked at me. She looked at my mother and she looked at me again. "Well, Danny," she said. "The train from Chicago was right on time. Miriam was dreading arriving home. It was a lovely warm Saturday . . ."

Saturday, July 28 – Sunday, July 29, 1894

The train was on time and pulled into the Camden Station at 3:43pm as scheduled. Tobias Wickham stepped from the train and surveyed everyone on the platform. When he didn't see Charlotte, he scowled. He turned and went to help his wife. Miriam saw the irritation on his face and felt the tension in his touch as he helped her step from the train. It bothered her so much she had to look away. Once on the platform, she straightened her dress and righted her bonnet. Her eyes roamed the platform, hoping she would see Charlotte. She knew deep down in her soul she wouldn't. A sick, panicky feeling rose from her stomach and her mouth went dry. A passage flashed through her mind as she watched Tobias. *Not one of them will survive. I will bring disaster on [you] . . . A day of reckoning is coming . . .* (Jer. 11:23) She trembled, unable to breathe as she watched her husband.

110

Tobias paced from one end of the platform to the other before stopping a few paces from Miriam. With his left hand tucked between his shirt and his jacket, he stood beside her and searched the platform for Charlotte. He was an imposing figure who stood over six feet with not an ounce of fat on his muscular body. For years he trained at his club at least four times a week. He was an expert in the fine art of boxing, Marquess of Queensberry style. He learned how to protect himself and there wasn't a visible mark on his face to prove it. He used his steel gray eyes, set close together like a predator's, to study his prey. His straight, narrow brows pointed downward like an eagle on the prowl. And between his eyes began his long, straight nose that almost reached his upper lip. It accentuated the squareness of his chin and face. His hair, trimmed around large, close-cropped ears, lay flat against his head. And his anger grew every moment he waited.

"Where is that girl?" irritated, he asked his wife. "She knew what time we were arriving."

"Calm yourself, Tobias," Miriam said, trying to hold herself together. "I'm sure there's an explanation for her . . ."

"Mr. Wickham, sir!" the cabbie called as he rushed to them. It was the same cabbie who had taken Charlotte to the first watering place so far from town two weeks earlier. "So sorry for being late, Mr. Wickham, my other fare was a good distance away. Let me get your bags. Right this way, ma'am, Mr. Wickham, sir."

"Is my daughter in the cab?" Tobias demanded before he took even one step forward.

"No, sir. She ain't with me," the cabbie said, looking at Tobias, sensing his anger. He was very uncomfortable. He removed his hat and fidgeted a bit.

"Then, where is she? Who sent you?" Tobias' voice grew sterner and more threatening with each syllable he spoke.

"She did, sir. Yes, she did. When I left her two weeks past, she arranged for me to be here. She paid in full. And tipped as well so I wouldn't forget."

"Two weeks past? You mean the day we departed for Chicago? The day it was your duty to return her to my home. Do you mean that very same day?" Tobias' voice was rising. He was at the point of striking the cabbie with his walking stick but thought better of it.

"Yes, sir. That same day I took her."

"Where did you take her?"

"To the first clearing, sir. The first clearing on the old Blackwoodtown Road, sir. That's where I took her. That's where she asked to go so, I left her there—in the clearing, just as she said."

"Alone. In the woods. Surrounded by Indians. You left my daughter there!"

"Yes, sir. Yes, I did as she asked, Mr. Wickham, sir, she asked that I be sure to be here to fetch you, sir. That she did. And she paid me well for it, so I comes to get you just like she said."

Tobias looked at Miriam and studied her face. "Did you know any of this?" His voice was odious, soft, and peppered with rage.

"She was secretive for weeks. I had no knowledge of this," Miriam said, looking Tobias in the eyes. Her stomach spasmed in fear as she spoke, dreading what would come.

Tobias glared at his wife for several moments. He turned to the cabbie and ordered, "What are you waiting for? Take us to our residence."

Without saying another word, the cabbie tied their

luggage to the cab. He climbed into the driver's seat and steered his horse from the station. They rode home in silence. The silence was so palpable Miriam imagined it was what a condemned man felt as he walked to the gallows.

Tobias stepped down from the cab and looked at his house. The neighbors were on their front porch and greeted him. He offered his greetings then turned to help his wife. He looked at her with a fierce stare and said in a hostile yet quiet voice, "Not one word to anyone. Do you understand me, Miriam?"

Miriam Wickham nodded her head. As cheerful as she was able to be, she said, "Why, good afternoon, Mr. and Mrs. Rayford. And how has everything been in Camden these past two weeks?"

"No news of note, but we did meet Charlotte's nice young gentleman." Mrs. Rayford turned toward her husband. "Didn't we dear; the day you went on your trip. Now what was his name? Do you remember, dear?" He mumbled a name to her, and she turned to the Wickhams. "Yes, it was Taylor. What was it again, dear?" she asked, turning back toward her husband. "Hamson. Is that right, dear?"

Mr. Rayford shook his head and smiled. He stood and walked to the railing. "Afternoon, Tobias, Miriam. What Henrietta is trying to remember is Taylor, and if I'm not mistaken, he pronounced his surname as Aihàmson. He seemed well bred and quite mannerly for a young man these days. Pity he lives out of town."

"Isn't it, though. Tell me, did Charlotte mention why he was with her?" Tobias asked.

"Yes. Charlotte said she was overcome at the station. The young fellow happened by and saw her home," Mrs.

Rayford answered. "Isn't that what you remember, my dear?"

"Yes. Exactly. A good-looking young man and a good catch for Charlotte, ay Tobias," Mr. Rayford joked.

Tobias forced himself to laugh. "We will surely discuss it with her. Now, if you will excuse us, it has been a long, tiring journey."

The Rayfords said their goodbyes and sat down in their porch rockers. Tobias opened the front door and directed the cabbie to carry their luggage up to the second floor. Miriam hurried into the house and up the stairs. The cabbie followed her with their luggage. After dismissing him Miriam stood in the doorway staring into Charlotte's bedroom. On Charlotte's dresser, across the room, was an envelope. Miriam flew across the room. She retrieved the envelope and hid it in her dress pocket. Two seconds later Tobias entered Charlotte's bedroom.

"Did you find anything? A note, a clue where she went, anything?" His voice rose in anger with every word.

He flung open the closet door and threw everything that remained onto the floor. He yanked open each drawer in her chest, tossing them aside. He lifted the mattress from her bed and tore off the coverings. He ravaged through the room, throwing each thing he touched to the floor with a forceful fury. When the room was in shambles, he stood, looking around it. His nostrils flared like a raging bull ready to tear apart anyone or anything that stood in its path.

He terrified Miriam. She stood in the doorway watching in horror as her husband rampaged through Charlotte's room. He turned from the bed to the bureau and stood staring into the mirror attached to it. For a brief moment he looked at his image before he screeched in anguish,

"Aaarrrgh!" holding the sound as long as he could. In the mirror he saw the horrific pain trapped inside him reflected on his face. He took both arms and swept the objects atop the bureau onto the floor. Then, breathless, he leaned on his outstretched arms, his hands clutching the top of the bureau. His knuckles were white; his head bent down as if in prayer as he stood there catching his breath. He stumbled to the chair next to the bureau and slumped into it. Then put his head in his hands. "What have you done?" he whispered. He lifted his head and shouted out, "Girl! What have you done?" He rose from the chair and looked at his wife with a venomous glare. A taste of bitter bile came from the pit of her stomach up to her tongue. He walked to Miriam's side. "I will find her," he said with a vengeful threat in each syllable. "I swear I will find her and bring her back. She will not lie with that savage. He must die. He will not have my daughter. Not as long as I am able to take a breath. I will kill them both first."

He pushed passed Miriam and went down the stairs. He opened the front door and flung it with such force that the doorknob left an indent in the wall. He took two more steps until he was clear of the frame and slammed the door behind him, shaking the whole house.

Miriam Wickham watched from the top of the stairs as her husband stormed through the front door. She choked back the nauseous feeling churning in her stomach. And she walked into Charlotte's room. She sat down in Charlotte's chair and cried until no more tears would come. A deep, foreboding emptiness enveloped her. Fears for her daughter's life glutted her mind, and she closed her eyes, wanting to shut her thoughts out. She forced herself to think of good things and happy memories. She conjured up pleasant visions to calm her fears, trying to fill the enormous void she felt in her heart. They were so real that she opened her eyes, hoping that Charlotte was there, right there in her bedroom.

But only shadows filled the room. "Charlotte," she whispered as she reached out into the gloomy gray darkness. But there was no answer. No one was there. A tomb-like empty blackness surrounded her. She shuddered and rose from the chair and began to put everything back in its place. She hung the few garments in the closet that, in his rampage, her husband had thrown on the floor. She struggled with the mattress, setting it square on its frame. She made the bed as it was before Tobias . . . *Tobias*, she thought.

Miriam went down the stairs and got the carpet sweeper and wastebasket. She carried them up to Charlotte's room. She righted everything that Tobias had overturned in his tirade. She swept the floor, picking up the debris with her dustpan, and threw it into the wastebasket. She smoothed Charlotte's bedspread again and looked around the room one more time. As she turned to leave, she straightened her skirt and felt the letter she had hidden in her pocket.

She walked down the hall to her bedroom. Locking the door behind her, she walked across the room and opened the left door of the armoire. She knelt down and removed two pairs of her shoes and placed them on the floor beside her. She reached into the armoire and lifted a loose floorboard, listening to be sure Tobias hadn't come home. With great care, she took the note from her pocket, held it to her lips. "My darling daughter," she whispered, "I must wait till later to read this. Your father could return at any moment." She kissed the note and turned her eyes upward as she petitioned the power above. "Oh, dear Lord, I pray, please take care of my child."

She held the note close to her breast for a moment more. Then she placed it in the empty space and covered it with the floorboard. Miriam sat on her heels and closed her eyes. Tears ran down her cheeks as visions of her daughter cascaded through her mind. She wiped the tears away and replaced her shoes exactly as they had been. When everything was in place she stood up, squared her shoulders and dried her eyes. She walked down the hall and retrieved the wastebasket and carpet sweeper. She took them down to the kitchen and started to prepare supper.

* * * * *

Tobias Wickham was a veritable tinderbox cloaked in composure. He walked into the Sheriff's office and approached the front desk. He was resolute and unswerving in his purpose and asked to speak with the Sheriff. "He's on a call," the deputy behind the desk answered.

"Have him contact me the second he returns. Do you understand?"

"Yes, Mr. Wickham," said the deputy. "The second he returns."

Tobias left the Sheriff's office and walked to his law firm. Clerks and apprentices were still working when he arrived. He walked through the reception area and headed to his office. He didn't speak to anyone as they bid him a good afternoon. He walked into his office and stood in front of the window, staring at nothing. He stood there for several minutes before he began wandering around the room. He grew more and more impatient as he waited to hear from the Sheriff. He looked out the window again to see if the Sheriff was heading his way. When he didn't see him, he slammed his hands on his desk and swore under his breath. It took several minutes until he regained his composure. He walked from his office to the far side of the firm's suite of rooms. There he stopped and waited in the doorway to the office of his law partner, Jedidiah Rue.

Tobias and Jedidiah met at Princeton. They were never friends. Tobias barely tolerated Jedidiah because Jedidiah Rue was half Lenape and half white. But after Tobias opened his practice, he realized he needed Jedidiah's expertise. So, Tobias contacted Jedidiah. At the time, Jedidiah was a senior official with the Bureau of Indian Affairs. They haggled for weeks over the terms of the partnership. Jedidiah finally brought his wife, a full-blood Cherokee, and daughter to see the town. With their approval he then accepted Tobias' offer of a full partnership in the firm.

Jedidiah and Tobias spoke to each other only when the topic had to do with a case the firm was handling. They rarely conversed otherwise and never met socially. So, when Jedidiah raised his head and saw Tobias standing in his doorway, he was a bit shocked.

"I'm usually summoned to your office when you call me on the carpet, Tobias. So, what brings you slumming today," Jedidiah asked with all the sarcasm he could muster.

"Cut the crap, Rue. I need answers, not snide remarks!"

"In that case, by all means, come in and sit. Oh, wait. Sitting and conversing with a half-breed is beneath you, isn't it, Wickham?"

"Rue, no more bullshit. I need help." The veins and arteries in Tobias' neck glowed crimson red and pulsed with each beat of his heart. Tobias spoke with a bitter ire in his voice as he tried to contain his rage.

Jedidiah stared at his partner. He saw Tobias stagger and noticed that he labored to breath with every step. Jedidiah had never seen his partner suffer from such severe emotional stress. Concerned, he walked to his partner, took him by the arm, and led him to a leather chair facing his desk. He turned and closed his office door. He walked to Tobias and attempted to open his collar, but Tobias fought him away.

"You dumb bastard. You can't breathe! The veins in your neck look like they're going to explode, and you won't open your tie! What's wrong with you?"

"G—give . . . me . . . a . . . minute. . . . I'll . . . be . . . alright . . . in a . . . min . . ."

Jedidiah poured a glass of water and offered it to Tobias, but he shoved it away.

"Afraid I spit in it? You—you . . . go ahead. Have an apoplectic fit. Even die if that's what you want. Damned if I'll stop you." Jedidiah turned and slammed the glass of water down on his desk well within Tobias' reach. He walked around his desk and sat in his chair.

Tobias gasped as he fought to breathe. He forced himself to inhale air deep into his lungs. He took deep breaths over and over until he was able to calm himself. As his breathing returned to normal the color came back to his face. He took a few extra deep breaths then stretched his neck. He straightened his tie and fixed his eyes on Rue. He reached for the glass and made a gesture like he was making a toast. He took a drink. "Thank you," he said in a low, hoarse voice.

"Why are you so distressed? Did something unforeseen happen in Chicago, Tobias?"

"This has nothing to do with my client."

"Then what? Are you going to tell me what this concerns?" Jedidiah moved his chair forward and put his elbows on his desk. "You said you needed help. Why? I can't help unless I know what this is about. So, talk, Tobias, for once, talk to me."

Tobias looked at Rue, knowing he had to take him into his confidence. He lowered his head. And in a quiet voice filled with the anger raging inside him, he said, "The Indian village, Jedidiah. The one that's out on the old Blackwoodtown Road; you know where I mean?" Tobias looked at Jedidiah.

"Yes. I know it. What of the village?"

Tobias took a deep breath. "I need to know the legal ramifications of searching every house, barn, shop, everything. I need to search every inch of the woods—every inch—how do I do it, so I don't violate a damn treaty; how, Jedidiah, how?" The red of his neck showed above his collar again.

Jedidiah's mouth dropped open. "Are you mad? Why in the hell would you want to do that? You must be insane. What do you think you would accomplish? Do you want to start a war with the Indians again? Are you that stupid?"

Tobias shouted back at Rue, "No! But I need to see if they are hiding her, that's why! How do I do it?"

Jedidiah, startled, searched his face for answers. "Who? Who do you think they are hiding? And for God's sake, why?"

Dropping his head Tobias said, "Charlotte. She must be there. They have her. I'm sure of it." He raised his head and looked at Rue. "If she's not there, they know where she is."

"Charlotte? Your daughter Charlotte?"

Tobias nodded.

"Why, Tobias?" Jedidiah said. "Are they holding her for ransom? Level with me. Tell me what's going on."

"Jedidiah, it's—" Tobias said, waving his hand as if dismissing Jedidiah's comment. "It's not ransom. Charlotte's with a boy. She thinks she's in love with this boy." Tobias sat straight and moved to the edge of the chair so he could rest his arm on Rue's desk. "When we returned from Chicago this afternoon she was gone. She'd taken her clothes and other belongings too. The day we left, our neighbor saw her return from the station with a young man named Taylor Aihàmson. Aihàmson, Jedidiah. Aihàm's son. The chief is Aihàm and that's the boy Charlotte refers to as Tey. Tey is Aihàm's son. Tey, Taylor. Damn it; it fits. She's run off with this, this young buck, and I will get her back, come hell or high water!"

"Whoa, Tobias, not so fast. Charlotte's eighteen now, isn't she?"

"Yes. What does that have to do with anything?"

"She's of age. We need to know if she married the boy. She could, with or without your consent. She is no longer a minor in the eyes of the law."

"Married! How the hell do I know if they married! I'll kill the bastard! I swear I will send her to a convent and never let her out. Married! That buck's been sniffing around her since grade school. I should never have let her out of the house. I trusted her to go to Millie's on her own. I should have taken her there myself." As Tobias slumped in his chair, Jedidiah heard him utter a faint cry.

Jedidiah watched Tobias for a few moments. "So, if you did, if you had taken her yourself, what do you think would have happened? In all probability, she would have gone off with him from there. I don't think you could have stopped it even if you were here, at home. So, what do you want from me? What do you want me to tell you that you don't already know?"

Tobias lifted his head and looked at Rue. "What to do, Jedidiah. I need to know a legal way I can go on their property."

"Tobias, you know damn well that you better have the law on our side before you put one toe on their property. So, going out there and making a fool of yourself is out of the question. You need to listen to me. First, we should have our clerks do a record search to see if they did get married. That village is in a different county, and they have their own Clerk's office. Still, we should start there. We'll need to see if a marriage certificate is on record. So, a timeframe, Tobias. Did it happen during these passed two weeks or before that? Think, because we need a range of dates to start looking. And names. Do you know the boy's Indian name? The license could be in that name. Did Charlotte ever mention an Indian name he called her? If they married by Lenape law, she would take a Lenape name. It could be that's how her name appears in the documents. Once we have that information we can proceed. But Tobias, prepare yourself for what we may uncover. If we discover they signed the statement of their own free will. And, they both are of legal age, then Indian or not, it is a legally binding marriage. Will you accept that?"

Jedidiah studied his partner for several minutes. The look on Tobias' face answered his question. He started laughing. "Of course not," he said. "Look, do yourself a favor. Don't do anything stupid like charging in there with a posse demanding to go house to house. You'll be in a federal penitentiary before nightfall. Let me do what I've outlined first. It's now 5:50 on Saturday—too late to do anything. So, go home and, for God's sake, relax. This isn't the worst thing in the world. I will get our staff working on this first thing Monday morning. I'm confident we will have answers before day's end. So, go home, Tobias. Miriam must be frantic with worry, not only about Charlotte but especially about you. Go home and have a nice supper with your lovely wife."

* * * * *

Miriam Wickham sat at the kitchen table, waiting for her husband to arrive. The table was set with the dishes she had planned to hand down to Charlotte when Charlotte married. She was deep in thought as she caressed a dinner plate in her hands when Tobias walked into the kitchen. She looked at him, smiled as she rose from her seat and walked to the stove.

"Nothing much in the house until I go shopping," she said as she stirred the pot she had simmering on the stove. "So, I opened a jar of the beef soup Char—" She stopped. Tears ran down her cheeks. She swatted her tears and cleared her throat. She took a second to compose herself before she spoke again. Her voice still trembled with thoughts of Charlotte in her head, "that we put up a few months ago."

Tobias said nothing to her. He sat brooding in his accustomed place at the table. Miriam placed a steaming bowl of beef soup in front of him. She sliced off a large piece of bread from the loaf she had baked. "Tobias," she said. "Please eat. You've had nothing since noon time." She turned, served herself soup and sat down in her place.

Tobias dropped his soup spoon to the table and turned to Miriam. "You said she was secretive for weeks." He paused and glared at his wife as the words she spoke when they arrived at the station resonated in his brain. "Yes. Secretive for weeks . . . is exactly what you said. So, why, Miriam? Why did you not think that strange? Why did you not press her and demand to know the cause?"

Miriam wasn't able to breathe as she put her trembling hands in her lap. She looked at her husband. "She said to let her be, Tobias, and she said nothing."

"Let her be. And you permitted her to keep her silence? Is that what I am to believe? You permitted that girl, who told you everything, to say nothing to you? Even when pressed? Nothing, Miriam?"

Miriam stared at her hands. She closed her eyes and mustered her strength. She sat straight in her chair and smoothed her apron. She turned to face her husband. "She said nothing. She said it was best I knew nothing."

Tobias slammed his palms down on the table and shouted at Miriam, "Then she did say something! Woman, why did you say nothing?" As he tried to control his temper his face got redder with every breath he took. And the more he tried to contain his anger, the more infuriated he got. He was seething as he rose from his seat and walked to her side. He reached down and closed his fingers around Miriam's throat and was pulling her from her chair when the doorbell rang. He glared at Miriam with pure hatred in his heart. He threw her back down into her chair. With his fist clenched and his jaw trembling, he turned and left the room to answer the front door.

He walked to the front door. He squared his shoulders, straightened his tie then took a moment more to collect himself before opening it.

"Evening, Tobias," the Sheriff said. "They told me you were looking for me."

"Yes. Yes, I am, Sheriff. Please come in." Tobias showed the Sheriff into the main parlor and offered him a seat.

"No, I can't stay long; big fight in Mick Town that we broke up this afternoon. Arrested close to thirty of 'em. Got to make sure they are booked properly, or Donavan will spring 'em sure as shit stinks."

"Understood. I'll make this brief. I need a posse—a large posse—tomorrow morning."

"What in hell for?"

"To find Charlotte. She's gone. Someone in the Indian village knows where she is. Can I count on you?"

"I've got no jurisdiction out there, Tobias. I can only back you up. Why would they know where Charlotte is? Do you think they've kidnapped her?"

"That's no concern of yours now. I need a posse. That's all I need. A show of force. That bastard Aihàm needs to know I mean business. Can you get a posse together by morning?"

"Well, I . . ."

"You owe me, and right now I'm calling in favors."

The Sheriff looked at the floor and played with his cap. "I'll see what I can do, Tobias."

"I want to know tonight."

"I understand," The Sheriff said as he turned to go to the front door. "I'll let you know tonight." The Sheriff nodded to Miriam, who was standing outside the parlor. "Evening, Miriam," he said as he put on his cap and walked past her and out the front door.

Miriam heard the whole conversation between Tobias

and the Sheriff. She turned to Tobias. "Don't do this, Tobias. She will hate you for the rest of her life. Please don't do this."

Tobias looked at his wife with enormous contempt. "We are legally bound together for life," he said with such disdain and antipathy that it shook Miriam to the bone. "But that is all! From this day forward you are no longer my companion. You are to be seen and not heard. You are to tend my house and prepare my meals as directed by me. You no longer have the privilege of access to my accounts. I will allot monies for specific things as I see fit. You will do exactly as I command. Woman, from this day on you live in hell. Have I made myself clear?"

Miriam stared at him as a festering anger churned inside her, growing with every word he said. She moved her foot and took a bold step toward him and stared into his eyes. "Perfectly," she said, filled with conviction. She did not move. She stood in his path. They stared into each other's eyes for several minutes until he walked around her and left the room.

* * * * *

It was a muggy, hot Sunday morning for late July. The clouds in the sky were threatening to burst open any minute. Tobias rode his horse from the livery stable to the Sheriff's office. Twenty-five men on horseback greeted him as he approached. He waved and called them by name and shook hands with a few. The Sheriff rode to meet him. "They're volunteers and none of us have any idea why we're here. So, we'll follow your lead. Tobias, I must warn you that it is my duty to arrest you if you cross the line."

"Of course; let's ride." Tobias steered his horse out of

town and sunk his heels into the animal's side. The horse responded with a whinny. They rode for the better part of an hour at a moderate pace until they reached the outskirts of the Indian village. There Tobias signaled to the men to get in a two by two formation.

With Tobias in the lead and the Sheriff by his side, the posse entered the village and rode into the center of town. Tobias signaled to stop as the posse reached the town square. A few people were milling around, and Tobias shouted down to them, "I want to speak to your Chief. Now!"

An elderly man looked at Tobias and tipped his hat. "Right away," he said, and as if in slow motion he took several steps across the square toward Aihàm's house.

"Now, you red bastard! I want to see him now," Tobias shouted at the man. The Sheriff leaned toward Tobias and said, "Calm down, Tobias, calm down."

In the distance, Tobias saw Aihàm walking toward him. Tobias dismounted and crossed the square, heading for Aihàm. When they were face to face, he demanded, "My daughter! Charlotte! Where is she?"

Aihàm stood within arm's length of Tobias and looked him in the eyes. "Today, I do not know."

Tobias lunged at him, grabbing him by the throat. "You do know, you red-skinned bastard, you do know and if I have to squeeze the air out of you, you will tell me."

"I can tell you what I know and no more." Aihàm rasped as he stood motionless with his arms by his sides.

"Don't give me that Indian crap! Where is Charlotte?"

"She is with my son." Aihàm's voice was near a whisper, but his posture didn't change.

"Where, God damn it, where?"

"That I do not know." Aihàm's voice was almost inaudible.

Tobias stared into Aihàm's eyes. Reluctant, with a violent, sadistic thrust, he released his hold. His lips snarled, he stepped back and lowered his head. For a fleeting moment, concern for his daughter's welfare was paramount in his heart. But as he raised his head and looked into Aihàm's eyes, his priority changed. "So, what do you know, Aihàm? What exactly do you know? Are they married?"

Aihàm still didn't move. "Yes," he said. "In both the way of the Lenape and the rite of the white man." His voice was as clear as if Tobias had never touched him.

"What do you know about my rite?"

"Only that which Charlotte requested."

"Requested? Charlotte requested you use our marriage rite in this heathen union. Is that what you are saying?"

"It was her request. The words were said. The papers filed. They are wed in the eyes of your God and mine. It is legal in your world and in mine. It is done."

Tobias felt Aihàm's words as if he was stabbed in his gut. And the look he saw in his adversary's eyes felt as if Aihàm was twisting the blade over and over again. A torrent of insufferable, excruciating pain bombarded Tobias' senses. He wanted to recoil, to cry out, but he fought the urge and stifled the growing wail that was stuck in his throat. He eyes fixed on Aihàm. He refused to back down—to flinch—to show any weakness. He stood immobile, glaring into Aihàm's eyes, and with every ounce of rancor in his body he spat on the ground at Aihàm's feet. "That," Tobias said with a hatred that spewed from his toes, "is what I think of this marriage."

Tobias turned and walked across the square. He

mounted his horse and rode to where Aihàm stood. "We are not through, Aihàm. This marriage will not be. They cannot hide from me. I will do everything in my power to end it. If that means death, either his or mine, so be it!" Tobias turned his horse, joined the posse, and led them out of town.

Chief Aihàm stood anchored in his spot with his eyes riveted on Tobias. He made not a single movement or gesture. He watched until the last horse disappeared from view, then he turned and walked to his house. Violet, anxious to know what had happened, came toward him from the kitchen.

"Aihàm, Tobias Wickham is satisfied?"

"No, Kishkikwentis. He has vowed to kill our son." Aihàm could not bear the look of horror on his wife's face. So, he turned his head, walked past her, and slumped into a kitchen chair.

* * * * *

Miriam Wickham took the last loaf of bread she had baked from the oven and put it on the sideboard to cool. She washed the few dishes left in the sink and coaxed the last loaf of bread from of its pan. She placed the bread on a cutting board with a knife beside it. She put them on the table with the other food items she found for Tobias' Sunday morning repast. Satisfied that her table was perfect, she went to her bedroom and locked the door. She reached into her armoire and took Charlotte's letter from its hiding place. She lifted the envelope to her nose to see if she could smell her daughter's fragrance. The faint scent of rose water and gardenia delighted her senses. She laughed as she pictured Charlotte unwrapping her birthday gift a short time ago. She removed the note from the envelope. It was dated July 14, 1894. Tears came to her eyes as she looked at the familiar handwriting, and a sob caught in her throat. Taking long, slow breaths, she waited until her eyes cleared and she was able to read the note.

My Dearest Mother,

Tey and I will be married tonight in an evening ceremony by firelight. Please be happy for us and please do not worry. Tey and I are well aware of Father's reach. That is why I have told you nothing. I did not want to force you to choose between being honest with your husband or protecting your daughter. My hope is that you will someday forgive me for what I am about to do. I hope, in your heart, you know my intent is not to hurt you or Father, but to be with the man I love. Trust that I am happy. Tey and I belong together. We are one for now and forever. We always were, and we always shall be. I love you, Mama. I will write when it is safe. Until you hear from me again know you are in my heart always.

Your loving daughter, Charlotte

Miriam read the note several times before she hid it back under the floorboard. She rose to her feet and went from her bedroom down the stairs into the middle room. She settled into her rocker. She reached into the basket she always kept beside her chair. And she lifted her knitting onto her lap. She righted the needles, made sure the wool was not tangled and rested her arms. She rocked and knitted and waited for Tobias Wickham's return.

* * * * *

Tobias dismounted at the livery stable and patted his horse. The turmoil inside him raged. He looked left and right as he measured the surroundings that he knew so well. Harley Griffith was tending the stalls. He smiled and bid Tobias a good morning. Tobias nodded and told Harley to curry his horse. "We've had a long, hard ride this morning, Harley. He needs the full treatment."

Harley smiled, showing a top row of teeth missing a front tooth. "Tie him there. I'll get to him right away, Mr. Wickham."

Tobias patted his horse once again and tied him to the post. "Thank you, Harley. I can always count on you." Tobias walked from the livery onto the main street of town. He stood there for a few moments, looking up and down the street as if he were wondering where he should go.

There wasn't a single person within a hundred miles who didn't respect or fear the name of Tobias Wickham. Still, Tobias knew that there wasn't one of those people that he could call a friend. At that moment he so needed a friend, someone to talk to. He couldn't go home and talk to Miriam any longer. He had made sure of that with his tirade of yesterday. It never occurred to him to apologize to Miriam for his words and deeds. Tobias Wickham made apologies to no one.

Tobias slapped his riding crop against his leg. He turned and walked back inside the livery stable. "Harley!" he yelled out. Harley's head popped up in a stall not far from where Tobias stood.

"Yes, sir."

"I'm taking him out again. Be back later this afternoon."

"Sure thing, Mr. Wickham, I'll be here."

Tobias mounted his horse and reined him toward the

street. His horse immediately followed his lead and trotted from the livery. A short distance ahead the road forked. Tobias stopped and pondered which road to take as a familiar old verse came to mind:

"Enter through the narrow gate. For wide is the gate and broad is the road that leads to destruction, and many enter through it. But small is the gate and narrow the road that leads to life, and only a few find it." Matt. 7:13-14

He patted his horse and said to him, "Which gate, old boy—is it life or destruction?" Tobias exhaled the air from his lungs through his clenched teeth. He snickered and coaxed his horse onto the road.

Tobias rode to the other side of town until he saw Jedidiah's home. It was a white two-story Victorian set back from the road on a large parcel of ground. He stopped his horse and watched. Jedidiah, his wife, and daughter carried trays of food and dinner dishes to a pavilion. They'd built the pavilion beside a small running stream that was a short distance from the house. Jedidiah put down what he was carrying and turned. As he turned, he spotted Tobias.

He approached Tobias and studied him for a few moments. "Well, I never thought I'd see this," Jedidiah said, trying not to be sarcastic. "Tobias, come join us. We are going to sit down and have our noon meal."

"No. I will not impose. I will speak with you some other time." Tobias pulled on the reins to guide his horse away. Jedidiah moved in front of his horse to stop him.

"You will not be imposing, Tobias. Please. I'd like you to join us. Besides, I'm sure you would not have come out here if you did not need to speak with me. So, please, join us."

Tobias hesitated for a few moments. Then he dismounted and followed Jedidiah to the pavilion.

Inside the pavilion sat Jedidiah's wife and daughter. Tobias stared at them for several minutes. His hatred of the Indian blood coursing through the bodies of his dinner hosts was blinding him. And he fought to get it under control. He looked back and forth from them to the food on the table. He'd had nothing to eat since the noon before. His stomach rumbled, begging for food. His hunger controlled his every move, his every thought, and he forced himself to sit down at the table. Within a few moments he was eating heartily.

After dinner, the two women cleared the pavilion and left the two men alone. Unable to look Jedidiah in the eye, Tobias lowered his head and said, "I went to the village this morning. I threatened the life of Aihàm's son."

"Why? I told you not to go, not to do that."

"I had to know." Tobias raised his head and looked Jedidiah in the eyes. "I had to know."

"Well? Did you find out?"

"They are married, Rue. It's legal. And Charlotte, Charlotte used the Christian . . . Why can I not accept it, Jedidiah, why?"

"In time. Hopefully, you will in time."

"No. I want to kill him. I want to kill you, your lovely wife, every Indian alive. Every second I breathe, my hate grows."

"Why such hate, Tobias? I never understood this irrational hate for me, for my kind. Why?"

Tobias sat silent for many minutes not looking at Rue. Then almost whispering, he began, "When I was a boy, just fourteen . . . I had to bury . . ." Tobias raised his head. A fierce, cruel, vicious look was in his eyes as he stared at Jedidiah. "They butchered them. My whole family butchered." Tobias' nostrils flared as images and memories rushed through his mind. "Retribution. That's what they said. Retribution." Tobias emphasized each syllable, then he spat on the ground as hard as he could. "Jedidiah," Tobias said, looking into his partner's eyes, "I was the only one left. I was the one who collected the pieces. Every member of my family: I buried them, one by one. Then I buried everyone in the whole damned town. I buried them all; every last one. I saw the looks on their faces. I am the one who closed their eyes. I am haunted by them. Jedidiah, I cannot find it in my heart to forgive because it is impossible for me to forget."

"I didn't know," Jedidiah said in a whisper.

Tobias stood and put on his riding gloves. "Thank you for the meal. Please thank your wife for her hospitality. Now I must go and do what I must do." He walked to his horse without shaking hands or looking back. He mounted his horse and rode to the livery stable.

Chapter 8
After Midnight, October 22, 1951

"What is he going to do, Auntie? Is he going to kill Tey? He's not, is he, Auntie?"

"Well, that's the rest of the story, Danny. That should wait until the morning. What do you think, Diana?"

"I agree. It's after midnight, Dan. You must be tired by now."

"No! I want to hear more. Pleassssse."

My mother looked at Auntie, and Auntie looked at my mother.

"Well, I do have a bottle of Porter left. What about you, Auntie? Another cup of tea?" Mother asked.

Auntie nodded, and Mother left the table to put the kettle on the stove. I ran to the bathroom. When I returned, they were sitting in their places around the table. Auntie looked at me and wagged her finger. "One more hour, young lady, do you understand? Because this old girl is getting tired."

Mother laughed, and I smiled and agreed to one more hour.

"All right; let me see. I don't want to tell you anything that may give you bad dreams tonight. So, I'll tell you what Tey and Charlotte were doing while Tobias was on his rampage. What do you think?"

"Yes. Please. I want to hear it all," I said.

"So do I," my mother said.

"Well, Charlotte and Tey were very happy. They were together, and they were so much in love. Charlotte decorated, primped, and personalized the flat. Doilies or tablecloths made by her mother covered every table. And bright and early Monday morning on, July . . ."

Monday, July 30, 1894

Charlotte and Tey walked hand in hand through the Princeton campus. They were going to the registrar's office to make sure all was in order. Charlotte sat down on a nearby bench to wait while Tey went inside. It was a beautiful summer's day with birds chirping and students wandering around the campus.

Good morning," someone said, and Charlotte turned to see who it was.

She smiled. "And a good morning to you also, Mr. Butcher."

"Please, don't be so formal. We are in the same boat here. Please call me Will. And where is your husband, if I may ask?"

"Inside checking with the registrar. He wanted to make sure everything is in order."

"Has he matriculated before?" Will asked.

"No. It's his first time. He's quite excited and a bit worried also." Charlotte replied.

"Quite a feather in his cap. Being accepted to Princeton and all," Will said. "It took me three tries before I could get in. Schools in Guiana don't meet Princeton standards so I'm still on probation. My grades, you know."

"For how long?" Charlotte asked, surprised. "I didn't know they did that. I assumed once you're in, well, you're in."

"No. That's not the way. Especially for first-year

students; you see, we must cut the mustard, or we are expelled in our first few weeks. Weeds out the herd, so to speak."

"Tey!" Charlotte shouted and waved. "Here he comes now, Will." She stood as he approached, and Tey took her in his arms. He kissed her before he turned and offered his hand to Will.

"Good morning. William Butcher, correct?"

"Yes, and you are Tey." He thought for a moment and said, "Tey is short for . . ."

"Taylor Aihàmson."

"Yes. That's right. Sorry, sometimes I worry about my memory, but I remembered your lovely bride all right. Didn't I, Charlotte? Must be only men I tend to forget."

Tey laughed. "It seems we are neighbors. We are in 301."

"Yes, we are. Well, I was on my way to meet a few fellows and stay on and dine with them. Why don't you join us? No time like the present to get to know classmates."

Tey looked at Charlotte, and she nodded. "We'd be delighted." Tey said.

The three of them walked down the street until they came to a ladies' apparel shop. Charlotte spied a sign in the window that read: *Help needed; apply within.*

Excited, she said, "Tey. Please wait. I want to talk to the proprietrix of this shop. Please, before someone else does."

Tey turned to Will. "She is determined to work and help with expenses. So please, if you don't mind, another time. But thank you for inviting us."

"Of course, old man, I understand completely. We

usually dine at Murphy's; that's the tavern on the corner. When Charlotte finishes come join us. Well, goodbye now."

Will walked on, and Tey turned to Charlotte and smiled. "I will be waiting right here."

Charlotte, a bit nervous yet full of anticipation, walked into the shop. She couldn't help but admire the clothes and array of women's undergarments on display. A tall woman approached Charlotte. She had chiseled features and golden hair piled high on top of her head.

"May I help you?" she asked with a slight accent and took hold of Charlotte's left hand and continued, "Madam."

A little embarrassed, Charlotte smiled and nodded, "Yes, please. May I speak with the proprietrix?"

"You are," the woman answered and nodded at Charlotte. "How may I help you?"

Charlotte looked into the woman's eyes. Confident, she said, "I am enquiring about the position you advertise in your window. Madam, I am well educated, and I've been taught a fine hand stitch. I also know how to operate both a treadle and an electric sewing machine. I keep abreast of today's styles, and I can make patterns to copy them. The dress I am wearing is an example of my work. I am available every day, and I am willing to take work home to finish at night. I am capable of doing whatever you require and doing it well. I am the person you seek."

The woman walked around Charlotte, inspecting her. She studied her design, assessed her sewing, then she leaned against her front counter. She eyed Charlotte once more and smiled. "And what is your name?"

"Charlotte Wick . . . Ah . . . Aihàmson, Madam."

"Well, Charlotte Wick . . . ah Aihàmson, I like your spirit. I am Giselle. Giselle LaFountaine." She put her hands on Charlotte's shoulders and turned her around once more. "I like what you did with your dress and your attitude tells me we will work well together." She smiled and offered her hand to Charlotte to shake. "When can you start?" she asked.

Charlotte chuckled as she grasped Giselle's hand and said, "Tomorrow! I can start tomorrow if you like." Charlotte looked at Giselle and they laughed.

"Yes, I like. And tell me; is that your husband pacing outside? Why not ask him in? I'd like to meet him."

Charlotte nodded and hurried outside. She told Tey she had the job. He hugged her, and she took hold of his hand. They were laughing as they neared Giselle. Charlotte, her eyes on Tey's, said to Giselle, "Madam Giselle LaFountaine, this is my Tey, Taylor Aihàmson."

Giselle offered Tey her hand. "Monsieur, may I address you as Tey and will you address me as Giselle?"

"I'm honored," Tey said as he shook Giselle's hand and smiled at Charlotte.

Tey listened as Giselle and Charlotte talk about the job and her starting wage. Satisfied with the arrangements Tey and Charlotte left the dress shop and headed to Murphy's. Charlotte's excitement was bubbling over. All she wanted to talk about was her new job that paid $1.50 per day. So, as they walked Charlotte babbled on. "And, Tey, did you hear Giselle say that many of her customers were very generous. Particularly if they liked someone's work. That means extra money because they will like mine. I am sure of it."

As soon as they entered Murphy's, they looked around

to see if William Butcher was still there. When they didn't see him, they found a quiet table and settled in. They ordered an inexpensive meal and shared a pint of beer. Tey also asked the barmaid to bring a slip of paper and a pencil to their table. The barmaid obliged and Tey and Charlotte set to work on their budget. They figured that Charlotte had the potential of earning nine dollars weekly. Tey told Charlotte that tomorrow he had a meeting with the superintendent of the plant to apply for a job.

He showed Charlotte the referral slip the registrar had given him. The referral said he qualified as an engineering trainee and quoted wages of $1.77 per day to start. The two were overjoyed. If the wage numbers came true, they wouldn't need to worry about expenses. Together they would earn more than twenty-one dollars a week. They needed to budget food, clothing, and other personal essentials. Housing was part of Tey's stipend, which also covered his books. Still, journals, paper, writing implements, and other essentials were his responsibility.

When they had finished their meal, they went to the grocery. They purchased supplies for supper, breakfast and items to pack for their noon meal the next day. Then they headed home to work on their budget, accounting for everything down to the last penny.

As soon as they entered their flat Tey set to work finalizing their budget. Charlotte sat next to him as he went over the numbers one last time to make sure everything was correct. She leaned over and kissed him on his cheek. He turned to look at her, smiled and turned back to his numbers. She reached out and lifted his chin and turned his face toward her. They gazed into each other's eyes for a moment before she leaned in and kissed him on his lips. "Tey eholàk," she whispered. "Enough playing with numbers; instead, let's . . ."

Tey rose from his chair and took her in his arms.

Chapter 9
Early Hours of October 22, 1951

"Well, it's now past one o'clock, young lady. Time for bed. And I am very tired," Auntie said as she rose from her chair. "What about you, Diana?"

"Me too. Give up, Dan. Pouting will do no good right now. So, go brush your teeth. Right now! Go. We will be right there."

I did what Mother told me to do. I was tired too, and very sleepy. I brushed my teeth and sat down on the top step waiting for them.

After my mother climbed the stairs, I followed her into the middle room. She folded down the bedspread and patted the bed, smiling at me. "Well, come on, get in and lay your head on this pillow."

It was a soft feather pillow, and it felt so good to rest my head on it. I looked at my mother and asked, "Are you sleeping in here? With me?"

"We'll see. I want to talk to Auntie a little longer so close your eyes, sweetheart. It's time to sleep. The sandman is long overdue."

Mother didn't sleep with me that night. When I awoke, I dressed and went in search of them. I found both Mother and Auntie still dressed asleep on Auntie's bed. They were facing each other. Auntie had her arm around my mother's waist and my mother had her arm around Auntie's shoulders. It was early. The clock read ten minutes to six and I thought and thought about whether I should wake them.

But the story. I wasn't sure how much more was left.

Tobias had said he would do what he must, and I was afraid that Tey was in danger and Charlotte too. Still I waited. I sat on the floor at the foot of Auntie's bed until the clock read 6:15. Auntie was always awake and dressed by six fifteen. She would be upset if I didn't wake her because she had things to do. That's what she told me all the time. Still, I was a little leery. She could be angry if I disturbed her, so I thought I'd nudge my mother and get her to rouse Auntie. But when I nudged Mother she didn't move. She didn't even push me away. So, I nudged her again and again until she asked, "What, Danny, what do you want?"

I bent down and whispered in her ear, "You need to wake up Auntie."

Mother rolled over and looked at me. "Why?" she asked. "Why would I ever do that?" I couldn't believe she asked me that question. I stood there with my hands on my hips and said, "Because it's after 6:15. She has things to do, that's why."

I heard a chuckle coming from Auntie's side of the bed and Mother laughed too.

After they changed and dressed we met in the kitchen. Auntie and Mother made blueberry waffles while frying thick slices of country bacon. The bacon was crisp and salty and the Vermont maple syrup on our waffles was sweet and sticky. I licked my fingers savoring every morsel.

I sat in my place enjoying breakfast, listening to them chat about everything but the story. As it dragged on, I got a bit frustrated. I wanted to hear the rest of the story. So, I got up and started clearing the table. Mother and Auntie took the hint and we washed the dishes. After we finished, Mother made another cup of tea for each of them, and the three of us sat down at the table.

"Well, what will we discuss now? Any ideas, Danny?" Auntie asked. I could tell she was playing with me, but I didn't care.

"The story! Finish the story, Auntie. Please finish it."

She smiled at me with her jesting smile. I looked at Mother. She had her head bent down, looking into her teacup. When she looked up the laughter that was in her eyes moments before had vanished.

"Yes," Mother said. "Please finish. You're getting to the murky parts, the parts that make no sense to me." She looked into Auntie's eyes. "They're what I need to know."

Auntie reached across the table and took hold of my mother's hand. "Ask anything you want. I will answer as honestly as my memories allow."

My mother looked into her eyes. An aggrieved confusion was in her voice when she asked, "There are so many questions. Charlotte and Tey—they were happy at Princeton? Were there problems, hard times? What happened?"

Auntie nodded. "Yes." She gazed off as if she were searching the firmament for every detail. "They were very happy at Princeton. For them, being together, no matter what hardship they may have had to endure, was heaven. She kept house and worked at the dress shop while he studied hard to keep up his grades. Tey found a farmer less than a mile from where they lived. He cordoned off a small piece of ground so Tey could plant a few crops. Tey went every day that fall. He tended his crops and nourished his small field so it would be ready for planting in the spring. But as each day passed, he grew more and more worried about Charlotte.

"At first, it seemed to happen only one or two mornings.

Soon it was every morning and sometimes in the afternoon and evening that she was sick. It became so bad she couldn't keep anything, not even soda crackers, in her stomach. And when he touched her breasts, she winced as if in pain. He worried that she had contracted a pernicious disease and he didn't know what to do for her. She wouldn't listen to him and go to see a doctor so before he went to work on Sunday, October . . ."

Sunday, October 14 – Friday, November 2, 1894

Tey tried to hide from view as he stared through the display window of Giselle's shop. It was Sunday. Giselle and Charlotte had a special order they needed to finish by Monday morning. Charlotte was in the work room at the back of the shop when Tey spied Giselle. He waved at her, urging her to come outside. Giselle, curious about what he wanted, came to the door. Tey pulled her from in front of the window so Charlotte wouldn't see them together. Tey pleaded with her, "Please, Giselle, please, you must speak with Charlotte." The urgency and concern in his voice alarmed Giselle.

"Why, Tey, what is wrong?" Giselle asked.

"I don't know. She needs to see a doctor. Tell her she must let me take her. Or she could go with you. Please, Giselle, if she will go, please take her."

Giselle, puzzled by Tey's angst, strained to think of a reason for Charlotte's condition.

"But . . . Tey, she seems fine. . . . She seems, well, she does seem . . . At times . . . yes . . . A bit out of sorts. Still, she seems . . . But . . . her humor has, well, sometimes I . . . and . . . She is so tired, so sluggish . . . yes, even sleepy . . . and her corselette seems . . . she has . . ." Giselle furrowed her brow as she pondered. Looking at Tey, she cocked her head to one side and asked, "She is having a sickness . . . in the morning, no?"

Tey nodded and said, "Yes. And in the afternoon and evening too. We don't know why, Giselle. It can't be what she's eating. I would have it too."

Giselle furrowed her brow and her eyes glazed almost as if she was in a trance. Several minutes passed before her eyes widened and a smile spread across her face. She threw her head back and began laughing. He looked at Giselle, bewildered. He had no idea what she could have found funny in what he said. Giselle took hold of Tey's hand and pulled him.

"Come. Come with me. We must speak with Charlotte. We will calm things now. Come." She led Tey into the shop to the backroom where Charlotte was working.

Charlotte raised her eyes at the sound of footsteps, and she saw Tey. "Why are you here? You should be at work. I told you I was fine. Go to work or you'll be fired. Stop worrying about me."

"It's Sunday, Charlotte. My shift doesn't start until one. Everything's all right."

"Then you should be studying," she said, and she burst into tears.

Tey turned to Giselle. "You see? You see what I mean?"

"I see," Giselle said, turning to face Charlotte. "Charlotte, please put that work down and speak with me a moment."

Charlotte was hesitant, yet the look on Giselle's face made her curious. She watched Giselle as she walked toward her. Giselle bent down and took the work from Charlotte's hands. She pulled a chair next to Charlotte and sat down facing her.

"Charlotte, your emotions, they are, how you say, *haut et bas*, ah, high and low, yes?" Giselle asked. Charlotte shot a look at Tey and stared at Giselle. "And, my Charlotte, here," she said, moving her hand across her bodice. "It is tight, tender also, yes?" Charlotte nodded. "And, you have a sickness, yes?" Charlotte looked at Tey and back to Giselle and nodded. Giselle leaned toward Charlotte. She whispered, "Your unclean days, they have not come for some time, yes?" Charlotte, embarrassed by the question, looked at Giselle and nodded yes. Giselle leaned back in her chair and laughed. She took Charlotte's face in her hands and kissed both cheeks. "My darling Charlotte, what a beautiful mother this baby will have." She walked to Tey. She put her hands on his arms, and she kissed both his cheeks. "And such a strong, wonderful father." Giselle turned so she could see both of them. "You must see the doctor. He will confirm this is so, and he will make sure everything is as it should be. So, you will see him, yes?"

Charlotte was flabbergasted. She sat in her chair, not moving a muscle, her mouth gaping open. She stared at Tey and watched a smile spread across his face. She turned to Giselle and searched her eyes for confirmation. As Giselle's words sunk into her head, she again turned to face Tey. She looked into his eyes. Her surprised, bewildered stare of moments before disappeared. She grimaced; she put her face in her hands and cried.

"Charlotte, what's wrong?" Tey rushed to her. Confused and concerned by her reaction, he knelt by her side, rubbing her arms, trying to comfort her. Charlotte looked at him with tears streaming down her face.

"Oh, Tey, I'm so stupid. I've been so afraid. I thought I

had an awful disease that was eating my insides away and, and, I had no idea. If I could have talked to Mother. She would have told me what was happening. Oh, Tey, no one ever told me . . ." Charlotte looked down and caressed her abdomen with her hands and whispered, "about when it is in there . . . How it grows." She raised her head to look at him, "inside me . . . What to expect . . . I am so stupid, Tey. I didn't know. I didn't mean to worry you. I didn't know."

Tey rubbed her hands and arms, trying to soothe her. He took her face in his hands and kissed her. "It's good, Chulëntët. Smile, my love. It is a time to be happy. We are going to have a baby, you and me. Our baby, Charlotte. Think of it; we are going to have a baby." Tey bubbled as he spoke. He overflowed with joy. His joy and excitement permeated the room. Charlotte finally felt it and smiled and finally laughed with him.

* * * * *

The next Wednesday Tey and Charlotte strolled to Dr. Mosby's clinic. The doctor was a member of the university staff. He had an office in a small private hospital he partially owned. And, because Tey was a student at the University, he gave them a much-discounted rate for his services. After he examined Charlotte, she forced herself to ask a few questions. His answers were cold; he spoke in a clinical manner as if reciting from a textbook. She left his office relieved knowing everything seemed normal. Yet she still had no idea about what was going to happen next.

As they enjoyed supper at a table in the corner of Murphy's Charlotte told Tey what happened in the doctor's office. ". . . And he reached under my dress with this listening thing. He put it on my belly to, he said, auscultate the baby's heart tones. He said he heard nothing of any concern. He told me to see him again when it is closer to my time. Mid to late January he wants me to come back so he can examine me again. He said I needed to be careful not to gain too much weight to avoid a condition called toxemia. He told me to stay as calm as I can to ensure a healthy baby, and he measured my belly. The fundal height indicated that the baby would be born five to six months from now. Think of it, Tey, in less than six months our baby will be here—sometime in April."

Tey watched as Charlotte's eyes danced when she talked about the baby. "Chulëntët. You seem so relieved. The doctor must have answered all our questions."

Charlotte's smile faded and she dropped her eyes from Tey's. "Not all, Tey. I'm more confused than ever and Tey, well, I, I didn't ask about that. I was so," she looked at him and blurted out, "embarrassed. I didn't ask much of anything. He was so abrupt when he asked questions about my days that I couldn't get the words out. I couldn't talk to him about anything. Please don't be angry with me."

"Charlotte, my love," Tey said, shaking his head and smiling, "I'm not angry. Please, Chulëntët, don't fret."

"But I should have. I, I never talked about things like that with anyone else but my mother and yours. But he's a man, Tey. It was embarrassing enough when he put his hand up my skirt. I closed my eyes and couldn't speak afterward. How could I talk to him of . . . of that? You're the only man I ever talked to about things like that."

"But he will be the one there when our baby is born. Charlotte, he will see and touch you. You must allow it."

Shocked by his words Charlotte stared at him for a long

time. "It hadn't occurred to me," she whispered, her face colored by the embarrassment she felt, "It never crossed my . . ."

Tey nodded his head. The look on his face brought tears to Charlotte's eyes. She was sure he was mocking her. She felt ashamed. Her ignorance overwhelmed her, and she yelled at herself that he had every right to mock her. In anguish, she cried out, "I'm so stupid on this subject, Tey! Why didn't I know that? You reasoned it out; why didn't I? Am I this stupid about it? I should have known. My mother would've made sure of it. She would've told me. If I could've talked to Mother I would know. I always went to her. I could ask her anything, and she would explain everything. I never felt embarrassed with her. She always told me and now, without her, I feel . . . Oh, Tey, how can I be this stupid?"

Tey moved his chair next to Charlotte's and took her in his arms. "Shush, Chulëntët. Hush now. It will be all right. Stop fretting."

Charlotte tears turned to a sob. "What are we going to do? Six more months. I can't control my emotions and, and I don't know what to do because I was too embarrassed to ask. I've been so worried that something was terribly wrong inside me. That's why I wouldn't let you touch me. I was afraid I'd give it to you. But now I know why my days stopped, but I don't know what to do . . . Oh, Tey, Mother would tell me what to do. She'd tell me what she did. She'd tell me how to be a proper wife to you. I don't know. Six more months—how will you ever put up with me?"

Tey kissed her forehead and held her tightly. He ran his fingers through her hair as he whispered, "Don't you worry about that, my love. Don't give it another thought. I'll find a way. I promise you; I will find a way."

* * * * *

Charlotte had a terrible night. Horrible dreams went round and round in her head. She dreamed of doctors laughing at her ignorance. She saw nurses holding babies. They wagged their fingers at her and called her stupid. In her dreams, she watched as babies grew in her womb. They questioned her, demanding answers. "How big? Do you know? But it's fundal – Charlotte," they scoffed. "It's fundal-mental!" They jeered and laughed. They were beautiful, healthy babies. And as she watched they transformed. They became little hideous, monstrous creatures screaming all around her, "Fat! Got fat! Look at me! Toxic! Too toxic! Must get out! I'll die! Let me out! Let me out!" But her body refused to give them up. She felt them scratching and clawing and tearing at her flesh. They were trying to get through layer after layer of her skin as fat engulfed them until—until—she woke in a cold sweat. She lay beside Tey, praying for the sunrise. As each second ticked by she became more determined to learn about childbirth.

In the morning she prepared breakfast. She urged him, "Please, Tey, please bring home anything you can find on the subject. Go to the library and bring home anything you can."

"But they are textbooks, Charlotte. Full of things you know nothing about," he answered.

"Do you think I am an idiot? I may be ignorant about what's happening to me, but I am not stupid, Tey. I can read and I can learn as well as you. Besides, Mother taught me Latin and Greek roots, prefixes, and suffixes. I can understand the meaning of most words, so bring the text home. Don't fight me on this, please."

So, after class Tey went to the library. He learned that the texts on prenatal care and childbirth were in the medical section. But that was a special reference section in the library. University policy said no books in that section could leave the library. And since he wasn't a medical student, he had no access to them anyway. He thought of seeking help from one of the medical students, but he didn't know any and didn't know anyone who did.

So, he asked the librarian to help find the information Charlotte longed for. She went through her card file and told him that there weren't any layman texts on the subject in the library. "With only men on campus, we don't have a call for them," she said. "But there may be some information in a few books of another nature." She directed him to a section full of lewd books, some quite pornographic. He perused Bernard Mandeville's *Mysteries of Virginity.* He leafed through Nicolas Venette's *Conjugal Love.* He looked through John Cleland's *Fanny Hill*, and Arthur Vincent's *Lives of Twelve Bad Women.* He decided that they were most unacceptable for Charlotte to read.

The library didn't have even a single paper on the subject that he was able to check out. When he told her, her disappointment overwhelmed him. Still hoping, he mentioned the bookstore where students resold their texts. She jumped at the suggestion and together they searched the stacks of books in the store. They found nothing on the shelves about a woman's reproductive system or childbirth.

Tey didn't know what else he could do. He wracked his brain trying to find answers. Charlotte needed to know about what was happening inside her body. He wanted to get Charlotte the answers she was looking for but, in his mind, he kept coming up short. Charlotte so hungered for advice from someone who knew the mysteries. And, as each day passed, she longed to talk to her mother and her yearning grew.

Tey watched Charlotte write letter after letter while he studied in the evenings. Letters that they both knew could never be delivered. Posting her letters to Miriam Wickham was impossible. Still he felt in his heart that there had to be more he could do. He had to put Charlotte in contact with another woman who had been through childbirth. He had to find someone she would trust and who could give her the advice and counseling she needed.

He made an appointment to speak with Dr. Mosby. He hoped the doctor would be able to recommend someone that Charlotte could talk to. The doctor gave Tey the name of a midwife in town. Dr. Mosby told Tey that he had never met the woman. She was highly respected and from what he'd heard she knew her business. Tey thanked the doctor for his help and asked him if there was a book that would satisfy Charlotte's curiosity. Dr. Mosby told him, *"The Married Woman's Adviser and Young Mother's Guide* by Francis Welch. It's the only decent discussion of the subject I know of."* But he told Tey, he would have to write to the publisher to see if he could get a copy. It was published in 1838 and never reprinted, as far as he knew, because it was banned in most places. He wrote down the publisher's name and address for Tey. He laughed, saying, "I'm willing to wager that you will see your child before you ever get hold of a copy of that book."

Tey wrote to the publisher anyway. And he made arrangements for Charlotte to meet with the midwife. But the meeting with the midwife didn't go well. Charlotte didn't feel any closeness with her. She thought the midwife was much too brash and intimidating. And the midwife thought Charlotte was a dim-witted child. She dismissed Charlotte's concerns as ridiculous musings of a spoiled brat. Charlotte felt lost, alone and even more stupid than she already felt. She longed for her mother more and more.

So Tey pleaded with Giselle to talk to her. But Giselle was uncomfortable assuming that role. She shied away from any discussion relating to the subject. She would do anything for the two of them. She treated them like her own children. Still, to talk to Charlotte like a mother Giselle found most disconcerting.

When Tey asked her why she was so hesitant, she shrugged and tilted her head to the side. "Tey, you are right," she said. "Charlotte needs someone to talk to, but that someone is not me. I have never been with child. I do not know what she is feeling. I do not know anything more than I have already said. It is as much a mystery to me as it is to Charlotte. If I told her what I heard and that was not right, I would not forgive myself ever. She needs to hear from one who knows and understands. And that I do not. A young woman turns to her mother at this time. It is most unfortunate she cannot, but I do not have the answers she seeks."

"I understand, truly, I understand how you feel. I also understand that I must do all I can. I fall short as a husband if I don't. I need to find a way to get her help. Giselle, I have got to find a way. I've tried everything else I could think of so if that's what she needs . . ." Tey straightened his shoulders and the look on his face alarmed Giselle.

"Tey, what you are thinking is impossible," she said. "Don't do it. It is reckless. If you contact her mother, how can you be sure she will not tell Charlotte's father? And if her father does find out, what will happen? He will know you are here and what will be the outcome? Will he kill you as you have said? Then what? What will happen to Charlotte and your child? Think. Before you act on your thoughts, think long and hard."

Tey knew Giselle was right. Still, Charlotte's peace of mind weighed heavily on him; it showed on his face, in his walk, in his posture. The following Sunday, as he walked into the plant, he ran into Barnaby Harrington.

Barnaby, a jovial, friendly sort, knew everyone at the plant. Barnaby was the ace salesman for the company. He hawked his wares in New Jersey, Pennsylvania, New York and Delaware. He was able to call his own hours and delineate his own territory. The company accommodated his every demand. He had a huge customer base. When he wanted to make a few extra dollars, he sold door to door. He sold the company's glassware and pottery lines to any homemaker who wanted them.

"What's wrong, old man?" Barnaby asked as he approached Tey. "You look like you've lost your best friend. Life can't be that bad now, can it?"

Tey smiled and said, "No. It isn't. I'm a little down, that's all. I'm worried about my wife. First baby and all. She misses her mother and there's no way . . . ." Tey stopped short, realizing he was saying more than he should.

Barnaby put his hands on Tey's shoulders. "Tey," he said, "you've come through for me a lot of times. You've fired up those boilers when I needed to cure pottery so I could meet my delivery times. You've stayed many a night for me, so today let me return a favor or two. Look, at the very least I can listen. I am a good listener. Besides, I've got four of my own, you know, and believe me I know how sensitive a woman can be during that time. So why not tell old Uncle Barnaby what's bothering you? Come on. I'll clear it with Cleary. He can spare you for a half hour or so. What do you say?"

Tey smiled and shook his head yes. "Thanks, Barnaby, I'm early anyway and, well, I do need to talk to someone before it eats my insides out."

Barnaby and Tey sat under a big, old oak tree near the boiler room where Tey always ate his lunch. Tey took Barnaby into his confidence and told him about Tobias Wickham. He explained why it was impossible for Charlotte to contact her mother. When he finished, he looked at Barnaby's face. Barnaby smiled and said, "Why is it impossible? I don't see a problem. I'll go to her neighborhood and sell our pottery door to door. Have Charlotte bundle her letters together and I'll hand them to her mother myself. No one will be the wiser."

Tey was skeptical. "You would do that for us?"

"Why not? I'm a good salesman. I'll get them in her hands and even she won't know what I'm doing. Trust me. Tobias Wickham will never know."

"If Miriam Wickham tells Tobias how you will . . ."

"Well, I don't know . . . there's this nice little town in Delaware where I could say we met and, look, don't give it another thought. From what you've said she won't tell him. He will never know."

"A reply, Barnaby, can you get a reply?"

"Leave that up to me. Have Charlotte bundle her notes tonight and give them to me tomorrow. Get here early. I'm scheduled to leave on the 10:12 to Newark and from there to Bloomfield. On Tuesday I have a few stops along the coast before Atlantic City. Wednesday I go to Camden. I'm there all day. I have lots of time. Thursday, I have one stop in Philadelphia and one in Dover Friday morning. Then I board the express headed for Trenton, where I catch the local home. I'll be on the 6:10 Friday evening. Meet me at the station. I'll find a way to get a reply for Charlotte."

Tey wasted no time telling Charlotte of Barnaby's plan, and she was overjoyed. She packaged her letters together and wrote one last one to her mother. Tey watched her in amazement. The change in her was immediate, instantaneous. When she finished writing, she addressed the envelope to *My Dearest Mother*. She wrote the address under it and she slipped the letter on top of the others. She sat in her chair, smiling as she stared at the package that she held it in her hands. Her smile faded as her brow tightened, and a worried look covered her face.

Tey reached across the table and touched her hand. "Charlotte, you were so happy a few moments ago, what is wrong?" he asked.

"If Father finds us," she said, grabbing his hand with hers. "Suppose he's there and he finds my notes? What will he do to Mother? I want so much to talk to her, but I am so scared he will find us. We've been so happy. Our baby! What will he do?"

Tey walked around the table and took her in his arms. "Oh, now my sweet, sweet Charlotte. Don't, my love, please don't fret so," he said. "We can only control that which we can control and nothing more. Barnaby knows our whole story. I took him into our confidence. If there is even a small chance Tobias Wickham could get wind of this, he will not proceed with our plan. That, my love, I can guarantee. So, think, in a few days you may hear from your mother. Good thoughts, Charlotte. Think good thoughts. Good thoughts to calm you and to keep our baby happy."

* * * * *

Wednesday was a crisp, sunny day. Barnaby Harrington was finding this new neighborhood very lucrative indeed. The sales he had made in the first three houses totaled more than fifty dollars, and he had only begun his day. By the afternoon he had made twelve more sales, and he now stood in front of the last house in the neighborhood. He gathered his thoughts and walked onto the front porch. He knocked and waited for someone to answer.

"Good afternoon, Madam. I'm Barnaby Harrington of the Freehold Pottery Works. If I may take a moment of your time to show you a new bowl. . . ." Barnaby lifted a deep-sided oblong bowl from his bag and held it so that Miriam Wickham was able to see inside it. In the bowl Barnaby had placed Charlotte's letters. ". . . in our new line of baking ware. It's the newest thing, and . . . note . . . the intricate . . . hand . . . work on the inside. You won't find another like it anywhere." He waited and watched.

Miriam looked down at the bowl and noticed that there were letters in it. Her mouth gaped open when she realized that the letters were from Charlotte. Her eyes welled with tears and she looked up at Barnaby. She took a step backward out of view from the opened door so no one could see her tears as she took the bowl from his hands. She slipped the letters into her apron pocket, cleared her throat and said as her voice quivered with joy and anticipation, "I thank you, sir . . ." She fought to regain her composure and stepped forward until she was standing in the doorway again. She had no idea what to do so she studied Barnaby for a sign and noticed him barely shake his head no. Miriam, unsure, shook her head no too, as if questioning him. Barnaby smiled and nodded once in answer and kept his eyes glued on hers.

Miriam smiled, realizing what he wanted her to do and half nodded her head. She looked into Barnaby's eyes and said, "But I'm not in the market for such a dish at the moment. I thank you for stopping by." Barnaby smiled and nodded yes. He put the dish back in his case and took out a brochure. He handed the brochure to Miriam. "I will be stocking the shelves at the Woolworths store all afternoon." he said. "Please peruse our brochure. If you wish to learn more write a note and bring it to the store this afternoon, and next Wednesday I will bring you a reply from our warehouse. I deliver my wares to the Woolworths every Wednesday." Barnaby stared into Miriam's eyes. He winked and smiled. "Thank you, Madam, for your time." Barnaby bowed and walked down the front steps. At the bottom of the steps, he turned to face Miriam, tipped his hat, turned onto the walkway and headed toward town.

Miriam closed the front door, leaning her weight against it, clutching the letters to her lips. Tears ran down her cheeks as visions of Charlotte streamed through her mind. A voice in her head, echoed the words, *write a note and he'll deliver it,* over and over again. She forced herself back to reality. *I haven't much time,* she thought. She ran up the stairs and locked herself in her bedroom and read Charlotte's letters. Tears gushed from her eyes.

"My baby is having a baby," she whispered to herself. Overwhelmed with emotion, she forced herself to calm down, to get in control. *There isn't much time,* she kept reminding herself. *I have much to do and there isn't much time. I must write my Charlotte and try to quell her fears.* She tried to cover the most important questions Charlotte asked. But she was afraid if she went into too much detail, she wouldn't make it to the store and back before Tobias came home. She cut her note short. She told Charlotte she would answer her questions in a letter she'd write during the week and she would look for Barnaby at Woolworths every week from now on. She'd exchange letters with him there because it would be much safer that way. She told her that since her disappearance no mail came to the house. Her father had the mail delivered to the office, thinking Charlotte would write. So, using the post was impossible. And, she told Charlotte, she went to the stores once a week anyway. And it made no difference what day it was so Tobias would think nothing of it.

She sealed the envelope and addressed it to *My Darling Daughter.* She put on her wrap and walked as fast as she could to Woolworths. She found Barnaby stocking shelves as he had said and slipped him her letter. She wanted to pull him to her and kiss his cheek but, instead, she thanked him and headed home. She got in well before Tobias was due to come home and went into the kitchen and started supper.

She stood by her stove, thinking about the wonderful turn of events of the day. A calm serenity spread through her. She knew her little girl was safe. She knew Charlotte was happy. And she knew her baby daughter was having a baby of her own.

* * * * *

Charlotte and Tey waited on the train platform on Friday evening. The 6:10 from Trenton was forty-five minutes late when they heard its whistle in the distance. As it pulled to a stop Charlotte kept looking at Tey, asking, "Do you see him? Tey! Do you see him?"

Tey looked left and right along the platform then spotted Barnaby. He was at the far end carrying bundles in his hands. They hurried to meet him, and Tey offered to help him carry his packages to a waiting cab.

"My youngest son's birthday. I bought a few things for him and my others, too. Always do when I have to miss one because of work." He dropped his packages in the cab and turned to face them. "You must be Charlotte. I am pleased to make your acquaintance, Charlotte. Tey has told me a lot about you. Oh! Before I forget." Barnaby reached into his coat pocket and frowned. He reached into another pocket and found the note he had for Charlotte. "I have this for you. She's a lovely woman. Your mother. It was a pleasure meeting her." He handed her the note.

Charlotte stood motionless, holding the letter in her hands staring at it for several seconds. A smile started at the corners of her mouth and she flung her arms around Barnaby's neck and kissed him on the cheek.

"Thank you. Thank you so very much." Charlotte clutched the note in one hand as she put her other hand to her lips. Tears welled in her eyes, and it was impossible for her to say anything more.

"You're a wonder, Barnaby, and a good friend. Thank you for doing this for Charlotte," Tey said, offering his hand to Barnaby.

"I told her I'd be there every week, so if she doesn't slip in front of the old man, I have no problem taking notes to her. A word of caution, though. Sometimes it seems too easy and that's when we make mistakes. So, stay vigilant and all's good. Now, I'd love to stay and chat, but I have a couple of babes and especially a birthday boy I want to hug tonight. See you at the plant, Tey. Charlotte, enjoy your reading." Barnaby waved and got into the cab, and the driver pulled out of the station.

Tey put his arm around Charlotte's shoulders and asked, "Where to, my love?"

"Home, please. Tey, I want to read her letter." Tey laughed. "Of course."

Chapter 10
Morning, October 22, 1951

"Well, Danny, life was good for them. Charlotte was communicating with her mother. And Tey was doing very well in his university studies. Months passed and Christmas drew near. Via Barnaby, Miriam sent booties, sweaters, and blankets she made for the baby. She also sent things that Tey's mother made for them. You see, Tobias watched every piece of mail sent or received in both Camden and in Aihàm's village. He laid in wait for Charlotte or Tey to slip up. He was certain that one of them would write to someone they knew. So, Miriam took Aihàm into her confidence, and they too corresponded with the children via Barnaby.

"Everyone was happy—everyone, that is, except for Tobias Wickham. Each day he grew more frustrated and angrier as he searched high and low for them to no avail. Now, sweetheart," Auntie said, drawing in a deep breath, "I need to take a break. My throat is a little dry from talking so much and that means it's time for a cup of tea. Diana, go put the kettle on and I'll get that tin of biscuits you like so much."

My mother looked at Auntie. "The imported ones that you used to get by mail?"

Auntie had an impish grin on her face when she went to the pantry and carried in a big blue tin. She put it in the middle of the table and looked at my mother. "These?" she asked, chuckling. "And you, Danny, what would you like? Juice or milk?"

"Milk, please. Auntie don't you know you always have milk with cookies. Anyway, does he find them? Did he find a letter or something? What happened?"

Auntie made the tea and brought the pot to the table. She sat down and fixed her tea, tasting it to make sure it was exactly as she liked. She looked into my eyes and smiled.

"Well," she said after taking another sip, "they were very careful but Tobias, Danny." Auntie paused. She took another sip. "At first," she continued, "he was looking in all the wrong places. He heard that Tey had applied for a scholarship at Rutgers, so he sent his detectives to New Brunswick. They searched for about a month but found nothing. Shortly after that, he heard that Tey was attending school in Philadelphia. So, he sent his detectives there."

Auntie took another sip of her tea. "He gave up that search shortly before Christmas. After that, he followed the lead he got from Millie's father that they had gone to New York. It took months to search the city. When he found nothing, he expanded his search to cover the whole state. By spring Tobias still had no answers. But something about Miriam attracted his attention." Auntie stopped and a serious look covered her face. "She had been acting strange since Charlotte disappeared. And he was certain she wasn't telling him all she knew. So, he decided it was time to pin her down. Now that triggered a strange turn of events. Miriam, instead of telling him everything she knew, did what she had vowed in her heart that she never would do. She lied. She downright lied. It happened on Wednesday, April . . ."

Wednesday, April 24 – Sunday, April 28, 1895

Tobias Wickham studied his wife as he sat across from her at their kitchen table. It was 7:30 on a Wednesday morning, the day he knew his wife always went to Woolworths. He had been having her followed for weeks. He knew that she had made an acquaintance with a traveling salesman. And this salesman delivered his wares to Woolworths every Wednesday. He also knew she exchanged envelopes with the salesman. And he wanted to know what was in those envelopes.

"Who is he, Miriam, this salesman in Woolworths? Every Wednesday you meet and exchange envelopes; I want to know who he is and now!"

"He is no concern of yours, Tobias." She looked into his eyes.

"He most certainly is! You have kept this relationship from me long enough. Now, who is he?" Tobias rose to his feet and pounded his fists on the table. His neck was reddening with every pulse going through his veins. "You will tell me now or you will not leave this house again! Have I made myself clear?"

Miriam rose from her chair and looked him straight in the eyes. Her stomach wrenched, sending a bitter taste to her tongue. Her eyes burned with the same ire she saw reflected on his face. She took an extra breath to gather her thoughts, and she said, "We are intimate, Tobias. He is my confidant and my dear friend. You will not give me what I need so I have looked elsewhere."

Tobias' mouth gaped open. "A lover! Am I to believe he is your lover?"

A rancorous grin curled her lips. "Believe as you wish."

His face turned ashen. His eyes stared at her in disbelief as anger consumed his whole being. He snarled and snorted. He clenched his teeth and fists as his body trembled and seethed, crazed by the fury inside him. Suddenly the fury in his eyes changed as if a switch in his brain had been turned off. He clutched his head and staggered back. He hit the sideboard behind him and fell to the floor. Miriam rushed to his side. She loosened his collar and opened his shirt so he could breathe. She straightened his rigid body, so he lay flat on the floor and ran into the next room to fetch a coverlet and pillows. She placed the pillows under his head and covered him with the blanket.

"Tobias," she said. "I'm going for help. Please don't die. Please don't die." Miriam stood and ran to the Rayfords next door. She pounded on their front door until Mrs. Rayford answered.

She was frantic. "Tobias! Please, it's Tobias! He needs help. Get a doctor. Please." She turned and ran down their front steps back into her house, leaving the front door wide open. She ran to the kitchen and knelt by Tobias' side. She took his rigid, claw-like hand in hers. She tried to comfort him. But as he lay there struggling to breathe, his fierce, menacing, sinister eyes scrutinized her every move.

The doctor arrived and examined Tobias. He told Miriam he could do nothing for him there. "He needs to go to the hospital for treatment," he said. "It looks like Tobias had a fit of apoplexy. I'll know more when I examined him at the hospital." A few minutes later the ambulance arrived. The emergency team lifted Tobias onto a stretcher and carried him out of the house.

"I will be at the hospital shortly, Doctor," Miriam said. "First, yes first, I must let his office know and I must go to . . . yes . . ." she said, looking at the doctor.

The doctor took a hold of Miriam by her shoulders and said, "Miriam. First, you must calm yourself. You can take all the time you need. Now I want you to," the doctor said as he reached into his bag, "take this powder." He handed Miriam a packet. "Stir it in a full glass of water. It will calm you. Afterward, do whatever you must. It will be quite a while until Tobias can have any visitors, even you, my dear. So, calm yourself or you will find yourself in the bed next to him." The doctor looked at his pocket watch and said, "I warned him about his temperament. I warned him this could happen if he didn't calm himself. So, mind my words, Miriam."

Miriam bid the doctor a good day and sat down at her kitchen table. She turned the packet over and over in her hands as thoughts raced through her mind. In a few minutes, she stood. She straightened up to her full height and tossed the packet onto the table. She turned off the burners on her stove and put the food she had prepared away. She removed her apron, laying it on the back of her chair, and smoothed the front of her dress. She went upstairs and retrieved the letter she had written to Charlotte and went downstairs to the kitchen. She checked to see if she had put everything away. Then, she turned off every light in the house as she walked to the front door. She stopped for a few moments at her door to finalize her thoughts before she squared her shoulders, and wrapped her shawl around her. She put her hat on her head, tilting it to the right side, and walked from her house, locking the door behind her. She headed straight for her husband's office. As she entered the receptionist rose to greet her, but she waved her off and walked to Jedidiah Rue's office. She walked in uninvited and shut the door behind her.

Jedidiah looked up at the sound of the door closing and was very surprised to see her in his office. Miriam had never been so bold before to walk in and sit down. After she removed her hat, she righted herself in her chair. She asked him to represent her legally in all present and future matters. Before she divulged anything, she wanted him to be bound by attorney-client privilege. She noticed the surprise on Jedidiah's face and smiled. Jedidiah, skeptical and confused, agreed to her terms. He asked why she thought she needed an attorney and why she didn't have her husband handle her affairs as he always did. Miriam told Jedidiah every detail surrounding Charlotte's disappearance. She told him about her marriage to Tey and what had happened that morning. She ended with, "And I told him Barnaby Harrington and I were intimate. Tobias assumed he was my lover. I believe that's what caused his fit."

"You told him what, Miriam?" Jedidiah was shocked yet thought it quite comical as he tried to hide the half smile on his face behind his hand.

"That we were intimate. I suppose it wasn't the best choice of words." She looked at Jedidiah, who sat spellbound by what she was saying. "Now, Jedidiah, don't look at me like that. I didn't mean to imply that we are, you know, but you see, I was planning to leave with Barnaby. That sounds improper too. What I mean is I was going to meet Barnaby this Friday in Trenton and he was taking me to Charlotte. Do you understand now?"

Jedidiah smiled and nodded. Miriam sighed with relief.

"Now please, I want you to go with me to Woolworths where I will introduce you to Barnaby Harrington. He will take you to Charlotte this Friday instead of me. She needs to know of her father's illness, but Jedidiah, nothing, and I mean nothing, is to upset her. She is due to have my grandchild any moment and I must find a way to go to her. But with this, I don't know when. I want so to bring her home; to bring them home to me. Help me Jedidiah, please help me." Miriam gave in to the emotions she had been holding inside, and she put her face in her hands and sobbed.

Jedidiah waited and let Miriam cry uninterrupted, watching and listening to her closely. When she looked up at him, he asked, "When would you like me to meet this Barnaby Harrington, Miriam?"

She wiped the last tears from her eyes. She smoothed her dress and adjusted her shawl. She sighed a heavy sigh of relief. "Now, Jedidiah," she said, "Right now." She stood and looked at him. "Right now, Jedidiah, please."

Jedidiah got to his feet immediately, put on his jacket, and together they walked from his office. At the front desk, Jedidiah dictated a short note to the receptionist. He instructed her to send the note by courier to Tobias' clients informing them of the situation. The courier was to wait for replies in the event some clients wished to reschedule their appointments with him. He made sure his receptionist understood his instructions. Then he and Miriam left the office to go meet with Barnaby Harrington.

Barnaby was stocking shelves as he always did, and he smiled as Miriam approached. "Well, a very good day to you, Miriam, and what have you for me today?"

"Barnaby, this is Jedidiah Rue," Miriam said, turning toward Jedidiah. "He is my husband's law partner."

Barnaby pulled back as he knitted his brow, wondering what was going on.

"No, Barnaby. He is a friend. Tobias was taken with a fit of apoplexy this morning, and I need you to take Jedidiah to Charlotte. He will meet you in Trenton this Friday instead of me." Her voice trembled as she spoke. "He will deliver my message and tell her of her father and, I hope, bring her home. Will you do that for me, please? Will you take Jedidiah to Charlotte?"

Barnaby eyed Jedidiah before he offered him his hand. "If he's all right with you, Miriam, I suppose he's all right with me. I'll be happy to take him."

Miriam smiled through closed lips and nodded. "Good. You are a good man, Barnaby Harrington. You have been a good friend to us all. Now, I leave you. I must go to the hospital and see to Tobias. Please, Jedidiah, see me before you go, and I'll explain what Barnaby and I arranged for this Friday."

"Certainly, Miriam. Certainly," Jedidiah said and kissed her cheek. She turned and reached out, pulling Barnaby to her. She hugged him and kissed his cheek. "We will meet again, if not in this world then in heaven, because you surely have made your place there." Miriam turned and hurried from the store, turning onto the street that led to the hospital.

* * * * *

Charlotte squirmed in her chair. She arched her back and moved side to side. She tried several positions. But nothing she did relieved the nagging discomfort she felt on both sides of her spine. She tried putting another pillow behind her and when that didn't help, she removed all of them.

"What is wrong, my Charlotte? Can I help you?" Giselle asked.

"Oh. I don't know. I just wish this were over. I'm so uncomfortable, Giselle. And today these nagging pains have started. I hope this baby comes soon because his mother is miserable."

The two women were laughing as Tey walked into the back room. "So, you agree; it is a he and not a she. I heard you say "his' mother," Tey said, joking as he kissed his wife.

"I agree to no such thing. A slip of the tongue, that's all."

Tey laughed and turned to Giselle. "Has she been impossible today? I don't know where her energy is coming from," he said, turning to his wife. "Giselle, last night I couldn't stop her from cleaning the cupboards. Then she ironed everything in sight. She told me she had to get it finished before the baby came. Didn't you, Charlotte?"

Charlotte chuckled and took hold of his arm for help to lift herself from of her chair. She grimaced in pain for several seconds as she straightened up.

"Are you all right?" Tey asked.

"Yes, yes, a bit stiff from sitting so long. Let's go home, Tey. I think I'd like to lie down for a few minutes before supper. My back is bothering me today."

They kissed Giselle and left the shop, taking their normal route home. They strolled along the street, window shopping, and laughing and dreaming about their future as they went. Several times Charlotte stopped to let a momentary painful cramp pass and when it subsided, they continued on their way. They walked past the hospital and turned onto their street when Charlotte cried out in pain. She looked at Tey's troubled face and tried to smile. "I'm sure I'm fine. Don't look so worried. I probably did too much today is all. Come on, take my arm and let's go home." She held Tey's arm as she took two more steps. Then another cramp squeezed her abdomen, forcing fluid to run down her legs.

Charlotte looked at Tey. "We should go to the hospital. I think this baby wants to be born today."

They turned around and headed to the hospital when Charlotte grabbed Tey's arm. Tey, frantic with worry as he watched Charlotte in so much pain, picked her up. He carried her the last half block to the hospital and into the lobby. He sat her in the nearest chair while he told the receptionist what had happened and asked her to get their doctor. In a few minutes, a nurse with a rolling chair came to get Charlotte. She kissed Tey goodbye and was taken to the delivery room. A courier went to fetch the doctor and Tey went to the waiting room on the second floor. The nurse told him the doctor would see him there after he examined Charlotte.

Tey waited. He paced. He sat wringing his hands. He paced, retracing his steps once more. Another man came into the waiting room and sat down to read his newspaper. After a while, the man asked, "First one?"

"Me?" Tey asked back. "Are you talking to me?"

"I don't see anyone else in the room, do you?" The man laughed. Tey looked around and blushed.

"Yes," Tey said. "It is our first one."

"Son settle down. It could take hours."

"Hours! What do you mean, hours?" Tey asked with alarm.

"First babies come when first babies choose to and not one second before. There's no rushing them. The Doc's a good man. He helped my wife through five so far. This will be our sixth one. No problems yet. Don't foresee any either. So, sit down. Your wife is in good hands."

Tey smiled. He shoved his hands in his pockets and walked to the window, trying to focus on the street below.

Dr. Mosby came into the room sometime later and went to greet the man reading the paper. "Another girl, Simon," he said. "A fine one; eight pounds with a good pair of lungs. Your wife is doing fine. She can go home on Saturday. You can see her now if you wish."

The man thanked him. They shook hands and the man left. Dr. Mosby turned to Tey.

"Tey . . ." he said, extending his hand.

"Is Charlotte all right, Doctor," Tey asked.

"She's comfortable right now. We have a while, though. The head hasn't presented yet. I'll have someone keep you informed. Why don't you go get a bite to eat? Ask a friend to come sit with you."

Tey nodded and said, "Yes, I need to tell my employer and Charlotte's what is happening. I will be back as quickly as I can. All I ask is keep my Charlotte safe. Please."

"She will be fine. Don't rush. You have plenty of time."

Tey shook the doctor's hand again and ran from the waiting room and returned to Giselle's shop. He pounded on the door. When there was no answer he went to the rear of the building and climbed the stairs to her flat. When Giselle opened the door, he told her what had happened. He said he was going to the plant to tell his boss that Charlotte was in the hospital. He didn't wait for her to answer; he turned and ran down the stairs. At the bottom of the stairs, he stopped. He pondered a moment, turned around, ran up the stairs and kissed Giselle. "We are having a baby. Tonight," he said and turned, running down the steps to the street.

When he arrived at the plant, he went in search of Jack Cleary, but he was told Jack had already gone home for the evening. So Tey headed to his house. Jack answered the door and listened as Tey told him what was happening. Tey asked for a little time off to be with Charlotte, and Jack told him to take off until his Monday shift. Tey thanked him and hurried to the hospital. Giselle was waiting for him when he arrived. Tey checked with the nurse at the desk to see how Charlotte was doing. The nurse told him she would tell the doctor that he had returned. Dr. Mosby came into the waiting room a few minutes later. He informed Tey that there was no change in Charlotte's condition, so he should relax and wait.

Tey and Giselle waited for hours. And more hours. A new day dawned and passed. The third day dawned. Dr. Mosby continually kept them informed. But as they waited, and the third day turned to early evening Tey was frantic. A little past 7:15 the doctor came in once more. This time, he had a grave look on his face. "I must take the child from her," Dr. Mosby said.

Tey, on the verge of hysteria, didn't understand what the doctor meant. He looked at Giselle before turning to face the doctor. "What does that mean?"

"I must operate. I've been unable to move the head of the infant into the proper position. Charlotte's contractions have slowed almost to a stop. She is exhausted. If I don't act right now it may be too late. I must take the child now."

Tey looked at the doctor, questioning, not understanding, disbelieving what the doctor said. Giselle grabbed Tey by the arms and spun him around to face her. "Tell him to do it, Tey, or Charlotte will die. Tell him right now!"

A look of shock, pure horror, covered his face as he turned to the doctor. "Is she right? Will my Charlotte die?"

"She could if I don't take the child now!"

"Promise me; promise me you will do everything in your power to make sure my Charlotte comes back to me. Dr.

Mosby, there is only one Charlotte Aihàmson. Promise me, Doc."

"I will do everything in my power to save them both. Now I must go. Precious minutes are ticking by."

* * * * *

Barnaby Harrington and Jedidiah Rue stepped onto the train platform. Barnaby looked at every face, searching for Tey and Charlotte. "I have no idea where they are," Barnaby said. "They usually come running toward me as soon as I get off the train. The first thing Charlotte asks for is her mother's letter. She is always so excited. Where can they be?"

"Something's happened. When is Charlotte due to have the baby?"

"Very soon. I'm not sure but do you think . . ."

"Yes, I do. Barnaby, do you know what doctor? Midwife? Hospital?"

"No. But the hospital isn't far from here."

"Good. Let's start there."

The two left the station and headed for the hospital. When they got to the hospital, Jedidiah went to the reception desk. He asked if they had a Charlotte Wickham or Aihàmson registered. The receptionist said yes and directed them to the second floor waiting room. She told them that the expectant father and his friend were waiting there. They approached the doorway and stopped when they heard voices. They waited outside and overheard the conversation between Dr. Mosby and Tey. As soon as the doctor left Barnaby moved to go inside but Jedidiah grabbed his arm holding him back.

"My friend needs me. Let me go," Barnaby said.

"Yes, he does, and you must go to him. But he doesn't need to know anything about Tobias Wickham at this moment, Barnaby. Say nothing to him. I think it best I leave you now and find a place to stay in town. When I know Charlotte is well, I will make my presence known. Thank you for your help, Barnaby."

"I understand. But wouldn't it be good to ease his mind by letting him know her father is unable to come after them?"

"Perhaps. But at this moment Tobias Wickham is the farthest thing from his mind, and right now he doesn't need a reminder. So, take care of your friend. But please say nothing."

* * * * *

Tey stood at the window watching the sunrise. Orange yellow spikes sliced through the dark early morning sky. The amber haze hugging the earth melted away as the sun inched its way above the horizon. It was Saturday, April 27, 1895. He and Giselle spent another night dozing off and on, waiting for news of Charlotte. He stretched and looked at Giselle as she opened her eyes. They had heard nothing all night. It was 5:55am. The shift was changing, and a different nurse was coming on duty as Tey walked to the waiting room door. He waved to her, and she waved back.

"Good morning and congratulations. You must be so happy. Have you seen him yet?"

"Happy? Who?" Tey asked. "Have I seen who?"

"Your handsome son. I just came from the nursery. I'll take you if you like," she said, giggling.

Tey's eyes lit up, and his mouth dropped open. He could hardly contain himself. "Wait, please," Tey said, laughing. "Let me get Giselle." He turned and ran into the room. "Giselle, he's a boy; I mean a male baby boy. I mean . . . come, let's go see him."

Tey grabbed Giselle's hands and as he looked into her eyes a fear, an overpowering fear, took him by the throat. He stood motionless, staring at her. "Tey! What's wrong?" Giselle asked.

Suddenly Tey turned and raced out to the nurse, took her by her arms and spun her toward him. "My wife! I've heard nothing about Charlotte. My wife; how is my wife?"

Doctor Mosby was turning the corner when he saw Tey with the nurse. "What's going on here?" he asked.

"She said he was born. But Charlotte . . . Doctor, what of my Charlotte? Tell me of Charlotte?"

Doctor Mosby put his hands on Tey's shoulders. "Calm yourself. Everything is fine. She is fine. Follow me and you can see for yourself. She will have much discomfort for a while, but both Charlotte and your child are doing very well."

The doctor led Tey to a room at the end of the hall. The room was sterile with bare white walls and bleached wood floors. The smell of the cleaning solution used to clean the room was astringent and offended Tey's nose. There were four beds, but Charlotte was alone in the room. Her bed was nearest the window, and Tey walked to her and stood beside her bed. She was asleep. She moved and grimaced when she moved, moaning quietly. Tey smiled, leaned over her, and kissed her lips. She opened her eyes. She smiled at him. He kissed her again. "Did you see him?" she whispered.

"Not yet, my love. I wanted to see you first."

"Go see him. Our son. Tey, he's beautiful. Go see him," Charlotte said and closed her eyes as she slipped off to sleep.

"I will. Right now. Sleep well, my love." Tey kissed her forehead. He stood straight and smiled as a tear ran down his cheek. He wiped it away. He turned to face Giselle and the nurse. "Please, will you show us my son?"

* * * * *

Early on Saturday morning, shortly after sunrise, Jedidiah Rue walked to the hospital. He checked on Charlotte's condition and learned of the birth. He sent a telegram to Miriam Wickham that read: *Caesar delivered mail this am. Stop. Returning 7 12 tonight. Stop. Will come by with details. Stop.*

Miriam heard the knock on her door and wondered who would be at her house before nine o'clock on a Saturday morning. She was shocked to find the Western Union delivery boy standing at her door. She accepted the telegram and told the boy to wait. She took two pennies from her change purse. Thinking better of it, she put the pennies in her apron pocket and found a nickel and gave it to the boy. The boy smiled, tipped his cap and rode off on his bike.

Miriam hurried into the kitchen and ripped open the envelope. She read and reread the cryptic note from Jedidiah. *Caesar delivered mail.* It's a boy! She laughed and she cried, and she twirled around. She calmed herself and sat down at the table, smiling as thoughts muddled in her brain. She spoke to the table in her empty kitchen. "Well, Grandmother. You are, you know, a grandmother. I am a grandmother." She looked down at the telegram again and reread the line: *Caesar delivered . . .* "My darling daughter.

What pain she must have endured. Is all well? He doesn't say. Jedidiah will tell me tonight. I am so happy. I want to tell the world. I want to tell . . ." She stopped short. "Who? Who can I tell? No one knows they wed. They will think the babe is . . . They will think Charlotte, my Charlotte, a strumpet. I cannot allow that. I must not allow it. I will get Jedidiah to—yes, Jedidiah—he will know what to do. Oh, I want her here. I want them home, here with me. They belong here. She needs to be here to recover from her ordeal. She must come home. She must bring my grandchild home. That's impossible, but I so want to see her and my new grandson."

For many minutes Miriam paced around the kitchen verbalizing whatever came to mind. One after the other so many disjointed thoughts tumbled out of her mouth until her brain finally rebelled and she stopped short. And standing in the center of her kitchen she loudly reprimanded herself. "Miriam! You are acting ridiculous. Get yourself together. Get dressed and do what you must do to keep up appearances." She pondered her statements for a moment nodding in agreement, then went upstairs, bathed, dressed and returned to the front door where she put on her bonnet and wrap. She looked through her purse to make sure there was enough money in it. She locked the door after her and walked down the street toward the hospital.

A middle-aged nurse was sitting by Tobias' side, reading to him, as Miriam walked into the room. They discussed Tobias' condition. Miriam told the nurse she could take a break if she wanted to, now that she was there. The nurse smiled and accepted Miriam's offer and left the room. Miriam followed her to the door and closed it. She walked to Tobias' side and stood, staring into his dark, cruel eyes.

"Well, Tobias, I have had exciting news this morning."

Tobias glared at her. Miriam could feel his hatred for her oozing from every one of his pores.

"We are grandparents. A boy, Tobias. Charlotte delivered a boy this very morning." Miriam said, watching his eyes as a fire raged that was so menacing it seemed to burn through her skin. But she didn't flinch. She didn't recoil. Miriam stood her ground. She stared at him and said, "I see it in your eyes. I see the hate. But if you should stand straight up at this very moment, I do not care because I no longer fear you. You have no power over me any longer. You will do as I wish, or you will be penniless. On Thursday, I had Jedidiah open your office for me. He furnished me with a set of keys so I would be able to come and go as I chose. So, I've spent many hours in your office going through my affairs. And I found the papers. I found my father's will, Tobias. I finished reading every last word last night and now I know the truth. The wording is quite specific. My father found a way to circumvent the societal dictates against women. He devised a way for me to own my own property and manage my own affairs. That's why you've hidden his will from me all these years. Because it is I, Tobias, who controls my father's estate, and as of this moment, it no longer is you. Monday morning, I will set the records straight."

From the depths somewhere in the farthest corner of hell came a sound from his mouth. The sound was so unearthly it reeled Miriam back.

"OOO BER BI BEB BOB BEEE!!"

Miriam stared at him, stunned. In a few moments her surprise turned to laughter, and she laughed until tears ran from her eyes. "Over my dead body? Is that what you tried to say, Tobias? Well, it very well may be."

The nurse, after hearing his cry, burst into the room. Miriam turned to her, still laughing and said, "He is yours. I've had my say. I will return later to check on him, as society dictates every good wife should. Isn't that correct, Tobias?" She was laughing as she walked to his side. She leaned down and kissed his forehead. "Because I am a good wife. Isn't that so, Tobias?" Miriam smiled down at him. She turned and put on her hat and wrap. She left Tobias' room and headed for the taxi stand outside the hospital.

There were several Hansom cabs waiting for fares. As Miriam approached a cabbie came forward and asked her if he could be of service.

"Why, yes you can," she said. "Do you know the village that's out the Old Blackwoodtown Road?"

"Yes, ma'am, I do."

"Please, I wish to be taken there," Miriam said, waiting for the cabbie to help her get into the cab.

The cabbie, shocked by her request, said. "That's a long way, ma'am. It will take close to an hour to get there and another to return. Are you sure that's where you want to go? That's an Injun village, ma'am. No one goes there that don't belong."

"That's exactly where I want to go. If you won't take me, I'm sure another cabbie will."

"No, ma'am. I mean, yes, ma'am. I'll be happy to take you. Just making sure . . . Here, please. Let me help you up."

He drove his horse and rig to the Old Blackwoodtown Road, and they traveled for close to an hour. As they rode into town Miriam saw older women and children all along the streets. The stores that lined the streets had stands in front so passers-by could examine their wares. *Same as in*

Camden, Miriam thought. Grandmothers played with their grandchildren in the town square. Others were sitting on benches under parasols watching the children play. *It's strange,* Miriam thought, *no young people or men around town.* She wondered where they could be.

The cabbie stopped at the town square and turned around to Miriam. "Where to now, ma'am?" he asked.

"I'm not sure. Please help me down and I'll ask someone." The cabbie helped Miriam from the cab and stayed with the horse. Miriam walked to where a few women were sitting together on a bench in the town square.

"Excuse me please," she said. "I am looking for Aihàm. Can you point me to his house?"

A woman close to Miriam's age stood and faced her. She looked straight in Miriam eyes. Skeptical yet inquisitive she asked, "Who asks for Aihàm?"

"My name is Miriam Wickham." The woman stepped backward as if threatened. Miriam saw a momentary flash of fear in her eyes. "Please. No. Aihàm knows me. I need to speak with him is all. Please, I need to tell him the wonderful news I learned this morning. That is all. I mean him no harm."

The suspicion on the woman's face changed to an embarrassed remorsefulness as she said, "Yes, of course not. And I am too careful at times." Violet smiled at Miriam. "I am happy to meet the one who carries our words to our son. For that I am grateful. I am called Violet. I am Aihàm's wife. He and the others are in the fields. We watch the children so they can pick asparagus. Will you let me carry your words to my husband; this news you have for him?"

Miriam smiled and tears came to her eyes. She put her hands to her lips and laughed. "Yes," she said. "Yes, you can.

We have a grandson. He was born this morning. I received word of it a little before nine this morning. I don't know more than that. Except all must be well with mother and child and I assume father too. I'm sure he would have told me otherwise. It was by Caesarian, though. Tonight. I will know more after Jedidiah Rue returns on the 7:12 tonight."

Violet stared at her. She didn't move. Her mouth was open. Her eyes went blank as she closed her lids over them. She sat down and slowly rocked back and forth, and Miriam heard her chant in a sweet, melodic tone. Violet bowed her head. She rose, walked to Miriam, and took her in her arms. "It is happy news," she whispered in Miriam's ear and released her hold on Miriam. She took a few steps backward and said, "And I thank you for the happy news. Aihàm will be most pleased."

Miriam nodded. She turned and started walking toward the cab. She stopped and turned to face Violet. "It was a pleasure to meet you. Thank you for taking care of my daughter. She speaks very highly of you."

"I too, speak highly of her."

"Thank you," Miriam said. She turned and again took steps toward the cab.

"Your husband? What should I think?" Violet asked.

Miriam laughed as she turned toward Violet. "Don't worry about him; well, at least not right now. He took a fit of apoplexy and was, when I left him, unable to speak or move a muscle. He is in the hospital in town and will be for quite a while."

Violet nodded and asked, "If I may be so bold, may Aihàm and I hear tonight also of our children?"

"Tonight? From Jedidiah? Why . . ." Miriam thought. She stared at Violet, tilted her head and nodded. "Why, you are most welcome in my home," she said, smiling. "Please. Yes. I would like that very much. Our children would like that. After all, we have a grandchild, a grandson in common now. Yes. I would like that very much. We will meet again tonight. Bye for now." Miriam smiled and waved goodbye. The cabbie helped her into the cab and drove Miriam to her house.

* * * * *

Jedidiah Rue walked to the nurse's desk on the second floor. He asked the woman behind it if it would be possible to speak with Mrs. Charlotte Aihàmson. He told her his name and waited while she went to Charlotte's room to announce him. Jedidiah watched Tey approach as he followed the nurse. Wary of Jedidiah's intentions Tey asked, "What do you want of her?"

"And you are Tey, I presume?" Jedidiah asked.

"Yes. What do you want? Why are you here? Did Tobias Wickham send you?"

"No. He did not."

"You are his law partner, are you not?" Tey asked.

"Yes. That is true. But he has no knowledge of this visit. Charlotte's mother sent me. Please. I mean you no harm. I am here on Mrs. Wickham's behalf to inform Charlotte of her father's health."

"She doesn't give a damn fig for his health. He has caused . . ." Tey stopped. He stared into Jedidiah's face for a second or two. He lowered his head and stood motionless for a few moments as he got his anger under control. He took a large breath and exhaled it through his teeth. He looked into Jedidiah's eyes. "Please excuse me. Charlotte has taught me better than that. But it has been a very long couple of days. I am sorry for my rudeness. Of course, Charlotte wants to know about her father. She loves him. Please, follow me."

Tey led Jedidiah down the hall into Charlotte's room. When they entered, Charlotte looked at Jedidiah. "Mister Rue," she said in a soft, quiet voice, then paused to catch her breath. "How are you, sir? I didn't think you would be the one who found us." She was pale, so very pale, Jedidiah thought, and she seemed very weak.

"I'm not, Charlotte. Your mother sent me. How are you feeling, my dear?" he asked as he moved a chair to Charlotte's side. Tey walked to the other side of the bed and sat down, taking Charlotte's hand in his.

"Oh, I'm doing well, aren't I, Tey?" she said, and she turned her head to smile at Tey. She moved with slow, deliberate motions as if to displace nagging pains and grimaced. "My mother is well?"

"Yes. She is fine and I am willing to wager very happy to hear of your son."

Charlotte smiled and grimaced again in pain. "How would she know? Did you tell her?"

"Yes. I wired her this morning. I will tell her more when I return tonight. But first—the reason I am here, Charlotte, is that she, ah, she, asked me to tell you of your father." Jedidiah paused and looked at Charlotte's face.

"What of him? Is he dead?"

Jedidiah lowered his head so Charlotte wouldn't see him smile. "No. He is not dead. At least when I left town, he still was alive. But he was taken with a fit of apoplexy on Wednesday. He is able to breathe and perform all his functions on his own. But he is unable . . . when I last saw him, he was unable to speak or move any part of his body. The doctors cannot say whether he will recover at this time."

Doctor Mosby walked into the room, and Jedidiah and Tey stood to greet him.

"Doctor Mosby, this is Jedidiah Rue, my mother's . . ." Charlotte was barely able to catch her breath, and she hesitated. "Attorney . . . yes, her attorney. My mother asked him . . . to see . . . how I am doing." Charlotte struggled for air, coughed, and grimaced. She wrapped her arms around herself, trying to ward off the pain. When the pain subsided, she squirmed to get comfortable. She continued, "Please tell him . . . anything he . . . wants to . . . to know. He will . . . relay the . . . inform . . . ma . . . tion . . . to my moth . . . h— her . . . this . . . eve—ning."

Doctor Mosby studied Charlotte as he extended his hand to Jedidiah and shook it. Then he shook Tey's hand still without taking his eyes from her. He cleared his throat, and in a concerned voice said, "First things first, my dear." He turned to Tey and Jedidiah and said, "Gentlemen, as nice as it is to meet you, you must excuse us, I need to check my patient. You must go now." The doctor ushered them through the door and shut it. He walked to Charlotte's bedside and lifted the covers from her body. Her clothes and bed linen around her were bathed in blood. He hurried to the door, opened it and yelled for a nurse. A nurse rushed into the room and the doctor ordered her to take Charlotte to surgery immediately.

* * * * *

Tey and Jedidiah walked along the hall to the waiting room. "I'm willing to wager that you've spent a lot of time in that room," Jedidiah said, trying to start a dialogue with the young man.

Tey stopped and turned toward Jedidiah. "Mister Rue, I don't mean to . . ."

"Jedidiah, please," Jedidiah interrupted. "Tey, Miriam hopes we can be friends. She hopes that once you get to know me you will put your trust in me the same way she has. From what Charlotte said, she may feel the same way. I am on your side. Let me tell you my background and you will understand why Miriam came to me. So, let's go in and sit down."

They found two chairs by the window and sat down. "I'm sure you don't know that I too, am Lenape," Jedidiah said. Tey turned his head to look at him. "My mother was Lenape," Jedidiah said. "And my father was white; both have since died. My wife is full Cherokee. We have a daughter who is half white. Before we married, human traffickers raped and beat my wife and left her for dead. I know your anguish better than you realize." Jedidiah's eyes never left Tey's. He watched as Tey's veil of distrust lifted.

Tey listened with his mouth wide open. He dropped his head and said, "I am so sorry. I didn't know. That's why Mrs. Wickham came to you. She knew you would understand our plight. I need to thank you, to thank you for helping her. Mrs. Wickham is a wonderful person. She has tried to walk that hard line with me, but I always saw through it. She has always been fair, honest and upfront with me. She told me what she wanted and accepted nothing less. I trust her. I trust her judgment and until I find that I am wrong, I will trust yours too. And Charlotte, I am sure, will feel as I do."

"Good. Now, Tey, I have a train to catch because there is an anxious grandmother on the other end who wants to know about her daughter's health so I must go speak with the doc. . . ."

Doctor Mosby walked into the room. He was wearing a surgical apron. The look on his face was troubling. Tey jumped up and walked to him asking, "What? What is wrong with her? Is she not healing? What's happening?"

"She is hemorrhaging and losing far too much blood. I'm afraid I must operate again. I must see why she is bleeding internally. It may take removing everything to stop it."

"Everything? What does that mean? What everything?"

"Everything inside. All her female parts. I must stop the bleeding, or she will die. Do you understand? I must operate on her immediately."

Tey's face drained of color as he listened with his mouth gaping open. He grabbed the doctor by the apron and shouted, "Do not let her die! Do you hear me? Do not let her die!"

Doctor Mosby pried his hands loose. He said, "I don't intend to, but I have no idea what God's plan is right now, so pray." Doctor Mosby turned and left the room.

Tey, horrified by the doctor's words, watched him leave. A moment later he ran from of the room and down the hall to Charlotte's room. He stared at the empty blood-soaked bed where Charlotte had lain moments before. "He didn't let me tell her . . ." he screamed into the empty room. He ran to the nurses' station and demanded, "Where have they taken her? Tell me or I will tear this hospital apart."

"Down the hall to the right; the last door on the left is surgery."

Tey turned and ran down the hall until he saw Charlotte. She was on a bed against the wall, waiting to go into surgery and she looked at him and smiled. "Don't worry my . . . Tey eholàk. . . . God has a—a fight . . . on his hands if . . . he wants to take . . . me from you . . . and our son."

Tey leaned down and kissed her lips. "I love you with all my heart, my Chulëntët."

The nurse said, "Sorry, but it's time to go in." As the nurse pushed the bed towards the surgery doors, Charlotte strained to speak. "I love you, Tey," she said and disappeared into surgery.

* * * * *

Jedidiah Rue walked to the nurses' station. He questioned the nurses about the procedure the Doctor was performing on Charlotte. One nurse in particular answered his questions as if she was reciting from a textbook. She knew exactly what the Doctor would look for and what he had to do to stop the internal bleeding.

Jedidiah looked at his watch. It was 11:19 in the morning. His train didn't leave until after 4:30 in the afternoon. He had plenty of time to wait so he could know the outcome of the operation before he had to alarm Miriam Wickham.

He looked down the hall and watched Tey Aihàmson as he approached. Tey's head hung low, his hands in his pockets. He looked despondent, so wretched, so filled with despair. Jedidiah thought as he watched Tey walk toward him, *this poor lad has been to hell and back these past few days.*

Tey turned to go into the waiting room, and Jedidiah touched his arm. "Tey, when was the last time you had a good meal?"

Tey tried to smile and shook his head. "Thanks, but I don't think I could eat right now."

"That's unacceptable. If you don't eat you can't be strong, and right now what Charlotte needs most is for you to be strong for her. So, you and I are going to that little café across the street and you are going to force yourself to eat. You don't want to faint in front of Charlotte, do you? Of course not." Jedidiah took Tey by the arm, turned to the nurse on duty and said, "We are going to get food in this young man's stomach. If you need us, we will be right across the street in the café." He ushered Tey to the stairwell, down the stairs and across the street.

Tey wasn't interested in the menu at all, so Jedidiah ordered the special of the day for the two of them. Then he tried to make small talk until their meals came. A plate of two juicy chops with savory sage dressing, potatoes browned crisp, caramelized onions, candied carrots, and apple chunks laced with cinnamon were placed on the table in front of Tey. Tey moved the food around the plate with his fork as the aromas played on his senses. He took a bite, and he took another. He was famished. He realized that he hadn't eaten since, he said between mouthfuls, ". . . since I don't remember, Jedidiah. Giselle brought a couple of sandwiches on Thursday, yes, Thursday, and I guess she brought a few buns. Was that Friday? I don't remember." He ate hungrily, cleaning his plate before he placed his fork across it.

"Why do I feel so guilty right now? Charlotte could be..."

"Fine. Do you hear me? Charlotte is going to be fine. Dr. Mosby will stop the bleeding and she will be fine." He studied Tey for a long time. "Have you slept at all, Tey?"

"Yes. Some. I dozed off in a chair a couple of times. I didn't want to fall into a deep sleep in case they needed me. So, I dozed."

"Well," Jedidiah said, looking at his pocket watch, "in about an hour you will see Charlotte. Then your mind will be at ease. After that, you will go home and get some sleep. Understood?"

Tey nodded. "But not until I'm sure she is all right. I won't go until I'm sure."

"Fair enough. So, let's go and see how everything is going. If what the nurse told me is true, we should hear quite soon."

All afternoon Jedidiah watched the time. He looked at Tey, who was standing at the window. He looked down at his watch again. It was 3:47. *Charlotte was in surgery at 11:15 so she's been in surgery more than four hours now, he thought. If everything's going well the doctor should be here soon. Any minute, in fact. If he isn't, I've got to send Miriam a telegram. That's a telegram I don't want to send.* He shuddered at the thought. *But she must know because I'm not leaving this young man alone until we hear. He needs someone, and he seems to be taking a liking to me. Come on, Doc. Where are you? She's a strong girl. She'll win this battle. I know her. She won't give up. She's . . ."*

"Well, she's a fighter. Of that I am certain," Dr. Mosby said as he entered the room. "She's strong-willed and definitely had no intentions of giving up. That's what kept her alive." Dr. Mosby walked to Tey and put his hand on Tey's shoulder, "I am certain the internal bleeding has stopped. Completely. She is still coming out of the anesthetic. She lost a lot of blood and is very weak, but you may see her for a moment or two. No more. She needs her rest. I am telling the desk no visitors tonight at all, not even you. So, go home and get some rest, Tey." He paused, looking into Tey's eyes. He pursed his lips and said, "I had hoped that I would be able to save or repair . . ." He paused again and shook his head. Then he continued, "But the uterine rupture causing the hemorrhaging made that impossible. She will bear no more children. So be very thankful you have such a beautiful, healthy baby boy." He patted Tey's shoulder and turned, taking a few steps away. "Now, I want to check that she is comfortable and make sure the desk has my new instructions, and I too will go home." The doctor continued to walk to the door. He turned to face Tey and Jedidiah. "Gentlemen, I bid you good afternoon."

"Doctor," Tey said. "Thank you. Thank you so much. I don't know what else to say."

Dr. Mosby smiled and waved. "You don't need to say anything more. Now, don't tire her. See her briefly, then go home. In a few days, you'll wish you had this time to sleep. Remember, you'll be taking a crying baby home soon. Go home and sleep."

Tey and Jedidiah walked down the hall to Charlotte's room. When they entered her room, her eyes were closed. She looked so peaceful. Tey walked to the bed, leaned down and kissed her lips. She opened her eyes. "My Tey eholàk. I was dreaming of you and our baby. I love you, Tey."

"And I love you, my Chulëntët. I'm going home now. You sleep, my love. You must get strong for . . . for këmi-mëntëtëna."

"What did you call him?"

"I said këmimëntëtëna. It means our baby. I don't know what else to call him. He has no name yet. We never picked a boy's name, only a girl's."

"Yes . . . It must be special . . . He is so beautiful," she said and closed her eyes.

"Yes, he is. My mother would call him wëlësu," he said

in a whisper.

Charlotte's eyes fluttered open. "What does that mean?"

"It means he is good-looking, handsome, perfect."

Charlotte smiled and nodded as she blinked and closed her eyes again. "Wel les . . . is that what you call . . ." and she drifted off to sleep.

Tey watched her sleep for several minutes. He kissed her forehead, and he and Jedidiah left the hospital. Jedidiah walked Tey home. He refused to leave until he extracted a promise from Tey. So Tey promised that he would get several hours sleep before he returned to the hospital. They shook hands and Jedidiah hurried to the train station. He arrived in time to board the 4:47 headed for Trenton. He relaxed in his compartment. He knew he would be on time to make his scheduled connection that would get him to Camden by 7:12 that evening.

He laid his head against the headrest and closed his eyes. Visions of Miriam, Charlotte, Tey and the child haunted his thoughts. But, in the back of his mind loomed Tobias Wickham. A shiver ran through his body. He couldn't shake the feeling that Tobias was devious enough to find a way to punish them all. He changed trains, and soon the train pulled into Camden station. He hailed a cab and went to the home of Miriam Wickham.

Miriam opened the door, her face beaming when she saw Jedidiah. "My daughter, Jedidiah, my daughter? Is she well?" Miriam asked as she showed Jedidiah into her front parlor.

"When I left, she was comfortable and resting. It's been quite an ordeal for her, but I am told the worst is past, and she will be fine."

Miriam heard a rap at her kitchen door. She stood and

looked at the street through her front window. "Come, Jedidiah, it is Aihàm, Tey's father. Aihàm will not come to the front door. He will only come into my kitchen. Please come." Miriam hurried through the house to the kitchen door.

"Aihàm! Welcome. Did you not bring . . ." A person moved from behind Aihàm and she saw Violet. "Violet. Please come into my home. Sit. This is Jedidiah Rue," she said, gesturing to them. "Jedidiah, these are Tey's parents. Jedidiah has seen Charlotte, Tey, and the baby. Jedidiah, the baby, is he beautiful?"

Jedidiah had never seen Miriam so emotional before. She was rambling on and on as if she were warding off tears that were about to burst from her eyes at any moment. "Miriam, please calm yourself. Sit down and I will tell you everything I know."

"First, I must brew a pot of tea, and I made a cake for . . ." and Miriam walked to the stove and stopped. "My baby, Jedidiah." Tears ran from her eyes. "My baby is well? Please tell me she is well."

Jedidiah walked to her and put his hands on her arms. "I will not soft-soap it, Miriam. She had a very hard time. They took the babe by Caesarian because the doctor was unable to turn him. Then complications forced Dr. Mosby to operate a second time. She had a uterine rupture that caused hemorrhaging. But when I left, her color was back, she seemed quite comfortable, and the doctor was well pleased with her situation. I am planning to return tomorrow to make sure." He turned to Tey's parents. "And Tey is well. He has had a rough time of it too. He had dinner this afternoon, and he promised me he would get a few hours of much-needed sleep."

"I must go with you, Jedidiah," Miriam said. "I must see my daughter. Make the arrangements. We will go. All of us. We must see our children. Please, I must. We can go after I see Tobias and return before suppertime. Can't we, Jedidiah?"

Jedidiah looked from face to face at the expectant stares. He smiled. "Yes, we can. The four of us then?"

"Of course, the four of us," Miriam said.

"It will be a long, tiring day, Miriam. We will need to leave on the . . ." Jedidiah took the train timetable from his inner pocket and spread it on the table, "The 7:10 from Camden. Aihàm, you will need to meet the train at Burlington at 8:32. If we should miss, we will wait in Trenton until either you or we arrive. Once in Trenton, we will go from there."

* * * * *

On Sunday, Miriam waited for the cab to arrive. Jedidiah had arranged with the cabbie who took him home the night before to fetch Miriam at 6:30am. When she saw the cabbie stop in front of her house she closed and locked her front door and walked down her front steps. The cabbie helped her into his coach, and they drove to the hospital.

Tobias heard her footsteps in the hallway, and he moved his head to watch her as she walked through the door. "I see you have head movement this morning as well, Tobias. I was told of your speech; the nurse said you are making distinguishable sounds. And that look in your eyes; unmistakable; it says you are not pleased I am here, so why not let me hear it from your lips. Tell me, Tobias, tell me what you are thinking."

"Ooo bbiisssssch. I ill eeee ov errr."

"I would be willing to wager you would. You will recover to spite me. Just to get even. Of that I am sure. But name calling is beneath you, Tobias. Although some say a lady in my position must be a bitch or she will be trod upon all the days of her life." Miriam walked to the side of his bed. She bent down over him, looking him in the eyes, "But that, my dear husband, ended last Wednesday. Remember that well." She kissed his forehead, and he pulled away. She flinched at his sudden movement and chuckled as she turned and walked toward the door. "I will check on him later this afternoon," she said to the nurse who was entering his room. She heard him mumble unintelligibly, and she turned to look at him. "It's not a bother at all, my dear husband," she said every word dripping with sarcasm. "That is what a good wife should do." She smiled at the nurse and left the room. She headed for the train station two blocks away.

Jedidiah was waiting in front of the station when she arrived and escorted her onto the train. They settled into their compartment. When the train pulled into the Burlington station, Jedidiah went to the platform to meet Aihàm and Violet. He showed them into Miriam's compartment, and the train left on time heading for Trenton. In Trenton, they switched trains and disembarked at the Princeton station. Miriam looked at Jedidiah surprised. "Princeton?" she asked.

Jedidiah smiled. "Smart boy. He's on scholarship here."

Miriam nodded and said, "Tobias and I spent his last years in school reading law here. I have many memories of this town."

Jedidiah hailed a coach and the four of them got on board. He told the driver the address and they left the station. When they arrived at the hospital Jedidiah made arrangements with the driver to fetch them later. He took them inside and up to the second floor to the waiting room. Tey was standing by the window; he looked toward the door as his parents entered. He ran to his mother as she ran to him. He hugged his father and turned to Miriam Wickham not knowing what to expect. She put her arms around him and kissed his cheek. He hugged her back and whispered "thank you," in her ear. Then he looked at Jedidiah Rue and extended his hand. "You really are on our side. Thank you. Especially for this."

"Enough," Miriam said. "Take me to my daughter."

Tey, a bit shocked by her change in attitude, stared at her. "Mother hen," he said, laughing, "put your claws away. No one threatens your chick. My Chulëntët will be so happy to see you. She is much better today."

"Why are you here and not with her?"

"She needed to . . . well . . . she had to . . ."

"I understand."

"Excuse me, Mr. Aihàmson, your wife is asking for you now," the nurse said popping into the waiting room.

"Thank you. Please, come meet our parents, Charlotte's mother and my mother and father. You know Mr. Rue from yesterday."

"Yes, I do. I am pleased to meet all of you. But this will be too much excitement for her, Mr. Aihàmson. She is doing very well, but she is not ready for a party."

"Nurse, if I may," Jedidiah interrupted, walking toward the nurse and took hold of her hand. He looked into her eyes and said, "Their parents cannot stay long. They have a train to catch in a short while. Please. They will not upset her. If anything, it will help her recovery. They simply want to make sure she is fine and see their grandchild."

"Well, all right, but if she is upset in any way, I must ask you to leave immediately."

"We understand. Thank you," Jedidiah said without taking his eyes from the nurse's. "Now, Tey, why don't you take them to Charlotte's room?"

Tey studied Jedidiah for a moment. Jedidiah nodded and winked at him. Tey smiled. He took his mother by the hand and Miriam by the other. His father followed as he led them to Charlotte's room.

The nurse heard Charlotte's scream and frowned as she moved to go to her room. Jedidiah took hold of her arm. "It was a scream of delight that you heard. She is fine. Please let them be. A few minutes more, please. We cannot stay long. We must board a train for home quite soon."

"If the doctor comes . . . if he finds such commotion . . . you don't understand. He left specific orders. He doesn't want her excited at all."

Jedidiah nodded as he caught a glimpse of Tey walking toward him. All he could see was Tey's smile as he approached the nurses' station. "I understand perfectly. Still, ask him if this visit is bad for Charlotte. Is it Tey?"

"She is so happy. She is so very happy," he said, beaming and turning toward the nurse. "She asked if it would be possible for them to see our son now? Please. They have come a long way. Charlotte asked me to ask. Please."

The nurse pursed her lips, looked at Jedidiah and turned to Tey. She sighed, saying, "Oh, why not? We've broken every rule so far, why not this one too?" She walked down the hall and Tey and Jedidiah followed. As they passed Charlotte's room Tey motioned to his parents and Miriam, and they fell in line behind him. They followed the nurse to the nursery, and she went inside. She reached in the crib and lifted the sleeping infant, cradling him in her arms. She walked to the glass and held him so everyone could see. They watched as the infant squirmed and tried to put his fists in his mouth. The nurse touched his cheek and he turned his head toward the window and stuck out his tongue. He stared wide-eyed as he knitted his brow, trying to focus while his tiny tongue darted between his lips. Then, closing his eyes, he turned his head toward his shoulder and went to sleep. The nurse held him at the window for a few minutes more before she put him in his crib and left the nursery.

"Please, some of you must go to the waiting room. Her husband and one other visitor are all the hospital allows. The doctor is due soon. I will get in trouble."

When they got to Charlotte's room, Aihàm and Violet kissed Charlotte and said their goodbyes. Miriam and Tey remained in the room. Jedidiah, Aihàm, and Violet returned to the waiting room. In a few minutes, Tey arrived. "Mister Rue, ah, Jedidiah, Charlotte would like to see you."

Jedidiah nodded and walked to Charlotte's room. He went to Charlotte's bedside and kissed her on the cheek. "You look a hundred times better today, my dear," he said. He turned to Miriam, who was standing at the window, looking at the street below and motioning to him.

"Jedidiah," Miriam said. "Take a look." She pointed to a man leaning against the side of a building across from the hospital. The man was pretending to read a newspaper. "Pinkerton, you think?" she asked.

Jedidiah watched the man for a few moments. "Could be, but I don't think so. Pinkertons are better trained than that. That one's not trying to hide his presence at all. It's as if he wants us to know."

"That's the same man who's been following me for weeks. I saw him several times when I met Barnaby. Tobias thought he'd shock me with that news, but I'd already spotted him. I knew."

"You knew you were being followed? Miriam, you didn't tell me that. When did Tobias tell you that you were being followed?"

"Wednesday, when I told him about Barnaby and caused his fit."

"Mother, what could you have said about Barnaby to cause his fit?"

"Well, Charlotte, I insinuated that . . . well . . . that Barnaby is my lover."

"Mother! You didn't!"

"Yes. I am afraid I did, Charlotte."

Dr. Mosby and Tey turned the corner into Charlotte's room and heard her laughing at her mother's statement. "Not too much of that or you may open your incision," the doctor said, smiling at Charlotte. "But it is a joy to hear you laugh."

"Dr. Mosby, my mother is here. Mother, this is Dr. Mosby and of course, you remember Jedidiah Rue. You met him yesterday," Charlotte said.

"Missus . . ." the doctor looked at Charlotte for help.

"Oh sorry, Doctor. It's Miriam Wickham, my mother," Charlotte added.

"Mrs. Wickham. It's nice to meet you. Mr. Rue, it's nice to see you again. Now I do not mean to be rude, but I need to discuss Charlotte's condition with Tey and Charlotte."

"Enough said." Jedidiah shook the doctor's hand. He turned toward Miriam and continued, "Besides, there's a fellow outside I need to speak with." Miriam nodded and

Jedidiah walked to Charlotte's bedside. He bent down and kissed her before leaving the room. The doctor looked at Miriam. Charlotte said, "Doctor, my mother isn't about to leave, are you, Mother?"

"No. I am not."

"Well, Tey, do you have any objection to Mrs. Wickham staying?" Dr. Mosby asked.

"None, Doctor."

"Fine, let's proceed."

* * * * *

Jedidiah walked along the street, looking left and right. He headed down the street and around the corner, looking in every doorway and alley to no avail. He crossed the street and walked along the other side. He looked in every shop window. But the man he and Miriam had spotted from the window of Charlotte's room was nowhere in sight. He returned to the hospital and stood half-hidden in the hospital doorway. He watched the street for five or six minutes before turning and entering the building. He went to the second floor and joined Tey's parents in the waiting room.

Jedidiah looked at his watch. In less than fifteen minutes the coach would arrive, and they must leave for the station. With five minutes remaining, he left the waiting room and started down the hall to Charlotte's room. He saw Miriam and Tey in the hallway waiting for Dr. Mosby to finish. They were deep in discussion when he approached. Miriam looked up. "Jedidiah, is it time?" Miriam asked.

"Yes, I'm afraid it is."

"Fine. Tey, I will go in. I don't care if the good doctor is through. I want to kiss my daughter once more, then if you will walk with us to say goodbye. . . ."

"Of course."

Miriam went into Charlotte's room and a few moments later joined Tey and Jedidiah. Tey went into the waiting room and escorted his parents out. Each one thanked the nurse. At the stairwell, one by one, they kissed Tey goodbye. They went down the stairs and waited a few moments until the coach arrived. Then they were on their way to the train station.

The train pulled to a stop at the Burlington Station where Jedidiah and Miriam said goodbye to Aihàm and Violet. Soon they were on their way again. When they arrived at the Camden Station Jedidiah helped Miriam into the cab and got in beside her. "I want to go to the hospital before I go home. He is making great strides. I want to keep abreast of his progress."

As they approached Tobias' room the man they had seen in Princeton exited the room. He attempted to hide his face as he walked past them.

"I must have a word with him, Miriam," Jedidiah said and turned and followed the man. Before Miriam went to Tobias' room, she stopped at the nurses' station for an update on his condition.

"Well, good evening, Tobias. I'm told you were able to ingest solid food this evening. You seem to be making great strides toward recovery. And look at you sitting up. Holding your head up on your own and following my every movement. Well, Tobias, you scare me not! We saw your henchman today. So, tell me, how do you intend to pay for his service after I cut the purse strings? I will have none of it."

"Mrs. Wickham," the night nurse said as she entered the room with Tobias' medications. "I need to get him ready for the night. He's been up quite a while this evening. Time for bed, Mr. Wickham." She laid Tobias down and fixed the blankets around him. She straightened his pillows and smiled, saying, "There you are. Ready for a good night's sleep." She turned to leave the room when Miriam said, "My husband's clothes. And his personal belongings. Will you bring them to me, please? His shirt must be laundered, and I will need his keys to handle his office affairs in the morning." She glared at Tobias as he glared at her. "His wallet is most important also. Thank you very much."

Miriam moved to the end of his bed in his clear view. She didn't take her eyes from his until the nurse brought Tobias' things. The nurse placed them on the end of the bed and Miriam went through each item. She made sure his office and bank vault keys were there. She searched his wallet until she found the combinations to the two massive office safes. Still, she continued searching his things. She looked up at the nurse and asked, "A key, a key with a blue fob attached. I do not see it in anything here. Could it have been misplaced somewhere?"

The nurse walked to Tobias' side. She reached under his bedclothes and lifted out a chain that was around his neck. "Is this what you are looking for?" the nurse asked. From the chain dangled a key with a blue fob. Tobias mumbled profanities and squirmed attempting to grab it.

"Yes," Miriam said as a smile curved her lips, "Yes. That is exactly what I was looking for. Thank you." The nurse handed Miriam the key and she bundled Tobias' belongings together.

Jedidiah walked into the room and Miriam handed the

bundle of clothes to him.

"Did you talk to him, Jedidiah?"

"Yes. He wants payment for his services. That's why he was here tonight. I am meeting with him tomorrow at my office and I will learn more."

Miriam nodded and placed Tobias' personal things in her purse. She walked to Tobias' bedside. "Now I hold the key to your kingdom, Tobias," she whispered into his ear. "So, call off your henchmen or I will play my ace in the hole." She kissed his forehead, turned and left the room.

Chapter 11
Lunchtime, October 22, 1951

"Well, I'm parched, and my stomach is screaming that it's time to eat."

"My stomach's rumbling too," my mother said. "Are you hungry, Dan?"

"Yes," I answered and turned to Auntie. "Do you have any of that sliced ham you always have? You know, the stuff you get from Mr. Englewood with—with your home-made ground mustard on it. And a slice of that holey cheese too, please."

"Humm . . . that does sound delicious on a nice slice of pumpernickel bread," Auntie said with a chuckle in her voice. "The same for you, Diana?"

Mother nodded. "Sounds good."

During lunch Auntie said, "Before it gets too much later, we should think about what we are doing for supper."

"Don't worry about supper. Daniel can take us to the diner. He'll be here by six."

"I didn't know you talked to him today?"

"I didn't. Before he left last night, he wanted me to give him an idea when to pick us up. He's taking the girls to his brother's today, and since this is on his way back, we agreed on six. Why? Is there a problem?"

"No. Not at all, Diana."

"Yes, there is, Mother. Auntie has to finish the story first. We can't go home. I've got to know what happens. Please let her finish it."

"Of course. I want her to finish it too. I still have many questions that need answers."

"Me too! Auntie, Tobias was really, really, really mad, wasn't he?"

"Angry, Danny, he was very angry." Auntie corrected me. "Mad connotes insanity, although there was a definite madness about him. Still, you should use the word angry."

I sighed and looked at Mother. "Don't look at me. I've lived with it most of my life," she said.

"Okay then, angry. Was he very angry? He must have been. Did he recover? Did he find Charlotte and Tey? What did he do to them? The baby, Auntie, does the baby have a name? Does he like the baby? What happens with the key, tell us about that blue key? What did it unlock?"

"Whoa, Danny. One thing at a time. Let's begin with his anger." Auntie took a sip of her tea and looked into my eyes. "Yes, Tobias Wickham was very angry. At first, he was angry that Miriam had his personal things and especially the key with the blue fob. He learned Miriam had his safe that the key with the blue fob opened removed from his office. He also learned she took it to an unknown location and that Jedidiah Rue was also aware of what the safe contained. So, until he had the contents of that safe in his hands, Miriam and Jedidiah must remain untouched.

"That made him even angrier and his anger consumed him. His anger became the driving force in his recovery, and he began to recover quickly. Within six weeks Tobias had regained substantial control of his speech. And he was able to use the entire right side of his body. He was still confined to a rolling chair because of the weakness of his left leg, and he had no control of his left arm. The left side of his face sagged, and his drooling was repulsive. When he spoke, he deliberately and painstakingly elongated his words. He punctuated each one with its ending sound like this—HaapPEEE or tiimmmedDA."

I laughed at the way Auntie was talking, and I tried to mimic her. "Like-ka dissaa, Auntee-a?" I asked.

"Yes, just like that, Danny," Auntie answered, chuckling at me.

"I guess when he got better Miriam took him home, didn't she, Auntie?"

"No, she didn't, Danny. She hired a man to help Tobias, and she moved him into his club, which was close to the hospital. She thought it would be easier for him to be near the hospital for rehabilitation. But she soon learned that her decision was a wrong one. You see, Tobias had incredible powers of persuasion. Soon Thomas Gravely, the male nurse Miriam hired to help him, became Tobias; he emulated him. He idolized him. Once that happened Tobias knew he owned Thomas, body, mind, and soul. And Tobias' manipulated Thomas so completely that in the end Thomas felt the same hate as Tobias.

"And Tobias hated with a hatred so deep that he couldn't breathe when he thought about Charlotte's baby. He referred to the baby as 'that thing' as if the child were not human and he cursed the infant every moment that it lived. Tobias could not accept the fact that his blood mixed with that of a Lenape. In Tobias' mind, Charlotte's child was an abomination of nature and must cease to be. No matter what it entailed, no matter what the consequences, it must not exist even one more moment. He felt completely justified, for so it is written: *'You shall not intermarry with them . . . [for] the anger of the Lord would be kindled against you, and he would destroy you quickly.'*

Deut. 7:3-4

"By October Tobias was able to resume his law practice. He came to his office every day and, of course, Thomas was always by his side. Most of Tobias' clients and his open cases were being handled by Jedidiah Rue. So, left with nothing to do the evil ever-present in Tobias' Cimmerian mind consumed him. And he spent every waking hour devising plots and secret plans to hurt Charlotte.

"One evening when Jedidiah was working late—that wicked evening of Wednesday, November ..."

Wednesday, November 6 – Thursday, November 7, 1895

Jedidiah walked through the reception area toward Tobias' office. He had a brief in his hands that he was preparing for his client. This client, formally one of Tobias', was most insistent. He wanted to take a position that Jedidiah thought was impossible to defend. Jedidiah hoped that Tobias may have a suggestion on how to handle him. As he approached, he heard voices coming from Tobias' office. He stopped to listen to see if he should interrupt now or wait until morning. Realizing that Tobias and Thomas were having a conversation, Jedidiah turned to walk away. He stopped when Thomas asked a question that piqued his interest. He turned back and strained to hear every word as Tobias and Thomas made plans to kidnap and murder Charlotte's baby. And once that was done, they were going to deal with Charlotte and Tey. Horrified, he knew he must conceal himself so that he could learn every detail of their plan. So, he moved into the shadows out of sight from the door and listened. He stayed hidden in the shadows until Thomas took Tobias from the office. When he heard the click of the office door latch, he hurried down the hall to his office. He closed it up and went to speak with Miriam.

"I heard it with my own ears, Miriam," Jedidiah said.

"I know him to be cruel but his own grandchild. Is he a monster?" she shouted as she pounded on her kitchen table. "Jedidiah, we must foil his plot. Are you sure of the dates? And the persons involved?"

"No. I didn't hear the whole of it from the beginning. That's why we should act right now and secret the baby away as soon as possible. We cannot wait to gather more information because I am unsure when Tobias is planning to act."

"You are correct. You must go to Charlotte and Tey tonight and tell them what you heard and of your plan. We must not waste a moment."

Jedidiah went to the train station and caught the 10:12 for Trenton. He shut his eyes, trying to sleep, but Tobias' words kept going round and round in his head. "That thing must cease to be, Thomas, for it has fouled my blood. Once done we will deal with the sow that bore him. As for its sire, he will die as mine did. I want him skinned alive the same way his skinned mine. I want her to bear witness. Remember Thomas, it is God's law. '*Vengeance is Mine, I will repay, says the Lord*'. *(Romans 12:19)* And so it will be, Thomas, so will it be."

It was very late when Jedidiah arrived in Princeton. He went to Tey and Charlotte's flat and knocked on the door. Tey opened the door as he buttoned his pants. He was very surprised to see Jedidiah standing there at this time of night.

"What's wrong? Is Miriam all right, Jedidiah?" Tey asked as he rubbed his eyes, gesturing to Jedidiah to come in.

"We must talk. Right now. Sit. Both of you. You must hear me out."

Jedidiah told them what he had overheard and presented his plan to protect Welles. He told them he would take the child tonight while no one suspected anything. He said he would hide him in the safest place he knew.

"Where will you take my child?" Charlotte asked, alarmed. "No! I cannot allow you to do that. How do I know he will be safe? How can you guarantee me, Jedidiah?"

"He will be in the safest place he could possibly be. He will be right under Tobias' nose and, Charlotte; Tobias won't be able to touch him. Not one hair on his head. Trust me, Charlotte. I will let no harm come to your child. Neither will the person that I will entrust him to. He will be safe."

"Where, Jedidiah? I must know where," Charlotte insisted.

"No, Charlotte. If you know you may tell whoever comes for him. You must not know until we are sure you are safe. Trust me, please. He will be well taken care of. And he will be very safe."

After much consternation Charlotte finally agreed. She took food she had prepared for her son from the icebox, and some clothes items he would need from the dresser. She put them in a sack along with the doctor's instructions and the recipe for his formula. She handed the sack to

Jedidiah before she picked up her sleeping child. She held him close and kissed his forehead. As tears escaped her eyes, she handed her son to Jedidiah, and he left with the child.

After they closed the door behind Jedidiah Charlotte ran to the door screaming, "What have I done? Tey, what have we done?"

"He will be safe. Charlotte, we must believe he will be safe." Tey took her in his arms and held her for the rest of the night.

* * * * *

Jedidiah boarded the train heading toward Trenton. The babe slept in his arms unaware that he was the object of his grandfather's wrath. Jedidiah and the sleeping child changed trains in Trenton and disembarked in Burlington. The sun was beginning to lighten the sky as Jedidiah knocked on Aihàm's front door. Violet was shocked to see Jedidiah, especially holding her grandchild. She took the child from him. The baby stirred and whimpered.

"What are you doing here and with Welles? He's waking. Did they send instructions on feeding him, Jedidiah? Did they send anything for him? Why is he here? What is going on?"

"In due time. First the babe. What you want to know is in this sack Charlotte packed. She said the doctor's instructions were in there as well as other things." Jedidiah turned and slumped into a chair.

Aihàm, who watched in silence, spoke. "Now you must tell us what is going on. Why is the child here?"

"No. Aihàm." Violet said. "You need to run and get

these things from the store. Hurry, Aihàm. The child is waking. Soon he will know his hunger, and we will hear about it."

Aihàm hurried through the door across the square to the mercantile store. He purchased everything on Charlotte's list and hurried home. Violet took the items from Aihàm and made the baby's breakfast as Aihàm settled in his chair with his grandson in his arms. "Now Jedidiah, tell us why our grandchild is here. Tell the whole of it."

Jedidiah told of the conversation he had overheard. He told Aihàm and Violet the exact details as he knew them and the plan he had devised to foil Tobias' plot. Aihàm and Violet listened.

"The next step is to take the child where Tobias wouldn't dare to go. When he learns there is a child there, he will suspect, but he will never know the truth. But for the next part of my plan, I need your help. I need a woman to go with me to Camden. We need to arrive when the women would be outside on their porches watching their children play. When would that be?" he asked Aihàm.

"In the afternoon after the children come home from school. Today is Thursday. The children will have homework to do so, 3:30, four, but, because the sun will go down early, no later than five. After five the women will be inside cooking supper. Why do you need a woman?"

Jedidiah looked from Aihàm to Violet. "Because," he said, "she will be the one to hand the child over. She must knock on the door and ask the person who answers to care for the child because she cannot. She must speak loud enough for the neighbors to hear. We must stage this well. We must draw a lot of attention, and everyone who sees us must believe this is real. I am hoping we are so convincing that someone tells the newspaper of the generous deed. I want it to be in the morning paper. So please find someone, because we must leave so we have plenty of time to get there while everyone is outside. Now, is there a telegraph office in this town?"

"Yes. Why?"

"I must send a wire to make sure the person who will receive the child will be home. Point me in the direction please."

Aihàm showed Jedidiah where to go, and he settled in his chair. Violet fed the baby and then changed him. She placed him in the makeshift bed she devised from one of her large dresser drawers.

In a short while, Jedidiah returned to the house. Violet put a plate of food in front of him. "Eat," she demanded. "You look exhausted. You have been traveling all night with no food in your belly. You must eat. And you will rest until it is time." Violet watched Jedidiah as he ate. "Will I do? Can I be the woman?" she asked.

Jedidiah stared at her as he pictured the chain of events that he had planned in his head. "Yes. You are perfect. You must bring two head coverings and two shawls. Aihàm, the three of us will go together and we will leave you at the railway station while Violet and I deliver the baby. After we deliver the child, we will come to the railroad station to get you. Then you and Violet will return to the house where we left the child so you can help get things settled, and I will go home. It works. The whole plan works."

"You are taking our grandson to Miriam," Violet said, smiling.

Jedidiah looked into Violet's eyes and nodded. "Yes," he said. "It is the safest place on God's earth for the babe. Tobias will suspect; all the days of his natural life he will suspect, but he will never know for sure. He wouldn't dare harm Miriam or the child because Miriam holds the key to Tobias Wickham. She knows facts about him that would destroy him. He will never risk it. The child is as safe as if he were in God's hands."

"And our children, Tey and Charlotte, what of them?"

"I need to rest a few hours. I must gather my thoughts before I can devise a way to keep them safe. They are aware. They know to be cautious. But where to take them? I'm not sure where yet. I don't know. I am hoping that if Tobias finds out that the baby is no longer there, he will leave Tey and Charlotte alone. That is my hope."

Someone knocked on Aihàm's front door, and he went to answer it.

"A telegram for you," Aihàm said, handing the wire to Jedidiah. Jedidiah opened it and smiled. "She says, of course, she will be there." Jedidiah sat there, staring at the telegram for a long time. His body relaxed, and his eyes closed as he tried to laugh. The telegram dropped from his hand down to the floor. His head nodded a few times until his chin drooped and rested on his chest. He fell fast asleep. Aihàm helped Jedidiah from the chair and led him into the parlor where he lay down on the sofa. Aihàm put a pillow under his head. He covered him with the knitted blanket that hung on the back of the sofa and left the room.

He walked into the kitchen and looked down at his sleeping grandson. "The plan is good," he said to Violet. "The plan will work. He will be safe. But I must go with Jedidiah, Kishkikwentis." He turned toward Violet. "After

214

we deliver the child, I must go with Jedidiah to make sure the children are also safe. I will not be able to rest if I do not. You will stay with Miriam until we return."

A few hours later Aihàm went into the parlor. "Jedidiah," he said as he shook him. "Jedidiah wake up. We must leave here soon. You must wake up."

Jedidiah opened his eyes and jumped with a start at first, not realizing where he was. As he remembered the happenings of the night, he smiled at Aihàm. "Yes. Of course," he said, still a bit groggy. "Have I slept long?"

"Several hours. But soon we must leave for town."

"Yes. What is the hour?"

"It is noon. Time for us to eat. Afterward, we will go."

Jedidiah nodded and followed Aihàm into the kitchen. He smiled at Violet and looked at the happy baby playing with his feet. Aihàm showed him the bath facilities. "Would you like to freshen up first?"

"Yes. Yes, I would." Scraping his chin with his hand, he asked, "You wouldn't have an extra razor hanging around, would you?"

Aihàm laughed. "We are not as hairy as white men."

Jedidiah nodded. "My father's side," he said, smiling.

"Yes," Aihàm said with a slight laugh. "I have a straight razor I use for shaving skins. It is very sharp." He handed Jedidiah the razor, and Jedidiah touched the blade.

"Yes. This will do nicely." Jedidiah went into the necessary and closed the door.

In a little while, Jedidiah came back into the kitchen. He looked like he had stepped from his own front door ready to tackle the day. Violet gestured to the table and served dinner. The three of them ate and talked while the baby played beside Violet.

As the clock struck two, Aihàm rose and said, "It is time. We must leave now. I will get the wagon and pull in front of the house." Violet packed the few things she had for the baby. She took two different shawls, two different hats and an extra dress from their hooks by the front door. She handed them to Jedidiah. She picked up the child and she and Jedidiah waited for Aihàm on the front porch. Aihàm pulled his horse and wagon to a stop in front of the house and Violet handed him the baby. Jedidiah helped Violet into the wagon and handed her the rest of the things she had brought. When Jedidiah was on board Aihàm pulled his horse to the left. Then he started him trotting around the square toward the Old Blackwoodtown Road.

They arrived at the train station at ten minutes after three. Aihàm jumped down, and Jedidiah slid across the seat and took hold of the reins. "Trot slowly. Do not rush through town. You have plenty of time," Aihàm instructed Jedidiah.

Jedidiah nodded. "Be back in an hour, I'd say," he said to Aihàm. He pulled the horse to the right and started trotting off toward Miriam Wickham's house. As he approached the Wickham house, he slowed the horse down even more. He wanted to gather the attention of the neighbors who were outside. He came to a stop in front of Miriam Wickham's house. He jumped down and noticed a woman standing on the porch of the house next to the Wickham's.

"Good afternoon, Madam," he said, tipping his hat to her. Before he put his hat back in place, he made sure she got a good look at him. "A fine afternoon, isn't it?" He turned toward Violet, who was hiding her face from view with her hat. "Come, my dear," Jedidiah said in a loud, distinct voice. "This is the home of the woman I told you about. She will surely care for the child." Violet nodded and handed the baby to Jedidiah. Jedidiah helped her down with his free hand. When her feet were firmly on the ground Jedidiah handed the child to Violet. "Do not be afraid. I've known Miriam Wickham a long time. She has the means and the heart to care for him." Jedidiah spoke in a voice loud enough for the neighbors to hear. They climbed the steps onto the front porch, and Jedidiah knocked. In a moment Miriam Wickham came to the door.

She stepped through her doorway onto the porch. In a loud voice she said, "Why, Jedidiah Rue. What brings you here at this hour?"

"Miriam, I am here to ask you to extend a Christian hand to this poor woman. She holds in her arms a babe not yet a year old that she can no longer care for. Her husband was taken with . . ." He paused quickly thinking. "Consumption," he said. "Yes, the consumption, a fortnight ago, and she has six other mouths to feed on the wages she makes in the fields." Jedidiah turned to Violet and nodded, prodding her to proceed. Violet looked at him and turned to face Miriam. She tried to look and sound pitiful when she said, "Please kind, Madam. He is a good boy, six months old. He cries very little. And as soon as I am able, I will come for him."

Miriam put her hand to her mouth to stop herself from smiling. In a moment she answered in her usual authoritarian tone, "Does this child have a name?"

"Yes, ma'am. He is called Welles in the white man's world." Violet said.

"Welles. Welles, you say. I like that name, Welles. And," she said, moving the cover from the child's face. "I like the look of this child. I should like to care for your Welles. Yes, Madam," she said nodding at Violet, taking the child from her. She nodded at Jedidiah. "Jedidiah, I will do the Christian thing. You know the particulars regarding his birth, I assume?"

"Yes. Of course. You will take him then, Miriam? And this poor woman no longer needs to fret about the future of this boy?"

"Yes, I will take him, Jedidiah. Madam, I will care for this child as I would my own grandchild."

"Thank you," Violet said, bowing her head.

"Miriam, I must take this woman to town. I will return to speak more with you in a short while." Jedidiah turned and escorted Violet to the wagon. He heard Miriam shout, "Jedidiah, if you see Aihàm in town would you ask him if his wife could help me for a few days? Just until I get the hang of it again, you understand. I would pay her handsomely."

Jedidiah turned around and smiled. "Why, most certainly, Miriam. I believe I saw him making deliveries as we came through town; both he and his wife if I'm not mistaken. I will go speak with them." He climbed up onto the seat, waved to Miriam and pulled the horse and wagon onto the roadway.

When Jedidiah and Violet arrived at the train station Aihàm motioned to pull up next to another rig. He said while he waited for their return, he saw the wagon from his village stop to make a delivery. And he thought they should switch wagons too, so no one suspects. Jedidiah agreed and the three men transferred the produce from the one wagon to the other. While the men worked Violet went into the station and changed her dress. After sending the driver of the other wagon on his way, they stood, saying nothing. Relieved that the plan had worked, and the baby was safe, they said their goodbyes. Aihàm and Violet headed to Miriam's house, and Jedidiah went home.

* * * * *

Miriam Wickham stood inside her front door, holding her grandson in her arms. Tears filled her eyes as she watched the smiling baby. She carried him into the middle parlor and sat down to play with him. He reached for her nose and grasped onto her glasses. She smiled, "You are safe, my dear Welles. You are safe. Now, young man, I must find a place to put you and see if I have anything in the house that you can eat. I'm sure you will be getting hungry soon. So why don't we go to the kitchen and see what's there." As she walked toward her kitchen, she heard a knocking at her front door. She walked to the door and opened it. There stood her next-door neighbor and several other women in the neighborhood. "Ladies," Miriam asked. "What can I do for you?"

"We thought," Mrs. Rayford said, "you could use a few things. Each one of us has saved baby things from our youngest child, and we thought you could put them to good use."

"How wonderful! How thoughtful of you. Please, I would appreciate anything you can spare," Miriam said.

The women poured into the house. They brought clothing, toys, a baby chair for feeding, a cradle and a crib that needed a small repair. They held the child, and Welles, delighted by the attention, smiled at them and laughed and cooed. As five o'clock approached, the women left to prepare supper for their families. And Aihàm and Violet arrived at Miriam's house.

The word rapidly spread of what a wonderful thing Miriam Wickham was doing. Soon there was no one in town who didn't know "the whole story" from someone who "was there," and had actually heard it with her very own ears. A reporter for the newspaper interviewed Miriam's neighbors, gathering tidbits of information. He was writing an article for the Friday morning edition of the daily paper on November 8th. Welles, in the course of a few hours, became the talk of the town.

Chapter 12
After Lunch, October 22, 1951

"Did Violet name him? When Jedidiah brings the baby to Violet; that's the first time you mentioned his name?" my mother asked.

"Well, in a way. Do you remember the part of the story when Tey tells Charlotte what his mother would call the baby?" Mother and I nodded, and Auntie said, "In Charlotte's drugged stupor she only remembered hearing Wel les. She said it over and over and then told Tey. He laughed but was happy with her choice. So, by the time Aihàm, Violet and Miriam arrived at the hospital, they had named their baby Welles Taylor Aihàmson.

"That's how Welles got his name, Diana. But when Tobias heard the rumors that Miriam had taken in Welles, it infuriated him. He had no proof, but he was positive that it was Charlotte's baby. His anger became insurmountable. He cursed Charlotte and damned her soul for giving birth to a child who was half Lenape. He referred to Welles as 'that thing,' and he told Thomas Gravely, 'That thing is now living in my house! She is rubbing my nose in her disobedience. She must be punished! She must pay dearly! She is Jezebel incarnate, and she has the curse of God upon her. She must be smoted and left to the dogs.'"

"He actually said that. He cursed his own daughter?"

"Yes. It was in his diaries. He kept meticulous records."

"What an absolute bastard he was!"

"Diana!"

"Well, I can't believe . . . I . . . what did he mean, make

her pay? What else happened? Why isn't it in the book?"

"Because the book was in Camden and Charlotte was in Princeton. She wrote a lot of it down when she was in Princeton and later. But the book is so tattered, and the extra pages she wrote, well some are here and some of them have been lost. So when, when . . ."

"When what? What a monster he must have been! What did he do?"

"I'm getting to that part. So, hold your horses. Let me get my thoughts straight. Some of this I learned later. But the next thing was the article. Yes, the article was published in the morning paper the next day. The article lauded Mrs. Miriam Wickham for her act of kindness and petitioned readers to do the same. Well, when Tobias read it, he went into a rage. He now knew it was impossible to touch the child or Miriam because she had the key with the blue fob. And, he was sure Jedidiah Rue knew everything. Still, in his twisted mind, he searched for a way to avenge this wrong Charlotte had committed against him. So, he called Thomas Gravely into his office. He closed the door and the two of them began formulating a scheme that took shape on the infamous morning of Friday, November . . ."

Friday, November 8 – Friday, November 15, 1895

Early Friday morning Thomas Gravely closed the door behind him. He moved his chair as close as he could so Tobias would be able to speak into his ear. Thomas listened and nodded and listened some more without interruption. When Tobias was through, he leaned back in his chair and studied Thomas.

"Yoouu unnerer sandda?" Tobias asked.

Thomas shook his head and looked askew at Tobias. "It will take money; lots of it. But I know the boys who can do it. I will need free rein. Tobias, once I set them loose, there will be no going back. You understand that, don't you? I will not be able to stop it."

"Mya namea no un too knowo."

"You will not be implicated nor will I. It will be in cash. All they will know is that Mr. Taylor Aihàmson must disappear forever. They will do unto him as his did unto yours. And his wife Charlotte will witness every moment of it before she is left to die. Tobias, you are sure that is the outcome you wish?"

Tobias shook his head yes.

"So be it. Write the note to the bank manager and I will see that you are in your rooms before I go arrange it."

Thomas wheeled Tobias through the office doors and took him to his suite of rooms at his club. He washed and dressed him for the night. He left word with the club manager that he had a vital meeting to attend and Mr. Wickham would be alone. Someone was to serve Mr. Wickham dinner at 1:00pm. and not one second later. Someone was to clear it at 2:00pm on the dot and help Mr. Wickham to the necessary. And if Thomas was detained, they were to serve supper at 7:00pm and clear at 8:00pm. Then, after supper someone needed to help him get into bed. He handed an envelope to the club manager containing a large sum of money to compensate for his time and trouble and left the club. He walked to the docks to wait for the ferry going to Philadelphia.

* * * * *

Jedidiah went to the office Friday morning. He wanted to check on things before he returned to Princeton. He had an uneasy night worrying about Charlotte and Tey. Keeping them safe was his main concern now. As he walked around the office, he noticed Tobias and Thomas, again with their heads together. He watched for a sign, a signal that evil was afoot. He slipped into an empty office out of view. He watched as Thomas wheeled Tobias through the lobby and out the office doors. Jedidiah felt his skin crawl, and his stomach draw into a knot as an eerie, macabre feeling took hold of him. He couldn't put his finger on it, but the peculiar and alarming look on Thomas' face raised his suspicions even more. He closed his office and went to the front desk. He spoke to his courier and instructed him to go to the Pinkerton office. He was to speak with Clancy Hepplewhite and speak to no one else. He was to ask Clancy to send a man to meet him at Farrell's, the café across the street from Tobias' club, as soon as possible. Then Jedidiah left the office.

Jedidiah reasoned that whatever Thomas was up to he would first see that Tobias was in his rooms and taken care of. So once outside the building, Jedidiah looked for Thomas. He caught a glimpse of him wheeling Tobias into his club two blocks away. Jedidiah walked to Farrell's and took a table near a window to watch for Thomas. In a few minutes he was joined by Henry Watts, a clean-shaven, nice looking young fellow. Jedidiah explained to Henry his concerns, and as they talked, Thomas appeared in the doorway of the club. He stood there a moment looking around before he walked to the ferry docks.

Henry shook Jedidiah's hand and followed Thomas to the ferry. Henry was unknown to Thomas. So, when Henry walked to the bulkhead and waited in full view of Thomas,

Thomas didn't give him a second glance. During the day Henry made sure Thomas never noticed or suspected he was tailing him.

When they returned to Camden, Thomas went from the dock directly to Tobias' club. Before entering the club, he looked around, tapped the large case he was holding, and then went inside.

* * * * *

Henry watched Thomas leave the ferry. He waited until Thomas walked a good distance before leaving the ferry. Once Thomas was out of sight he headed to Jedidiah's office. As soon as Jedidiah saw him, he waved for him to come in and closed his office door. He listened as Henry told him the details of his day.

"When we got to Philly Thomas went into a tavern on Delaware Avenue. A seedy place packed with dockworkers having lunch. I hid in a dark corner and watched as Thomas made his way across the room. He singled out an unsavory character who was sitting with three others. They talked a bit before this person led Thomas down a hallway in the rear of the bar. Forty-five minutes later Thomas came back and headed out the front door for the trolley car.

"It was 12:47pm. He boarded a trolley heading west toward City Hall and got off at the Taldmadge Bank and Trust. I followed him inside and watched from a counter against the far wall. Thomas met with the bank manager and handed him a note. The bank manager read the note, went into the vault and came out carrying a large case. He made Thomas sign for the case, and Thomas left and returned to the same seedy bar. The place was now empty.

The person Thomas spoke with earlier was sitting alone, and Thomas joined him. I saw Thomas open the case and hand him an envelope. It looked like this person counted the money inside the envelope. Then he nodded in agreement to Thomas' terms. As Thomas stood up, I heard him say, 'Soon. I don't want to know when but do it soon. Send word when it is done.' We took the ferry to the Camden docks, and I came here. That's all I know. What would you like me to do now?"

Jedidiah looked at him for a few minutes as if he were looking through him at the wall behind him. After several seconds, Jedidiah's eyes narrowed, and he looked into Henry's face. He slammed his palm on his desk and said, "I knew it! Henry, we need to go to your office right now." Jedidiah locked his office and both men left the building. They went to the Pinkerton office. Jedidiah asked the first person he saw to show him to Clancy Hepplewhite's office.

Clancy Hepplewhite was a big burly man in his early sixties. He stood six feet two inches tall and weighed about three hundred and fifty pounds. Clancy had been the Camden Office Chief for many years, and he knew Jedidiah well. "What a pleasure." Clancy said as Jedidiah entered his office. "It must be big to bring you in here, Jedidiah."

"It is Clancy. And thanks for sending Henry Watts. Good man. Did what I ask. Now you need to hear what he found out."

Clancy hollered down the hall for Henry Watts. Henry arrived in a few seconds. Clancy settled himself in the big over-stuffed leather chair behind his desk. "Now tell me what this is about."

Jedidiah told him what he knew and then Henry told him what he saw. Then Clancy grilled Henry on a few more points. He reclined in his chair and pondered the information he heard. Then he leaned forward and crossed his arms on his desk.

"Jedidiah, we have a murder plot on our hands. We don't have an office in Princeton or Trenton. And the authorities will do nothing until an incident occurs. So, I need to dispatch a few men to make sure those two are safe. I know just the ones." Clancy rose and opened his door. He hollered out, "Milford, Delancy, Keegan, front and center!" In a few seconds, the three men were standing in front of him. He gave them explicit instructions. He opened the safe behind his chair, handed each man an envelope and sent them on their way. He told them he wanted a report no later than midnight. He turned to Henry. "From this moment on, your eyes stay glued to Thomas Gravely. I want to know if he even thinks about farting on his way to the men's room."

"Yes, sir," Henry said and left the room.

"Well, Jedidiah. It looks to me like Tobias Wickham has crossed that line. I will do everything in my power to protect that young couple. My hope is those scoundrels didn't get too much of a head start on us. We will know in a few hours when the first report comes through. I will send word to you as soon as I hear."

Jedidiah stood and extended his hand to Clancy. "I couldn't ask for more."

* * * * *

Before she retired for the night Charlotte walked down the hall to the necessary. She bathed and changed into her night-clothes. She brushed her hair and cleaned the necessary then turned off the light. She left the door ajar and started to walk down the hall. She was startled by a loud commotion coming from the direction of her flat. She saw Will Butcher burst from his room and demand to know what the commotion was about. She watched, frozen in place, as a man with shoulders twice as broad as Will's and a face full of unshaven whiskers put his hand around Will's throat. He wrenched him off the ground and pinned Will against the wall. "It's none of yar business." He spat, "if ya don't want to end up like that bastard red-skinned Injun shut up and keep the door closed." He threw Will into his flat and slam the door.

Charlotte's body trembled with fear as she watched two unkempt, crude men drag something out of her flat. She strained to see then gasped loudly when she realized it was Tey they were dragging into the hall. Tey's whole face was bloody and he didn't appear to be conscious. She tried to cry out and go to him but Martin, her neighbor in Flat 304, grabbed hold of her and covered her mouth before she could. He pulled her inside his flat and locked the door.

The men stopped in the hall when they heard her cry. They waited a few moments. When she didn't appear, one of the men shouted out, "Yar next, you Injun whore. The rest of ya, watch what we do to no good red-skinned Injun shit!" He signaled to the men holding Tey and they threw him to the ground and kicked him again and again. Charlotte fought Martin and tried to open the door. She shouted at him, "I must —!"

Martin threw his back against the door. He held her in his arms with his hand over her mouth until there were no more sounds in the hall. He was relaxing his hold on her when they heard one of the men say, "Get 'im out of here. We'll skin 'im at the old farm outside of town."

Charlotte cried and Martin held his hand tighter over her mouth. They listened as Tey was dragged down the stairs. When everything seemed silent Martin loosened his hold on Charlotte. As he inched open the door Charlotte ran through it. She ran to the stairwell and stopped at the top of the stairs. She heard one of the men shout," Ya stay and find the whore!" Martin grabbed her and pulled her inside. "SSSSH!" he said. "Get under the bed. Hide under this blanket. They may come door to door looking and for God's sake, stay there. You can't help him. Only God can now, so pray."

Charlotte lay huddled under the bed, watching Martin. He listened and spied through a crack in the door as the thug outside began prowling the hallways in search of her. Somewhere there was a scuffle and a very loud shout.

"Milford, cuff that bastard so he can't move and start questioning him. He knows about the girl so beat him to a pulp if he won't talk. Keegan, you get the police and head to the old farmhouse. They'll know where it is. Go, man! Time's a wasting. I'll start going door to door to see what the neighbors know. Go!"

Charlotte heard loud knocking on a door down the hall. "I don't think the men are the same ones," Martin said. "Stay where you are while I check." He opened the door and walked into the hall locking his flat door behind him. At the same time Michael Delancy of the Pinkerton Agency was leaving Will Butcher's room. "Is he all right?" Martin asked. Will stuck his head around the door frame. His collar was torn, and his neck was purple. His voice was raspy and soft when he croaked out, "I think so. Did they get you too, Martin?"

Michael Delancy walked down the hall and showed Martin his credentials. "Mr. Martin, is it?" Delancy asked?

"Yes, it is," Martin said as he read Delancy's credentials. "You are Pinkerton?"

"Yes. Mr. Martin. Is that your given or your surname?" Delancy said, eying Martin. Martin was a tall dark-skinned man in his early thirties. His black eyes watched Delancy's every move.

"My name is Martin Maartèn." He emphasized the last syllable. "I'm from the islands, you see. But here they call me Martin Martin, so I get used to it. I no longer fight it."

Delancy's facial expressions didn't change. He asked, "Did you see anything that happened, or can you tell me what you heard? I'm looking for information on the whereabouts of Mr. Taylor Aihàmson's wife, Charlotte. They live in Flat 302. There was an altercation there this evening. Did you see or hear anything that may help us locate her?"

"How do I know you are not in cahoots, as they say, with the others?"

"Mr. Martin, Jedidiah Rue sent us. He's Mrs. Aihàmson's attorney. He suspected foul play was afoot. . . ."

Charlotte started pounding on the door and shouting, "Let me out! It's safe, Martin. He is on our side, please let me out." Martin looked at Delancy who, not taking his eyes from Martin, shouted through the door. "Charlotte Aihàmson, is that you inside?"

"Yes, it is," Charlotte said. "Martin, unlock the door."

"Step aside, son," Delancy said sternly.

"How do I know she will be safe with you?" Martin asked.

"I've been hired to protect her."

"Well, you have done a shit job of it to this point."

"Martin, please. Unlock the door. The Pinkertons are here to help me. Please, Martin." Charlotte said through the door.

Martin turned and unlocked the door and opened it wide. Charlotte Aihàmson, now frantic, darted out of the doorway into Delancy's arms.

"Mrs. Aihàmson," Michael Delancy said, and Charlotte looked up at him. "It is good to see you, ma'am." Charlotte stepped back as he continued to speak. "Our agent Daniel Keegan and the police are on their way to the old farm as we speak. If the information we obtained from the one we've got cuffed is correct, they took your husband there. We should have news soon. Ma'am, is there anything you need? Did they hurt you in any way?"

"Get him back alive. Please. Please, that's what I need. I'm . . . I'm . . . fine. You need to find Tey. Please find Tey. Don't let them hurt him anymore. Please, Mr. Delancy. Please, find Tey." Charlotte slumped to the floor, sobbing.

Martin and Will ran to her side and knelt beside her. They helped her to her feet and walked her to her flat. As she entered, she gasped and recoiled when she looked around the room. There was blood on the floor, the walls, on the sheets and blankets covering the bed. Lamps were overturned and curios broken. Chairs had been thrown against walls, and the mirrors on the armoire doors were shattered. Then she saw the man who was cuffed sitting in her straight-backed chair. A rage, a fury exploded inside her. She walked to him and stood there for a few moments, studying him. From deep inside her came a cry so terrifying it rocked the men back. She lunged at the cuffed man, flailing at him with every ounce of strength she had in her. She screamed every obscenity she could think of until Delancy pulled her from him. He gradually released his hold on Charlotte as he felt her body relax. She stood staring at the man for a moment. She dropped her fists to her sides, turned, and walked through her flat door.

She stood in the hallway, not knowing what to do next. "Charlotte Wickham Aihàmson," she reprimanded herself. Then she tossed her head back and looked at the ceiling. *Get control of yourself. Somewhere there is a child who needs you. Somewhere there is a husband . . .* Her eyes welled up. She raised her hands to her lips, trying to stifle her cries. *How do I know,* she thought, *how do I know my baby is safe? How do I know they will find Tey?* Her mind raced with thought after thought. She wasn't sure she was safe. She wasn't sure Welles was safe. And Tey. Where was Tey? What had they done with him? "It's because of me," she said. "I am responsible for this. If Tey and I had never wed this would never have happened. It is my father who sent them . . . because of me. Because I disobeyed him." She closed her eyes. She chastised herself for being the impetus Tobias used to vent his hate against Indians. Then her self-recriminations turned to anger, and with the anger came rage. And with rage now coursing through her veins she wanted revenge. "No!" She looked to the ceiling as if calling upon the Herald Angels to carry her message. "It is you, Father, who will regret this. I swear on my life you will rue the day you set this plan in action."

Charlotte's whole body shuddered as if waking from a bad dream. She straightened her shoulders, put her chin up, smoothed her clothes and walked into her flat. "Mister Delancy," she said. "Would you remove that despicable person? I don't want him in my home. Would all of you please take chairs and move to the hallway? I must clean up this mess before Tey comes home."

"Certainly, Mrs. Aihàmson," Delancy said. "Everyone out. Move him into the hallway. Cuff him to the banister. Make sure he doesn't try anything."

"Why don't you take him to the jailhouse?" Will asked.

"Because once we hand him over, we lose control. I want to get Keegan's report first." Delancy answered.

"Charlotte," Martin said. "I'd be more than happy to help you."

"Thank you, Martin," Charlotte said, touching his arm. "But you have schoolwork to do, and besides, I need to do this myself."

Martin nodded his head. "Yes, I'll go home then. Call me anytime, and I will come."

"I will," Charlotte said. Martin was turning toward the door when Charlotte yelled his name.

"Charlotte, what is wrong?" he asked.

Charlotte stood there staring at him for several seconds. "You saved me tonight. You may have saved my life. I haven't thanked you. I need to thank you."

Martin took several steps until he was in front of her. He took her in his arms. "You are unharmed, and that is good. But tonight, Charlotte . . ." Martin hesitated and stepped backward. He dropped his head. "Tonight, I was a coward. I knew you were there because I watched from the crack in my door, and I did nothing while they beat my friend. If I had . . ."

"If you had shown yourself," Delancy interrupted, "you would be with Mr. Aihàmson right now or dead in this hallway. These men were out for blood. You couldn't have stopped them or even slowed them down. So, go home,

Mr. Maartèn. You did a good thing protecting Mrs. Aihàmson. Go home and feel glad you helped her."

Martin nodded his head. He reached out and squeezed Charlotte's hand. "Good night, Charlotte," he said, and he went down the hall to his flat.

Charlotte turned and walked into her flat. She wandered around at first, setting lamps on tables. She got her broom and swept up the broken glass. Piece by piece she put her furniture in the place where it belonged. She stripped the bed, soaking the bloody bed coverings in the sink. She scrubbed them until every blood stain disappeared. She wrung them dry and hung them in her small necessary room to dry. She filled a bucket and scrubbed the blood from the walls. With each stroke she invoked every God she knew or had ever heard of, begging them to keep Tey safe. Tears ran down her cheeks as she fell on her knees. She scrubbed the floor while pleading, begging, and bargaining for his life. When she had scrubbed the last spot of blood away, she sat back on her heels. She whispered into the empty room, "I know you are alive. I feel you. Stay strong; please don't give up. We will find you and bring you home. Fight, Tey, please fight. God, please go to him. Show him how. He is strong." She extended her arms, raising her palms toward the ceiling. She cried out, "Kishelëmùkònk, creator of us all, please help your son Miltëwakàn. Show him the path. I love you so, my Tey eholàk."

Loud voices came from the hallway, forcing her back to reality, and she fought to hear what they were saying. She walked into the hallway and asked Delancy what was happening.

"Keegan rode up." Delancy turned from Charlotte and

addressed Keegan, who was walking toward him. "Well, man, did you find them?"

"We got the other two, but the Indian, Mr. Aihàmson; he got away and crawled off into the woods before we got there. One of them told us they were going to scalp and skin him alive. But when they went to get him, he was gone. So, right now, there are nine policemen looking, but when I left, they hadn't found him or any trace of him yet."

"He's alive?" Charlotte asked, pulling at Keegan's sleeve. "Please, is he alive? Tell me if he is alive."

"I think he was when I rode off, but ma'am," Keegan said, pursing his lips and parsing his words. "I can't say for sure. They beat him up bad. I don't know if he's alive. Sorry, ma'am."

Charlotte nodded and turned away. She walked toward her flat but stopped when she heard Keegan say, "Delancy, he's Indian so there's no trail. As hurt as that poor fellow is, he's leaving no trail behind. There are only a few drops of blood that we saw that led us to where he went into the woods. After that, there is nothing, not even a bent twig, nothing. We've called his name, but he either can't or won't answer us. He doesn't know who we are. We should get an Indian tracker on this one."

Charlotte turned and said, "He knows me! He knows my voice. He will answer me. Take me there. Take me there now!"

"Mrs. Aihàmson," Delancy said, about to placate Charlotte until he turned and stared into her eyes. He paused for several seconds in deep thought and studied her for several seconds more. "Yes," he said, nodding his head. "Yes, I think so. Yes, you'd better put on warm clothes first and sturdy shoes. You are correct. He will answer you. Keegan, go get a wagon for us to take Mrs. Aihàmson. Wake up anyone you need to but get it now. Milford, go with Keegan and take that piece of shit to the jailhouse. Keegan, on your way, wire Clancy. Let him know what's happening, and Milford, you stand guard in the jail until I get back."

Charlotte ran inside her flat and changed. She returned to the hall, dressed in Tey's trousers and a pair of his heavy work boots. She had piled her hair on top of her head and put on one of Tey's caps to hold it in place. Delancy smiled when he saw her.

"Are you ready, ma'am?" he asked.

"Yes, sir, Mr. Delancy. Let's go."

They rode six miles on a desolate road and stopped at an old farmhouse that looked like it should have been demolished years before. Shutters were rotting on the ground or barely hanging by a single nail. Most of the windows were broken and the paint had peeled off long ago. Vines covered its wall and the dilapidated barn that was a few yards away. The surrounding fields were overgrown with thorn bushes and weeds that were taller than the fence posts. And the fences surrounding the property were rotting, falling apart and beyond repair.

In the distance they heard voices calling Tey's name and saw glimpses of torches glowing as they moved between the trees in the woods. Delancy spotted the Police Captain and the Sheriff, who were directing the manhunt. They were in deep conversation about where they should look next when Delancy walked up.

Delancy introduced himself and told them he had brought Tey Aihàmson's wife with him. He explained what he thought should be the next step, and they both agreed with him. Delancy came to the wagon and helped Charlotte down. He led Charlotte to the Sheriff and Police Captain, introduced her, and explained what he wanted her to do.

"It's deep woods out there, so I want you to walk in my footsteps and hold on to my jacket the whole time. We will make a sweep, a section at a time, beginning west of the area where Keegan spotted the blood. Every tenth step we will stop, and you will call his name as loud as you can. Don't shout or scream, simply say it loudly. Mrs. Aihàmson, if there is a pet name only you call him, use it. Now remember, it is very dark, and the underbrush is dangerous. So please hang on to me. Are you ready?"

"Yes. Of course. Let's go."

They started into the woods and on the tenth step Charlotte called out his name, but there wasn't any reply. They took another ten steps and she called out again but heard nothing. They walked on for ninety paces more, and every tenth step she called to him, but he still didn't answer. They turned left and walked twenty paces more. Her voice grew louder as she called to him, but she heard nothing in return. They turned left, heading toward the farmhouse. Charlotte was getting more frantic with every step she took. As they neared the farmhouse, in desperation, Charlotte shouted out, "Tey eholàk, where are you? Answer me. I am here. Your Chulëntët. Please answer me." She stained to hear his voice and in despair, she whispered into the night, "Please, Tey, answer me."

A rustling in the breeze whispered *Chulëntët* as it passed by her ears.

"Stop!" Charlotte screamed. "Don't move. Don't make a sound." Everyone stopped and turned toward her.

"Hush! —Oh dear God, let it be him." Charlotte took a deep breath, closed her eyes and called out, "Tey eholàk! My Tey eholàk. Please say my name again." She held her hands against her mouth so she wouldn't make a sound and listened. In a moment, she heard a rustle of leaves and, "Chul . . . ënt . . . ët."

"He's here! He's here. He's right here somewhere. Be careful. Please don't step on him. He's alive. Oh, thank God. Tey. Tey, where are you? Talk to me. Tell me where you are. These men are good men. They are here to help you. Please talk to me."

"I'm. Here. Chul . . ." His words were almost inaudible. Then there was silence.

His hand was all that Charlotte saw when she found him. He was lying under a layer of leaves that covered his whole body. She swept off every leaf that covered him until she exposed his entire frame. He was unconscious. She bent down, kissed his lips and whispered in his ear, "My Tey eholàk. Let these men take you where you will be safe." She touched his face once more then took hold of Delancy's hand. She got to her feet. "Don't hurt him anymore, please, don't hurt him anymore."

By the time he reached the hospital he had lost a tremendous amount of blood. After Dr. Mosby examined him, he said it was a miracle that he was alive at all. He had broken bones in his lower left leg, left forearm, most of his ribs and several bones in his face. He had deep abrasions on his knees and elbows and thistles, brambles, and thorns embedded in his skin. Of major concern to the doctor was his suspicion that a rib may have pierced Tey's left lung. But he told Charlotte, Tey was too weak and had lost too much blood for him to operate to find out.

* * * * *

"Stop pounding. You'll wake my family." Jedidiah Rue said as he opened the door.

"Western Union, Mr. Rue. This one is marked urgent too, sir."

"I pray this one's good news," Jedidiah said as he signed for the wire. He made the courier wait while he read the telegram from Delancy. "I need to send a reply, son." He looked at his watch and at the courier. "When does the next train north leave?"

"Don't know for sure, sir."

"I'm not sure either. So, here's my reply to Delancy: Leaving first train out. Stop. Trust your judgment. Stop. Meet at hospital. Stop. That's it. No, wait. I need to send telegrams to Miriam Wickham and Chief Aihàm too. The wires are to read: Found alive. Stop. Leaving first train out. Stop. Wire when I know more. Stop. Got that, son?" Jedidiah asked.

"Yes, sir, Mr. Rue," the courier replied and handed Jedidiah his pad. Jedidiah read the messages and nodded. "You're the boy, who came earlier, aren't you?"

"Yes, sir, I am, Mr. Rue," the boy answered. Jedidiah smiled at him. He wrote down the addresses where the telegrams to Miriam and Aihàm were to be delivered. He asked the courier to wait a minute more and he went to the dresser by the door, chose a few coins and handed them to the lad. "Thanks for speedy service tonight, son. Now, please make sure those wires are sent as soon as you get to the office. You'll do that, son?"

"Yes, sir, Mr. Rue." The courier tipped his hat, got on his

bike, and peddled away.

Jedidiah closed his door and ran up the stairs. He dressed, kissed his wife and daughter, and headed to the train station. Before sunrise, he walked into Tey Aihàmson's room without making a sound. Tey was still unconscious when Jedidiah arrived.

Jedidiah stopped short when he saw Charlotte. Her face was smudged with dirt, and she was dressed in men's clothing with her hair stuffed under a cap. She was asleep with her head lying next to Tey's, holding onto his hand. He moved to the chair next to the window and sat down to wait. In a few minutes, Charlotte stirred and felt someone's presence in the room. She turned her head and smiled when she saw it was Jedidiah.

"He's alive. Mr. Rue, he's alive," she whispered. "He's a fighter. I think he's going to be all right. We must wait and see."

"Yes. I know. I checked on his condition. Charlotte . . ." Jedidiah said. He moved forward in his chair. He had his elbows on his knees and he was ringing his hands. He looked at the floor before his eyes met Charlotte's.

"I am so sorry, Charlotte. I should have seen this coming. I didn't act soon enough. I should have made sure the two of you were safe. I am so very sorry."

"Sorry?" Charlotte said. "You saved our baby. You warned us. I should have listened. I should have listened because, Mr. Rue, he warned me. Many times he warned me, still I refused to believe my father was capable of this. But you . . . you saved our baby from harm. You shouldn't feel any guilt about this."

Jedidiah got to his feet and lifted Charlotte from her seat. He held her in his arms. "Thank you, my dear, for those kind words," he whispered in her ear. He loosened his hold and held her at arm's length. "But my guilt cannot be absolved that easily. I know your father. I know what he is capable of. I should have known, Charlotte. I, of all people, should have known. I didn't read the signs quickly enough. I am so very sorry."

A few hours later, Aihàm and Violet arrived at the hospital. They left home as soon as they received Jedidiah's telegram that Tey had been found alive. The next day Jedidiah learned that the man they called Mean Joe Biggs was arrested. Thomas' contact in the seedy bar was telling everything he knew to save his neck. On the third day, they learned that Thomas Gravely and Tobias Wickham were arrested. Each was charged with three counts of conspiracy to commit murder.

Tobias learned that loyalty cannot be bought at any price once Thomas was in handcuffs. Thomas told every detail of Tobias' plan to murder Tey, Welles, and his daughter. Tobias was shattered by Thomas' betrayal. Furious that his plan had failed, he succumbed to another fit of apoplexy. He was admitted to the prison unit at the hospital. He was kept under twenty-four-hour police guard.

During those three days, Dr. Mosby set Tey's bones and treated his wounds. Jedidiah didn't leave Charlotte's side. He conducted his business from Tey's hospital room. And he continually sent word to Miriam about Tey's condition. But by the fourth day, the doctor was sure that Tey had developed pneumonia. He ceased restorative measures and concentrated on clearing Tey's lungs.

As Tey's condition worsened, Jedidiah, Aihàm and Violet grew more worried about Charlotte. Nothing they did or said could coax her to leave Tey's side. She was exhausted.

But she refused to leave him even for an hour to have dinner. She sat holding his hand. She helped the nurses bathe him, moisten his lips with water; she did whatever she could.

And she talked to him constantly. She laid her head on the pillow next to his and spoke into his ear. She told him how much she loved him over and over again. She explained what the doctors were doing to make him well and what Jedidiah was doing to bring him justice.

She sat in the same place for hours on end. She held his left hand against her heart while stroking his hair. She spoke in his ear, reassuring him that everything that could be done to make him well was being done. She told him not to worry. She told him he must use all his energy to make himself well so that he could come home to them.

On the fifth day, as the sun was beginning to rise, Charlotte was stroking his hair and watching him sleep. Aihàm and Violet were seated on the right side of Tey's bed, and Violet was holding her son's hand. Jedidiah sat in the chair behind Charlotte as he had for the last four days. And Charlotte sat on Tey's left, holding his left hand to her heart.

Charlotte detected a faint, breathless whisper. It stunned her, and she jolted up. She leaned forward and listened as he said, "Chu-lë-nt-ët, I . . . heard you." She smiled, half-laughing and half-crying. She tried to hold back her tears as the smile broadened across her face. Everyone in the room heard him speak, and they were awake, watching him. His eyes were open, and he was trying hard to smile. "You were . . . with me." Tears ran down her face as she bent over him and kissed his lips.

"I want to hold you in my arms, my Tey eholàk," Charlotte whispered into his ear.

He smiled and said, "Close your eyes . . . I am there . . .

Now . . . Forever . . . We are one . . . Do you feel...?"

She laid her head next to his. "Yes. I do. I feel you holding me."

"I heard you . . . as you washed. . ." He stopped to catch his breath.

Charlotte, in disbelief, raised her head and looked into his eyes.

"The wall . . . you called . . . Kishelëmùkònk . . . to show me the path . . . I was shown."

He closed his eyes. "My Chulëntët . . . ktaholël . . . close your eyes . . . I am there . . ."

"I love you too, my Tey eholàk. Rest, my love. We have the rest of our lives to talk. Now you must heal. Go to sleep and make yourself well. I love you, Tey. My Tey eholàk."

Charlotte kissed his forehead and smoothed his hair. She touched his cheek and smiled a tentative, happy half smile. She watched him sleep and listened to him struggle to breathe. His breaths became shallower and shallower. For many minutes he labored until he inhaled one long, deep breath. A scowl narrowed Charlotte's eyes. She clenched her fists and her whole body trembled. Her face turned crimson with the rage that smoldered inside her. She stood up and she lowered her eyes to his torso. She watched his body. Then she pounded his chest with her clenched fists. She hit him with such force his body jolted upward. Jedidiah rose to his feet and tried to put his arms around her, but Charlotte pushed him away. "No. Leave me be!" Furious, she pounded Tey's chest once more. "Tey! Breathe out. Tey. Open your eyes. I will not allow you to die. Tey. Please breathe." Charlotte watched his eyes for a few moments before she took his face in her hands. She held his face so close to hers their noses touched. She pleaded with him, "Please. . . please,

Tey, please, please breathe, Tey, please, open your eyes."
Tears ran down her cheeks as she laid her lips on his.

Violet walked around her son's bed and opened the
window; then she returned to her son's side. She reached
into the small satchel she was carrying that was lying on the
floor beside her chair. She removed a small, white,
embroidered handkerchief from the satchel. She reached out
and touched Charlotte's shoulder. Charlotte looked at Violet
and nodded. She sat down beside Tey and watched Violet
place the handkerchief over her son's face.

* * * * *

The body of Miltëwakàn, Tey, Taylor Aihàmson was
taken from the hospital to the nearest mortuary. There he
was prepared for transportation to the village where he was
born. Charlotte and Violet stayed with Tey's body to watch
over its preparation. Aihàm went to the telegraph office to
arrange for Tey's arrival in his village. And Jedidiah went to
make the railroad arrangements to transport Tey's body
home.

Following Lenape custom, Aihàm sent telegrams to five
people, not related to the family. He asked each one to
perform a specific task. Aihàm sent telegrams to two women
that he and Violet trusted. He asked them to take care of the
food and oversee the cooking. He sent telegrams to two men
asking them to help the women with all the heavy work
involved. The last one Aihàm sent to Tey's oldest friend. He
asked Lainipën to be the one to keep the vigil over his son's
body.

Lainipën and Tey had been friends since Tey was four
years old. He was two years older than Tey and he was the

youngest of three children. His parents died trying to extinguish a fire that consumed their barn. He and his siblings were then taken in by their grandfather. Lainipën's grandfather was the tribal historian/record keeper. He vehemently opposed the white man's interference in tribal affairs. He would not allow his grandchildren to attend public school. He forbid them to associate with the white man or work outside of the village. But Lainipën longed to be part of the world outside of his village. He envied Tey's ability to move between the two with ease. So, at sixteen, after his grandfather died, he left the village. He earned an apprenticeship with a small fire department on the outskirts of Camden.

When Lainipën received Aihàm's wire he felt honored to be the one chosen to keep Tey's vigil. He made arrangements to leave his post at the firehouse and traveled back to the village. He followed Aihàm's instructions in the wire he sent, and he contacted three of Tey's friends. They met the train when it arrived at the Burlington Station. And they transferred Tey's body to a covered wagon for his final journey home.

Tey's body arrived at the funeral home at 11:22 the same morning. There he was washed, dressed and laid in the coffin that would hold his physical remains for eternity. His parents placed his hunting knife, a warm blanket, a change of clothes, food to eat and other things in the casket. These were things they thought his spirit would need on its journey. At 3:30pm, townspeople, relatives, and friends started filing past the casket. One by one they took a seat for the evening vigil. Miriam Wickham and Welles arrived late in the afternoon. And Charlotte smiled for the first time in a long while when she took her son from her mother's arms.

During the long hours of the vigil, Lainipën stayed at the head of Tey's casket. He didn't leave him alone for a moment until he was laid to rest in the burial grounds. Welles slept in a makeshift crib by his father's side. And a group of mourners played the traditional moccasin game. At midnight, everyone except Lainipën went outside. Someone raised a rifle into the air and fired one shot. Then everyone went inside and gathered around the body. The speaker prayed for the departed and the bereaved. He lifted the embroidered handkerchief and painted Tey's face with three red stripes. This marked Tey so the creator knew he was a good son of the Lenape. Once the speaker finished, the two women, chosen by Aihàm and Violet, served the midnight meal.

Charlotte, Aihàm, Violet, Miriam and Welles kept the vigil for their beloved Tey through the night. At dawn someone with a rifle again fired one shot into the air and breakfast was served. Precisely at twelve noon, the burial procession began. Leading the procession was the speaker, followed by Aihàm, Violet, Charlotte, and Welles. They were followed by Miriam and the other relatives and friends. The casket, escorted by Lainipën, was last as they walked to the burial grounds. No one turned to look back at the casket, ensuring that Tey's spirit stayed with his body and did not fall behind. Once the casket arrived, six men dug the grave where Tey's physical remains would rest in perpetuity. The speaker said words of comfort to the bereaved. He asked the Creator to guide this good son of the Lenape on his journey. And Lainipën said his final farewell to Tey.

Everyone, one after the other, circled the casket counterclockwise, beginning in the east. A notch was cut in the casket near Tey's head. The notch was painted red so that Tey's soul had a way to leave his body and find its place in the spirit world. They lowered the casket into the grave with Tey's head pointing east. They covered it with only the soil that they removed to make the grave. Then they put dry soil, pieces of bark and dry leaves on top so no fresh ground could be seen. The kìkinhikàn, painted red, was set in place at the head of Tey's grave in the east. It marked the location of his grave. It was a wood board, straight and tall, with a diamond carved at the top, and it pointed Tey to the spirit world. No name was carved on the kìkinhikàn, and the Lenape name of the departed would never be said again. Two canvas sheets were laid on the ground at the head of the grave. The family put the food they'd prepared on one sheet, and on the second sheet others put the food they had prepared. A small fire was started that would be restarted at sunset for the next three nights. It would keep Tey's spirit warm as it journeyed to the spirit world. And vittles would be placed on the grave to nourish the soul as it searched for eternal peace. The speaker said some final words after two bundles of Tey's clothes were given to helpers who were his same size. Then everyone went home.

* * * * *

Charlotte kissed her mother and son goodbye. They boarded the carriage with Jedidiah, his wife, and daughter for the return trip to Camden. Miriam leaned out of the carriage window and said, "We will see you on the twelfth day, Charlotte. If you need anything, if Aihàm or Violet need anything, send a wire. I want to do whatever I can to help. Charlotte, please make sure they know that."

"We know that, Mother. Right now, taking care of

Welles is what we need. I love you, Mother. Jedidiah, take care of them for me please." Charlotte waved as the carriage left the town square. She watched until they were no longer in view. Then she walked across the square to the home of Aihàm and Violet. There she'd stay for the twelve days of mourning that began minutes before.

Her hair blew into her eyes as a gust of wind passed by. She brushed it from her face, shaking her head so it would fall into place. In keeping with Tey's traditions, she hadn't pulled her hair back or tied it up, and it hung around her shoulders. She had no idea how she looked. Every mirror in the house was covered, and they would remain that way until the twelfth day. The Lenape believed by the twelfth day Tey's spirit would have found its place in the happy hunting ground. In the olden times, the twelve days of mourning came before the burial. But now, because of state health laws, the mourning period followed the burial. It made no difference to Charlotte. With or without his body present, she missed him so.

She opened the door and entered Aihàm and Violet's house. It was full of people. She walked along the hallway that led to the kitchen, politely speaking with everyone. *My in-laws' home*, she thought, *but I feel so ill at ease, like I don't belong.* Her wedding day flashed through her mind and Violet's words echoed in her brain. "Only you can make you feel like you do not." She smiled to herself. *How right she is,* she thought, *I do belong, especially today.* She walked into the kitchen and found a place where she would be out of the way. The kitchen was full of women she didn't know who were busy cooking more food. She was leaning against a wall, watching them, when she felt a hand take hold of one of hers. She looked down at the hand and followed the arm attached to it up until she saw a person's face. Violet smiled and whispered, "Come, I will show you where you will sleep."

Sleep, Charlotte thought. *None of us has had any sleep since before Tey died. I am so very tired but if I close my eyes and he isn't there. If there's only darkness, emptiness...* She shuddered at the thought and felt an ache within herself she'd never known before.

Violet led Charlotte upstairs to the second floor. As they walked along the hallway, they passed a room with a Phillies cap and pennant hanging on the wall. Charlotte gasped and stopped short. She stood at the doorway to the bedroom as her eyes toured the room. A photograph of her was in a frame sitting on the nightstand next to the bed. And lying next to it was a book of poetry she had given Tey. A blanket, one she had knitted for him, was folded over the back of the chair next to the nightstand. And his headdress, the one he wore at their wedding, was mounted on a stand that stood on a chest across the room. Charlotte turned and looked at Violet. "Is this. . ?"

Violet nodded and said, "Yes. I cannot bring myself to give his things away. I should have done it by now, but I cannot yet. I touch his things, I remember. I feel him, and I cannot part with it yet."

Charlotte turned again to look into Tey's bedroom. She saw the cap, and Sundays in the old mansion during the Phillies games replayed in her mind. She closed her eyes and pictured him lying on their featherbed, beckoning to her to join him. She wrapped her arms around herself and felt his touch. She remembered his smile, the one that always fluttered her heart. For a second, she couldn't breathe as tears ran down her cheeks. She sighed and wiped at her tears. She stood there for a moment more without saying a word.

"I understand," she whispered. "That's what I must face when I pack our things in Princeton. Oh, how I dread it. But the hardest thing for me right now is not being able to say his name. I don't know if I can do it."

"Chulëntët, you may not say his Lenape name, but Tey and Taylor are his white man's names. It is his Lenape name that no longer is said. But please, in front of others, I ask you be careful. . . ."

"Yes. Of course. I promised you when you came to the hospital that I would abide by your traditions, and I will not break that promise. I will not embarrass you, Violet, I promise."

"Yes. I know you will not. Thank you."

"Why don't you hate me? It's my father who's caused this pain, so why don't you hate me?"

Violet touched Charlotte's cheek. "That is why, Chulëntët—because you are not your father. What I feel for your father is between my Creator and me. I will deal with it in my own way. What I feel for you is between us, and we will deal with that together." Violet smiled and turned. She walked further down the hall and stopped. She turned to face Charlotte and asked, "Would you like to sleep there, Chulëntët, instead of in this room?" Tears were falling from Charlotte's eyes when she turned to Violet. "Yes, please."

"Yes. I will have your things moved." Violet walked to where Charlotte stood. She caressed Charlotte and went down the stairs.

Chapter 13
Early Afternoon, October 22, 1951

"It's okay, Dan." my mother said, putting her arms around me.

"I liked him." I was trying not to sob. "I didn't want him to die." I straightened up and looked at Auntie and my mother.

There was a puzzled look on my mother's face. "I liked him too. . . and . . . all my life . . . I always thought he was . . ." She turned toward Auntie as a strange, hostile look crossed her face. "But he died. He couldn't have been, could he? You just told us about his death."

Auntie didn't answer. She had a look of such remorse on her face that it made me uncomfortable, and I turned away. I looked at my mother and watched as her eyes narrowed and she set her jaw. I knew that look. She was getting angrier as each second ticked by, and so was I.

The story of Tey's death kept going round and round in my brain. I stopped crying as my anger grew. "Tobias Wickham should have been skinned. He was a bad man, a very bad man." I said, breaking the onerous silence in the room.

My mother turned to me and said, "Yes, he was. Yes, he was indeed." And I watched my mother's face change even more. It hardened as anger sharpened the few lines she had around her brow and eyes. She turned and glared at Auntie. "Just who was he?" She hurled the words at Auntie. "Am I supposed to now believe that fairytale? And Charlotte. . . Is she someone else too? Tell me, Auntie; tell me, how did Charlotte feel? Was she angry? Did she hate him? It escapes me. I don't understand. I don't understand why I was never told!"

"Because I vowed, Diana."

"A damn vow! Is that what I am supposed to believe? A damn vow made you lie! You lied to everyone. You lied to me. Why? Why did this—this vow take such precedence that you, everyone, lived a lie. Why? How can you explain that?"

"Let me try. Please listen and let me tell you what happened. Please, listen."

"Listen! Listen to what? More lies! Did anyone ever think how it felt . . . not to belong? Everyone needs to belong, especially to someone. But this damn vow. I don't understand this damn vow at all. Why was the secret still kept after everyone died? Why?"

"Because it was 1895 when it began, Diana. There was good reason for it and later, well, later there was no way to change it. And so, the secret went on."

For a brief moment my mother stared at Auntie before she retorted, "That's hard for me to believe. In 1917 Welles and Alice had a child. Welles died in 1918, Alice in 1920. Everyone else, everyone who knew, died within months of each other. They were all gone except for the two who raised their child. Why? Why didn't they tell her? Why did it take sixty years? An absolute twist of fate that an eight-year-old finds the tattered black book. And the secret is, at long last, revealed? What is so bad about it that it couldn't be told? It doesn't make sense to me. I find it hard to believe."

"Let me finish my story and we can discuss the decisions made, right or wrong. But first, I think you need to know the rationale for those decisions. Please, Diana, hear me out."

My mother stared at Auntie for a long time. "Yes. All right. I will." Mother looked at the clock. "But I need to call Daniel because I don't see how you'll tie this story up with a pretty little bow by six o'clock." Mother stood, knocking over her chair, and walked into the middle room to telephone Pop.

I stared at my mother's back as she walked into the middle room. I was confused by her anger and mystified by her resentment. So, I turned to Auntie, looking for answers. Her eyes were rimmed with tears as she tried to smile a funny, half-hearted smile.

"Danny, I am sorry. I should have taken care of this a long time ago. But even I procrastinate when faced with a difficult situation." Auntie got to her feet. "Do you want a cookie or milk or a scoop of ice cream?"

She looked at me, and in her eyes I saw a sorrow, an agonizing regret that I didn't understand. She turned and, like a beaten dog, she walked to her kitchen sink with her head down and her shoulders slumped.

Mother came into the kitchen. She picked up her chair and stood next to me. Mother looked at Auntie, who had her back toward us. "I told Daniel to take the girls out for supper; that we needed to finish this. Is that all right with you?"

Auntie turned around and nodded her head. There may have been tears in her eyes. I wasn't sure. She looked down and wiped her hands on her apron. My mother sighed and said, "I'm . . . I'm sorry. . . . I. . ."

"Diana. . ." Auntie interrupted and put her hand up as if to tell her to stop. She rinsed the teacups. When she was finished, she braced herself on the sink. She stood looking out the window, her shoulders going up and down with each breath she took. After several minutes she turned around to face my mother.

"I have a pound of ground beef in the Frigidaire," she said. "There's enough to make a meatloaf."

"Sure. That's fine," Mother said, not looking at her. "What would you like us to do?"

In silence, we peeled potatoes, diced onions and did whatever was needed. Then Auntie put the meatloaf surrounded by potatoes on her sideboard to be popped in the oven a little later.

She stood at the sink washing her hands for a long time. As she reached for the hand towel her head popped up. She spun around to face my mother and said, "Diana. Down in the root cellar, there are a couple of bottles of wine."

"That's just what the doctor ordered," Mother said and headed for the root cellar. In a few minutes, she returned with a dusty bottle in her hands. "This is a good wine, Auntie. Where did you get it?"

"Every Christmas, Fireman Harriman brings me a gift from the fire company. It was a little thank you for the cakes and pies. He brought those three bottles last year. I put them in the root cellar. I was going to give them to you, but it slipped my mind."

Mother opened the wine and took a sip. "Well, I should thank him. This is an excellent wine." She sat down at the table. She spun her wine glass in her hands for a minute. She watched the wine inside the glass curl up the sides until she raised her eyes and asked, "If yesterday..."

"Go on. If yesterday, what? Ask your question. If

yesterday…" Auntie asked as she took her place at the table.

"If yesterday we had been later; say, an hour later . . . would you have told all of this?"

"No. The story would have ended with the wedding."

Mother nodded and pursed her lips. "Another 'and they lived happily ever after fairytale,' I suppose, and the secret would still be a secret?"

"Yes," Auntie said, avoiding looking into my mother's eyes.

Mother watched Auntie for several minutes before asking, "So this is because of me?"

"Yes. We should have had this talk a long time ago," Auntie said, dropping her head down. "I am feeling very remorseful right now, Diana." Auntie raised her head and looked at my mother.

My mother stared at her. "And I am having a hard time with the secret. Why the secret? Why all these years? Am I wrong to be so. . ."?

"Diana," Auntie said, reaching across the table and putting her hand on top of my mother's. "The year was 1895. A girl, a nineteen-year-old girl lost the love of her life at the hands of her father—her father, Diana. Her father was so blinded by hate that he did everything in his power to expunge every record of her marriage to a Lenape Indian boy. She had a six-month-old child and no husband, not one piece of paper and not one witness to corroborate her claim. Sure, there were the Indians in the village, but they were of no account. They had no standing in the community. No one would take their word over that of Tobias Wickham. There was no one. No one could verify or bear witness to the fact that she had married Tey. It was her word against her father's. Her father made her a prime target for that big A to be painted upon her chest, just like the one Hester Prynne wore. Does that make any sense to you?"

Mother sat back and looked at Auntie for a few moments. "Yeah. . . whatever. . ." She looked away and clasped her hands together in front of her on the table.

"Auntie, who is Ester Pine?"

"Hester Prynne, Danny. She is the main character in Nathaniel Hawthorne's novel *The Scarlet Letter*. The letter was a big capital A," Auntie said and waited until my mother looked at her. When their eyes met, she reached across the table and placed her hand on top of my mother's.

"Diana, you must understand that it was a whole different world back then. Diana, in 1895 women were second class citizens. We had no rights. We never dared dream we'd have the freedoms women have today. Women in 1895 were bound into a life governed by the whims of their husbands or fathers. We were unable to own property; we had no legal claim to monies we earned or inherited, and we didn't have the right to vote. Our husbands and fathers did not permit us to work outside the home. The only exception was for the survival of the family. And women couldn't even dream of going to universities. We were not allowed to think or reason or express an opinion. We were expected to stay in the home and cook, clean, mend clothes and bear children. We were to be seen but not to be heard. And sports, Diana? Sports like you participated in were beyond the realm of possibility. That's why the Women's Suffrage movement took hold. Women across the nation took off their aprons and marched, willing to die for the cause."

"But Miriam, you said Miriam. . ."

"Diana, Miriam Wickham was the exception, not the rule. Will you listen and let me tell you what happened? Please?"

Mother leaned forward and put her elbow on the table. Her fingers traced her chin and mouth as she studied Auntie for several minutes. She put her other elbow on the table and intertwined her fingers. She rested her chin on her hands and said, "Yes. . . go on."

Auntie nodded. "Miriam Wickham was the exception because her father was a free thinker. Some thought him cut from a different cloth. She often wondered why he chose Tobias as her mate. Tobias was such a strict and demanding man and he considered women chattel. Tobias despised her father's views and his railing against keeping women in their place. But that was what Miriam's father believed. He recognized that women had thinking minds. He believed women's thought processes were every bit equal to that of men. He believed all they needed was a little nurturing. He educated Miriam and gave her the independence that a woman of that time very seldom had. In his will, he established trusts for her with peculiar stipulations. His will gave her complete control, circumventing the conventions of the times.

"Miriam had no knowledge of these stipulations until Tobias had his fit. But once armed with proof of Tobias' affliction, she assumed control of her own affairs. She asserted herself. She realized she was a wealthy woman and needed to answer to no one ever again. However, that didn't extend to her daughter. And the welfare of her daughter and her grandson preyed on her mind.

"So, after the mourning period the three of them boarded a train for Princeton. Miriam and Jedidiah helped Charlotte pack up the flat. And they discussed Charlotte's options for the future of both her and her son.

"Charlotte knew she had life changing decisions to make. She hadn't set foot in Camden since she'd married Tey. She needed a plausible story that explained where she had disappeared to for the last two years. And her baby? How would she explain Welles?"

"Why didn't they tell the truth?" Mother asked. "They could have set the record straight right then and there. Why didn't they?"

"Diana, if she had, she knew she couldn't prove what she said. There was no one who could vouch for her. Not a single person, not even her mother, could say she was not a common paramour. And there were the big questions about her father. Would he recover? Would he be able to stand trial for his crimes? Would he be punished to the full extent of the law? Or would a judge be sympathetic? Would he get a compassionate release from prison for his dastardly deeds? And would Tobias mesmerize another unwitting person who'd become his accomplice again? And once enabled, would he put in motion another nefarious scheme to kill Welles? The whole thing boiled down to protecting Welles.

"And so, she wrestled with it but, in the end, she realized that if the truth were told it would incite Tobias anew. He was diabolical enough to find a way to besmirch her character, which would harm her child. And she couldn't defend herself against his accusations. Worst of all, she couldn't defend Welles against the injustice of being known as her bastard child. To Charlotte, the most important thing in life was to protect her son and ensure his legitimacy. So, she swallowed that bitter pill and made the decision. She knew full well that Miriam would be the one Welles would know as his mother. But she recognized that a name wasn't worth the cost it extracted.

"So, the decision was made to leave the story about Welles intact. Now the only thing that remained was explaining Charlotte's absence. To do that they concocted another story. The story was she went to school in Princeton. She studied dress design under the tutelage of Madam Giselle Lafontaine. And she returned when she learned of her father's illness.

"When they arrived in Camden, they took Aihàm and Violet into their confidence. The five of them made a pact. They vowed on Welles' life and the life of his progeny. They vowed that they would never reveal a word of what happened on that train from Princeton. They swore that the truth of Welles' lineage would die with them."

"And the lie begins, doesn't it, Auntie!" my mother almost spit the words out at her.

"No, Diana. The lie began the day Jedidiah uncovered Tobias Wickham's plot. And that lie told in 1895 made it possible for Welles' issue to be born."

I was so confused. I had no idea what Auntie was talking about. "Will someone explain that to me, please?" I asked. I looked from Auntie to my mother, searching for an answer. My mother put her arm around my shoulder and said, "It's nothing, Dan. Honestly, nothing."

"Did you understand what she meant?"

"Well, yes. . . but. . . but, if we listen to the rest of the story, we both will know what she's talking about." Mother looked at Auntie. "Won't we, Auntie?"

"Yes. That's true. Let me finish my story, and you will understand everything. Will you?" Mother watched Auntie for several seconds before she nodded yes.

"And, well, the days passed into years. Welles, what a wonderful boy." Auntie gasped as she said the name Welles. Her eyes clouded as if a memory crossed her mind and tears filled her eyes. "So bright, so charming; he loved everyone. He grew like the beautiful flowers in spring, straight and tall, full of color and life. He looked so much like his father, and Charlotte doted on him. But when he said his first words and he called Miriam 'Mama,' Charlotte thought she would die; a pang that went straight to her heart. Violet felt her pain and suggested they teach Welles to call Charlotte Àna. In Lenape, àna means 'mom' or 'mommy.' Well, Charlotte loved that idea and from that day on, Welles called her Àna.

"A few weeks after Welles took his first steps, Mean Joe Biggs and two other thugs went on trial, followed by Thomas Gravely. Tobias was last. His trial started on Monday, May . . ."

Monday, May 16 – Friday, May 27, 1898

On May 16, 1898, Tobias Wickham went on trial in Princeton. The officers of the court, along with the County doctors, said Tobias was well enough to go to Princeton to stand trial. Tobias had regained some speech after his second bout, but not enough to be understood by most people. After he was arrested, the court appointed a guardian to take care of him. Once again, the guardian discerned the inflections and slurring in Tobias' speech patterns well enough to understand everything Tobias said. But unbeknown to Tobias, this guardian was not taken in by him. He reported every threat Tobias uttered about Welles and Charlotte to the court.

Tobias waived a jury trial in hopes that he would garner the sympathy of the court due to his condition. Thomas Gravely, Mean Joe Biggs, and their cohorts had already been tried in Princeton. They were convicted on all counts. Tobias Wickham went to trial last. And Jedidiah Rue helped the prosecution prepare their case against Tobias.

Before the trial began, Jedidiah petitioned the presiding Judge. In his petition, he asked that the trial be in-camera. He wrote that it was for the protection of the minor child, Welles. His identity and relationship to Tobias Wickham must be kept out of the public purview at all costs. He petitioned the court for all previous trials and was granted favorable rulings. But as this trial neared, he still had not been notified of a ruling. So, when the courtroom was called to order on the first day of the trial, Jedidiah immediately stood. He asked the Judge for a ruling on his petition. The Judge smiled and told Jedidiah, "Sit down, Mr. Rue; I will get to that in a moment. Have patience."

He turned his attention to everyone in the courtroom and laid down the law. He told them the decorum he expected to be maintained at all times, and he addressed Jedidiah's petition. He said that the proceedings of this court would be held in-camera. The transcripts of the trial are to be sealed. And from this day forward, his courtroom would be closed to the public and all news agencies. The Judge invoked the "gag rule," stressing to those involved the seriousness of this case. He threatened charging anyone violating his orders with contempt of court. No one was permitted to talk about or discuss this case outside of his courtroom. He said he would release a statement after a verdict was reached. Then, after sentencing, he would disclose the final disposition of Tobias Wickham and nothing more. And the courtroom was cleared.

Before opening arguments were heard, Tobias Wickham was helped to a standing position. The Judge read the charges against him. He was charged with two counts of conspiracy to commit murder, one count of accessory to the murder, and one count as joint principal to the murder of Taylor Aihàmson. No charge was proffered concerning attempted kidnapping. Nothing was placed into the record of this trial that even hinted at the involvement of a minor child.

Outside the courtroom, the rumor mill ran rampant. The news agencies staked out areas surrounding the courthouse entrance. They tried to garner any tidbit of information they could from anyone who went in or came out. Welles was never connected to the case. But cameras flashed as Aihàm, Violet, Miriam, and Charlotte made their way into the courtroom. Their faces made the front pages of every daily for miles around throughout the trial.

The Camden paper plastered Charlotte's picture on the front page of every edition that came off their press. Their reporters quoted neighbors and supposed "old friends" regarding Charlotte's illicit affair with "that Indian boy from Kuwehòki." That was the boy Tobias Wickham allegedly had killed. He lived in the Indian town out the old Blackwoodtown Road. One quote read, "They've tried to convince us that Charlotte was at an out-of-town school somewhere. But I'm sure she ran off with that Indian buck.

Why else would a fine, upstanding member of our community like Tobias Wickham ever commit such a dastardly deed?" Another quote read, "Disgraceful! It should be her on trial, not Tobias Wickham." But through it all, the press never made mention that there was a child involved. Welles remained unscathed by the rumors and innuendos. So, Charlotte kept her head up, smiled, and thanked God every moment that he was above the fray.

The trial lasted eight days. Tobias' defense was weak and based on his health. His lawyer was Stanfield Richardson Williams, who practiced in Trenton. He called as expert witnesses four doctors with four different specialties. He attempted to prove that Tobias had a severe mental condition caused by his affliction. Counselor Williams was unable to find even one character witness, nor was he able to supply the court with any other evidence to support his claim. Consequently, the defense rested its case before lunch on the second day of the trial.

After lunch, the prosecution began its case. They entered into evidence sworn statements from Thomas Gravely, Mean Joe Biggs, and the other thugs involved with this crime. All of them implicated Tobias Wickham as the mastermind and financier behind the plot to kill Taylor Aihàmson and his wife. No mention of a child was made.

The prosecution began calling witnesses to the stand. First, he called those present the night of the assault; William Butcher and Martin Maartèn. Then he called Dr. Mosby, who was the attending physician for Tey. Next came the Princeton Sheriff, the Police Captain and several persons from Princeton. And then he called the Pinkerton agents assigned to the case. The last witness for the prosecution, the wife of Taylor Aihàmson, took the stand on Tuesday, May 24, 1898.

Charlotte relived that horrible night of November 8, 1895. She told the Judge what she remembered. The Judge asked Charlotte, "Do you believe if Tobias Wickham had been there, in person, that evening, he would have struck the fatal blow?"

Charlotte turned and looked at her father. "Yes, your Honor, I do, and he would have relished every moment."

"The accused is your father, is he not?"

"Yes, he is."

"You disobeyed his directive and allegedly married without his consent, is that correct?"

"I was of age, your Honor, and Tey and I were legally married."

The Judge looked at Charlotte sympathetically. "The legality of your marriage, Miss Wickham, must be determined in another courtroom. Today I will only hear testimony pertaining to this trial. Do you understand?"

Charlotte looked at the Judge and nodded. "Yes, your Honor."

The Judge smiled and looked down at the papers on his bench. He cleared his throat. "From what you've said, I can assume that there is a great deal of acrimony between you and your father, Tobias Wickham."

"Your Honor, until the evening of Friday, November 8, 1895, the acrimony, as you call it, was one-sided. I loved my father and prayed every night that someday he would know Tey as I knew him. I wanted him to love our son, his grandson. I hoped that. . ."

The prosecutor was on his feet, requesting that Charlotte's last statement or any statement made by her or anyone else in the courtroom pertaining to a child be stricken from the record. The Judge agreed, and Charlotte was instructed to continue her testimony.

"Yes, your Honor. It will not happen again." Charlotte said before she resumed her testimony. "You see, your Honor," she said. "since we were seven years old there wasn't anyone else for Tey or me. There were boys, suitors, one's Father was considering as . . . But none . . ."

Charlotte turned to her father. "Father, I never ever thought you would welcome Tey as a son. My hope was that, in time, you'd tolerate him. I hoped that once you saw what a fine man Tey was; how smart and industrious he was and realized how much I loved him you'd relent. There were times when you did. There were times you felt a special tenderness for me, and I hoped this was one of those times. But, that was not to be. So, I had a decision to make—to choose you or Tey—and you hate me for choosing Tey."

Charlotte looked down at her hands and paused for a moment, turned and looked at the Judge. "It's his hate, Your Honor; his hate is so irrational. My father harbors so much hate for Indians he sees nothing else—not one drop of good in any of them, not even the Lenape. Oh, I understand why. I've heard the story over and over again. But his hate made it impossible for us.

"Still, I never could ever, not in my wildest imagination, believe my father capable of this. I loved him—unconditionally. With all his faults I loved him. But," Charlotte straightened up and turned to face her father. She squared her shoulders, raised her chin. "But on that evening, my every hope, every smidgen of love I felt, was lost forever. Because on that evening—the evening of November 8th, 1895—Tobias Wickham murdered my husband. He used the hands of his henchmen as willfully as if he had stood over Tey himself."

Charlotte left the stand. Closing arguments were heard, and court was adjourned. The Judge deliberated two full days before court was reconvened for sentencing. Once everyone was seated, the Judge looked around the courtroom and down at his hands folded on his bench. He cleared his throat and turned, looking at Charlotte.

"I'm having difficulty choosing an adequate sentence. The sentence must be commensurate with the crimes committed in this case. Because Tobias Wickham is infirm, I should be inclined to leniency. However," he said, lifting his head to look at Tobias, "the nature of this crime is so heinous that I am finding that distasteful. So before sentencing, I want to ask the parents." He looked at Aihàm and Violet. "And the named wife of the deceased." He turned toward Charlotte. "If they have any preferences as to the disposition of Tobias Wickham."

Immediately, Jedidiah Rue was on his feet and addressed the court. "Your Honor," he said. "The family of the deceased has appointed me as their spokesman. May I address the court on their behalf?"

The Judge looked at Jedidiah and nodded. "Yes counselor, proceed," he said.

Jedidiah walked to the center of the room and faced Tobias. "Your Honor," he said. "As an officer of the court I've taken the liberty of explaining to the family the various sentences you are bound by law to consider and may impose on Tobias Wickham. Unanimously, your Honor, they agree that if you sentenced Tobias Wickham to an eternity in hell, that sentence would be far too lenient. However, your Honor, the family does have an alternative to offer the court."

Jedidiah walked to the prosecutor's table and picked up a folder. He turned and faced the Judge. "Your Honor, they propose incarcerating Tobias Wickham in a facility that will be erected at a place that was purchased yesterday and named Eaglet's Rest. If I may, I would like to enter these documents into the record." Jedidiah put the folder on the Judge's bench and stepped back. The Judge perused the documents for six minutes before he lifted his head and spoke to Jedidiah. "Counselor, this is a paradise compared to the facility I have in mind. Please explain to the court why this is the family's preference."

"Of course, your Honor," Jedidiah smiled. He walked to the center of the courtroom. He unbuttoned his jacket and tucked his thumbs in the sleeve sides of his vest. "For months, Miriam Wickham knew that Tobias Wickham was having her followed. She was certain the reason for it was to locate their daughter. And as hate and anger consumed Tobias Wickham, she feared for her daughter's life. An animosity between her and her husband festered. It grew deeper and deeper as his irrational behavior propelled him onward."

Jedidiah walked around the courtroom. "At that time, Miriam Wickham had no knowledge that she was a woman of great means. She was well aware that her father had left her sizable assets and that said assets were managed by her husband." Jedidiah stopped and pointed to Tobias as he said, "Tobias Wickham. But," he said. He turned and faced the Judge. "Your Honor. She was determined that not one penny of those assets be used by Tobias Wickham in his irrational quest." He turned again and looked over the scant audience in the courtroom. With his head to the side he said, "The problem was she didn't know how to stop him." He straightened up and smiled. "A quandary. A quandary soon to be resolved, your Honor. After Tobias Wickham was taken with his first fit of apoplexy, Miriam Wickham went to his office. There she found and read, for the first time, her father's will. A will that had been hidden from her since her father's demise in 1884." He walked to Tobias and looked at him. "That is when she realized she had the means to stop Tobias Wickham." He stood there, savoring the moment before he turned and faced the bench.

"In her father's will, your Honor, were specific clauses relating to Miriam Wickham's legal rights. Those clauses give her the authority to take control of her assets managed by Tobias Wickham. Among those assets were bankbooks and securities hidden in a small safe. The safe was hidden under Tobias Wickham's desk. And that safe, your Honor, was opened by using a key with a blue fob." Jedidiah walked around the courtroom once more. "Mrs. Wickham first became aware of this key two years prior. At that time, Tobias Wickham was hospitalized with an inflamed vermiform appendix. At the time, she didn't give much thought to the key or what it opened." He turned back to face the bench. "That is, not until the recent turn of events prompted her to take a closer look at her affairs. And she found the safe that was opened by the key with the blue fob." Jedidiah held up the key and turned, showing it to everyone in the courtroom.

"In that safe, your Honor," he said. He put the key back in his vest pocket. "Mrs. Wickham found ledgers with detailed transactions. She realized he was systematically embezzling funds. Funds from both her father's law firm, in which she is a principal, and her inheritance, both managed by . . ." He wheeled around and pointed to Tobias. "Tobias Wickham." He walked to Tobias and looked him in the eyes. "And with those ledgers were others detailing investments he made using the pilfered monies." As Jedidiah said the next sentence, his eyes rested on Charlotte. "Tobias Wickham did not know that Miriam Wickham had any knowledge of this key. He learned of it the evening she returned from seeing her daughter on Sunday, April 28, 1895. A blessed event occurred that day." He smiled at Charlotte and turned to face the bench. "The prosecution has proved Tobias Wickham had Miriam Wickham followed on that day. And it was on that day Miriam Wickham stood at the foot of Tobias' bed. She demanded the hospital staff produce his belongings and the key with the blue fob." He walked to Tobias and looked at him again. "It was in that moment Tobias Wickham knew. He knew his wife, Miriam Wickham, had evidence enough to incarcerate him for the rest of his life."

He turned and faced the Judge. "The next day, your Honor, Miriam Wickham and I met and went through the safe. Armed with her father's will, we then met with all of the bank managers and the security investment firms involved. We changed control of the accounts to Mrs. Wickham, femme sole. At that time, we were unaware of the bank account that Tobias Wickham used to finance his dastardly deeds. That was the account he had opened in the Taldmadge Bank and Trust. We first learned of it after his arrest on accessory-to-murder charges. Once informed of the arrest, Mrs. Wickham and I went to the rooms he occupied at his club. There we found yet another secret safe.

"Your Honor, we were astounded when we learned the total of the monies Tobias Wickham had stolen. The amount verified by the various institutions totaled . . ." Jedidiah stopped and looked around the courtroom. He waited until he had everyone's complete attention before he continued. ". . . It totaled five hundred fifty-one thousand, seven hundred thirty-four dollars and twelve cents." He turned and looked at Tobias, enjoying every second as their eyes met. A slight smile curled Jedidiah's lips as he shifted his glance and nodded to Miriam.

"Your Honor," he said. He turned to face the Judge. "Mrs. Miriam Harrington Wickham, the principal owner, and yours truly, the sole law-abiding partner of the firm of Harrington, Wickham, and Rue, and with the complete sanction of all family members, wish to put those funds to good use."

"Consequently, we ask the court," he said. He turned again. He walked toward Tobias and stared down at him. "What better hell is there for Tobias Wickham than to live the rest of his natural days in a facility called the Tey Aihàmson Memorial Hospital and Convalescent Home at Eaglet's Rest?" He lifted his head and looked at each one of the few faces who were in the courtroom, moving around the room as he spoke. "The funds will be used for the construction and maintenance of the facility. It will be built on the grounds purchased yesterday. And Dr. Charles Black, Sëkinehënaonkès, or 'Black Horse' in English, who is a highly qualified professional in the field, will oversee the general operations of the facility. All of the staff will be trained and educated at accredited institutions of higher learning. And this hospital will employ the Lenape along with other qualified professionals. They will be responsible for the care of Tobias Wickham." He turned to face Tobias. "Until the facility is operational, the family wishes he be sent to the hospital in the town of Kuwehòki. There, for the rest of his natural life, he will be dependent on a Lenape for his survival." He paused, watching Tobias' eyes. He turned to face the Judge. In closing, he said, "This is what the family of the deceased requests, if it pleases the court, your Honor." Jedidiah bowed, walked to the prosecutor's table and sat down.

The Judge, his chin in his hand with his fingers hiding the smile on his face, watched Jedidiah as he took his seat. He looked down at the documents and paged through them once more. "This certainly isn't what I had in mind but what a unique solution it presents," he said to no one in particular. He took several more minutes as he went through the documents. Then he closed the file and cleared his throat. He straightened his body in his chair and addressed Tobias Wickham. "Tobias Wickham," he said. "Having been found guilty of all charges presented before this court, from this day forward you will be remanded into the custody of Dr. Charles Sëkinehënaonkès Black. And, from here you will be taken to the hospital in the town of Kuwehòki, where every day for the remainder of your natural life you will be dependent on a Lenape, and only a Lenape, for your survival. Court is adjourned." He slammed his gavel down and left the bench."

Chapter 14
Mid Afternoon, October 22, 1951

My mother laughed. "Did that really happen? Did the Judge actually send him to the Lenapes? I think it is hysterical, Auntie."

"Yes, well, so did they—Aihàm, Violet, Miriam, Jedidiah, and Charlotte. The look on Tobias' face when he heard the sentence was priceless. But, as his guardian was wheeling him from of the courtroom, Miriam walked to his rolling chair. She looked at him and said, 'Who is in hell now, Tobias?' He looked like he was going to cry. He tried to reach for her hand, but she pulled away. He said things, unintelligible things that sounded like he was begging her. She was so angry that she cut him to shreds with her look. 'You will get no sympathy from me.' She spoke with a steely sternness that could have turned water at a full boil to ice. 'Nor from my daughter. You have burned that bridge for all time, and now you will wallow in its rubble.'

"And," Auntie said with a sigh, "it was over. The court gave Dr. Charlie Black custody of Tobias, and he took him to the hospital in Kuwehòki. Everyone else went home to pick up their lives where they had left off. Aihàm and Violet returned to their home in Kuwehòki, and Miriam and Jedidiah went back to life as they knew it in Camden. They seemed to do all right. It didn't seem too difficult for them to return to their normal routines. But Charlotte—Charlotte floundered. She poured herself into Welles. She lived vicariously through him, so much so everyone close to her worried about her state of mind. She had no other interests, nor did she wish to find any other than doting on her son. It wasn't normal, they thought. What will happen to Charlotte when she is separated from him? What will she do when Welles goes to school? He would be five on April 27, 1900, and he was due to start school in September the next year. So, they put their heads together and figured they had to find another interest for Charlotte. They began throwing soirées of a sort."

"What's a soirées?" I asked.

"Parties. They are parties, Danny," Auntie said.

"Like birthday parties?"

"No. They were dinner or supper parties. Every Friday supper and every Sunday dinner, all spring and summer, Miriam had a dinner party. An unsuspecting young man or two were always invited to her soirées. If memory serves me, there were the four new clerks Jedidiah had hired and, of course, his two new partners in the firm. And Aihàm and Violet invited several young men from their community. And Miriam invited quite a few young men she knew from her church group. They invited the sons and nephews of neighbors. They pressed Charlotte's old school chums for names of anyone they could think of."

"Did they ask you, Auntie? Did you give them names too?"

"Well, no. They never asked me, but Charlotte found it very amusing. She was always polite, and she enjoyed the evenings. Yet, she never accepted an invitation from any one of the young men. She wasn't interested in exploring the possibility of a relationship of any sort. She was quite content with life as it was. So, nothing changed. Time went by and soon a new century was ushered in. She and Welles enjoyed the spring and summer. She watched the excitement grow in her son as he anticipated going to school once he turned six in April 1901.

"Welles and Charlotte loved to take long walks. During the cold January and February of 1901, she'd bundle Welles up. They would embark on a new expedition that they had planned at breakfast that morning. She'd often pack a luncheon and, most times, their expedition led them to the park that was a block away. There they fed the ducks the stale bread that Miriam saved for them and had lunch by the old weeping willow tree. With the changing weather as spring approached, they wandered farther from the house. Sometimes they crossed Federal Street and visited the firehouse or window shopped. They always stopped at Reed's Confectionary Store for a stick of licorice. Then in March, on a sunshiney day with the puffy wind blowing, they neared the firehouse. The hook and ladder truck was outside. On that particular day, it was Tuesday. . . ."

Tuesday, March 26, 1901

Charlotte and Welles walked along Federal Street toward the firehouse. The hook and ladder truck was blocking the sidewalk. A fireman was washing it down after returning from an early morning run. Welles loved fire trucks. He loved firemen and firehouses and wanted to know everything there was to know about them.

"Here, Àna," Welles said with excitement as he handed his licorice to Charlotte, "I want to see it." Before Charlotte could stop him, he ran to the truck and started climbing up the side, trying to get on board.

"Welles," Charlotte scolded as she reached the truck. "Come down from there immediately. Do you hear me?"

"It's all right, ma'am," a man said from over Charlotte's shoulder. Charlotte turned in the direction of the man and stopped, transfixed by his mystique. His handsome brawn seemed to fight with the alluring gentleness she heard in his voice and saw in his eyes. She was sure she knew him and yet she didn't remember ever meeting this man who stood smiling before her.

"Youngsters do it all the time. I'd like to show him our toys and gadgets, ah, that is, if you don't mind? If memory serves me his name is Welles, isn't it?"

"Yes," Charlotte said, wondering how he knew that. "Yes, it is." She watched the fireman lift Welles onto the truck and climb up next to him. She studied his face. *I know this man from somewhere,* she thought, *but I cannot place him.*

The fireman explained to Welles how they filled the water tanks. Then showed him how they raised and lowered the ladders. After he explained every part on the top of the truck he and Welles climbed down. And he explained each of the gadgets and fittings along the side of the truck. Charlotte followed behind them, studying the man, racking her brain as she tried to place him. Several times the fireman glanced at Charlotte and smiled. When he finished telling Welles how everything worked, he lifted Welles up into the driver's seat. Then, in a low firm voice, he said, "New Recruit Welles, there's a three-alarm on Twenty-Seventh Street. I need you to go and help those people, so you'd better get a move on."

"Yes, sir!" Welles said, and he scooted across the seat, grabbing hold of the reins. The excited child shouted down to Charlotte, "Look, Àna, I'm driving the truck!"

"I see, Welles. Don't run anyone down on your way."

Charlotte laughed at Welles. And she turned toward the fireman, who was looking straight at her, smiling. Their eyes locked for several seconds until he said, "You don't remember me, do you?"

"I am so sorry. You are so familiar, and yet I cannot place you. Have we met before?" Charlotte asked, a bit embarrassed that she couldn't remember.

"Yes, but I had much longer hair then, Charlotte, ah, may I take the liberty and call you that?"

Charlotte shook her head yes and answered, "Yes, of course. You obviously know us. Please feel free. And you are, if I may be so bold?"

"Jules," he said and smiled. Charlotte furrowed her brow. She bit her bottom lip as she searched her memory for any recollection of him. "When did we meet?" she asked.

"At the wedding and then again when . . ." Jules watched her face and saw her bewilderment.

"Ah," he said. "I was introduced as Lainipën." Charlotte was still puzzled. He saw her confusion, and he touched her arm. Quietly he said, "I am the one who kept his vigil." And he waited to see her reaction.

Charlotte looked into his eyes, bewildered for a few moments. Then she breathed in sharply as the picture of a young man sitting at the head of Tey's casket flashed in her mind. Jules saw the pain in her eyes. He started chattering, saying anything that popped into his mind.

"Lainipën," he said, "means July in Lenape. You see, I was born in July, so my mother named me, ah, well, I'm not alone. I have a brother named January, and my sister is called August. And my father was called Sunday Monday. I guess my grandmother wasn't sure on which day he was born. And . . . well." Jules studied her face. He watched the momentary pain dissipate, and he shrugged with a roguish grin. A half smile curled Charlotte's lips as she surveyed this handsome man standing in front of her. He watched her eyes, and he tilted his head to one side. "Anyway, I needed an English name when I went to university. I didn't want to be known as July. I always took a lot of ribbing for my name; since I had a choice, I wanted a name that sounded professional. Everyone I know calls me Jul, so I changed it to Jules. I may have been inspired by Jules Verne. I can't say for sure, but I do enjoy his works. And I needed a middle and a last name to fill in the forms, so I thought to myself I'll break my name apart and . . ." Charlotte's smile now was spread across her face. "Ah, and I am babbling on. So, ah, Charlotte Aihàmson," he said, bowing from the waist. "I am known as Jules Laine Penn, and I'm turning the conversation over to you."

He smiled, and his eyes twinkled, lighting up his whole face when he looked at Charlotte. The way he looked at her and smiled was so familiar. It touched Charlotte's heart so that for a moment she couldn't think. She couldn't speak. She couldn't breathe.

She turned away to catch her breath. Then she cocked her head and turned to face him. She fixed her eyes on his. They looked at each other, lingering for a moment. She smiled and said, "Jules, it is a pleasure to see you again."

"Yes. It is a pleasure, Charlotte, yes, it is."

* * * * *

Jules began calling on Charlotte, and within six months they were keeping company. They talked a great deal about Tey and when they met. Jules told Charlotte that he fell in love with her that very day that she stepped off the train in Burlington. He told her he wanted so much to comfort her during those awful hours, but he couldn't. The wire Aihàm had sent asked him to take charge of the arrangements. "It was a great honor to be the one chosen and entrusted with keeping the vigil for Tey." Still, Jules said, "As I sat at his casket's head, I watched you. I couldn't take my eyes off of you. With every hour that passed my heart grew fuller and fuller. I knew someday, if the Creator deemed it so, we would meet again. And so now it has happened."

Charlotte too felt an immediate closeness to Jules that she had felt for no one other than Tey. She worried that what she was feeling wasn't an attraction but loneliness. She questioned if her loneliness would drive her to try reshaping Jules in Tey's image. For weeks, she whispered into the night darkness, calling Tey. She'd feel him in the quiet moments between her thoughts. She asked if he had sent Jules to her. She begged to know if this was the right path for her now. She knew he felt what was in her heart. And each time she asked, she sensed a certainty, an assurance that eased her disquiet. Still, she longed to know if he was comfortable with another man holding her as he had. And she yearned to know how he felt about another man raising Welles as he dreamed. And in that darkness came the signs that gave her reassurance and clarity. Jules knew her. He knew everything about her. Tey had shared his feelings, his hopes, and dreams with Jules as if he were grooming Jules to take his place. She knew no one could ever fill the void that Tey had left in her heart. But she grew certain Jules could fill the emptiness around it.

Chapter 15
Late Afternoon, October 22, 1951

"You see, it wasn't a fairytale, Diana," Auntie said as she smiled at my mother. "Or maybe it was. Either way on Saturday, March 28, 1903, Charlotte and Jules were married. The civil ceremony took place in the front parlor of Miriam Wickham's house."

My mother blushed when Auntie teased her, and grinned at her aunt, nodding in agreement.

"Officiating at the service was . . ."

"Jedidiah Rue," Mother whispered.

Auntie nodded. "Yes, Judge Jedidiah Rue who, at that time, sat on the bench of the Federal District Court of Camden County. In attendance were Aihàm and Violet, Jules' family, and a dozen close friends. After the reception, Charlotte and Jules went off to Atlantic City. They had a brief, four-day honeymoon."

"I liked Atlantic City when we went, didn't I, Mother?"

"Yes, you did. But, Dan, it's a lot different today than it was then."

"Did they see the diving horse, Auntie? Did they?"

"No, child. They had other things in mind, Danny."

"Like what, Auntie? Welles and Miriam—were they on their minds?"

"Well, yes, actually, they were. What school Welles should attend and Miriam. . . ." Auntie paused. "Danny, Charlotte was very worried about her mother." Auntie sighed. The sigh came from deep within her as if it were a lament. "You see, Charlotte and Jules lived with Miriam for several years. They watched as guilt ate her alive, powerless to stop it. It began when she went to the hospital herself to have Tobias sign a document. She thought it better than sending a clerk from the law firm. She said it would reaffirm her anger since she hadn't seen him since the trial. However, when she returned, she was distraught. Charlotte questioned her. She thought Tobias was being mistreated, but Miriam reassured her that it had nothing to do with his care. He was not being mistreated, she told Charlotte. In fact, he was being treated very well, and he looked very healthy. Charlotte pressed the issue, trying to determine what was bothering her. But Miriam became irritated and upset, and she retreated to her bedroom.

"As the next few weeks passed Miriam spent more and more time alone, brooding about Tobias. She exaggerated and amplified events that she felt were her transgressions against him. She'd tell Charlotte, 'if I hadn't said that about Barnaby,' or 'if I hadn't confronted him after the trial, he would never have suffered his fits.' And Charlotte would remind her about the hate he carried in his heart. And remind her that he was still determined to have Welles killed. And they would argue, back and forth, on and on.

"Miriam would listen to Charlotte, but nothing Charlotte said satisfied her. She didn't believe a single thing, and her guilt multiplied. And that guilt she amassed and carried on her shoulders was staggering. She tried to convince Charlotte that she was neglecting Tobias. But Charlotte's patience was wearing thin, so she chided her mother for it. 'But a good wife knows her duty and her duty is to see that her husband is well cared for,' was all Miriam would say in reply. She discounted every bit of sane reasoning and logic. She made up her mind that it was her duty and started going to the hospital to see him every day."

"But why, Auntie? He was such a bad, bad man."

"I know, Danny, but I guess deep down inside, Miriam cared for him. So, she started going to see him. She spent countless hours sitting by his side reading to him. She talked to him about the events happening in town as he glowered and spoke obnoxiously to her. She never made mention of Welles or Charlotte. Even when he prodded and insisted, she refused to discuss anything about them. When she came home, she was emotionally spent, and she would withdraw from the family.

"Charlotte knew in her heart that he was insidiously gnawing away at Miriam. Still, Charlotte couldn't convince her not to go and she'd go the next day and the next and the next until he finally died. She was with him. She wouldn't leave his side. She held his hand as he took his last breath, and it killed her. I am sure of it."

Auntie paused and rubbed her hands together. Mother reached across and touched Auntie's hand. "It's all right. Skip some details. I don't need to know everything."

Auntie patted Mother's hand and tried to smile. "Yes, you do. So, let me finish while it is in me to tell. . . . So . . . So after . . . after his funeral, she blamed herself even more. She blamed herself for his illness and his death. Every indiscretion he had ever committed she took upon her shoulders as a cross she must bear. She had convinced herself that she was the reason he suffered so. She assumed the blame for his deeds, especially Tey's death. She told Charlotte if she had been stronger with her, none of it would have happened. If she had not flaunted Welles' birth, Tey might have lived. And she affixed the hurt and sorrow Charlotte, Aihàm, and Violet endured to, what she truly believed, were her sins.

"Charlotte tried to console her, but Miriam's hopelessness and despair stymied her. And Miriam's depression worsened. Charlotte found it impossible to pull her back from her abyss. Still, Charlotte was determined that her mother would never succumb to it. So, each morning she fought with her to get dressed. She forced Miriam to come down the stairs, to socialize, to be with everyone. But every day Miriam refused to respond. And she sank deeper into her dark, despondent melancholia. She found no solace in prayer. Yet for hours she stayed on her knees in her bedroom praying night and day, begging for forgiveness for her sins. And each time Charlotte heard her pray, each time Charlotte saw her on her knees, she cursed her father. And when she did, Charlotte heard her father's laughter echo in her brain.

"In her last days, there was nothing, not even her precious Welles, that could save Miriam from her abyss. Her depression became so deep she didn't sleep and wouldn't or couldn't eat. She rarely spoke and she wasted away to nothing. It was nine months after the death of Tobias Wickham that Miriam Wickham succumbed to her demons.

"Welles was fifteen years old. Her death overwhelmed him with such grief as he sat at the supper table the night she died. And the pain and sorrow he felt because of losing the only woman he'd ever known as his mother came gushing out. It was a horrible . . . horrible evening . . . the evening of Tuesday, May . . ."

Tuesday, May 3 – Thursday, May 5, 1910

Welles pushed his food around his plate, staring down in deep thought. He was being tormented by more than Miriam's death that morning.

"It may help if you talk about what's bothering you, Welles," Charlotte said. She reached across the table to take his hand. He jerked his hand backward, looking up. He saw the concern spread across her face. He shook his head from side to side. He clenched his lips together until they were blue and scowled as he looked at her.

"I . . . I don't, I can't help thinking that . . ." he paused as anger lit his eyes.

Charlotte watched him and saw the fury, the fire inside him. It had been building for months. Every day after he came from Miriam's room, he was more and more troubled. He refused to talk to Charlotte. He refused to talk to anyone. He'd go to his room, shut the door, and keep the emotions he was feeling bottled up inside.

As Charlotte sat across the table from him, she watched his face, so full of sorrow. She could feel his anguish as it permeated the air around her. She waited as another silent minute passed. "Tell me," she said, pleading with him. "Tell me what you're thinking. Please tell me. Force yourself to talk it out or it will eat at you like the demons inside Mother consumed her."

"Demons. Yes. That's it. That's what I'm thinking. Those demons—she never should have had those demons. What happen to her never would have happened if . . . if . . . It's because of me. I caused her demons. I'm the reason they plagued her. That . . . that miserable, despicable, hateful man. He should have hung for his crimes. Instead, they allowed him to live so he could prey upon Mother. His vileness ate at her and sucked her dry. And to think I bear his name. Every time I went to see her, he was all she talked about. She thought she had betrayed him. Betrayed him, mind you. Why? Why did her mind go there? He was the guilty one. He hated, and he extracted his pound of flesh from her. Why not me? It was me he hated. It was every Indian alive that he hated. Me! I'm one of them. He hated me, and so he berated her. Why did she go? Àna, why did you allow her? Why didn't you stop her? Why did she listen to him? Why did she ever listen to such outlandish talk from such a loathsome individual? Was it because of me? If she had never taken me in, she would be alive. She would be our mother. That wonderful . . ." he paused and glared into space.

"Welles, that's not true," Charlotte said. "You are not the reason for her death. She loved you more than life itself. You were her reason to wake in the morning. Whatever filth my father filled her head with had nothing to do with you. You must believe that."

Welles stared at Charlotte as a frenzied calm came into his eyes. "That's not true. It had everything to do with me. Mother told me he called that Indian whore, 'the Jezebel that spawned me.' She told me he wanted to see her dead. Mother told me he condemned her for taking me in and helping that whore. That's what she told me. And each time she said it, I cringed. Inside me, I felt dirty. I feel a hate for a person I don't know, that I can't remember. That's the person I hold responsible for Mother's death. She is the cause of this. She is the guilty one, not Mother." He stopped. Charlotte's ears reverberated with the sound of each breath he took. "I asked Aihàm and Violet, but they wouldn't tell me anything. They won't talk about her. I asked people in the village, but no one will tell me anything. Why, Àna? Not even you. You won't tell me either. Mother wouldn't tell me. Who was this . . . this . . . this whore, this Jezebel who . . ? At times I think about her and I wonder what type of woman could do that. How could she have left me like that? And not a word since! She's never tried to even . . . not once did she try to contact me. What sort of a woman could do that? She has caused this. Her irresponsibility caused me to be. And because I was no use to her, she pushed me off on Mother like unwanted garbage. And that was all the ammunition Tobias Wickham needed, and he used it against Mother. So, am I wrong? Should I not hate her? Am I wrong?" He stood on the other side of the table, grasping the back of his chair and looking down at Charlotte.

Shocked and paralyzed by his words, Charlotte sat staring into his eyes. She moved her tongue across her lips and in a quiet, unfaltering voice she said, "Yes. Yes, Welles. You are wrong. She gave you this. She gave you Mother. Don't you see that? Do you think you could pause your hate for a moment and take a look around you? Could you take a moment and think about what Mother did and remember what she wanted for you? Would this have been possible otherwise? If Mother had not taken you in, where would you be? I know in my heart that the woman who gave you to Mother loved you every bit as much as I do. She loved you so much, in fact, that she gave you up . . . she gave you to Mother so you could have this. Can't you see that?" Charlotte stared at him. Her heart was pounding in her chest, and she was unable to breathe.

Welles shook his head. "No. No, I don't. But it doesn't

matter now. Mother is dead. She is dead because that Indian whore who bore me couldn't keep her knees together. That's what matters. And I will hate her till the day I die!"

Charlotte studied the face of her son, her mouth gaping open. And for the first time in his life she was not able to respond to him. Jules reached out and put his hand on Charlotte's shoulder. As he moved to her side he said, "Welles, there is more to the story than you are aware of. There are reasons that . . ."

"No, Jules," Charlotte interrupted. "Let him be. Please . . . Please . . . Please, let it be." She stood and smoothed her apron with her trembling hands. She cleared the table and carried the dishes to the sink. She said nothing more. She didn't turn to look at either of them. She washed the supper dishes and left the room.

Miriam Wickham was laid to rest two days later. The minister of the church where Miriam had worshiped her whole life presided. Charlotte held Welles in her arms during the final gravesite service. When his tears subsided, she kissed his forehead and asked him to go to the carriage. "I'll follow in a few minutes," she told him. "I have an issue to settle with my father. It doesn't concern you. It is between my father and me." Welles nodded and left with the minister. They followed behind the other mourners as they walked from the grave.

Jules ignored Charlotte's urgings and refused to leave her. He stood and watched as Charlotte walked to her father's side of the burial plot where his remains were laid to rest. The last time they were there was the day of his funeral. Charlotte had no desire to return again. But today it was Charlotte's duty and responsibility to follow her mother's wishes to the letter. And Miriam Wickham was buried beside her husband, Tobias Wickham.

Charlotte stood next to her mother looking at her father's headstone for a long time. She felt no sorrow. She felt no grief. All she felt was an ever-present anger and a hate that churned inside her whenever she thought of him. "Well, Father," she said in a voice filled with venomous rancor. "You've claimed your second victim. You sucked the life from Mother as willfully as you took Tey's. And she succumbed to your will. But Father, I never will nor will my son. You robbed me of his father. You robbed me of a title, but in spite of everything you did I still have had the joy of raising him. And you will never touch him, ever. You taught me well, Father. And every day that I live I will never forgive you because it is impossible for me to forget. I will do all in my power to fan the flames of the hell-fires that burn around you. And I will pay the Devil his due to keep you asunder. So, mark my words, Father—your reach is no more. It stops here. You will not claim my son! You will not claim me . . . ever!"

She turned and walked to her mother's open grave. She looked down at her mother's casket. She stood in silent prayer with tears running down her face for many minutes. Unable to stifle her sobs she said, "Oh Mother, my dearest Mother, I've done what you wished and . . . I hate it. I just hate it." She fought back more tears as she bent down to pick up a stray flower by the open grave. "The thought of you next to him makes me sick." She threw the flower into the open grave. "In my heart, I know he is responsible for this. From his grave, he pulled you in. He wheedled his way into your soul and ate you alive. When he had consumed every morsel, he left you to die. I felt it. From the depths of hell, I felt him. I heard his laughter, and I saw his satisfaction at leaving you a broken shell. I despise him, Mother, and all that he ever stood for. He hated with a hate unparalleled and he taught me well. So, mark my words, Mother, he will never take our precious Welles. I swear as God is my witness, he will never possess my son. Never!" Charlotte opened her clenched fists. She stared into the open grave as tears continued to run down her cheeks. She crouched down next to the open grave and picked up a handful of dirt. She raised her hands to her lips and said, "I love you, Mama. I will miss you every day I live. I will pray every day that you find the peace you so well deserve. Goodbye, my darling Mother." She kissed the dirt in her hands and tossed it on top of the coffin. She rose to her full height and raised her eyes, looking to the heavens. "Dear God, Lord of all Creation, please take my mother into your arms. I beg you, Lord. Look after her . . . please." She lowered her head. She turned, took Jules' arm, and they walked from the grave.

Chapter 16
Almost Suppertime, October 22, 1951

"The truth! Why wasn't the truth told?" Diana asked. "It was perfect timing. Welles needed to know. Why wasn't he told?"

"Because, Diana, sometimes things are better left unsaid. True, they'd broached the subject. But, the state of mind that Welles was in after Miriam's death was tenuous. Charlotte knew that it could cause a rift that she may never be able to repair. In her mind, that was too great a price to pay. She had made her choice long ago, and she knew that 'Curses are like young chickens, they always come home to roost.' She had steeled herself for it.

"So, Charlotte and Jules sold the old house and moved away. They purchased a brand-new home on 27th Street. The new house was across the street from the firehouse where Jules was stationed.

"Near here, Auntie? Your house is on 27th Street and the firehouse is across the street too."

"Yes, it is, Danny, the house where Welles grew up. He was smart, like you. Quick-witted and eager to learn, and in 1912, at the age of seventeen, he was accepted at Princeton where he read law. Jedidiah was thrilled that he chose to study law, and he took him under his wing. He tutored him every chance he could, and Welles loved it. Welles worked at the firm every free moment he had. He pumped Jedidiah for any tidbits of knowledge he could get out of him.

"By the time Welles was twenty, he had grown to be

an attractive young man. He looked very much like his father with dark, brown-black hair and eyebrows. He had dazzling, bright, dark brown eyes that seemed to shine and twinkle from within. His smile was quick and always genuine, and he laughed at the smallest things. He stood over six feet and was as muscular and agile as his father had been. And he gave no quarter to anyone about his heritage. Charlotte was so proud of her son. She found it hard to stop the tears of joy that always came into her eyes every time he entered a room.

"That same year Jedidiah Rue resigned from the bench of the Federal District Court. He was in his sixties now and he told Charlotte and Jules he missed his private practice and wanted to return to it. Charlotte and Jules thought it was due to the threats he was receiving. Several times he ruled against the crime syndicates that had recently sprung up. You see, a new evolving tide became prevalent after the turn of the century. Urban conditions changed considerably. This change created an excellent environment for organized crime to grow and grow it did. Crime syndicates sprang up in a lot of cities. They gained prominence and notoriety from Camden to Atlantic City, and from New York to Chicago.

"Al Capone. He was in Chicago. I read about Al Capone in our new encyclopedias. There is a whole section on gangster stuff. Did you know any gangsters, Auntie?"

"Afraid not, Danny. We were much too straitlaced for them."

"What about Welles? Did he know any boys in school who worked for them?"

"Not that I'm aware of. Danny, Al Capone didn't become notorious until the 1920's. Welles went to

Princeton in 1912. I don't think Princeton had that problem then. But in 1915, he met someone and fell in love. Would you like me to tell you about that?"

"I would," Mother said. "Everything you remember."

Auntie nodded and said, "And so I shall. Well . . . One evening, when Welles was on spring vacation, he met Alice Hardtack at a church supper. Alice and her mother, Missus Elmira Hardtack, lived in rented rooms. Their house was across Federal Street from where Charlotte, Jules, and Welles lived. They recently moved in after Alice's father died. He left them with limited resources.

"Welles and Alice kept company for two years. And against all entreaties from Charlotte, Jules, and Jedidiah, Welles decided to marry Alice. Charlotte didn't like it one bit but accepted it. He was of age and could do whatever he chose without her consent. Besides, she told Jules and Jedidiah, "I have no right to interfere. Remember, I too went against both my parents' wishes when I married his father. I'd be an absolute hypocrite if I tried to stand in his way now." Jules and Jedidiah agreed with Charlotte, and, even though they didn't like it, they acquiesced.

"So, Welles and Alice were married on Saturday, February 10, 1917. The ceremony took place in the front parlor of the home of Charlotte and Jules Penn. Unbeknown to them was the fact that Alice was pregnant at the time. A week later, Welles told Charlotte of Alice's delicate condition. Quite shocked by the news, Charlotte tried to quell her disappointment. And she welcomed Alice into their family. But she worried that with a new wife and a child on the way, Welles wouldn't finish school. He still had several months to go until he graduated.

"With that in mind, Charlotte tried to convince Welles

and Alice to move into their large, empty house to no avail. Alice wouldn't even consider it. She was adamant that they were moving in with her mother. She would not discuss any other options. That proved to be a much bigger problem than Charlotte ever imagined.

"Alice's mother, Elmira Hardtack, didn't like Charlotte. When they first met at the wedding they didn't get off to a good start. Elmira thought Charlotte had uppity ways. She was convinced that Charlotte thought Alice beneath her and not worthy of Welles at all. But during the wedding reception Charlotte tried to make Elmira and especially Alice comfortable. She went to extremes, introducing them to everyone. She made sure they were part of every conversation. Welles later told Charlotte that they felt that she had put them on exhibition—that she made them the brunt of cruel jokes for her own amusement instead. Charlotte had no idea what to do to correct the situation. The two women were both surly sorts and Charlotte had never dealt with their likes before. And, every time Charlotte tried to mend the relationship it made things worse.

"Alice didn't seem to care what her new husband's family thought. Nor did she make any effort to rectify the situation. In fact, it was as if she enjoyed throwing more wood on the fire. Every time they met, she chided Charlotte, saying things like, 'You are not his mother. A sister, that's all. And not even his blood. Stop trying to control him and leave us alone.'

"Charlotte was finding it difficult to contain her anger. She assumed, right or wrong, that Alice's remarks were at the insistence of her mother. So, to keep peace, Charlotte decided it best to stay away. She seethed inside as she watched the way Alice and Elmira treated Welles. Still, she kept her distance and left them alone. And as Alice's pregnancy advanced, her humor grew even more caustic and matters between Charlotte, Elmira, and Alice deteriorated even more. Welles tried and tried to smooth things. But Alice, fueled by her mother's animosity toward Charlotte, was having none of it.

"The struggle to see Welles became an unmitigated fight for Charlotte. If she saw him, he was alone, and Charlotte knew he would face Alice's wrath because of it. But none of it seemed to bother him. Welles took it all in stride. He stayed in good humor and at the top of his class, and he graduated from Princeton with honors in May of 1917. He turned on his charm and made the best of his situation. He had this incredible ability, and he rolled with the punches as the whole world changed around him. And change it most certainly did.

* * * * *

"Well, I am quite parched. Would anyone like a glass of pop? Danny, a bottle of that soda you like so much is in the pantry."

"Yes, please," I said and jumped out of my chair to get the soda. When I returned, Auntie was leaning over the kitchen sink prying ice cubes from her ice tray. On her sideboard were three glasses. She put several cubes in each of the glasses and took the bottle of soda from my hands.

"You too, Diana?"

"No," Mother said. "We are so close; don't stop now."

Mother's tone made Auntie spin around and look at

her. Auntie frowned until her nose wrinkled. "I have no intentions of stopping. My intent is to tell you everything. I thought that's what you wanted."

Mother nodded. "Yes. Yes, I do. Please. I didn't mean to . . . Do you understand at all my need to know?"

Auntie filled the three glasses with soda. She handed one glass to me and carried the two remaining glasses back to the table. She placed a glass in front of my mother and stood there for a moment gazing at her. She took her place at the table and tilted her soda glass from side to side. She listened to the clink of the ice cubes and watched the soda's foam climb up the sides. "And so, you shall," she said. "You will know every detail that my memory allows me to recall. Every last one. . . ."

She took a sip and placed the glass in front of her. She kept her eyes on her glass as she expelled air through puckered lips. "I believe I was telling you about Welles and about . . . Yes. . . . Well . . . When Welles came home from Princeton for the last time, he stepped from the train into a city he didn't recognize. Miles and miles of hard surface roadways had replaced the rutted dirt roads of the past. Automobiles raced down city streets, replacing the horse and buggy by the dozens. Trolley cars and buses ran along every highway and byway, taking passengers far and wide. Indoor plumbing with hot and cold running water, with flushing toilets, had become the law. And the DAT&T serviced many homes and businesses in town with an implement called the telephone. Every day new lines were being strung from the Atlantic Ocean to all points west. People found the convenience of the telephone astounding. It was a marvel of the time.

"After graduation, Welles went to work as an

apprentice in the firm. He obtained the needed certification from the court. They declared he was of good moral character. And Jedidiah assigned him to several cases where another set of eyes were needed. Welles was diligent and smart, and Jedidiah was so proud of him. And then on June 6, 1917," Auntie looked into my mother's eyes.

"June 6th! That's your birthday, Mother."

"Danny, hush. Please. I need to hear this. Please go on."

"On June 6, 1917, Welles received the call that Alice was in labor and he needed to go home. He rushed to her side. By seven forty-five that evening he held in his arms the most beautiful little girl he thought he had ever seen." Auntie smiled at my mother. "Alice delivered the baby without any complications. The baby was small but healthy. And within minutes of her birth, she became the most important person in Welles Taylor Wickham's life."

Auntie stopped for a moment. She wiped her nose with her handkerchief. "Welles adored his baby girl. He also knew that Charlotte and Jules would never see his precious Diana unless he made the effort. So, he threw caution to the wind and didn't give a damn what repercussions there were. And every evening, from the time Diana was three days old, after he had supper with Alice he bundled up his baby daughter. He put her in the pram, and he walked to the Penn house so Charlotte and Jules could see his baby daughter. Even on evenings when the snow was too deep to push the pram, Welles held his baby daughter in his arms. And he trudged through the snow to the Penn house. He didn't let a day pass without making sure Charlotte and Jules saw Diana.

"Then," Auntie said and closed her eyes. "In 1918 . . .

the unthinkable happened." Auntie got to her feet, turned and walked to the sideboard. She braced herself on her sink and rocked back and forth for a few moments. Then she turned and put the meatloaf in the oven. She stood there staring at the wall and, after an exaggerated sigh, she walked to the table and sat down.

Auntie stared at Mother for several moments as a horrific, pained look painted her face. Her voice quivered as she said, "On . . . On Friday, September 27, 1918 . . ."

Friday, September 27 – Saturday, December 14, 1918

The headline in the evening paper read: INFLUENZA IS HERE. The article said: The first case of the influenza pandemic was reported in the State of New Jersey. A soldier at Fort Dix, who had returned from Europe days before, was its first victim in New Jersey today. For months, an influenza pandemic had been sweeping across Europe. . .

By October 22, 1918, it was estimated that there were 150,000 cases with 4,400 deaths in New Jersey alone. It spread so rapidly it seemed unstoppable, and so many people were victims of it. So many people that Charlotte and Jules knew and loved died in the pandemic. Aihàm and Violet were first. They died on October 11, 1918, within hours of each other. The community of Kuwehòki held a beautiful funeral for them. Aihàm and Violet had the full Lenape rite, and they were buried beside their beloved son Tey, Miltëwakàn. Charlotte, Jules, and Jedidiah attended the services.

And still the deaths kept coming. They came so fast

there was barely time to grieve. Next were Jedidiah's wife and daughter. They died within two days of one another. But he was fortunate. He was able to bury them. How odd to even think Jedidiah fortunate because he was able to have a funeral for them.

But shortly after Jedidiah lost his wife, funerals were banned. Health officials thought that funerals helped the disease spread. But it didn't help. And the nightmare continued. People were dying so fast that dead bodies accumulated everywhere without being buried. It was a common occurrence to go outside and see dead bodies lying in the streets. Sanitary workers with wagons came along every day and picked up the dead. They piled them on their wagons one on top of the other. They used teams of horses to dig mass graves so they could bury those they collected. Thousands of people were thrown into unmarked mass graves. But, no one thought to make note of the location of the graves. No one even bothered to write down the names of those buried in them.

Late in November 1918, Welles felt achy and feverish. He was exhibiting the first symptoms of the influenza. And everyone agreed that he should go to the Penn house so the baby wouldn't be near him. So, Welles moved upstairs to his bedroom where Charlotte nursed him.

Jules went through a bout of the disease ten days before. Those moments when Jules' temperature soared were so vivid in Charlotte's mind. So as soon as she knew Welles was in his bed, she gathered everything she needed and took it to his bedside. For four days she bathed him as his fever raged, and on the fourth night it broke. But Charlotte knew the disease was insidious. She had witnessed it firsthand with Jules. She knew she must continue, or the disease still might take him. So, she kept her vigil, sitting right by his side. All through the night she bathed him, cooling his body. She prayed his fever would stay down but when dawn broke, his fever rose again. She and Jules worked and worked to bring his body temperature down. Welles labored to take every breath and as exhaustion set in on his ravaged body, he lost the fight. On the afternoon of November 28, 1918, Welles Taylor Aihàmson Wickham, Charlotte's darling child, died in her arms.

The funeral ban was in effect when Welles died. But Charlotte wouldn't call the authorities. She refused to bury Welles in a mass grave. She would not under any circumstances. She knew it was against the law. Still she told Jules, in no uncertain terms, "I'll bury him myself in my own backyard before I allow that!"

Jules understood how she felt and suggested that they give him the full Lenape rite. "After all," Jules said, "he is the son of a warrior and the grandson of a Chief." Charlotte was so relieved. "It is the perfect solution," she told him.

Late in the evening on the day Welles died, Charlotte and Jules wrapped his body in a blanket. They carried his body from their house and placed him in the backseat of their car. Then they drove along the old Blackwoodtown Road to the Indian burial grounds. As they drove, Jules explained the old traditional ways to Charlotte. He stressed that his grandfather felt white man's laws infringed on Lenape beliefs. Jules said his grandfather insisted that he learn the many Lenape traditions he knew. He was afraid, with time, these traditions would be lost. He had hopes that someday Jules would tell the young

Lenape of the true traditional ways. "And tonight," he said, "my grandfather would be proud to know that we are giving this good son of the Lenape a proper traditional funeral."

So, on a mild, starlit November night, they chose the perfect place to bury Charlotte's beloved son. It was the empty space between Welles' grandparents, Aihàm and Violet, and his father Tey, Miltëwakàn. They removed Welles from their car and laid his body on the ground wrapped in his favorite blanket. Jules removed the handkerchief Charlotte had placed over Welles' face. He painted Welles' face with three red stripes so that the creator would know he was a son of the Lenape. Then he chanted a Lenape prayer over the body.

They dug the grave as long, wide, and deep as Lenape tradition dictated. And Charlotte wrapped her son in his favorite blanket. They placed Welles in the grave on his side. Then they curled his body into the fetal position with his head pointing east. They placed in the grave things for his spirit to use as it searched for its place in the happy hunting ground. They covered his body with the soil they had removed to make the grave. And they topped it with a layer of dry soil and leaves so the ground looked undisturbed.

When they finished, Jules recited and chanted the Lenape prayers his grandfather had taught him. And Charlotte read a few passages from her Bible. Then, as was Lenape custom, they spread a blanket at the head of his grave and ate the food Charlotte had prepared. They camped near the burial grounds for the next three nights, keeping a vigil at his grave. Each evening as the sun was setting, they lit a fire. All through the night they tended the fire. This ensured that Welles' spirit could join his grandparents and father in the happy hunting ground. For the twelve days that followed, every mirror in their house was covered. And Charlotte let her hair down in keeping with the Lenape customs.

During those twelve days of mourning that followed, Jules spent hours carving a kìkinhikàn. He engraved it with a fire truck and finished it in a polished, bright, fire-engine-red hue. On the twelfth day, he and Charlotte returned to the burial grounds. They placed the kìkinhikàn in the east at the head of the grave containing Welles Taylor Aihàmson Wickham.

The pandemic that took the life of Welles Taylor Aihàmson Wickham continued until it ran its course in 1919.

Chapter 17
Early Evening, October 22, 1951

Tears were running down Auntie's face. My mother reached across the table and took hold of her hands. "It's all right. We can stop if you want. You don't have to tell us anymore. It's all right."

Auntie shook her head yes as her voice raised an octave and trembled with sorrow. "Yes, I do. You should have heard all this a long time ago."

She rose from her chair and walked to the stove and peeked in on her meatloaf. She went to the sink and washed her hands. Several moments passed before she sat down in her chair. She didn't look at either Mother or me. She looked at the table and smoothed the surface as if there was a tablecloth on it. She heaved a long sigh, expelling the air through puckered lips. She looked across the table at my mother and spoke. There was such pain, heartache in her voice it brought tears to my eyes.

"And afterward . . . afterward, the carnage of the influenza continued and . . . Charlotte, once again, floundered. It was almost impossible for anyone to console her. She was in so much pain. Deep inside her she felt an aching emptiness after Welles' death. She seemed to care about nothing. People they were close to or that they knew continued to die. Every day someone died. Every day . . . but their deaths didn't seem to touch her at all. She couldn't even find it in her heart to extend her condolences. Her grief was consuming her. As hard as Jules tried, there was nothing he could do. At the mere mention of his name or glance at a photograph, Charlotte dissolved in tears. Then, a little less than two weeks after his death, rumors started. The rumors concerned Welles.

"Rumors about him?" Mother asked. "What about? What could anyone possible say about him?"

"Well, shortly after Welles' death, Millie Hertzog Jennings, came to see Charlotte. She was Charlotte's oldest and dearest friend. She told Charlotte an outlandish rumor she had heard. She hoped it would jolt Charlotte out of her depression and get her to laugh.

"She told her that everyone they knew was passing it off as the musings of an envious, jealous woman. She said they were quite amused by it. But Charlotte found nothing amusing in the rumors at all. Instead, she seethed as she listened to Millie.

"The rumor Millie heard came from the mouth of Elmira Hardtack. She was saying that Welles never provided for them. She said that that's what she'd expected from someone reared by that woman, Charlotte Penn! Elmira claimed his equity in the law firm belonged to Alice, not Charlotte. She claimed that Charlotte wouldn't release even a penny of it to Alice. She said it was Charlotte's doing that Alice was stripped of her rightful inheritance. Millie said Elmira was indignant, even hostile when speaking of Welles. She told everyone how he was spineless for not making sure 'that woman' wouldn't starve us all."

Auntie stopped and gazed off into space. She rubbed her palms together and for a long time I don't think she took even one breath. When she inhaled, she filled her chest and held it in. Then she puffed out her cheeks and I heard the air escape as she forced it through her lips. She turned to Mother and in an anguished, yet resolute voice asked, "Are you sure you want to hear all of this?"

"Yes! I want to know everything about Welles and Alice," Mother answered. "As much as you remember—Please."

Auntie nodded. "Alright then. Well, Charlotte, anxious to hear what else Elmira was saying, started visiting people. She invited herself to the homes of friends and acquaintances. She had to hear the rumors for herself even though the rumors upset her and made her angry. Then when she heard a new accusation that Elmira made, she'd talk to Jules then ask Jedidiah if she could sue her for slander. Both told Charlotte to bite her tongue and let it pass. But as each day passed Charlotte found that harder and harder to do.

"For three months Elmira slandered Charlotte and Welles. She lay in wait for Charlotte to respond in kind. But, when no response came from Charlotte, Elmira marched into Jedidiah's office. She went right to his desk and confronted him with her accusations. She stood in front of Jedidiah and demanded that her daughter reap the benefits she deserved. She threatened to file suit against the firm it that didn't happen.

"Well, Jedidiah mollified the situation. He chalked up her outburst to a frivolous, idle threat. Then the papers were served. She had seen a lawyer in Philadelphia.

"Why didn't the firm give Alice a pension, Auntie?" my mother asked.

"Because there was no such thing as a pension at that time. Besides, even if the firm had one, she wasn't entitled to it. Welles wasn't a partner, Diana. He wasn't vested in the firm. He wasn't even a clerk. He was an apprentice. He made a good salary, more than the other apprentices. Charlotte saw to that. And Welles handled his finances well. He had saved quite a tidy sum. But being a partner, well, that may have happened. Still, it was several years down the road. Welles had much to learn about the practice of law before the other partners would even consider it. And Elmira's suit, well . . . Jedidiah felt that it wasn't worth his or anyone else's time to fight. So even thought her claim was outlandish, he opted to settle shortly after he received the papers.

"Still, Elmira's animosity toward Charlotte continued to grow. And after she and Alice signed the agreement with the firm, a rumor about Diana started. Elmira told everyone she hated the fact that her daughter married a half-breed Lenape. Now they must raise his squalling half-breed brat. So, Charlotte pressed Jedidiah on what she should do. He reminded her she had no legal standing where the child was concerned. He advised her to remain silent and keep her distance.

"Then, four months after Welles' death the rumors changed. Charlotte heard that Elmira had arranged a marriage for her daughter. Alice and Mr. Herman Ganns, a man thirty-seven years Alice's senior, were now betrothed. Herman Ganns was a good man. He was highly respected in the community. He was a jeweler in town who had a thriving business. And he was a man of considerable means. Within days of hearing the rumor Herman Ganns moved into the Hardtack's home. The next week they wed, and Herman had the responsibility of supporting the family.

"Several months passed before the whole neighborhood buzzed anew. The rumor went around that

Alice was pregnant with Herman Ganns' child and that he was delighted. He had no children by any previous marriages, and he had longed for an heir. But Herman Ganns, like Elmira Hardtack, wanted nothing to do with Alice's first child."

"Was he good to her, Auntie?" Mother asked. "And her daughter . . . what happened ..."

"Wait." Auntie held up her hand, interrupting my mother. She hesitated for several moments before tilting her head to one side. She grimaced and said, "Diana, again rumors were all Charlotte heard. And rumor had it that Herman Ganns was an irrational, demanding sort. She heard that everyone in his household was forced to kowtow to his every whim, and Alice had a hard time with it all. The rumor was that Alice didn't particularly care for the man. She married him to gain financial security for the family in exchange for producing an heir. However, producing his heir became more difficult for her each day.

"She was miserable. She found it impossible to please her new husband. And she had many health problems that began in her second month. Her health problems plagued her throughout her pregnancy. Then, on April 24, 1920, she started hemorrhaging. Her mother rushed her to the hospital in excruciating pain. Her attending physician had to take the child immediately or Alice would die. So, they took Alice into surgery. A few hours later Herman Ganns learned that he had a son but that his wife's condition was critical. For three days Alice suffered. An infection set in and coursed through her body, causing her death on April 27, 1920.

"Faced with raising his infant son, Herman Ganns turned to Elmira Hardtack. Elmira told everyone she offered to care for the infant. It was and I quote, 'Out of the goodness of my heart.' In truth, Elmira Hardtack had no option. Herman Ganns was her sole support. So, she and Herman took the infant home.

"Less than a week later Charlotte heard rumors about Diana. 'That poor little thing,' the rumors said. "So young to wander the streets alone. It's all her grandmother can do to take care of the infant. Is it any wonder the girl is unkempt? The babe is such a handful and her poor grandmother has no one to help.' That was all Charlotte kept hearing.

"For several days after the rumors started, Charlotte walked to the corner of her street. She would cross Federal Street and search in the direction of the Hardtack house, hoping to see Diana. The rumors could be wrong, and she is fine, she thought. She was frantic about the child, so she broke down and talked to Jules. She told him what she had heard and asked him if he thought she should go talk to Elmira. Jules warned Charlotte not to interfere. He told her nothing but trouble would follow. Charlotte went to Jedidiah for advice, but he told her the same thing. Still, every day Charlotte grew more and more apprehensive. She couldn't stand by and do nothing. Charlotte paced the halls of her house until she couldn't stand it anymore. Then, on a May morning, she walked across Federal Street heading toward Elmira's house."

Auntie twirled her soda in her glass before she looked at my mother. Mother leaned forward and put her elbows on the table. She clasped her fingers together and put her chin on her out-stretched thumbs. She smiled. "And," she said.

Auntie smiled. "She had no idea what would happen

once she arrived, but as she neared, she saw little Diana sitting on the front steps. It was a cool, nasty day in the early part of May. The sky threatened to rain any second. Diana was sitting on the front stoop with barely any clothes on," she said as she looked into my mother's eyes. "Diana looked up and saw her and beamed." Auntie smiled wider than I had ever seen her smile before. "Diana recognized her and ran down the steps into Charlotte's welcoming arms.

"The last time Diana saw Charlotte was two weeks before her mother died. She came with Alice to Charlotte's house to pick up a check. It was a payment for Welles' work on a case that the firm recently settled. It was a nice visit. Alice stayed for quite a while and Charlotte was able to play with Diana and Diana remembered her.

"So, as she held Diana in her arms Charlotte thought about talking to Elmira. But, she thought, if I ask for permission an altercation would surely ensue. She dismissed that thought and, instead, asked Diana if she would like to come and have lunch with her. Diana smiled at Charlotte and nodded. That was how it started.

"Every day for several weeks after that, even when Jules had off, Charlotte walked to Elmira's house. She'd take Diana home to spend the day and Diana looked forward to seeing Charlotte. She trusted that Charlotte would come for her. So, every morning after Elmira sent her outside for the day, she scurried down the steps. Then she ran to the corner of her street and watch and wait for Charlotte to come. When Diana saw Charlotte in the distance she'd jump up and down, so excited to see her. She never crossed the street. Diana knew she wasn't allowed to. She just waited, watching Charlotte until she was near enough to run into her arms. Then they'd walk hand in hand to Charlotte's house where Charlotte bathed her and washed her clothes. She dressed her in pretty, clean dresses she had purchased for her and fed her good things to eat. They played and talked, and Diana loved it. But they both knew when evening came it was time for Charlotte to walk Diana back to Elmira's house. And Charlotte knew she had to leave Diana there. It tore Charlotte's heart to shreds.

"When Elmira Hardtack realized it was Charlotte who fed and clothed Diana, she became incensed. She was so infuriated that she went back to her lawyer. And, with great pleasure she served Charlotte with a Cease and Desist Order. She told Charlotte, 'The next time you even think about taking Diana, you will find your ass in jail!' She slapped the order into Charlotte's hand and stared into Charlotte's eyes with a look that could freeze Satan's lair. Then she turned and walked away five or six paces and looked back over her shoulder at Charlotte. She had such a smug smirk on her face that Charlotte took it as a signal for war.

"Charlotte knew she was in the wrong. She should never have taken Diana without permission. Still, she seethed as she watched Elmira cross Federal Street. And with every step Elmira took Charlotte vowed she would get Diana away from her. But the law was on Elmira's side. Diana's mother had no will, she named no guardian and so the child went to the next of kin. That was Elmira. Still, there had to be a way and Charlotte was sure Jedidiah knew what that way was. So, she donned her bonnet and marched into Jedidiah's office with the Cease and Desist Order in hand.

"I need your help, Jedidiah," Charlotte said as she handed him the order.

"Elmira Hardtack, Charlotte?" Jedidiah asked, smiling at her.

And what a glorious series of events were set in motion. Jedidiah went right to work on the problem, and by Tuesday, July. . ."

Tuesday, July 27, 1920

Diana sat on the front steps of her house, trying to pick up the large glass of milk that was on the step beside her. The nice lady who came for her every day didn't come anymore and she blamed herself. Still she didn't know what she had done wrong that made her grandmother so angry about her. But her grandmother said she couldn't go with her ever again. Grandmother said if she did, she would be severely punished. But Diana liked her. She liked going to her house. She was sad she didn't come to get her anymore.

Diana, a bright three-year-old, had sparkling dark-brown eyes like her father's. Her curly golden-brown hair was unkempt and in need of a good brushing. She was quite small for her age, and she looked like there wasn't a drop of fat on her tiny frame. Remnants of her last meal smudged her face and her underpants smelled like they hadn't been changed in a week. Her dress was filthy, as were her hands, and she had no shoes on her little feet. She looked up as a police officer and a woman wearing a red dress approached her. They smiled at Diana and Diana like them instantly.

"Hello," she said. "My name is Diana. Do you want to

see Grandmother?" She spoke very distinctly for a three-year-old, and she constructed sentences that were beyond her years.

"Yes. Yes, I do," the officer said. "But first, we'd like to talk to you, Diana. Is that all right with you?"

Diana clapped her hands, smiling. "Yes! Yes! I love to talk to people but so few stop to talk to me. There was a . . . a lady who used to come and talk to me, but she doesn't come anymore." Diana looked from the officer to the woman. They sat down on the steps beside her.

"Is this your breakfast, Diana?" the woman asked.

Diana shook her head yes. "But I have to dunk the bread because I can't lift the glass. It's too big. It keeps slipping out of my hands."

"Here," the officer said. "Let me help you." He lifted the glass to Diana's lips, and she drank hungrily from it. When the milk was gone the officer put the glass down, and Diana said, "Thank you for your help."

"You are a smart little thing," the officer said and looked at the woman.

"Grandmother says I'm too smart for my own good. She doesn't like it one bit."

"Well, I want to talk to your grandmother now; Diana, please go with Mrs. Harris," he said, pointing to the woman in the red dress. "She is going to take you to the van parked in front of your house, right there." He pointed to the van. "Will you do that for us?"

Diana looked at the officer and at the woman. Both were smiling at her. She turned back to face the officer and shook her head no, saying, "Grandmother won't like it one bit." Diana turned toward the woman and said, "A nice lady like you used to come every day and take me to a nice place. My grandmother didn't like that one bit. She punished me for going with her. Now she doesn't come anymore. I liked her. She made me look pretty. She gave me good things to eat. But she doesn't come for me anymore. Grandmother will make you go away too, won't she?"

"That lady didn't go away, Diana. That lady sent us to bring you to her. She is in the van waiting for you. Will you go to the van with me?"

"Will I get in trouble again? I don't want to get punished again."

"No one is going to punish you, Diana. I promise."

"Then I will. Yes. I will." Diana took hold of Mrs. Harris' hand and started down the steps and stopped. "That nice lady, the one who lives across the big street; she is in the van?"

"Yes, she is. Mrs. Penn, will you please show yourself!" Mrs. Harris shouted. Charlotte opened the van door and waved at Diana. Diana laughed when she saw her, and she jumped down a step to go to Charlotte. She stopped short before she went down any further and looked at Charlotte pondering. Slowly, Diana shook her head from side to side.

"I'm not allowed. Grandmother says you are bad, and I am not to go with you anymore. She said she would punish me severely if I do. I can't go." Diana's bottom lip quivered, and a tear ran down her cheek. "So, go away."

"It's all right, Diana. You are coming to live at my house. No one is going to punish you."

Diana looked at Charlotte for several seconds, thinking about what Charlotte said. "It's all right for you to take me?"

"Yes, Diana, it is."

"My grandmother said so?"

"No, sweetheart. But this afternoon a Judge will say so."

"What's a Judge?"

"I'll explain everything to you in the van."

Diana looked at Charlotte with her big, brown, trusting eyes and smiled. She nodded and she walked down the steps, holding on to Mrs. Harris' hand and climbed into the van.

The officer turned and signaled to the two men who were waiting in a car parked behind the van. The two men walked up the front steps to Elmira Hardtack's house and one of them knocked on the front door. In a few moments, Elmira Hardtack opened the door and asked what the men wanted. The two men in black suits showed Elmira credentials. They identified themselves as officers of the court working for the Child Welfare Department.

Chapter 18
Evening, October 22, 1951

"Well, in 1920, that department was worthless because there weren't any child welfare regulations to speak of. The only thing the government seemed to want to regulate was alcohol consumption. And Prohibition became the law of the land. The Roaring Twenties were ushered in and if ever a decade was aptly named, that one was. In the 1920s a party atmosphere seemed to be the order of the day. It was a game for those who had the means to outwit the police and circumvent the prohibition laws. And speakeasies opened by the dozens and illegal liquor flowed by the barrel. For the average Joe, however, times were tough. Jobs were scarce. So, running rum or working in speakeasies owned by organized crime were opportunities. It was a way to earn a living for those who couldn't otherwise support their families. The women who refused to prostitute themselves were relegated to work in sweatshops for pennies a week. It was barely enough to feed their children and survive. There were scant labor laws then and virtually no welfare laws. It was a happy-go-lucky time for the fortunate and hell on earth for the downtrodden. No statutes existed to cover things like child neglect or child endangerment. Certainly not like there are today. But, as luck would have it, Elmira Hardtack didn't know that.

"You see, Jedidiah had a list of charges he could threaten Elmira with to get her to relinquish custody of Diana. So, by the time the two men finished speaking with Elmira she was so scared she'd go to jail or be fined or both she signed everything and anything they handed her.

"That afternoon Jedidiah presented the documents to the court and the Judge signed the order giving Charlotte permanent custody of Diana. So, on July 27, 1920, Diana came to live with Charlotte and Jules. She was three years old."

Auntie paused for a long time. Her head down she whispered, "And the lie kept going on like a snowball rolling down an endless hill."

"Why?" Mother asked, pleading with her. "I don't understand why."

"Because Diana, it couldn't stop. Legitimacy kept the lie alive. You see, what began with one legal document, a document that named Miriam Harrington Wickham femme sole, sole legal parental guardian of the . . ." Auntie stopped. A tear fell from her eye. She knitted her brow and set her lips and said, ". . . the abandoned child known only as Welles, led to the issuing of a birth certificate that legitimized him." As the words escaped her lips she seemed as if she were relieved. "And," she continued, "it saved Charlotte from being catapulted into ignominy. It kept her reputation intact. Who knew those two documents would mushroom into thousands of pieces of paper? There were legal documents, school, medical, and church records. It even involved United States Census statistics and tax returns. Jedidiah warned everyone in 1896. He warned that this adoption would be impossible to undo, and he was correct as usual. Nevertheless, everyone agreed that it was in Welles' best interest. And, once Jedidiah filed the papers, Welles had a respectable name and could take his place in society. And Charlotte? Well, Charlotte had all the joys anyway. She reared Welles and his daughter the same as if they knew their actual relationship. So, Diana, does it matter what they called her? Would a name have changed anything? Would a name have changed how much she loves them?" Auntie looked at my mother as if she were searching her face for answers.

My mother stared into her eyes and her face softened. The angry lines around her eyes disappeared as she shook her head from side to side. "No." she whispered, and she lowered her eyes. She studied her hands as she played with her wedding rings. A few moments passed until she looked back at Auntie.

"I wanted to know, to hear it told, that's all."

Auntie nodded at Mother and said, "Yes, a huge mistake—one that can never be undone. But do you think it can be forgiven? Do you think that's possible, Diana?"

Mother bit her bottom lip as she looked into Auntie's eyes. Gradually, she smiled with her lips closed as if she were holding back tears. She nodded her head and a tear escaped and lingered on her cheek a moment. Auntie closed her eyes, took a deep breath, and exhaled. She looked at my mother and shook her head yes. "Thank you," she said. Her voice was so soft I barely heard her.

There wasn't a sound in the room for several minutes until Auntie cleared her throat. "Well, Danny," she said, "that's the story, all of it as best as I can remember; the tale about a Lenape Indian boy named Tey and a white girl named Charlotte."

I looked from Auntie to my mother and back to Auntie. My mind was racing as I put the pieces together. So, I asked, "Charlotte, she's Diana's grandmother, isn't she?"

Neither my mother nor Auntie answered me. They smiled at each other and nodded their heads yes. After several seconds Auntie asked, "Is there anything else you want to know, Dan?" She turned her head to look into my eyes. I didn't answer her right away. I needed to put the last piece in place first. When I was sure I said, "Yes, there's one more thing."

Auntie smiled and cocked her head, "What, Dan, what do you want to know?"

My eyes were glued on her when I asked, "Auntie, isn't your name Charlotte?"

About Atmosphere Press

Atmosphere Press is an independent, full-service publisher for excellent books in all genres and for all audiences. Learn more about what we do at atmospherepress.com.

We encourage you to check out some of Atmosphere's latest releases, which are available at Amazon.com and via order from your local bookstore:

Home is Not This Body, a novel by Karahn Washington
Whose Mary Kate, a novel by Jane Laclere Doyle
Stuck and Drunk in Shadyside, a novel by M. Byerly
These Things Happen, a novel by Chris Caldwell
Vanity: Murder in the Name of Sin, a novel by Rhiannon Garrard
Blood of the True Believer, a novel by Brandann R. Hill-Mann
In the Cloakroom of Proper Musings, a lyric narrative by Kristina Moriconi
The Dark Secrets of Barth and Williams College: A Comedy in Two Semesters, a novel by Glen Weissenberger
Lucid_Malware.zip, poetry by Dylan Sonderman
The Glorious Between, a novel by Doug Reid
An Expectation of Plenty, a novel by Thomas Bazar
Sink or Swim, Brooklyn, a novel by Ron Kemper
Lost and Found, a novel by Kevin Gardner
The Unordering of Days, poetry by Jessica Palmer
It's Not About You, poetry by Daniel Casey

About the Author

A former Philadelphian, Lexy Duck presently lives in Daytona Beach, FL, with her spouse, two dogs, and two cats. Her professional career encompassed writing, designing and producing books, teaching guides, project proposals, reports, and sales materials for clients such as the U.S. Department of Transportation, the Washington Metropolitan Transit Authority, the American Bankers Association, and the Transportation Research Board. Her accolades for writing fiction were in Freshmen English many years ago. After she retired, she found she had an enormous amount of time on her hands. And, at her sister's urging, she rekindled her passion for writing fiction and *The Tattered Black Book* was born.

CPSIA information can be obtained
at www.ICGtesting.com
Printed in the USA
FSHW010709290920
74220FS